The Blue Phoenix

Gabriel Goode

Published by True Phoenix Publishing

ISBN: 978-0-9966167-0-6

Printed by Amazon in the United States of America
Printed elsewhere when appropriate

Dedicated to Cheryl and Libby.
The first inspired me as a student.
The second inspired me as a teacher.

Contents

Father told him not to come home until he was covered in blood. As Kaerisk lay panting, one useless wing folded uncomfortably beneath his scaly back, he hoped his father wasn't being literal. The way his day was going, the only blood he might end up covered with would be his own.

"He makes this look so easy. When he showed me how, he just pounced. Of course, one of his bounds is four of-"

Birds scattered from the nearby trees as his frustration caused his voice to rise. His golden eyes rolled in his head as he wallowed in his second amateur mistake of the day.

Never let the prey know where you are. Great.

Kaerisk stared up at the sky. His bent wing below him began to throb as his blood forced its way through his circulation, but he didn't make any effort to move it. As his eyes tracked a bird fleeing the scene, he caught sight of a small pinprick of light, shining in spite of the sun that had yet to set.

Solaris – the Daystar. A light so bright that it burns even during the day.

Slowly, Kaerisk rolled onto his belly, freeing his wing. Though sore, he stretched it out a few times until he could ignore the dull ache. He scanned the forest, seeking any signs of his prey. The deer had left a clearly visible trail in its haste, but the young dragon was certain it would have kept running long after he had keeled over from fatigue.

The method Father taught me is not physically possible for me. It's no different than when he showed me his dive; these wings of mine won't work until I'm older. Then perhaps the lesson is to innovate. He has often said the dragon's reason is what separates us from the dakael, *after all.*

He walked forward and placed a paw on one of the trees. The old forest grew tall here, separate from the ash that stunted the growth of the trees closer to home. Claws digging into the ancient bark, he hop-climbed the tree and perched upon

[1]

one of the branches. The leaves swished against one another, causing further birds to flee.

Not perfect, but it will do. Now to the second part of the plan...

Hopping down, Kaerisk followed the trail of the escaped deer, nose close to the dirt. Sweat, driven into the ground by the heavy hoofs of the animal, interrupted the earthy smell of the forest. It had left signs of its passing everywhere: broken branches, parted bushes, bits of fur so easily found with his snout. Nose to guide him, Kaerisk trudged forward.

An hour passed. He paused abruptly, pulling his head back from the trail and grinning. He had nearly walked right into steaming pile of spoor left by his deer. Not only had he saved himself from quite spoiling his appetite by getting feces on his snout, he had the sign he sought: the deer had stopped running, and was close. His forked tongue darted from his mouth and hung there. His head turned left, then right.

Wind from the east.

He crouched down, walking into the breeze. Every few steps, he would rub his body against the thick trees. After traveling some distance, he turned south to continue his tree marking, his draconic scent lingering behind him. Finally, he curved away from the wind, completing his half-circle. As quietly as possible, he slinked to the middle of his marked territory and climbed the sturdiest tree he could find. He took a deep breath as the wind rustled through the leaves and crashed against his chest.

I can smell it.

Bushes rattled ahead of him. The brown coat of the deer slowly crept through the parting brush. Its black eyes scanned for predators on its level. Its ears twitched back and forth. Its snout lifted, eyes fixated on the tree in which Kaerisk lay. He held his breath. Slowly, tentatively, the deer moved forward.

[2]

Step by step, it came nearer. Every muscle in Kaerisk's body tensed. Step. Step. Its head bent down to nibble on some errant grass.

Kaerisk leapt.

The deer startled, but it was too late. The blue hatchling landed squarely on the back of the beast, his powerful jaws sinking into the deer's neck. Kaerisk's claws had latched onto its flanks and it collapsed under the weight. As the warm blood dripped onto his snout, he held the deer in a final embrace. The animal slowly twitched and then at last was still. He released the deer's throat with a bloody grin.

Father had nothing to worry about.

He ate his fill of the carcass. When he finished, he dabbed a bit of the animal's blood on his wing – just in case Father was being literal. Satisfied with himself and his hunt, he began back through the forest. When he reached the semicircle ring of his scent marking, he paused; something was out of place about them, something unfamiliar. He lifted his snout and sniffed the air, realizing he must have looked much like the deer had minutes prior. The unfamiliar scent had stopped at the line for some time. Pulling back the brush, he saw a pair of tracks and immediately tensed.

These are no deer – they are dakael!

Carefully, Kaerisk crept through the vegetation, causing as little sound as possible. Through the tangle of trees, he spied them: two humans. They carried the pointed sticks Father had warned of, the so-called spears. They seemed to be making a wide circle around the path that he had laid.

Are they hunting me?

He crouched down, almost to the point where he lost sight of them. He had been warned of their kind. They will kill without hesitation if they can, Father had said, because it gives them a better chance of surviving. They are the cleverest of animals and should never be underestimated.

They continued out of sight. Only when he was certain that the forest returned to its natural sounds did Kaerisk rise up and bolt towards civilization.

He traveled north, through trees covered in ash. A plume of ashen dust rose behind him, but he would not risk stealth while there were others who might be caught by these dakael hunters unprepared. His sister was still being taught by the other elders; they might take their charges into the forest for a hunt. His claws scraped against the igneous stone as he rose to the top of the crater.

Below, San'Lux rested in its full glory. Dominating the crater-city was a massive statue standing over a pool of molten lava. Depicted was a great dragon, reared on its hind legs with claws splayed viciously, with wings spread out behind it. Surrounding it and connected to it were several platforms, wreathing the dragon like flames. Crystals of yellow, orange, and red adorned the twisting pathways. Each path led to a higher level and each level was used for some common part of dragon life; the lowest levels near the lava were dotted with dragons basking in the heat. The second, at chest level with the statue, held the elders who taught the other hatchlings. He narrowed his eyes; the hatchlings were already gone and the elders were packing up tablets of stone like Father used to teach him.

Is she home then? Is she safe?

Kaerisk rounded the crater, heading west. Rising above him, leagues into the sky so high that even a dragon would have difficulty passing them, was the Deep Mountains. Near the foot of those mountains, hidden in an outcropping of stone, lay the home he had known all his life. The opening was wide, but shadows cast over it made it blend almost perfectly into the obsidian around it.

Sprinting down the ramp into the lair, he entered the main chamber. A large dais rose above him. Sheets of water fell around it like tapestries and collected in a pool that, through some magic of the Riftwind, recycled back up into the ceiling from whence the water came. Father sat on the platform impassively, peering down at his son. The mighty elder was muscular, with talons half as large as Kaerisk's head. They scraped against the granite platform as his son entered. His head lifted; six horns protruded from the back of the elder's skull like a crown. His golden eyes narrowed on the hatchling before him. His thick, muscular tail twitched only slightly; the rest of him was as still as stone.

"You are back sooner than I expected. You have completed your task?" Father's voice, deep and firm, echoed through the stone hall.

"Is Zala here?" Kaerisk asked, trying to catch his breath. He peered off to the side. Halfway up the circular room was a stone walkway, connected by ramps to both the dais and to the floor where he stood. They also led to the brood-chamber, where he and his sister slept at night.

"What an odd answer." Father cocked his head to one side. "Yes, she is here." With that information, Kaerisk finally relaxed. Father stretched out his long neck to his son's level, his head nearly half the size of the hatchling's body. His nostrils flared as he drew in air. "I smell deer blood on you."

"Yes, Father, I was successful."

The elder jerked his head forward, preening the blood from Kaerisk's wing and then nuzzling him warmly. "You have made me proud my son. But how did you catch it? The method I taught you requires sheer luck or extreme Patience – the latter of which being the purpose of the exercise."

Kaerisk pressed his body against his father's mighty head as pride swelled in his chest. "I chose another Dragon Virtue, Father: Wisdom." Father chuckled, but Kaerisk suddenly pulled back. "Father, there is another reason I came back as I did. I saw two humans in the forest."

The effect of that one word, humans, was immediate and violent. Father's blue scales bristled and his head rose up like a serpent ready to strike. His words came like a rumbling volcano. "Dakael? In the Ashen Forest? Did you slaughter them?"

"No Father. They carried spears and followed a trail I had made of my scent. I thought they might have been prepared to hunt me and did not risk it." Kaerisk's gaze fixated on the floor.

Maybe I should have tried it.

His father's growling ceased after a time and his head returned to his son, lifting Kaerisk's chin up with the tip of his snout. "You are Wise, my son, wiser than I was at your age. Be Proud, for you did the right thing in coming here. Now go, be with your sister. I will hunt them down, and then we shall speak of your success in full." Father's head retreated, but his body slithered down from the dais. The elder moved around his son with grace, his heavy weight never once endangering his offspring, before sauntering out through the exit.

Kaerisk climbed the incline leading up to the second level and poked his head into the brood-chamber. Zala lounged on the brood shelf, playing with a stone statuette. The two of them had long outgrown the small stone nest, but Zala still liked to curl on it, even though her tail fell from it in a most inelegant way. The sight of it caused him to huff.

Undignified as usual. And Father got her another gift. When will I get one?

As he padded closer, she looked up from her play. Her ear fins perked and she smiled. "Risky! You're back! Father said you might be gone for some time."

Kaerisk crossed his wings in front of his chest, clasping them with the tiny thumb at the tips. "I was worried about you. I saw humans in the forest. I don't know when your teacher will send you on your hunt, but I want you to be careful."

Zala giggled. "We don't do anything like that, Kaerisk. You have it much different, but that's because you chose to become like Sanrex."

It had been some time since their lessons had diverged. Zala was sent from the lair, but Kaerisk had been given a choice: join her, or stay with Father and learn as the San clan had before they all died out. He still wasn't quite sure what he was being trained to be, but he always liked the stories Father had told of Sanrex, the hero and founder of San'Lux.

Kaerisk padded up to the shelf and tucked his paws below him as he sat. "Well, just stay away from the forest, okay?"

Zala nuzzled his head. "Brother, will you tell me about Mother Mountain again?"

Kaerisk's vision lingered on the toy Zala clutched in her paw. "I don't feel like it. And I haven't forgiven you for what you did in front of the Council."

"I said I'm sorry! I was just so excited to meet all the elders - I wasn't thinking."

"You emasculated me in front of everyone important in San'Lux. I'd be lying if I didn't say part of the reason I stayed with Father is a fear to show my face out there."

Zala's cheeks puffed out, her tail slapping against the side of the shelf. "Just because I called you Risky?"

One of Kaerisk's eyes fixated on his sister. "Only females drop the clan name. That's why we call you Zala instead of Kaezala all the time."

"I know that! C'mon Kaerisk… I don't remember like you do. I sit here and I try to think of where I was and what I saw, but I can't. The smell is gone. I can't remember the smell." Kaezala lowered her head, her fingers squeezing the little grey statue.

Kaerisk sighed. He couldn't remember the smell either. "Alright, alright." He rested his head against his sister's side. Closing his eyes, he tried to imagine the room growing larger and larger, until the shelf was like a mesa amidst a great valley of stone. Curled around that mesa was Mother Mountain. "The first thing I remember was Mother Mountain. Slopes of beautiful sapphire, as far as I could see. I wandered up the slopes, moving from ridge to ridge, finding just the right spot of territory I could call my own. Then I lay down and rested."

"Then I came along!" Zala exclaimed.

One of Kaerisk's eyes shot open to glare at her. "I'm getting there."

Zala's head drooped. "Sorry."

"And I thought it was so strange to see someone like me but not like me. We were blue, but you had those strange ear fins and I had horns. I reared up and roared as loud as I could, and you went running. But Mother Mountain scolded me. She told me that as she shared of herself with me, I had to share with you. And so we shared my territory."

"Our territory."

"Ours." Kaerisk smiled. "We fought off the buzzing six legged monsters. When food stopped appearing, we traveled to the highest peak of Mother Mountain. There we found the valley of rust and the fat white worms which we defeated. And after our battle, Mother Mountain called us down. She spoke to us."

"What did she say?"

"She gave us our names. She gave me the name of Kaerisk, which means Dawnbringer in the old tongue. And you she called Kaezala, which means Twilight. She told us not to be sad, for loss is a trial and all trials make a dragon strong. She told us to survive. You must tell him when he comes."

Tell him I do not blame him, Kaerisk. Tell him I died happy.

"Kaerisk?"

Kaerisk's eyes opened again. Zala sat staring at him with a furrowed brow. Her tail pressed against the shelf that had once been large enough to take a whole day to cross.

"What was Mother Mountain's real name?"

Kaerisk frowned, closing his eyes and resting his head against his sister. Through her scales, he could hear her heart beat slowly in her chest. "I don't know, Zala. Father never told me." There he rested, wondering when he would ever be able to fulfill the final charge of Mother Mountain.

Dangerous Game

"…isolated. It's not unheard of, but it might be signs of something greater. We just don't have enough details."

Father's voice echoed into the brood-chamber as Kaerisk woke. His sister had fallen from the shelf onto her back. Despite the odd posture, she continued to sleep, oblivious. He slid away from the pedestal and peered into the main chamber. Father stood on the lower level with another dragon. The gold elder sat with a dignified pose, tail curled around his forepaws.

"While I share your concerns, the Council is not ready to call the Flights to order. We must be patient, Kaevaeri. If this is a sign of things to come, there will be more. They are not that clever."

Father's tail whipped about. He stood much like the fighting stances that he had taught Kaerisk. "I know that, Luxari. But I still felt it necessary to voice my thoughts."

The gold smiled, unperturbed by Father's agitation. "You know you always have my ear, old friend. But I must admit: it was uncharacteristic of you. Why was there not more blood?"

Father finally sat. His pose was a mirror of Luxari's. "I've some use for them. And, perhaps, they might yet lead to other clues."

"With your son, I take it?"

"I've quite a lesson planned for him today."

Luxari chuckled. "He is still a hatchling. I trust you have supplies on hand?"

Father frowned. "Of course. A Wise dragon does not make the same mistake twice."

There was a pause. The running water of the dais falls seemed to be a roar in the sudden silence.

"I meant no disrespect, Kaevaeri. I know how precious they-"

The ground started to shake under Kaerisk's feet. It was slow, deep rumble, like his father growling, that began to rise. The rumble rose in volume and intensity as the entire cavern began to sway.

Not again!

Dust and bits of rock fell from the ceiling as Kaerisk struggled to remain on all four paws; he braced himself against the doorway. The elders, who had been sitting, rose to their paws as well, holding still. Father's head darted upwards towards the chamber, spotting the eavesdropper. Had Kaerisk not been terrified the trembling ceiling would fall on him, he might have felt shame.

"Not another quake!" Zala exclaimed; she rushed to her brother's side, dust falling on her wings and speckling them with metamorphic flakes of stone.

Then, as suddenly as it had come, the shaking stopped. Kaerisk righted himself. Father smiled almost imperceptibly, and then turned his eyes to the ceiling. Zala leaned into her brother, shaking as much as the ground had moments before.

"Those quakes are becoming unusually frequent. I have to be careful with my digging lately," Father said.

Luxari shook out his wings. "The city experiences them too, but they feel stronger here." Father's brow rose. "I know what you're thinking, but it is not evidence enough. But it may be another piece if this continues."

"I hope they are unrelated, but I shall prepare for all eventualities." Father sat, turning his gaze to his children. "Little ones, come say hello to Luxari. You met him at the Council meeting."

How could I ever forget.

Kaerisk and his sister descended the walkway on wobbly legs. They bowed their heads and necks to him reverently and he returned the courtesy in kind. Kaerisk couldn't help but look away when the elder's black eyes fell on him.

"Your children are growing well, Kaevaeri. But if you will excuse me, I should see if there are any damages in the city or to the statue."

"Of course. I thank you, my friend, for your compliments and your ear. Might I impose one last favor on you today? Please take Zala with you to her teacher."

"Father?" Zala asked, her head lifting.

"Run along, Zala; it's time for school," Father said.

The gold smiled to her. "We can start lessons early today, Kaezala." Father peered up from his child to the gold with a raised brow. "I have been teaching her personally."

Father frowned. "I did not ask that of you."

"You are my eldest and dearest friend, Kaevaeri. I expect no favors in return and, though I disagree with your wishes, I do respect them. She still has her blood though." Luxari smiled at Zala. "Come along, little one."

Zala nodded and silently scampered alongside the gold as he left. Father watched the gold for a time, and then turned his attention back to Kaerisk.

"You were eavesdropping. Such covert methods should not be employed in your own lair, little one."

Kaerisk shrunk back a bit. "I'm sorry Father."

"It is alright. But as you heard me say – a wise dragon never makes the same mistakes twice, yes?" Kaerisk nodded. "Good. At least you remembered to hide in the arch for the quake. Now – as you know, you have an important and dangerous lesson today. Come with me."

Dangerous?

Kaerisk trailed behind his father as the elder dragon ducked into a tunnel on the lower level. He paused, standing before it. Father spent most of his time in those tunnels, but Kaerisk had been forbidden to enter; he always believed that it was just Father's brood-chamber. Standing on the threshold, he peeked inside. The chamber was large enough to fit two elders comfortably, with four other exits flanked by colored Riftcrystals. His father stood before the pathway marked with blue crystal; it was made further unique by the large stone columns that had been pressed against the entrance, barring egress.

"Come, Kaerisk. It is alright. I have been working on these tunnels since you were born. Many of our future lessons will take place here, as will today's."

Kaerisk padded inside and stared into the barred chamber. The room beyond was large and poorly lit; unusual spikes of stone rose from the ground and hung from the ceiling like dragon's teeth.

"You are curious. You should be. The area behind has been modeled to look like the internal chambers of the Deep Mountains. It is a place where biped live."

"Why would you make a biped place in our lair, Father?"

The elder grinned, his sharp white teeth flashing in the well-lit chamber. "Because there's a human in there." Kaerisk hopped back from the gate, muscles tense. "I found the humans that tracked you with ease. One I slaughtered. The other I brought back alive. Today, you will hunt it in unfamiliar tunnels."

Kaerisk strained his neck to look up into his father's eyes. "But why, Father?"

Father's wings flared and he snarled. "The only threat to a dragon is a biped, Kaerisk. There is no greater challenge than hunting one. No duty more important than killing one. They are monsters, pure and simple: the Rage of the Firstbourne and a swift death are their only birthrights. The sooner you learn how dangerous they can be and how to cull them, the safer you will be. Do you understand?"

Kaerisk nodded as firmly as he could muster.

"I shall remove the gate. It has been in there for some time; be wary of traps. I shall wait in the foyer and ensure he does not escape the lair. Come to me only if you are covered in blood."

"I understand, Father. I will make you proud."

The elder's bristled scales settled with a smile. "I know you will son." He pulled the large gate from the entrance, stepped aside, and then returned to the waterfall room.

Kaerisk peered into the chamber. Two blue crystals flanked the inside of the door, giving the only light to the area; the rest of the room was exceptionally dark. Kaerisk had only seen that darkness once, when the crystals in his brood-chamber had been damaged by the quakes. His sister had clung to him and he held her, but really he felt like clinging to her himself. He wished she was there to cling to now.

Taking a deep breath, he pressed into the dark room. Quiet as he could be, he placed one foot at a time. He lifted his head sideways, listening: the sound of running water, splashing into a pool. The stillness of the cave. He tucked his wings tightly to him, maneuvering in the narrow space of the stone columns.

Where is the human hiding?

He froze. He thought he heard someone breathing heavily. On careful paws, he stalked up to the stalagmite. He

[14]

kept his tail high for balance, steeled himself, and leapt around the pillar.

No one was there.

He sniffed the ground. The prey was close. It had a strange, moist odor, foul and salty. It led off into the darker part of the chamber. He listened again for anything that might give away his prey, but he could not see anything but the dim outline of stalagmites.

He kept his head close to the ground, following the trail by scent. A great blackness rose up before him, which he realized was the wall before nearly colliding with it. He could smell the trail left by the human as its palm had led the way into the dark.

I can follow this to him.

Step by step, the chamber grew darker, the scent stronger. He could hear the breathing now, close. His heavy feet rose, one at a time and landed quietly against the smooth stone ground. Another step. Another step.

Crack!

He had stepped in something unseen, something crystalline. Shaking the shards from his paws, he realized that there once had been lights in this part of the chamber – and were no longer.

A scream. He could hear the biped charging, but he couldn't see it. In the darkness, something sharp stabbed into the scales of his neck, piercing deeply. It snapped as hot, red blood dripped from the wound. Kaerisk lashed out but caught nothing but another stalagmite. Heavy, rapid steps, an unnerving one, two, one, two – the biped was running away! Squinting, he could see the shape of the human as it disappeared out the door that had been barred. Tenderly, Kaerisk pried the sharp object free of his neck. He could feel the blood flow more readily from the wound. Had it been any

[15]

deeper, he would have surely perished. Awkwardly, he stumbled into the light on three legs, the last holding the weapon: a small shard of the light crystal. The biped had created a weapon out of something utterly innocuous!

Father is right, these things are clever and deadly. I should get help for this –

He growled, his tail lashing out and hitting one of the stalagmites so hard that it cracked.

I will make you proud Father. I'll tear out his liver!

Kaerisk tossed the shard aside and sprinted into adjacent chamber. The four other exits left many places to hide. Kaerisk pressed his snout to the ground, trying to scent it; instead, he found the unsettling smell of his own blood. Though the human had lost the weapon, it had not lost the blood on its hands, and a trail of it led right to the yellow crystal chamber. Again, the biped had shattered the lights and was hiding somewhere within, but this chamber was not as large. It housed what Kaerisk thought to be stalagmites. As he neared one, a broken crystal began to shine. In the sudden light, a towering biped rose up with a menacing weapon drawn. Kaerisk cowered back until he realized the biped did not move; the entire area had been filled with dakael statues, many types unlike the humans he knew.

Kaerisk took the piece of crystal that had reacted to his presence. He cloaked it under his wing to mask his location. Father had explained to him about the crystals and Riftwind, the magic of the dragons, though he had not yet told him how to control it.

I won't need to control it for this, though… I just need to get close. Reason, Kaerisk. That is what separates us. That's what you always say, Father.

The wound felt cold as the blood slowly congealed in a trail down his neck. He growled, stalking into the midst of the biped statues. He continued his low growl, sniffing and listening.

A scream.

He took the bait!

Kaerisk spread his wings, the sudden light of the crystal blinding his attacker. He lunged, his powerful claws rending flesh from bone while his teeth tore loose the throat of the human. The taste was sweet and he took a moment to savor its liver. His father always told him to do what he said he would.

Kaerisk dragged the carcass into the main chamber. His father smiled brightly upon his return.

"You have done well, my son. You will recount your hunt to me after you are done eating. And…" His father paused to look at the hatchling's neck, which Kaerisk tried to hide. "You are injured."

"It is just a scratch, Father."

"All wounds should be taken seriously, my son." Kaerisk held still as his father gently took his neck. "You can see just how dangerous humans are. This is deep. You should have come to me."

"I was able to finish my hunt," Kaerisk said.

Father's eyes became distant. "So was I, once."

From his scalepack, Father procured two objects: the first was a plant of some kind, and the second was a dragon scale that had been infused with Riftwind. He placed the herb onto Kaerisk's wound. It burned severely, but the hatchling curled his claws, clenched his teeth, and would not make a sound. Father then placed the scale over the wound and herb, sealing it with Riftwind.

"I only learned how to do that after-" He paused as though he had forgotten something, or almost forgotten something. "It is something I shall teach you in time, son. Now, enjoy your meal and your accomplishments – and your mistakes. Experience is the best teacher."

"Father, I saw the room with the statues. Just how many types of dakael are there?"

Father growled a bit. "More than you can count on your forepaws, my son."

"Do they all hate us? Are they all dangerous?"

"Yes. Some, more than others."

Kaerisk winced as he turned his head towards the corpse. The herbs stung worse than the wound did.

The animal tried to survive by killing me. Was my killing him any different?

"Why do they hate us, Father?"

"Eat your kill, Kaerisk. You can recount your story when Zala gets home. For now, just rest." Father rose up and slinked into the chambers where Kaerisk had fought.

The hatchling tore away a bit of meat from his prey and chewed on it in thought.

Inequity

"Where is it?" Zala shrieked. She paced all around Kaerisk, sniffing at him. The brood-chamber walls echoed her anger.

"I don't know what you're talking about." Kaerisk sat impassively as he could, just like Father. Of course, Father didn't hide his sister's dragon statuette under his belly when he sat. The wings of obsidian poked uncomfortably into his scales.

I never get anything. Father will just give you another.

"I know you have it, Kaerisk! Move!" Zala pushed her body against his, trying to roll him off his position. Kaerisk dug his claws into the ground.

A vicious growl froze them in place. Father's head had snaked into the chamber from where he rested on the dais, his teeth bared. Zala pulled back and Kaerisk lowered his head. Father had never physically harmed them, but the threat of it was ever present when it would take one bite to cut them in half.

"Now. What is it that has you squabbling?" Father asked.

Zala stood, timidly at first. "Kaerisk stole my statue!" Her grip on the ground grew more firm with each word.

"And where is the statue now?" Father asked.

"It's under him!"

Father glared at him. The command was clear. Slowly, Kaerisk rose, his tail drooping between his legs. Below him was the statue; however, the wings had torn lose when Zala had pushed at him.

"You broke it!" Zala shrieked, snatching the pieces out from under him.

"It broke because you pushed me!" Kaerisk exclaimed.

[19]

"Enough!" Father's voice boomed so loud that Kaerisk felt as though his father surrounded him on all sides. He cowered down, as did Zala. "Stealing is far below a dragon of standing, Kaerisk. Go out and play, Zala."

"But Father-" she tried.

"Go."

Dragging her feet, Zala took the broken pieces of the statue into her maw and ambled out of the room. Kaerisk could hear the scraping of her tail against the rock echoing through the cavern.

Father glared down at him. "I am disappointed in you. Sanrex would never have restored to thievery to satisfy his desire for hoard."

"Even Sanrex had Luxstra! I only ever leave the lair to hunt and Zala's class never goes hunting."

Father turned his head one way, and then the other, his harsh eyes never leaving Kaerisk. It made the hatchling squirm a bit, tail shaking against the stone. Finally, Father's deep growl faded. "I want you to be as great as Sanrex, nearly as great as the Firstbourne. Perhaps there is a lesson that might remedy this." The growl and glare returned for but a moment. "You are not to leave this room until I return." Father then turned and slid out the doorway. His heavy steps dropped a bit of dust from the ceiling; it landed on Kaerisk's nose, causing him to sneeze. By the time he had recovered, Father was gone.

For a time, Kaerisk curled around the brood shelf, claws over his eyes. He thought about his Father and his sister. They were all he truly had.

I love them both, I do. But I don't understand it! Why does Father give Zala everything and keep me away from everyone? Zala probably has tons of friends and she always has little trinkets to play with...

Kaerisk growled. His tail slapped against the ground as hard as he could, but no dust came from the ceiling at his motion. Uncurling from the shelf, he trotted over to the invisible line marking the boundary between the brood-chamber and the rest of the lair. He paced about it like an animal caged, heart racing.

It's not right. I'm going to get back at Zala. I don't know what I'm going to do, but I'm going to make her look like a fool!

Steeled by his thoughts, Kaerisk crossed the line.

Father had taught Kaerisk much of tracking. Zala, who had no reason to hide her trail or fear anyone, had left visible footprints and familiar smells so easy to follow that they could have been a painted line on the ground. Where her tail had dragged through the ash, it actually became a line. Kaerisk followed it towards the city, but it veered away just as the grand statue of San'Lux came into view. The trail led to the southeast of the city crater, to a much smaller depression. Within it, Kaerisk could hear voices. Sneaking up to the top, he peered down silently as though he were preparing to pounce on a deer.

Within the small crater were four hatchlings, sitting around a slow-bubbling pool of lava. Zala was among them, listening to a green dragon speak. Next to the green was a red with well-preened scales that shimmered in the light of the pool. A silver dragon, with scales splotched with opaque tones, rested beside Zala. Her breath seemed labored, as though she had been running earlier.

"And when the hatchling reached for the hoard his friends had left by the pit, a great flame monster rose up from it and grabbed him! Screaming, the hatchling was dragged into the pool and never seen again!" As the green hatchling, her underbelly yellowed like teeth, reached the climax of her story, a small bit of Riftwind danced through her form. It caused the lava to rise up in the shape of a blob with a mouth; the others all cringed in fear. And, as the magic faded, the blob retreated back into the depths and everyone began to laugh.

"You always tell the story so well, Rilla," the red said. She too had a feminine voice.

"Yes, thank you for telling it," the silver said. Her voice was soft and barely audible. Kaerisk watched her closely. Something about the shimmer of her scales entranced him.

"Yeah, well. Mom said I have to play nice with you and this is about all you're good for," Rilla said. Her stomach growled and she regarded the red. "Adra, let's go home and get some lunch. This Riftwind stuff makes me hungry."

Adra, the red, rose up. "See if you can try to play a game of tag next time, huh?"

"You know it's hard for Icia!" Zala exclaimed, also rising to her feet.

"That isn't our problem and it shouldn't be yours either. Why do you bother hanging around her anyway? You know she's just going to-"

Zala growled viciously. "Don't you dare say it, Senadra!" Kaerisk's claws gripped the ridge a bit tighter.

Senadra? That makes the red part of the Sen clan – Father really doesn't like them for some reason. If they're all like her, I think I might see why.

The silver's head hung, looking off to the side. "You can go play with them, Zala. I don't mind."

Adra snorted out a laugh. "Who said she was invited? C'mon Rilla." Head raised high, tail swinging back and forth as though striking the air, Adra led the green up the opposite side of the hill.

I thought Zala had lots of friends, but all she seems to have is...

[22]

"You don't have to defend me Zala. It's alright," the silver said.

"No it's not, Icia." Zala turned towards the silver and came to sit with her. Kaerisk realized she had not even attempted to rise with the others. "You and I made a promise, remember? We're going to see the sky together someday."

"Zala-"

"We made a promise. An honorable dragon doesn't go back on her promises. It doesn't matter; Luxari said you could grow out of it. I know you will! You're the strongest dragon I know!" Zala's paws rested on Icia's. She smiled, but Kaerisk had never seen her squint her eyes like that when smiling before. It looked as though her face was made of sapphire that had cracked along the eyes.

Icia also smiled, but hers seemed completely genuine. "Okay, Zala, you win. Show me the statue again?"

Zala's smile faded when she gathered up the pieces and laid them before her. "My stupid brother broke it." With those words, Kaerisk almost remembered what he had actually come out here to do. "You don't have to make another. I'll get it fixed somehow."

"I can do it." Icia scooped up the pieces. "It's my statue and repairing it isn't as hard as making one."

Father didn't give her the statue? Are all of Zala's trinkets coming from Icia?

"But-"

Zala didn't get a chance to continue. The silvery dragon struggled for a moment, her whole body shivering as she summoned up the Riftwind Kaerisk had seen his father use many times. Unlike with him or with Rilla, it seemed to harm Icia; she winced as she moved. Calling a bit of lava from the pit, she sealed the wing to the back of the statue once more. The lava quickly cooled, cementing the bonds between them. When

[23]

Icia smiled, there was blood on her teeth. "See? It's not that bad," she said.

Zala reached forward and hugged her neck with her wings. "Thank you so much, Icia." Her head rested behind the silver's, eyes closed tightly.

I was wrong to come here. I'd better get back before Father-

The ground suddenly shook; another earthquake tore through the land, shaking the hatchling from his feet. The lip of the crater gave way and Kaerisk went skidding down the ashen slope of the hole.

As the quake faded, Zala jerked to her feet, wings flared. "Kaerisk! What are you doing here?"

"I, um." Kaerisk struggled to his feet, glancing between the silver and the blue. He didn't want to look like a complete jerk in front of the silver. "Father told me to come apologize to you."

Zala shook her head. "I doubt that. But fine. Apology accepted. Go home."

Kaerisk gave Icia the best smile he could give. "It is nice to meet you Icia!"

The silver hatchling lowered her head bashfully, looking away with a small smile.

"Go, Risky, now!" Zala exclaimed.

Kaerisk grumbled as his sister emasculated him again, but the silver didn't seem to have noticed. She still looked off to the side, as though afraid to catch eyes with him. With some careful jumping, Kaerisk escaped to the top of the crater and shuffled home. He could not stop thinking about Icia, a frown creasing his face.

What is wrong with her? And if Icia is the one giving her the gifts... what has Father given to Zala?

So consumed in his thoughts, he did not see his father standing in the doorway of the lair until he had nearly impacted him. He glowered at his offspring, his wings folded in front of him like a shield.

"Kaerisk, my son and heir, you are incorrigible! Have I not taught you of the Virtues? You break all of them, and then have the audacity to test my Patience! Do you not remember? To leave my lair without permission is to be disowned. All rights, all status, even your very name would be taken from you! And now you return to me and expect entrance into this home? It could very well not be your home anymore."

"I'm sorry, Father. I was so angry, but I was wrong. I have no Wisdom - I don't understand anything." He did not quail at his Father's anger. He was still too numb from what he had seen and the lesson he had inadvertently learned.

The elder examined his son and his hard eyes softened with relief. "Please, Kaerisk, do not do that again. You matter to me more than anything else."

But… what about Zala?

"What troubles you? What did you see in your unauthorized exodus?"

"I saw Icia. I wanted to play a joke on Zala for getting me in trouble, but…"

"I see."

"Father, why is Icia so ill?"

The elder sat down upon his belly and opened the crook of his arm to the hatchling. Kaerisk took it readily, finding comfort in his father's closeness. "Some hatchlings are born ill. Icia is unlucky enough to be one of them. Some of us manage to grow out of that early sickness. Most… simply perish."

"But why, Father?"

"There is nothing to be done for them. No poultice or potion can cure them of the very blood in their veins. Kaerisk,

[25]

you may think that I am overbearing and cruel to keep you so close, to teach you at length, and to supervise you always. But in truth, most hatchlings, even those who hatch healthy, do not tame the sky. I worry about you greatly, Orban. Always. You are my only son, and… that is how it will always be. If I were to lose you, I do not know what would become of me."

"What about Zala – if Icia doesn't grow out of it…"

"Zala is much like her mother in that regard. She always fought the hopeless fight. But that is what made her, and your sister, strong. When the time comes, we must all deal with what we have lost."

"I still haven't."

"Neither have I, son."

Kaerisk opened his mouth to speak, to say those last words he had promised to say. But when he tried to find voice, none came. Father gazed towards the last rays of light, falling behind the horizon.

<u>An Unexpected Gift</u>

Father had not allowed Kaerisk into the lower chambers since his dakael hunt, so it was a treat to be able to visit again. The elder dragon watched over his son as Kaerisk sniffed about. The hatchling paused when he noticed a glimmer in the path beyond a green crystal. Father smiled when Kaerisk looked to him curiously. "That is my hoard, little one. Someday, you shall have all of it and you will need it to properly utilize the Riftwind. But that gift is not the one I wish to give you."

A gift for me? After what happened yesterday?

Father moved around his son to the cavern where Kaerisk first encountered his human prey. Unlike before, five bars made of stone connected by two more now adorned the entrance. Only one of them actually set into the ceiling and ground, while the others rested atop the ground with all their weight. They bore the marks of shaping by Riftwind, too smooth and scoured to be cut naturally. Inside, Kaerisk could hear a strange, whining sound. It rose just above the din of the water, falling in the darkened chamber. Again, he looked to his father.

"No, son, it is not another biped hunt. Go and see."

Kaerisk pressed at the bars as hard he could; inch by inch the makeshift door gave way. The hatchling slipped inside as Father stood in the archway. Kaerisk crouched low, slinking across the ground as close as he could without dragging his scales, tracking the whining noise by sound. As the scent hit his nose, he glanced back to the entrance; that smell was dakael – and it was fresh.

If this is not a hunt, then what is it Father?

[27]

Kaerisk came within striking distance, hidden by a small cluster of stalagmites. Between them and the blue light of the crystals, his approach had been quite easy. Cautiously, he poked half of his head around the barrier.

Sitting there was a human dakael, but it was much smaller than the one he had hunted. It had wrapped its arms around its legs and pulled itself into a ball. Strange liquid fell from its cheeks. It shivered, but Kaerisk did not find the chamber cold.

This is a dakael? Is it a threat?

Kaerisk stepped out from behind the barrier. "Father! This biped is tiny!"

The dakael jerked up at his voice and began emitting a horrible wail. The soft-skin bolted to the other side of the cavern, and then appeared to choke off its own wailing, perhaps in an attempt to hide.

It is not a threat. Could it be a child?

"Kaerisk, come here," Father said. With the threat gone, Kaerisk sauntered over to him. He peered up at his father, even though it was quite a strain to lift his neck so high. "I know that your recent transgressions are sparked by a desire for companionship. But for me to teach you as the San have taught for generations, outside contact with other dragons is forbidden before a certain age. I know this is a sacrifice. But there is one thing that I can do to give you companionship other than myself."

Kaerisk blinked, and then peered back to the dakael. "You mean that?"

"I do," Father said. Kaerisk shook his head in disbelief. "You will someday learn an important lesson from her. But for now, she is your pet and your responsibility. You must care for her, show her kindness, and of course feed and clean up after her."

"Father, I don't know the first thing about it."

"You will learn or the dakael will die. It is very simple; it is nature – as the Firstbourne intends. But she could prove a suitable playmate, so do not treat my gift too harshly." Father turned away from the entrance and pulled the bars shut behind him, sealing Kaerisk in with the girl. "In the future, you must hunt for her. But, for today, I have left a stag in there for you both. Enjoy your new pet, my son." With that, Father ambled away.

Kaerisk peered back to the girl, who had been peeking at the events. When their eyes met, she shrieked and ducked behind a stalagmite again. Kaerisk sighed.

What kind of pet is this, anyway? Maybe I should just eat her.

Kaerisk walked over to the stalagmite and poked his head around it. The girl stumbled backwards, falling to her rear with another wail. Cowering, she covered her head with her arms.

"You seem so helpless. You're not like the one that injured me."

At his words, the biped peered through her arms and scooted back.

"You probably think I'm growling at you, huh?" Kaerisk looked off to the side. "Father said never to make eye contact with animals. He meant for hunting, but it probably will help now, right?"

Out of the corner of his eye, he could see the girl struggling to her feet, leg muscles tense as though ready to bolt.

Two legs. It seems like such a silly method of motion. They must always be falling – wait, what if I showed her I am like a biped too?

Kaerisk lifted up, standing on his hindlegs. "See? It's okay," he said, trying awkwardly to move forward with just his

[29]

hind paws. His spine ached and his muscles strained to keep him erect. His wings and tail provided some balance, but he could do little more than waddle forward. "See?"

The girl screamed and ran for the other side of the room again. Even once she had hidden herself again, she continued to screech at him. Kaerisk fell to his four feet again with a huff, rubbing his head with a wing.

"Maybe that was a bad idea." Sniffing, he located the deer carcass. It was still fresh, but warmth had left the deer's body some time ago. With some effort, he dragged the neck of the beast in his teeth, pulling it to the other side of the room where the biped hid. The girl collapsed into a ball upon seeing Kaerisk, shaking her head and shivering. "Well, at least you're not running." He took a cut of meat from the deer, placed it before the biped, and then stepped back. He lowered his head and body to the ground, tightly curled up like she was.

After a moment, the wailing stopped. The girl looked at him, right in the eyes, and she did not flee. Crawling forward like a dragon, she sniffed at the meat, but soon turned away. She returned to her cluster of stalagmites and balled up again.

Kaerisk sighed. "Is it not fresh enough? Maybe it's not warm enough." He pondered over it, tail flicking back and forth in agitation. There was only one way he knew to warm a meal: fire. But his father had told him that he was not yet old enough for his First Flame.

When the time comes for your First Flame, you will know it. It represents the indomitable will that we have, and the willingness to do what is right, even if no one else does. Use it only in defense of your life or these principles, my son. That's what Father said. Is this the right thing to do?

Kaerisk crept up and moved the meat away from the biped, turning sidelong. He tried to smile at the biped, and then turned his head back to the meat. He focused inward, trying to breath out the flame. Inhaling and exhaling, he could feel the muscles in his throat Father had told him about. He coughed. An acrid liquid touched his tongue, boiling up from his throat.

I have to do this. To impress Father. To help this dakael.

The biped had uncurled from her ball, but she was no longer wailing or running. She stared at Kaerisk, wrinkles creasing her brow. He struggled once, twice more and then finally a spark; the liquid ignited in a short, but intense fire, which seared the piece of meat wholly. The biped jumped and cried out, but she still did not run. Kaerisk panted and his mouth burned and he felt as though his insides were on fire, but he had his First Flame. Timidly, he nosed the hot meat towards the girl. With small, slender fingers, she took it. She switched hands a few times, but when she bit down she made a sound that wasn't wailing or crying – it was a moan that chased away the wrinkles on her face. When Kaerisk heard that sound and saw what it had done for her, he smiled and knew he had done the right thing.

"Maybe dakael aren't really that bad." Slowly, he crept along her side and kept his head low. She tensed a moment before letting her hand fall on his head, rubbing it. He could barely feel it through the scales, but somehow it still felt nice to have that contact. When she seemed comfortable, he lifted his head and peered at her. Her eyes were the color of his scales: a rich, blue color. It reminded him of something he had almost forgotten. "I will call you Sapphire. Don't worry. I'll take care of you. I promise."

When she finished her meal, Sapphire curled up into a ball beside him; she seemed to find some comfort in his presence. Kaerisk stretched his neck to the deer to eat what he could without disturbing her. Though he was likely noisy, the girl did not move from his side. He watched over her for the rest of the day.

A scraping of stone against stone roused him from his near doze. It startled Sapphire as well who dug into Kaerisk's side while poking her head over his wings. At the door was Zala, who did not have the strength to open the door on her own. Kaerisk rose slowly, trying not to alarm the girl. Once on his feet, he left her to assist his sister. Taking one of the bars in his claws, he pulled as she pushed, allowing her to slink inside. He then shut the door behind her.

"I heard you got a new friend," Zala said. Her voice was a bit flat. Her eyes focused on Sapphire, who had taken to hiding behind the nearest pillar of stone.

Kaerisk trotted over to the girl, lowering his head to show her it was alright. "Seems we both have friends the other doesn't know about."

"It's not a contest, you know." Zala followed him cautiously. The girl hid behind Kaerisk, causing the male to smile. "Does she bite?"

"Most of her teeth are as flat as a deer's. I don't know how she was able to eat the meat earlier." Kaerisk churred to Sapphire, trying to coax her out. Timidly, the human looked to Zala. She stretched one hand towards her, but did not come too close. Eventually, Zala lowered herself so that the girl could reach out and rub her head as she had Kaerisk. "I know it's not a contest. But I'd still like to know more about Icia."

Zala's attention moved away from the human and she lifted her head. Sapphire ducked behind Kaerisk, as though afraid she had done something wrong. "What, are you against me being friends with her too? Everyone else is."

"No, it's not that. She just seems so nice."

Zala pulled her head back, tilted it, and then grinned widely. "You have a crush on her, don't you?" The shrieking, teasing tone must not have translated as playful to the human, for she abandoned Kaerisk's side to watch from a greater distance.

"I-I never suggested anything of the sort! I just thought it would be nice if you invited her here, since I'm not allowed to go out on my own!" Kaerisk exclaimed, turning sideways. Trying to look bigger was his only real defense to such a statement.

Zala giggled and bounded a few times. "You do! Father really does keep you shut in here, doesn't he?" Kaerisk grumbled and sat down, turning his head from her. "Oh, don't be like that." She came over to sit beside him. "I'll ask. But it's a bit of a walk for her, so no promises."

Kaerisk glanced to her. "Thank you… and I am sorry about spying on you two."

She leaned into him. "It's fine. I'm just glad Father didn't get too mad at you."

"I really thought that you had it so much easier than I did, Zala. That you got whatever you wanted from Father."

Zala's head drooped a bit, the playfulness gone. "No. For the most part, it's just me and Icia. And you, when you're not a complete pain in the tail."

He nosed her. "And Father. I know he loves you too."

Zala said nothing. Her attention was drawn away to the biped, who had crept from her hiding spot to nestle against Kaerisk again. "Seems she likes you. What did you call her?"

"Sapphire."

Zala smiled a bit and rested her head on her brother's paws. "Like the slopes of Mother Mountain."

Kaerisk watched his sister closely for a time, and then rested his head beside hers. Once he was certain Sapphire was comfortable, he drifted off to sleep.

Ingenuity and Faith

In the months that followed, Sapphire began to grow. Nightly, Kaerisk would retreat to her room and tell her all about his day, sometimes pantomiming the events. He knew she couldn't understand, but she still seemed fascinated by him and he enjoyed the attention. She in turn grew closer to him and always enjoyed the food he brought home. He had discovered a small trail of lava not far from town and used the Riftwind to shape stone as his father had taught him. It formed a makeshift grill, onto which he would place Sapphire's meal before bringing it home to her.

As she became taller, more pink skin began to show while the brown furry parts of her seemed to shrink and tighten. At some point, Kaerisk grew interested in the phenomenon and pulled experimentally at a piece of the brown fur that was loose. A moment of horror passed through Kaerisk as he tore the piece off, revealing still more pink skin below. Sapphire herself seemed quite flustered by it and hid behind a stalagmite for a long time, but she gave no wails of pain.

Though he was curious, he could not speak to his father about it. While she had been a gift from Father, the elder himself wanted nothing to do with the creature. He frequently spoke in sharp tones when he called Kaerisk to lessons.

Instead, Kaerisk turned to Zala, who didn't know about the coverings either; however, they did determine that the coverings came from a deer, though they had no idea what purpose they served. When Zala compared the loss of Sapphire's coverings to the loss of all Kaerisk's scales, he felt quite bad about having torn it off and decided to help her 'scales' grow back.

Retrieving a deer from the woods, he brought it back to the lair as he always did. Sapphire came out, arms around her chest, but she seemed somewhat perturbed that her usual warm steak was not waiting for her. Ignoring that, Kaerisk skinned the deer and promptly delivered the pelt onto the girl. Sapphire wailed as the bloody skin covered her, shook it loose, and finally jumped into the water to wash off the blood. Kaerisk laughed at this, though he immediately felt bad for doing so. He forced up another bit of dragon flame to cook the meat for her.

In the days that followed, the skin he had left for her began to change. At first he thought it was natural decay, but the back of the skin seemed to have been cleaned. He discovered a rock with a sharpened edge, fresh with bits of deer flesh. At first he thought that Sapphire was plotting something as Father warned him she someday might, but Sapphire lowered herself to the ground as he had months before, trying to display submissiveness. Curious, he let her keep it.

Days after that, the cave began to smell a bit; he realized it came from the deer skin and that Sapphire had done something to it. He made to remove the object, but Sapphire stepped onto it, shaking her head and waving her arms. Kaerisk decided to sleep in the brood-chamber, but again let her keep the skin.

As he exited into the foyer, he discovered an unusual sight. Father was not sitting on his dais, but standing before it. Zala and Icia stood in the entrance of the lair. The latter appeared out of breath, her eyes downcast.

"She will leave at once. You did not have my permission to invite her here," Father said.

Zala stood before her. "I don't need your permission! Can't you see how exhausted she is?"

Kaerisk trotted over to them. Icia smiled at Kaerisk, trying to hide the blood on her teeth at the same time, making

[35]

the smile seem forced. Kaerisk's tail whipped about behind him nervously before he turned to his father. "I will take her home, Father."

Father clasped his wings together with his wing-thumbs. "And how would you propose to do that?"

"I'll carry her on my back if I have to." His words caused Icia to become rather bashful, which in turn threw him a bit off balance. Zala, despite the situation, started to grin.

"You will do no such thing. You've already been emasculated before the city once; I don't need them seeing you with a dragon on your back too."

Kaerisk wasn't sure how that could emasculate him, but he continued regardless. "Then she must return under her own power, but she is currently unable to do that. Therefore, the only Honorable thing to do is to give her a place to rest until she is able."

Father growled a bit. "Don't lecture me on the Virtues, Kaerisk. Not when you do not fully understand what cost this might have." The elder regarded the three, and then sighed. "Take her to the brood-chamber. She can rest there. I will get something for you to eat."

Zala and Kaerisk beamed up at their sire. "Thank you Father!" Icia herself also gave her thanks, but it was muted against the chorus of siblings. The three hatchlings began up the path leading to the brood-chamber with Zala darting ahead.

Father stopped him as he passed by the elder's head. "Kaerisk." His voice was quiet. He waited until Icia had ambled past them to continue. "I do not want you to get too close to Icia. Not only for the lessons that I teach you requiring no outside influence, but because I know the heartbreak it might lead to."

Kaerisk frowned. "You have praised my Wisdom before, Father. Do you not think I will make the right choice?"

Father fixated on the exit. "Love has a way of perverting even the virtue of Wisdom, my son. As does hate..." A moment passed. Kaerisk thought he might continue, but without a further word, Father left the lair.

Kaerisk put the admonishment out of his mind and scrambled into the brood-chamber. Icia had already lain down before Zala, who took the brood shelf and pretended to sit like Father did on his foyer dais.

"Grrr, grr, Zala, grrr!" Zala exclaimed, giggling.

Kaerisk smirked at her. "He looks a lot more regal since his back end isn't hanging off the shelf." Zala snorted and lifted her head.

Icia smiled to him. She had cleaned the blood from her teeth. "Thank you for standing up for me, Kaerisk."

Kaerisk's heart started racing and he averted his eyes, scratching the back of his head with his wing claw. "It, er, wasn't anything. Just the right thing to do."

Zala grinned as she slid off the shelf and bumped her head under Kaerisk's chin. She then turned back to Icia and shook her tail. "Want to play Claws and Kills?" Icia nodded.

Kaerisk tilted his head. "What's that?"

Zala gave him a jaded look. "You don't even know Claws and Kills? Sheesh. Well, watch us." Zala sat down in front of Icia and scratched out two parallel lines vertically, then two more crossing them horizontally. Into the center box created, she scratched two more lines.

Icia went next, carving an X into one of the other boxes. "Let me win this one so we can show him." Zala agreed. They took turns, Zala filling in spaces with parallel lines and Icia with the cross lines. Eventually, Icia filled three in a row and scratched a line through them. "See? You have to get a line to win – all claws, or all kills."

[37]

Kaerisk understood, played the game with his sister, then Icia, and then watched them again, enjoying the simple moment. He leaned into his sister's side and Icia smiled at him. He tried to smile back, but he felt terribly awkward and so focused more on the game ahead of him. After a time, Father returned with a meal for them and delivered it to the doorway. Kaerisk took it to Icia and Zala and they ate their fill.

As the meal wound down, Icia looked up at the shelf again. "This is where Mother Mountain was, isn't it?" The question caught Kaerisk off guard.

Zala, too, hesitated before speaking. "Yes."

"You told her the story?" Kaerisk asked.

"What I can remember of it."

Icia smiled softly and stood. Her legs were wobbly, but the rest and the meal had seemed to strengthen her. "Thank you for the hospitality. I know elder Kaevaeri will ask me to leave shortly, so I might as well start heading back now."

Zala frowned. "You don't have to leave just to please him."

"No. But I probably should be getting back for my Riftwind lessons."

"You are learning the Riftwind? Father has only just started teaching me about it," Kaerisk said.

"A sage that visited my family said it might help my Illness if I do. I do feel stronger at least." Icia smiled to Zala. "Can you go on ahead?"

Zala grinned and bounced to her feet. "Don't do anything I wouldn't!" she exclaimed in sing-song voice as she hopped out of the room. Kaerisk's scales bristled in embarrassment and he ducked his head.

Icia giggled. It was a soft melodious sound that made Kaerisk relax. "I know that you have a different way of learning

[38]

and you might not get the same sense of San'Lux that Zala or I do. But I think your Father is right."

Kaerisk jerked his head up. "You heard him?"

"Some of it. I have heard similar words many times, enough to know what they are even if I hear nothing at all." Kaerisk frowned as she continued. "We females have things a little differently in San'Lux. All we need be is healthy, fit, and sharp. You come from a very prestigious family, Kaerisk. I'm just another dragon. You should focus your efforts on someone else." She turned her gaze from him.

"I – I have learned differently, Icia." She pulled her head back, ear fins perked almost as though she were startled. "I learned about the Virtues, and compassion, and - I know that you could have those things as well as any other. No, I know you have compassion, plenty of it! I don't know where my sister would be without you."

"Kaerisk…"

"I want you to have Pride in yourself. Even if you have the Illness. A dragon deserves no less, no matter their circumstance, right?"

She looked up at him and smiled, which made Kaerisk acutely aware of what he had just said. She walked by him, but paused before passing out of his flank. "Thank you Kaerisk, for giving me another reason to keep my promise to Zala. I'll try to visit again soon." She buried her head against his side in a tender nuzzle before ambling out of the brood-chamber.

Kaerisk stood there for a time before finally relaxing and smiling, placing on claw on the brood shelf.

I think she'll be okay. And Zala's with her too. Would you approve, Mother Mountain?

When he turned, he caught Father staring at him. Before he could speak, the elder slinked down into the lower chambers.

[39]

Over the next several days, Icia would visit. Sometimes Kaerisk could not spend time with her, as Father became insistent on lessons when she was present, but other times she arrived after lessons were over or he ran into them on return from his hunt with Sapphire's dinner. Kaerisk had sworn Icia to secrecy over the matter of his pet; for her part, Icia just smiled and agreed to keep it.

Finally, the smell had faded enough for Kaerisk to enjoy visiting Sapphire again. He discovered she had used the stone tool to cut the skin into parts, and that the back had somehow been cured and did not decay as he expected. He stared at it in wonder.

Using nothing but rocks and waste, she's turned discarded skin into something new. Father is right; dakael are clever animals!

She turned to Kaerisk and rubbed her stomach – a sign she wanted food. Before he could leave to hunt, she stepped in front of him, made the same sign again, and then lifted her arms as high as she could. Kaerisk wasn't sure what it meant, but he went to hunt again and returned home with her steak. She looked frustrated with it. She shook the pieces of skin aimlessly as she ate her meal.

Does she want another carcass?

Deciding to try, he brought the rest of the deer in from the forest where he had left it. He had already devoured most of it, but several of the chewy parts remained. Upon seeing it, she ran up and hugged him. She then turned to the carcass and started pulling out pieces of sinew from the muscles. She took these, cleaned them, and then attempted to use a small stone needle to press through the deerskin. Try as she might, it would not penetrate the skin and she again grew frustrated.

Kaerisk joined her and examined the piece of stone. Water fell from her eyes again. He took it from her. She tried to take it back but he growled a bit and she backed down. Closing his eyes, he let the Riftwind enter him. The magic of the dragons felt like an internal chill that began to burn as the energy became stronger. Using it always left him furiously hungry, but with the carcass nearby he wasn't concerned. Placing a careful claw to the piece of stone, he let the energy transfer into it, carving the rock as though he were carving wood with his claws. After several passes, he brought the tip to a fine point. Finally, he released the energy, which left him feeling heavy and hungry, and then returned the sharpened spindle of stone to Sapphire.

Father would flip if he knew I gave her a sharp piece of stone.

Sapphire did rush him after receiving it, but only to hug his neck as tightly as she could. She then tied the sinew around the back of the needle, poked it through the skin easily, and repeated this process again and again. Before long, the skin was sown together with the sinew and she struggled into it. It fit a bit loosely, but more of her pink parts were covered again and she looked happier than Kaerisk had ever seen her. Again she embraced him, muttering something into his earhole several times. Kaerisk smiled.

I trust you, Sapphire. I will further test that trust.

<u>Revelation</u>

Again and again, Father had spoken about the dangers of bipeds. He had called them animals, clever little monsters, demons – who used their ingenuity to craft devices of death. He had seen the spears of the humans in the forest and he had felt terror when they looked for him. His neck still bore the scars of one desperate victim of his hunt. And now he would risk everything to learn more about the dakael.

Pushing open the gate, he urged Sapphire to follow him. It took some coaxing to draw her from the prison-home in which she had lived for the past several months, but obediently she followed Kaerisk out into the main chamber.

Father sat on the waterfall dais, his attention focused on a tablet. His golden eyes scanned the words adorning the stone before peering up from it. Spotting the biped, his lips curled into a snarl, but no snarl came. "Why is that thing wandering the lair?"

Kaerisk winced, gazing up nervously. "I wish to take her hunting with me."

Father tilted his head, and then loosed a small laugh. "You are serious, aren't you? You'll never catch anything with her stumbling around and she's just as likely to bolt as soon as she sees the forest as the deer you might hunt."

"I want to see if I can trust her out there, Father. And it would be nice if I did not have to drag my kill back to the lair and clean her cavern all the time."

"I admit, I find it demeaning that my son is having to clean up after a dakael. Fine. Go hunting with her and see what happens. If the hunt fails, you can always eat her, right?" Father's lips drew back in a toothy grin. Sapphire cowered back.

No, she was already cowering back – did she understand the words?

Sapphire's face cracked with worry, but he nosed her and urged her along. Behind him, he could feel the disapproving stares of his father.

Of course, if he really knew what I was planning, he'd be even angrier with me.

Kaerisk kept his speed low. Sapphire took to holding the tip of his tail as he led her into the Ashen Forest. Sniffing the air, he located the scent trail he had left for himself. He followed it directly to the fallen log he had been using. Carefully, he withdrew a long piece of timber which he had sanded down with his scales and sharpened with his claws. Awkwardly, he handed it to Sapphire, who stared at it with wide eyes.

"Take it, Sapphire. We are going to go hunting."

Like a deer scenting nearby danger, she tensed, inspecting everywhere around her before timidly grasping hold of the spear with her oddly-shaped forepaws. She pulled the weapon back to herself, almost cradling it.

"Can I trust you, Sapphire?"

She peered at him curiously. Slowly, Kaerisk turned his back to her. He closed his eyes, his mind swimming through every lesson his father had taught him about how dakael were monsters that would kill hatchlings the moment they had a chance. Every lesson begged him to turn around and strike her down now that she was armed, the threat of losing to an inferior race scraping at his Pride – the greatest dragon virtue.

Movement. Sapphire's feet pressed against the ashen dirt behind him, shuffling around. Kaerisk stood tense. And then he felt her hand on his side. He turned his head to her, opening his eyes. She examined him as though concerned he was ill. He pressed his head into her stomach, churring happily,

[43]

and the girl hugged it. Her spear rested awkwardly against his neck where a different dakael had taken a chunk from it.

"I knew I could. Now let's go hunting."

Sapphire seemed to understand, but she still appeared nervous. He led her into the forest, her hand taking his tail again. They were in luck; a small family of deer had moved closer to the Ashen Forest. The dark, sooty trees broke up their shape to his eyes, but Kaerisk could smell them and just barely see the motion as they pawed at the ash for hidden roots.

He nosed Sapphire away from his tail and towards the deer. She hesitated at first, and then walked forward, stumbling much as his father had warned Kaerisk she would. He moved alongside her for a time, but slowly drifted downwind and hid in some dark bushes. Sapphire paused to watch him, but Kaerisk waved a wing towards her. She winced and moved closer to the deer.

Kaerisk judged the wind; the deer had to have been able to smell her from her position and they could certainly see her. She stood only a little over twenty-five feet away, and yet the most the deer did was step a little bit away from her.

The deer know fear of dragons – why are dragons to fear humans if the deer do not?

Sapphire lifted her spear, gripping it so tightly her knuckles turned white. Almost looking away, she threw it. It flew through the air and impacted squarely in one of the smaller deer, getting stuck in one of the shoulder muscles. The animal blared out and the whole herd began to run, but it could only hobble. Sapphire stood there, horrified. Kaerisk took this moment to leap from the bushes and charge the animal. Unlike its uninjured and fleet family, the small deer had no chance of outrunning the dragon and was quickly silenced.

Kaerisk drew the spear out and tossed it aside. Sapphire approached slowly and stared down at the deer as though she were shocked. Kaerisk, maw bloodied and claws covered in viscera, just stared at her half expecting her to join him in the meager, but acceptable meal. Instead, she murmured something and then turned her attention to the surrounding forest. Kaerisk postponed dinner – it certainly wasn't going anywhere – to watch her.

Bit by bit, Sapphire gathered parts of the forest: dried dead leaves from the ash-choked oak, bits of branches from the local bushes, and a larger piece of wood from a rotting log. She piled these and then began to rub two of the sticks together as fast as she could, resting them against the dried leaves. Just as Kaerisk began to get bored with her antics, smoke rose from the leaves and fire burst from it. He jerked his head back.

Dakael can create flames as well? Maybe they are monsters as Father says! But if so, why has Sapphire stayed with me?

The human peered at him expectantly. Kaerisk realized she wanted her meal now, and so he took a piece of the deer and gave it to her. She in turn stabbed the meat with her spear and stuck it over the fire. There she held it, turning it slowly, allowing it to cook as Kaerisk had over the lava pits. It took longer, but he was astounded by Sapphire's ingenuity.

There must be something more to this. We will go hunting again tomorrow.

Kaerisk ate his meal and Sapphire ate hers. They sat together in the calm forest, birds singing overhead oblivious to the two below.

The next day, Kaerisk set out with Sapphire again, but instead of the Ashen Forest, Kaerisk went north. He knew little of what lay in the north; Father never took him there, telling him the area was mountainous and ill-suited for hunting. Such places were fit only for scavenging dakael – and learning more about Sapphire and the dakael was worth the potential loss of a meal.

Gravel crunched with every step his heavy body made as he clamored through the northern hills. The earthquakes had caused several rockslides, making travel through the narrow passes treacherous. More than once he had to rear up on his hind legs and stretch his neck out to see if there was safe footing on the other side. The rock that had survived the fall from the hillside seemed to consist of only tiny jagged stone or large boulders; before long, he noticed Sapphire slowing down with a grimace painting her face. He paused and she came to a stop on a large stone, picking the rocks out of her fur-protected feet. Kaerisk sniffed. He could smell blood.

If this is what dakael normally have to deal with, it is no wonder they are resourceful.

He considered turning around for more ashen pastures, but they had already pushed on for two hours and it would take another two hours to return; light would almost be gone by then, but not enough to encourage out the nightly rabbits. Instead, he came near Sapphire and knelt down, motioning with a wing towards his back. She reached out hesitantly, rubbing his side, before climbing onto him. At first, he carried her as he would a carcass, splayed out on his back and half-pinned by his wing claws, but she struggled around for a bit, ultimately coming to a sitting position at the base of his neck. He grinned up at her and she smiled.

Father would die from shame if he saw me doing this. Thank the Firstbourne no one comes this far north.

Kaerisk carried her for another thirty minutes. A cloud passed over the Firstbourne's Eye, casting a dim shadow over the region. He wondered if it was an omen, but Sapphire pointed at something and began to articulate. Ahead, two large buzzards pecked at something just inside a bush. Kaerisk sped up. Sapphire's legs dug into his neck and her hands gripped his wings as she fell backwards with his charge. With a taunting shriek, they took to the air before Kaerisk could arrive, circling above him.

Lousy birds. My wings will work someday. I'll get you then - just you wait.

The corpse they picked at was buried in the rocks. One of the hapless animals of the region had been crushed by the earthquakes. The parts exposed were already picked clean. Sapphire slid from his back, already beginning to dig at the rubble. Kaerisk sighed.

It will have to do.

He was about to join her when he noticed one of the vultures land. Its pink-skinned neck curled up as though insulted. He turned and charged the bird again; however, the loose ground made for poor footholds and he soon slipped and slid along the harsh gravel. His scales protected him from serious harm, but not the cawing of the vulture. It sounded like laughter, further injuring his Pride.

Growling, he planted his feet and stood up. When he turned back to Sapphire, he noticed that the hill beside her possessed a gaping chasm in the side of the rock. Through the dimness, Kaerisk could discern columns within the cave. He drew close to it, almost as though the sight was somehow inviting. As the cloud moved away from the Eye, light shone into the cavern. Carved stone reliefs not yet worn away by time danced around the columns. Angular shapes began to appear, too straight to be natural, but too imperfect to have been shaped by Riftwind. The overhang protected from the sun, but with all the gravel atop it, he doubted the vultures – or a dragon – could spot it from the air.

Sapphire joined him, having given up the meal. She rested a hand against his wing, squeezing a bit. He could feel

[47]

her hand tremble. He followed her gaze to a relief at the back of the cave. The shadows made it difficult to make out, but it looked alarmingly like the open maw of a dragon.

Kaerisk churred a bit. "You don't need to fear me, Sapphire. It's alright."

Rocks shifted. Kaerisk whipped his head towards the sound. Standing there was a human, unarmed. His lack of chest covering marked him as a male, but his face was strange; colors had been painted on it, making it look as though he had two additional eyes. When his real eyes caught Kaerisk's, he began to scream and turned to run. Kaerisk tensed, every lesson Father taught him urging him to follow and kill.

Suddenly, Sapphire was between them. She spread out her arms. Kaerisk's head bobbed over and under them, trying to get past, but she adamantly refused to move. She began to growl. At first, the dragon thought it was some sort of challenge. But then, slowly, the growling began to form together into a squeak.

"… no."

Kaerisk blinked, pulling his head back like a startled snake. "What?"

Again she growled out the best draconic she could muster, her words stretched but understandable. "No hunt."

Kaerisk hardly registered the male human making his escape. He stared into Sapphire's blue eyes like the male had his only moments ago. "Sapphire - you can talk?"

Glossophobia

In the week that followed, Kaerisk spent every free moment he had with Sapphire. When he took her hunting with him to the Ashen Forest, they talked. When they ate their meal, they talked. When they returned home to rest, they talked late into the night. They talked first thing in the morning, when Father called Kaerisk to lessons, sometimes making him late.

Their communication was simplistic. Sapphire had picked up only the simplest of draconic words and had no syntax or structure to clarify; however, she was able to relate that dakael spoke a language of their own, called Lindorm – the Deep Speak. Kaerisk sought to know all about it and how to speak it. He hid his own disappointment well when he realized the grunts and cries she had been making before had always been words of her own language.

Father interrupted one morning, a deep growl rumbling in his throat. Sapphire immediately cowered behind one of the stalagmites. Kaerisk tried to urge her forward, but Father shook his head and called his son away from the cavern. After sealing it, he led his son towards the waterfall room. "I am disappointed."

Kaerisk felt as though his heart had sunk into his stomach. "Why Father?"

"Do you still intend to fulfill your dreams? To become the next San?"

Kaerisk growled as firmly as he could. "Of course!"

Father turned at the dais, walking out of the lair as Kaerisk struggled to follow. "Most dragons do not see their ambitions fulfilled. We like to delude ourselves into believing that each and every dragon has an equal chance at doing so, but this is a lie. Some of us possess clout and hoard far above our peers. But this alone does not necessarily aid or prevent one from achieving their goals."

"What then, Father?"

"Being willing to sacrifice for it. This, above all, is the most important part of seeing your desires met. It is easy to become distracted, complacent, or disillusioned. It requires Patience and the willingness to fight for what you believe in to see your dreams realized."

Father's heavy steps shook the ground, leaving deep imprints in the ashen earth. Kaerisk stepped into one, his paws only a fraction of his father's step. He paused to look at it before scampering after him.

"My son, you have invested too much time into that dakael of yours. You don't even know what today is, do you?"

"Yes I do! It's Windday!"

"And what is happening on this particular Windday?"

Kaerisk blinked and then paused in his tracks. He stared ahead to San'Lux, the massive silver statue shining in the early rays of the Firstbourne's Eye. Already, a large group of dragons flew to the top ring of platforms swirling above the statue's head, fire-colored crystals twinkling in the morning light.

This is when I'm supposed to join Father at the council meeting...

The hatchling scampered after his father as the elder dragon passed over the crest of the crater. Kaerisk half-slid down the side of the igneous bowl, earning a level, narrow gaze from his father. He lifted his head and tried to look dignified, but some ash had clung to his underbelly. He shook it off before ascending the statue.

The Path of Fire, the various circling platforms around the statue of the Firstbourne, was bejeweled by hundreds of red and orange riftcrystals. The last time Kaerisk had passed through here was on his father's back nearly three years ago. It was then he was introduced to the Council, the ruling body of all dragons, by his father – or more specifically, by his sister. When he had tried to speak, no words came. All the elders staring at him, expecting great things from him, sapped all sound from his throat. Instead, Zala introduced herself and him – as Risky. His emasculation drew more than a few chuckles from the venerated councilmen. The thought of standing before these same elders again terrified him.

Though Zala had been a source of stress, both then and at home, he could not help but think of her now. After all, this was only the second time he had ascended the Path of Fire, but his sister did so nearly every day to learn from Luxari with other hatchlings at school. While this moment was both terrifying and exhilarating for him, to Zala it must only have been another Windday. The second level, normally filled with hatchlings and elders at this time pouring over tomes and standing before the grand chest of the Firstbourne, was deserted. The weight of a meeting that could shut down the normal procedure of San'Lux burdened Kaerisk as he struggled to further ascend the path.

The third level of the walkway sloped down into a circular platform. The grand gaze of the statue had been fixed in the center of that ring, maw agape and snarling, as if to devour the unworthy that stood before it. Kaerisk had never seen it used, but Father had once explained that the ring served two purposes: the settling of disputes and the asking of blessings. The first was usually done in combat; though occasionally a great debate, it was more common for two dragons to fight and push the other from the circle. As for the second, Father explained that while all dragons venerated the Firstbourne, few were true religious disciples of him. Those that considered him a gift from, and now part of, the heavens came to this place as a holy site to worship from time to time.

[51]

The Path of Fire arched up at the other side of the platform. Kaerisk continued following its corkscrew to the top.

The path diverged just before the final level, making two winding paths that then connected to each other in an intricate halo. Though it appeared the flame crowned the dragon, one half of it was anchored to the statue's horns, providing solid footing. Kaerisk and his father had to weave between dragons perched all along the path, facing inwards where a circular platform rested. Standing upon it was the gold, Luxari, waiting for everyone to finish arriving. He smiled when he saw Father and the blue dragon returned the gesture. Father then led Kaerisk to one of the upper platforms, not far from a path directly connected to the central speaking platform. The hatchling stared at all the gathered dragons.

I'm going to have to speak in front of all these elders?

He tried to hide his shivers by pressing into Father's side, but the elder discretely pushed him away.

"Stand on your own four feet, Kaerisk. Show your Pride," Father admonished.

Luxari cleared his throat and then called the meeting to order; somehow, the bend of the circle amplified his voice, making it easy to hear his words. "Welcome, kyn, to this Council meeting. There are only two orders of business we must discuss. We shall start with the lighter one: The Festival of Flame is within two weeks. All roles and responsibilities have been designated. I will call them out; when I do so, those responsible must reply with an update." The gold waited for total silence before he continued. "Food."

A green stood and spoke, though it was harder to hear him. "Hunts continue and storage is arduous, but we will have plenty for the festivities."

"Messages," Luxari called.

A copper-hued dragon stood. "All have been delivered with haste."

"Good, that would have been quite a snag. Entertainment?"

A blue with baggy eyes rose slowly. Even among elders, she seemed ancient. "The storytellers prepare to weave their tales, the race coordinator has prepared the traditional test of skill, and the grand parade shall again circle the statue with the Pride of the dragons. I remind all present to be prepared for the trading of hoard-gifts."

Luxari bowed his head to her as she sat. "A good reminder indeed. Accommodations?"

This time, a red dragon and a white dragon stood, though only the red spoke. "We have not yet secured sufficient space for all those who will be present. There are fewer volunteers this year."

"That is a problem. Are there any present who might change their minds?" Luxari asked.

The same red spoke again. "I wish to donate the whole of my lair, but with my hatchlings soon to come, I cannot do this. Instead, I suggest the following: the northern mountains have long been considered part of our territory here in San'Lux, but we have little explored them and few have thought to take to the higher places. If my clan is given leave to build a home there, my entire lair might be used for the Festival."

Luxari's face contorted into a fierce frown. He was silent for so long that Kaerisk began to squirm, almost feeling as though he were the one who had done something wrong.

"Father, what's going on?" Kaerisk whispered.

"This is a good lesson for you, my son. The red there is Yenrick. He is unsatisfied with his home for whatever reason, but has found, through the responsibility of accommodations, a clever way to press for a new one." Father's bemused smile put Kaerisk at some ease.

"But Father, what does this have to do with the festival?"

Father chuckled. "Nothing, until now. Kaerisk, sometimes the best way to attack an opponent is to strike from the side instead of head on. Such maneuvering as this is quite common and allows for personal gain, as well as the possibility of prestige. The Council is an important governing body; who it recognizes often receives rewards."

I still don't see how they can make decisions with such maneuvering going on...

Luxari finally lifted his head and spoke. "The northern mountains are frontier lands. We know little of what rests there, only that the hunting is bad for at least a flight-mile. Moreover, one lair alone might not suffice if fewer dragons have volunteered."

"If I may?" Another red stood up. He was thick-muscled, with a deep voice and narrowed eyes. He strode down the path to the central platform as though he were the only dragon worthy of standing there. Luxari moved out of the way for him, though the same frown returned.

Father's smile twisted wider. "This should be good. Watch and learn, son."

"The frontier lands are likely dangerous. Even I have rarely visited there - we know not what kind of creatures might exist. Undiscovered biped civilizations might live there, huddled in the hills, waiting for any dragon fool enough to make it their home. And so, our only recourse is to go in force. I move that someone goes with the Yen clan to their new home and helps to protect them. This dragon should be strong, powerful, and well-trained in battle. He should give up his lair for the Festival, but it should be maintained for him should he

[54]

desire to return after a tour of one year is made. And he should be compensated for his trouble." The red paused for a time before lifting his head, ear frills flapping against his horns. "Of course, I shall volunteer for this."

Luxari's frown had faded as the red's speech progressed. He came to stand beside the red at his last line. "I agree. Your service is noted, Junrys. As the family is to be protected, compensation should be paid from their hoard. Under these conditions, I grant you both a lair-space of land in the northern mountains. Is this acceptable?"

"I accept. I shall serve with Honor!" Junrys exclaimed.

Yenrick lowered his head. The white next to him, likely his mate, shook her head. Despite this, he lifted his neck and spoke. "The Yen clan also accepts."

Father muffled his chuckle as Junrys returned to his seat. "Well played, Junrys. Remember, son – you may not always be the only one with your eyes on a potential prize. Yenrick attacked at the side, but did not see Junrys coming up from behind." Kaerisk blinked at him, having a difficult time understanding why this was funny.

"This concludes our first order of business. The second, however, is something I am certain you have all felt these past few months." Luxari's words caused a hush in the crowd. "The earthquakes have become far more frequent of late. Several lair entrances have been buried, though there are no reported deaths from this inconvenience. The good news is that it has nothing to do with the lava below – the scholars have examined the pool and the surrounding area, but there is no indication of imminent eruption, as what happened to the ancient city of Ton'Plu. Unfortunately, the scholars have been unable to determine an exact cause for the quakes. We shall now open the floor to the Flight to decide our course."

There was a moment's pause where several dragons spoke amongst themselves. Father said nothing. Instead, he rose from his seat. The same hush that had occurred when Luxari had changed to this topic occurred again. He glanced down to his son only once in a silent command to follow. The hatchling did, almost in a trance. The gold moved to one side for them as they took the central platform. Kaerisk looked around at all the faces of the elders, rapt attention focused on them. He pushed closer to his Father, but the elder blue discretely pushed him away with a low growl.

Father lifted his head. "It is well known my lair is close to the Deep Mountains. My clan has, for generations, seen themselves as the first line of defense against dakael incursion. Many of you know me – of the hunts undertaken against the Great Escape half a century ago. Many know my anger and my passion. But today, I wish to speak with my Wisdom – the Wisdom of experience. My lair has been beset with the strongest quakes of our area. The minor inconvenience within San'Lux proper from the insignificant shifting is in no compare to the sensation at my lair. The scholars, while they are of little use in a proper fight, do have knowledge and they have explained to me that quakes originate from a source, and become less powerful the further from it – like a dragon landing hard against the ground, those nearby will feel it, and those a mile away will not. If the quakes are stronger near the Deep, then there is only one obvious answer: the dakael are the source of the quakes."

As the crowd spoke in hushed tones amongst themselves, Father pressed Kaerisk forward with his tail. Kaerisk got his cue; however, when elders turned their gazes back to him, he froze. He opened his mouth, but no words came. All he could remember was standing here before, when Zala had made him look like a complete fool.

A red rose up from the crowd, as if sensing the weakness. With a cruel smile, he demanded, "How can bipeds create such shifting? How can they hope to move enough earth to even attempt such a thing?" Father growled.

"D-Dakael are more clever than we realize…" Kaerisk uttered, the sound echoing up through the platforms filled with elder dragons. It was louder than he realized, made more apparent by the silence that followed, almost as if the hatchling had spoken some horrific heresy that had ground the meeting to a halt.

Father stepped forward, eclipsing Kaerisk completely. "The Dakael are animals, but they are clever. It is entirely possible that they are tunneling and we must be prepared for it. San'Lux must not fall." With that last word, he shepherded Kaerisk back up the platform to their original seats.

As they settled, the red was quick to take their place, smirking up at the two. "As the revered elder has said – the dakael are clever animals. It is possible that they are digging, however unlikely, but this information is ultimately useless to us. The only one who we might have asked for assistance in this matter would have been the Matron Laniela, but the only one could have asked is no longer welcome within that Flight. I therefore suggest a different course of action." The red bowed his head, and then returned to his seat without actually suggesting any course at all.

Father growled deeply, but kept his voice hushed. "Sengex… there is no strategy, no elegance in you; you are no better than the dakael themselves!"

Sengex? Isn't that Senadra's father? I see why he doesn't like them…

Two more figures came to the front: a pair of black dragons. One was an elder, but the other was a hatchling like Kaerisk. When they stood on the platform, the elder did not speak as Kaerisk had expected. Instead, the hatchling came to the center, smiling wide to the Council.

Luxari lifted his head. "We have a visitor whom most of you know by now, from the Flight of Ur'Del. Go ahead and speak Delaan."

The hatchling nodded and raised his tiny voice to the crowd. "Esteemed members of the Council of San'Lux, I am still young and so my advice may not be the most sound among you. But as you are venerated elders, I trust that you will have the Wisdom to judge this for yourselves. In the short time I have been here, I have felt few quakes and they caused scarcely a grain of dust to fall from the ceiling of my beloved uncle's lair. His lair is far from the Deep, on the eastern side of San'Lux. Therefore, we can be certain that the epicenter is close to or within the Deep Mountains. However, this fact is not necessarily significant. We of Ur'Del know that dakael can be very clever indeed, but the feral creatures living in the Deep hardly possess any kind of large-scale technology or magic to cause so many quakes in so short a time. This must be a natural phenomenon."

The elders spoke amongst themselves in the short pause Delaan allowed. They seemed genuinely interested. It made Kaerisk's blood boil.

"My suggestion is to send a team as high into the Deep Mountains as they can go and survey the top of the peaks there. If it is natural, we cannot stop it, but we might be able to predict damage once we know its exact epicenter. If it is not, we still should know where the Deep might slide down upon us and make plans to prevent or mitigate it. I know that I am but a hatchling and know few things in this world. But I do know that I would hate to lose my beloved uncle or any of the kind elders I have met and spoken with here in San'Lux. We should therefore take measures to prevent such needless loss of life."

With his words finished, Delaan bowed his head and then smiled up to his uncle. The two returned to their seats.

None came to replace them and the Council fell silent. Luxari cleared his throat and spoke again. "Very well. Raise your wings if you are against Delaan's plan of survey and mitigation." The gold waited a time, but none raised their wings. "Then our course is set. After the Festival is over, we shall meet again to discuss the results. This adjourns our Council meeting."

As the elders stood and began to shuffle or fly away, Kaerisk's eyes locked on the black hatchling. He was grinning up to his uncle, looking exceptionally proud of himself. It filled Kaerisk with as much anger as his father had for Sengex. His scales bristled and he growled deeply.

He completely showed me up! I won't ever forgive him!

Father stood and pushed at his son with his tail once more. The elder did not look at him and said nothing. Kaerisk's rage vanished, feeling his father's disappointment. As the two winded down the Path of Fire, Kaerisk glanced over his shoulder, memorizing the grinning face of the black for later.

The Festival of Flame

Zala bounded around the waterfall chamber, eagerly watching the entryway that led deeper into the lair. Kaerisk sat beside her, marveling at her energy. When their eyes met, Zala trotted over to him and rested her belly against the ground. "I'm so excited!"

Kaerisk smirked. "I can see that."

"Father didn't let you go last year, did he?"

Kaerisk crossed one forepaw over the other, glancing off to the side. "I didn't even realize a Festival was going on."

She nuzzled her snout into his side tenderly. "You'll love it! There are so many dragons there, and there's all kinds of events, and rare foods I've never seen before, and the best part is no lessons for a whole week!"

Kaerisk chuckled. "No lessons for you, maybe. Father's been exceptionally harsh with his lessons lately." Kaerisk trailed off as he considered why. Since the Council meeting, Father had constantly insisted that Kaerisk defend any statement he made. If he didn't speak clearly or have a good argument, the elder would rap his tail against the floor hard enough to shake the hatchling nearly off his feet; if Kaerisk's spoken defense was particularly banal, Father would have him run two laps around the lair.

"I'm sure even Father would let you have some time to enjoy the Festival, brother."

"I hope so. I could use some entertainment."

"Icia will be there. She's been wondering where you've been."

Kaerisk tapped his claws nervously. "I guess she would be there too."

Zala ruffled her wings. "What kind of thing is that to say? She thinks you've chosen a dakael over her, I'll have you know."

Kaerisk ducked. "No, it's – Zala. Do you think you can keep a secret?"

She rested her wings against her back, stalking around to his side to look him in the eyes. "What about?"

"It's about Sapphire. I found out something important-"

Father's footfalls shook the ground. Kaerisk immediately silenced himself, standing at attention with his wings clasped before him. Zala gave him a bemused smirk, but when Kaerisk stood like that, as regal as he could muster, Father was always a bit more attentive to him. "Son, daughter. Here." He reached into one of his scale pouches – artificial flaps of scale fused by Riftwind onto the body – and withdrew two shining pieces of platinum. One was an intricately carved statue much like the one Kaerisk had stolen from Zala months ago, but with finer details and material. The other was a shining orb of pure platinum. The statue he gave to Zala.

Kaerisk took the orb. "What is this for, Father?"

The elder smiled. "I forget this is your first Festival, little one. Take it with you and when the parade begins, you'll figure it out."

"The hoard parade!" Zala exclaimed, rear lifting high with her tail waggling.

The elder's gaze fell on his daughter. "Zala, keep yourself more dignified." The statement seemed to deflate Zala considerably. "Someday, you shall have a hoard as well, son. And it is used for many functions."

"Like draining it for Riftwind?" Kaerisk asked.

"Mm. So you have been learning. Yes – such precious metals can be broken down for energy, saving us from starvation-sickness. But it is also used in the community, for trading and for status. And for brotherhood. Now come along." Father turned, tail sweeping over their heads as he ambled towards the exit.

Those two community uses make sense, but what did he mean by brotherhood?

Kaerisk and Zala scampered after him. The elder moved somewhat swiftly; the span of his legs made it hard for the two to keep up. Rather than walk as he did, both of the hatchlings bounded from one rock to another. By the time they reached the edge of San'Lux they were already tired, but the sight below did more to take their breath away than the run.

Hundreds of dragons sat on a circuit around the crater, more than Kaerisk had ever seen in San'Lux before. They had arranged themselves in four circles around the statue, leaving walking space between them. Only one dragon stood on the statue itself: Luxari. He watched the proceedings like a bird of prey from the perch in front of the statue's face.

Father squeezed into the outer line. The hatchlings pressed between him and a black. All around them, the dragons chatted absently with those near to them. The black to their side was engaged in a loud conversation about flight with the bronze next to him. The bronze kept nodding his crested head to the point where Kaerisk wasn't sure if he was following along or falling asleep. Father sat stoically above them, not engaging with anyone. His gaze was fixated on a far invisible horizon, his jaw set firm. His tail had bent around his side and up to his forepaws, curling around his left foreleg. Kaerisk attempted to emulate him.

"Father! Father! I see Icia!" Zala exclaimed. Kaerisk's near-regal pose was quite interrupted as he lurched his head forward into the gap. About four dragons down from them on the other side of the ring, Icia and her parents stood together. "Can I go stand with her?"

Father sighed. "Very well."

"May I go as well, Father?" Kaerisk asked.

The elder turned his vision from the horizon to his son. "I suppose this is to have fun, too. Zala, make sure you help your brother with the parade."

"Okay! C'mon Kaerisk!" Zala bounced into the open area, earning a few stares from the elders present. Kaerisk followed with a bit of apprehension.

Icia smiled as the two arrived. She was looking remarkably healthier; her silver scales seemed to shine even more in the warm light of molten crater. She lowered her head and pawed absently at one of her ear frills. "Nice to see the two of you again."

"It's been awhile. I know I've been really busy lately, but I have missed you coming over," Kaerisk said.

Zala rolled her eyes. "She has been coming over; you've just been too busy to notice!"

Kaerisk scratched the back of his head with a wingclaw. "I-I'm sorry. I didn't know. But I do have something to tell you, so -"

Before Kaerisk could complete his sentence, the voice of Luxari boomed across the crater. He tilted his head towards the gold, towering above them.

He must be using Riftwind. It seems like there is nothing it cannot do.

"Welcome, my kyn, to the Festival of Flame. All dragons burn with a spark of flame from the wildfire that the Firstbourne swallowed untold centuries ago. Together, that spark always burns brighter. The connections we share transcend all other things, no matter the Flight, no matter the place. Together, we are all brothers in flame. Let us share our spark. Step into the ring and walk the path. Give unto those along that path as though they were your family, for everyone here is family in flame!"

The lines began to shift. The outer line where Father stood came forward onto the cleared path, while behind them, the inner rings coalesced into a thicker line of dragons. When they came forward, they procured various artifacts of gold, silver, and platinum. They had been shaped into various forms: statues, orbs, urns, wafers. Kaerisk had no idea which was more valuable, but suddenly it didn't matter. They began trading these items with dragons from the other line, and then marching down and trading those new pieces for still more new pieces.

"Zala, what's going on?" Kaerisk asked.

"We trade hoard to show that we are all family, silly!" Zala seemed to be watching a black hatchling in the line, slowly meandering towards them with the crowd.

"But no one gets any richer from these trades." Kaerisk frowned when he recognized the black as the hatchling who had humiliated him at the council meeting.

"That's not the point, Kaerisk," Icia said. She stepped around Zala and handed him a small statue of gold, shaped into a snarling dragon. "The point is to share a moment together, without worries or strife. Will you trade with me, Kaerisk?"

Kaerisk faltered a bit. "Um, sure." He took out the orb his father had given him and traded with her. When she took it, her smile cracked wide and she pressed her snout to his.

"Thank you, Kaerisk."

He scratched the back of his head with a wingclaw sheepishly. "Well, uh. It's part of the festival, so I was happy to." The claw got stuck on his horns, leaving him in a somewhat awkward position when the black hatchling arrived. Delaan flashed that winning smirk at him and passed over Icia and Kaerisk completely, stepping up to Zala.

"Happy festival, Zala," Delaan said, handing her a small statue of silver. This one was shaped like a dragon lifting its tail proudly.

"Happy festival, Delaan." Rather than trade the hoard that father gave her, she instead procured a small statue of a dragon with his head lifted high as though in contempt.

Delaan took the statue and grinned at her. "I get the message. Say hello to your brother for me." With this, he bounded after his uncle and rejoined the line.

Kaerisk unhooked his wingclaw and joined his sister. "What was that about? How do you know him?"

Icia followed. "Delaan's been going to school with us for the past few weeks now. I think he's a bit of a sleaze, honestly."

Zala flicked her tail against Icia's, and then giggled. "If you can have a love interest, why can't I?" Icia and Kaerisk glanced at each other, and then quickly looked away. "Besides, I only like him. He's got his eyes on Senadra too, which tells me he's just taking part in San'Lux's customs. And that's not something I want for myself."

Kaerisk tilted his head. "What customs?"

Zala regarded him. "I guess Father hasn't explained that sort of thing to you, huh? Well, females really only have one role here and that's to attract the best male as a mate. Males have to choose the best connected and influential. Guess it's a tossup between me and Senadra."

Icia stuck her tongue out after him. "I just think he's in it for the preening."

Zala giggled. "Icia! Honestly." Her laughter faded as she turned her attention down the line. "Besides, I don't want that. I want someone to love me for who I am and not worry about politics. I guess that's why I've always been so close to you two."

[65]

Icia's mouth hung open for a time, her eyes wide. She then walked over to Zala and leaned into her. "Thank you." Kaerisk watched the two, feeling almost like an outsider.

Zala, what life have you lived out here while I've been inside?

"Hey Kaerisk, are you going to race?" Zala asked.

He blinked. "Race?"

She giggled. "Sorry, first time and all. After the parades, there's a race around the outer crater. I've seen Father making you run around lately. I thought he was training you for it."

Maybe he was. But...

"I don't really feel like it."

"Why?" Icia asked.

"Things didn't go so well at the council meeting."

Zala frowned, and then came alongside him. He leaned into her with a sigh. Zala didn't say anything.

She never has to.

The carousel of dragons completed their circle around their kyn; Kaerisk was surprised at how many hatchlings there were, far more than he ever saw studying with Luxari. As he wondered if they were taught at home as he was, Luxari's booming voice proclaimed an end to the hoard trading and the start of the festival. The circle broke as adult dragons ambled towards the caves along the crater, spoke amongst themselves, or departed for the crater's rim. Zala and Icia trekked up the hill and Kaerisk followed. The smell of cooked meat wafted from the caverns, tempting him to stray. As they crested the rim, Kaerisk discovered most of the hatchlings he had seen before bouncing about under the watchful eyes of several elders, lining the cleared track.

Cleared wasn't the right word. Ash had covered the circuit around the rim, presumably to fill in the earthen cracks and mark the track. As the group crossed it, they kicked up small clouds of dirt and soot, steps imprinted behind them. Luxari flew overhead as Zala and Icia sat down near the start of the track; he landed nearby and started to collect hatchlings for the first round of the races.

"The hatchlings go first. After that, it'll be the adults. The flight race is much more spectacular," Zala explained. She motioned to several boulders that Kaerisk didn't remember being there the day before. "The elders lift the boulders into the air with Riftwind and the racers have to avoid them."

"Why do they do these races?" Kaerisk asked.

"No one really remembers anymore. They said it was an old training exercise the Firstbourne devised in preparation for some big battle, but no one knows with what," Icia said.

"Tradition holds it was with the flame elemental that the Firstbourne swallowed to give us the gift of fire." It took Kaerisk a moment to realize that the voice didn't belong to Icia or Zala. Off to the left, three hatchlings down, was the red dragoness Senadra. Her eyes locked on Kaerisk and a twisted smirk painted her lips. "Not surprised none of you know that. Zala never pays attention in class, Icia has a terrible memory, and well. I hear you don't really have anything to say, Kaerisk."

"Oh, hello Adra." Zala's head turned away from her, looking straight ahead. Her tone was deadpan.

"What's that supposed to mean?" Kaerisk asked.

Senadra waved a wing absently, staring at the wingclaw as it moved. "Daddy has been raving about how badly you performed in front of the council. Delaan completely showed you up."

Zala snorted, tail striking against the ground. "Just ignore her, Kaerisk. Ornery Addy just likes to say things that don't mean anything."

Adra's smirk mutated into a grin with Zala's words. "I see you're not lining up for the race, Risky. What, did you hear

Delaan was participating and didn't want to look completely pathetic?"

Kaerisk turned to the starting line of the race. Delaan stood amongst the other hatchlings. He waved a wing to the group when he saw Kaerisk and Adra looking, flashing those white teeth that seemed so bright against the black scales. Kaerisk's claws pierced the ground as he fought the urge to snarl.

Adra waved a wing to the black. Her smile was, for a moment, more genuine. "Probably for the best. Sooner or later, Daddy's going to have a son that will be the true heir to the San clan. It's pretty obvious you're not cut out for it, Risky."

"You don't know what I'm capable of, Adra." Kaerisk snarled, stepping onto the track.

"Brother!" Zala exclaimed.

Icia pressed forward, brushing her wing against him. "You don't have to prove anything, Kaerisk. We know you're better than she is."

Kaerisk paused a moment, leaning into the wing. And as the moment passed, he pulled away, hopping over to the line. When Luxari saw him, he smiled brightly, but said nothing. Kaerisk muscled his way to the front of the line – right next to Delaan. He growled low and the black looked at him.

"What?" Delaan asked.

"I haven't forgiven you," Kaerisk said.

"What are you talking about?" Delaan asked.

Kaerisk didn't reply. He stretched out his legs and wings as he did before he hunted. The black titled his head and then turned his attention to the track.

Luxari lifted his wings. "Crowd, are you ready?" In response, the dragons on the sideline roared. "Racers, are you ready?"

More than you can know, elder.

[68]

The racers roared. A moment passed and Luxari roared, retracting his wings to his body. The racers took off, at least a hundred hatchling feet thundering down the track. A large number of hatchlings raced past him. Kaerisk covered his face with his wing to protect from the ash as he paced himself, going at a manageable speed. The crater was large; he had skirted it a few times, and knew that running like a deer could not last long – not even for the deer. The hatchlings that bolted ahead as fast as they could quickly came to a trot and then a slow walk, panting for breath. Kaerisk and the others bounded around the unexpected obstacles and kept going.

The ring of elders and hatchlings around the track cheered and roared for them. Out of the corner of his eye, he kept an eye on the black. Less than five minutes into the race, Delaan was already winded. It made him grin until he looked at the other hatchlings, who were as tired as Delaan.

Is this all they can do?

In his mind, he played out several fantasies of Delaan the deer, chasing him down. He was broken from his trance by a familiar roar. Down the track, Kaerisk saw Father standing amongst the others, as regal as he always did, but a look of pride on his face that Kaerisk had missed.

I will fulfill my dreams, Father. I will be the next Sanrex. And I'm going to throw it in Adra and Delaan's faces!

He grinned sidewise at Delaan, not unlike Adra before the race. "Hey, Delaan."

"W-what?" he asked, breathless.

"Better not get any ash on those pretty teeth of yours when you eat my dust!"

Delaan tried to ask what he meant, but Kaerisk broke into his full stride. His heavy claws dug into the ash and the ground below, propelling him forward at a relatively astounding speed. Large clouds of ash kicked up behind him, coating his fellow competitors in grey. The crowd cheered in surprise as Kaerisk raced around the crater faster than he ever had before. He chased his thoughts like a deer and salivated the same. When Luxari came into view, he pushed himself even harder, certain now that if there had been a deer, it could not have escaped. The elder's wings went up declaring his victory, but Kaerisk kept running - just a little further, so that he could come skidding to a halt right in front of Adra. A wave of ash washed over her and the unfortunate hatchlings beside her, dirtying her red scales. Her mouth hung half open, shaking herself off and grunting. Kaerisk lifted his head proudly and trotted over to Luxari who, grinning, nodded to him.

"I see the Kaer-Sen rivalry continues into another generation." Luxari folded his wings to his body, the other hatchlings still far off.

"I just had something to prove," Kaerisk said, shaking his paws of some of the ash.

"Not many hatchlings have to hunt for themselves as extensively as you do. Take Pride, but temper yourself with Honor, little one."

"Yes sir. Though I can't make any promises where Adra is concerned."

Or Delaan.

The gold chuckled. "Your families will be the death of me. I hope you enjoy the rest of the festival, little one. Meet with as many dragons as you can. Now is the time to truly prove yourself."

As Delaan and the others huffed and puffed to the finish line, Kaerisk sat in the most regal pose he could, turning his attention from the race to the crowd surrounding it. He wanted to meet the elders as Luxari suggested, but when his eyes fell onto Icia and Zala who waved to him wildly, he couldn't help but smile and feel all those thoughts of elders melt away.

[70]

<u>Discovery</u>

"Want I could see it."

"Wish you could see it?"

Sapphire struggled a moment, taking a deep breath. Communicating with her had been very difficult at first, but she had been learning his language long before he had begun learning hers. As a result, the two generally spoke draconic, which for her meant deep breaths and careful word choice. And an exceptionally cute growl that still occasionally made Kaerisk smile.

"Wish, yes."

She leaned into his side as they rested together. He had related to her about the race and the victory and how Delaan's pretty white teeth had a tint of grey soot on them when he gave a half smile at the end of the track. He wasn't sure how much had translated, but Sapphire always seemed to be enthralled by his stories.

"Kaerisk?"

"What?"

"I thought dragon.... Monsters. I wrong. I wish all dragon like you." Her head turned, looking down his long neck. He could only see her with one eye, but her smile calmed him.

"I wish all dakael were like you, Sapphire." He rested his head on his forepaws and closed his eyes. Behind the lids, he played out every story of Sanrex, the great founder of San'Lux. He battled the horrible hordes of dakael who raided and pillaged dragon lairs with spears and other horrible weapons destroyed in ages past. When he was younger, these stories exploded his imagination: grand elders with battered bodies, scuffed scales, and wings pierced in countless battles against a faceless enemy, standing atop a glorious mountain and watching those enemies scatter into the darkest Deep. Since learning Sapphire could speak, he suddenly had a face to put upon that enemy. Seeing Sanrex stand over the subjugation of someone who had been a loyal and trusted companion as Sapphire had become, the scene lost its epic feel and was less worthy of Pride.

Sapphire shifted. He opened an eye as she rolled from his side and crawled forward, coming to rest before him. His head lifted a bit as she spoke. "Dakael are like me. Live in fear. Live on scraps. Killed if found. Dakael killed like animals, but dakael not animals."

Kaerisk returned his head to his forepaws, frowning. "We don't know you like I do."

She pulled back onto her hind quarters, hands resting in her lap. "Not ever change?"

"I don't know. I'm just a hatchling. But I want to."

"Wish to?"

"Want to."

She huffed, rubbing her head fur with one hand. "Draconic hard."

Kaerisk smiled a bit. "The topic is hard. Sleep now. We can speak later." Sapphire nodded and crawled beside him, curling up against him. As she drifted off to sleep, a new dream struck him. He stood as Sanrex on that lofty mountain, but shepherded the dakael out of the Deep as a great savior.

In the morning, he left the chamber. Father rested on the waterfall dais, stretching out his wings. Upon spotting his son, he smiled. "You did well to reclaim your Pride yesterday."

Kaerisk lifted his head, curling his tail around him in regal pose. "I had much to prove, Father."

"The festival lasts the week. No more lessons until it is over. I want you to go out and learn from your kyn for now.

[72]

Many Flights are here and you have earned a little fun, too. Hunt for your pet and hurry to the city."

The hatchling beamed. "Thank you Father!" He hopped out of the lair, rear end struggling for traction. Behind him his father chuckled, but he didn't stop. He wanted to spend more time with Icia and Zala and see all the festival had to offer.

After a successful hunt and one last visit to Sapphire, he bounded to the festival. The great throng of dragons had lessened from the first day, but the crater was still considerably filled. Most congregated around the caverns that dotted the crater. Sweet-meat smell wafted from some of them. Squeezing into one, he discovered a large table wreathed in flame beside a great freezing chest. Both were tended by well-fed masters of Riftwind, keeping the elemental effects in place. Another dragon placed various meats from the frozen box into the flame and cooked them as Kaerisk did for Sapphire. The jovial bronze cook stopped his conversation with other dragons and offered a small scrap from a large smoldering animal to Kaerisk. The meat was a little tough, but it had a rich smoky flavor that caused Kaerisk's wings to curl a bit. The cook laughed and returned to his conversation.

Kaerisk scurried from that cave when his meal was finished, intent on trying all of the meals that caused him to salivate, but the next cave he visited lacked one of the fire-forges he had seen. Instead, an elder rested upon a dais, regaling his audience with a mighty tale. Dragons of all size and color came together to battle their most hated ancient enemy, the dakael. Again and again the dragons clashed with them. The horrible weapons caused the dragons great losses, but the survivors rallied for a great final charge that scattered the lines of dakael and struck down their leaders. Without a strong leader to guide them, the bipeds became weak and cowardly, retreating into the holes of the Deep. Many of the

[73]

dragons present cheered at this conclusion, but Kaerisk noted several who had a more thoughtful expression on their muzzles. He began towards them, intent on speaking to them about the story.

"Kaerisk! There you are!" Zala's voice derailed him. She stood in the cave entrance with Icia, both hatchlings avoiding the careful steps of the elders that shuffled out of the cave with the completion of the story. "C'mon, let's get out of the way!"

Kaerisk hopped over to them, glancing back over his right wing at the speaker who grinned proudly, either at the story or his telling of it. "Oh! I forgot, with the races I forgot to talk to you about-"

Maybe I shouldn't say it here.

"About what, brother?" Zala asked.

"Let's talk elsewhere! We'll never see the sky if we get crushed!" Icia exclaimed. The elders that passed her chuckled, though their large clawed feet did come rather close to her.

Kaerisk agreed and Zala led them out of the cave and up the ridge of the crater. Safely out of the way, Kaerisk could watch the whole city in action from his perch on the rim. Near-head height with the statue, he could see several dragons on the upper levels. A pair of dragons crouched in battle stance before the watchful gaze of the Firstbourne.

"What did you want to tell us, Kaerisk?" Icia asked.

Kaerisk carefully stretched his forepaws out, coming to rest on his belly. He glanced at Icia, her blue eyes fully on him. "It has to do with Sapphire. I know I've seen spending a lot of time with her, but there's a reason." Icia and Zala came to lie beside him.

"What reason, brother?" Zala asked.

"Sapphire is sentient. I've been talking with her."

The two dragonesses pushed their heads forward, looking at each other with mouth half agape.

Kaerisk pawed at the ground. "It happened when I went hunting with her. She stopped me from killing another human - and spoke. She's been learning draconic from me and I've even learned a bit of her language! The bipeds don't have to be our enemies if we can talk with them, right?"

Icia twiddled her claws together. "Well, no Kaerisk, but…"

"Brother…" Zala pressed her neck against his, golden eye locking to golden eye. "Sanrex was the great hero that put the dakael in their place. The whole city of San'Lux was founded on the principles of the superiority of dragons and that only dragons have right to the land. Father had to have told you this."

So many times…

"But does it have to be?" Kaerisk jerked his head up and away from her. "We can be superior maybe, but I've seen what Sapphire can do. She is clever and courageous. She has to be, just to survive! Maybe she's not a dragon, but she should be. Why can't we stop killing each other?"

A laugh. Icia's head lowered, frills rattling against her head in annoyance or fear. Down the ridge from them was the sneering red, Senadra. She was flanked by Delaan and Nerilla.

"Oh, this is too rich. Delaan, did you hear all of that?" Adra asked.

He scratched the back of his head with a wingclaw, glancing off to the side. "Yeah, I did."

"What are you doing here, Adra? Didn't get enough ash last time?" Zala asked. She bat a clawful of it at the red, who hopped back.

Adra grinned. "I'd not do that if you care a lick about that stupid brother of yours, Zala."

Zala lifted to her feet. "What are you talking about?"

"Isn't it obvious? If I tell my father about this, or any of the elders, Risky'll be the laughing stock of San'Lux! To think, someone supposedly of Sanrex's blood could be so soft-scaled!" She laughed, joined a moment later by Rilla. Delaan just kept looking off to the side, like the stone there was particularly interesting.

Kaerisk tilted his head, flicking a small pebble towards them. "No one'll believe you. The rivalry of our family is well known."

Senadra crouched down, batting the pebble away with far more force than necessary. It clattered into a crack and disappeared. "Oh, maybe not. But they'll believe a third party, who has no reason to lie for you or for me. Right Delaan?"

Delaan sighed. "Yeah, yeah. Look, this isn't a big deal to me-"

The red brushed her side against him. "You're still honor bound to tell the truth and that's all I care about."

Rilla giggled gleefully. "You'll have to do what we say now!"

Zala stepped forward, threatening to slide down the hill, her wing partly obscuring Kaerisk's view of them. "What do you want, Adra?" Zala asked. Kaerisk grimaced a bit.

Does she go out of her way to emasculate me or does it just happen?

Kaerisk looked sidelong to Icia, but she didn't seem to notice that Zala was protecting him. Rather, she had lifted to her paws as well and stood much as Zala did, though her frail form was not as intimidating as his sister's.

Adra's black eyes were practically twinkling. "I want to challenge Kaerisk to a race again. I want to show you all that Delaan's the better dragon. And since I am so generous, I'll even let Risky determine the track."

Zala snorted. "Don't let her intimidate you, brother. She's just blowing hot air instead of proper fire."

I wish that were true, Zala. But if Delaan is any dragon at all, he'll follow the Virtues – and Honor is honesty, too. And I can't do anything for the dakael, for Sapphire, or even for myself, if this witch makes good on her threat. My only hope is that I can convince Delaan to keep the matter to himself, but I would need time, and to talk to him alone… Wait.

"I can choose any track I want, huh?" Kaerisk asked, lifting to his feet.

"Brother-"

"That's what I said, Risky. Hope you're not going deaf, too." Senadra's tail tip bent back and forth in rhythmic motions.

"There is a hidden location, far to the north. A cave with murals. That is the place I choose. It's a bit far for your delicate constitution, though."

She glowered at him. "Trying to make it hard on me? Fine. I'll make it hard on you, too. If Delaan beats you, I'll tell everyone what I heard. But in order to beat him, you're going to have to make it to the finish line with your precious biped in tow, too!"

Kaerisk floundered a bit before standing upright. "Alright. Meet me just north of my lair and I'll get her."

Rilla laughed again. The high pitch of her laugh and its odd placement made it sound as though she didn't really have any idea why she was laughing at all. "You'll never beat Delaan dragging a deadweight along. This'll be fun!" The three climbed the hill and walked by them.

Adra's tail swept some ash onto Zala's paws as she passed. "We'll see you fools there." Zala swiped at her, but Adra was surprisingly swift and hopped out of the way. Delaan followed behind them, shaking his wings out.

Zala stepped in front of Kaerisk. "Brother, there has to be another way."

He pushed past her. "There isn't. Don't worry, just stay here."

"I want to go too! – I mean, we have to go." Icia's voice started strong, but tapered off at the end, her eyes not making contact with Kaerisk's.

Zala trotted alongside him. "Icia's right. I don't trust that girl. I think she's plotting something. We're going with you." Icia struggled to keep up, shuffling behind them.

This is not what I had planned... but it's not like I can ever get Zala to change her mind.

"Fine. Wait with them and I'll sneak into the lair to grab Sapphire." Zala agreed and Kaerisk scampered off. His heart raced in his chest as he rushed home, pausing at the entrance to let it slow, only to realize it was not the run that had made it pulse so quickly.

Father had vacated his dais, perhaps to enjoy the Festival himself; it put Kaerisk at some ease. Down the ramp he went, past the waterfalls and into the four-way passage. With a grunt, he pushed back the bars, startling Sapphire, who had been half-dozing. Her brow creased with lines as her skin moved so unnaturally compared to Kaerisk's more solid scales, which were just as furrowed but far more taut.

"What wrong?" she asked.

"Everything. Sapphire, I need your help. Can I trust you?"

She paused a moment, and then nodded and forced out a growl. "Always."

"My future and yours depend on it. We have to go back to the cave we saw to the north."

She shivered and placed a hand against his shoulder. "I help if I can."

[78]

He smiled. "I have faith in you. Come." As he led her out, he was surprisingly calm. All he could think about was how good a test it would be for Sapphire and how their success would prove his faith justified.

Fateful Race

"This is not turning out to be as fun as I thought it would be…" Rilla paused again, picking sharp pebbles out of her soft green scales. Kaerisk couldn't help but smirk a bit, but he knew this wasn't easy on Sapphire either.

"Shut up, Rilla! If we don't get there soon, Kaerisk, I swear to the Firstbourne, there won't be a Flight in all the world that doesn't know about your biped fetish!" Adra shouted. The sound echoed up through the hills, scattering some buzzards that had perched on the few remaining trees clinging to life on the side of the cracked mountains.

"Delaan and I could have gone alone. Or do you not trust him?" Kaerisk said.

She sneered. "I want to be there when he beats you." She was as winded as Rilla and her hide seemed even thinner. Delaan, for his part, had been surprisingly quiet. Kaerisk had expected at least a winning smile or two out of him, but his maw had remained shut.

"At this rate, you'll expire before they even race!" Zala exclaimed. Her snout lifted high to the air, as though she avoided some particularly foul carrion on the ground. She had held up well on the journey. Kaerisk could only wonder at why her paws were more calloused than her peers, especially since Icia couldn't play outdoors as much as others might.

Icia held up the rear. She had been taking her time, moving carefully over the earthen barriers put in place by the quake-riddled ground. She was as tired as Adra or Rilla, but she had never complained, nor stopped moving. The thought of it made Kaerisk smile.

Never give up, Icia. If you don't, I won't.

Adra sneered. "What are you grinning about, Risky? How much further?"

Kaerisk huffed, lifting his head to the sky and taking a deep breath. The curve of the hills in this area seemed to go on forever and it made Kaerisk wonder just how large the world might be. "We should be nearby. Look for pair of bushes between two hills."

Adra groaned. "Oh, how exceptionally specific. We're going back."

Sapphire hopped ahead of them. "Near." She knelt in the pebbles and took a handful of them. Kaerisk came beside her and she opened her palm. Most of the rocks were chips from the hills, but a few were off-color purple gemstones.

"What are these?" he asked.

"Deep stone."

Adra laughed. "Now you're following a biped? Some San you are."

Zala snorted. "You're following her too, you know." Adra had no other reply but an irritated hiss.

Kaerisk furrowed her brow at her. "What do they mean? Are other dakael here?"

Sapphire shook her head, dropping the crystal shards to the ground. "Don't know. Not safe."

Delaan walked forward to them, causing Sapphire to cower behind Kaerisk. "It's okay. Do you know something about this place we're going, dakael?"

Sapphire lifted her head over Kaerisk's wing. "Not safe. Not to go."

Delaan began to scan the ridges. "I don't like this. Maybe we should head back." Kaerisk peered at him.

He doesn't seem that shocked that Sapphire can talk... and he is listening to her?

"Forget it! If we're close, we're going to do this now! Where is it, you stupid animal?" Adra shouted, storming up to the group. Sapphire rounded Kaerisk and broke into a run, somehow keeping her balance on the uneven ground. Adra followed her, as did the rest of the group. The human disappeared around a hill, finally coming to a stop. Adra and the rest joined her, staring into the same yawning chasm that she did. Inside, the familiar carved relief opened its massive maw as if beckoning them to be eaten.

Zala pressed near Kaerisk. "Brother – what is this place?"

"A better question is how this is any kind of proper race track!" Adra exclaimed. She descended a small slope and entered into the cavern mouth.

"Adra, wait!" Delaan exclaimed, going after her.

As Kaerisk followed, the full extent of the cavern came into view. Larger even than a dragon's cave, the weight of the hill was supported by several massive columns. A pit of ash and wood rested in front of the relief. Purple crystals were sprinkled all around it. Light from the Eye cast shadows all about, but as Delaan examined the pit, the off-color crystals began to glow.

Riftcrystals? Do the bipeds use them for light in the Deep?

The purple light chased away the shadows of the columns and cast the shadows of the reliefs. They depicted a mighty battle. Dragons cast their stone wings at the top of the carving gloriously. Their stone breath burned fleeing bipeds, who eternally escaped to the left side of the mural. A huge maw, dragon shaped, rose from the center with ruby eyes. They gleamed, but Kaerisk couldn't tell if it was from the presence of dragons with Riftwind or if it was a trick of the light. Strangely, the maw seemed to form some sort of blockade for the fleeing bipeds, as no dragons could be seen on the left side of the relief.

"What does it mean?" Rilla near-whispered to Adra. The stillness or perhaps the open chamber and its domed ceiling amplified the sound of her voice.

"I don't care. What, are you going to race around the pit? This is a joke!" Adra exclaimed. She wandered away from the basin of ash, pausing as she looked down a slant. "There. There's some sort of way further in."

Kaerisk padded over to her. There was an arched opening, nearly pitch black due to the angle. "You want us to race in total darkness?"

"The thought crossed my mind." Adra spit at his feet.

"There's another entrance on this side," Rilla said. She stood over a similar slant on the other side.

Delaan rested a wingclaw against his chin. "Symmetry. It's possible that it continues further in, but-"

"Then it's settled!" Adra exclaimed. "You and Delaan, and the stupid dakael, will choose a side and race to the deepest part of the cave." She plodded over to the scattered purple shards and threw a pawful at them at Kaerisk. A few of the pieces stuck in his hide. "You can use these to see."

"We don't know that it's safe. We should go elsewhere," Delaan said.

Adra groaned. "I am not going back until Kaerisk gets beaten! If you're so worried, I'll go and protect you, Delaan. Rilla, you come with me too."

"Then we're going with brother!" Zala exclaimed. She took a pawful of purple shards and covered herself.

Kaerisk walked up to her. "Zala, maybe you shouldn't..."

"It's settled! We'll take this side," Adra said. Rilla hesitantly joined her at the right side, while Delaan looked between the cave and the entrance before sighing and joining the other two.

Kaerisk also sighed. Sapphire placed a hand on his side and tried to smile. He nodded to her and took his position on the left with Zala. Icia crept up behind them. When Kaerisk saw her, he shook his head. "No, you should stay here, Icia."

She came beside him, lifting her wings, showing a few purple shards she had placed in them. "I don't want to, Kaerisk. If something happened in there, to you or Zala, I don't know what I'd do. I know I'll slow you down, but please. You know I've been feeling stronger. Let me go with you. I want to be there when you beat Delaan."

He sighed. "Alright." He faced the cavern entrance.

"Ready, go!" Adra exclaimed from the other side of the cavern, charging into the breach. Kaerisk could hear her companions follow suit. Kaerisk examined his unexpected entourage. Speckled with the stones, Zala and Icia looked like they were ready for a party, not an adventure. Sapphire kept twitching nervously, her eyes on the exit.

If only there was another choice.

Kaerisk led them into the darkness. The path was straight at first, uneven floors causing the dragons to stumble from time to time. The walls were large enough to handle an older drake, but a full-grown dragon would have found maneuvering the tunnel to be impossible. The turn of the passage was sudden and abrupt, leading to the left. As they passed down a short slope, one of Kaerisk's paws brushed against the wall, feeling the uneven marks made by something that was not quite claw and certainly not dakael nail.

Another turn revealed a sudden split in the path. To the left, the walls became wavy and curved, like the undulation of a tail. The right was straight and led up what looked to be an easy slope. Kaerisk moved towards the easy path, but Sapphire grabbed his tail. Not expecting the contact, he jerked a bit;

Sapphire in turn leapt back, pressing herself against one of the walls.

"I'm sorry – what is it Sapphire?" Kaerisk asked.

Sapphire regarded Icia and Zala, who crowded around her, before speaking. "Short path, long path. Long path, short path. All I know."

Kaerisk scratched his head, glancing back at the divergence. "You're sure? I thought you didn't know about this place."

Sapphire picked at her fur coverings. "Don't know all. Important. Pieces. Father say, walk long path."

"We should take the upper path. It'd be easier for Icia," Zala said.

Icia smiled, but she appeared even more nervous than Sapphire. Her tail moved erratically in short, sudden bursts. "Don't worry about me."

Kaerisk considered a moment and then nodded. "If Sapphire knows something, then we should listen. We take the long path."

The purple light made it somewhat difficult to tell where one curve ended and another began. Kaerisk moved slowly around the twists and turns of the serpentine path. Zala bit his tail a little harder than necessary and Icia kept trying to look back at the biped that held her tail, but they kept a steady pace. After a few minutes, they came out of the corridor. The new area consisted of a pit and cliff: before them, a dark opening loomed while the far wall led upwards into another dark space above. Uneven stones served as steps, leading both up and down. The stones were covered in large cracks and seams, as were the walls in the area. Kaerisk shuddered as he realized just how much rock rested above them.

"Any idea Sapphire?" Kaerisk asked.

She stepped in front of him and paced along the edge of the pit. "Saying. Um. Up?"

"Up?" Icia asked. The dakael regarded her and she smiled as best she could. So did Kaerisk, despite the situation.

This is how it should have always been. Is this the world I didn't get to experience in Father's lair?

"Saying. Future, up."

Zala was a bit less patient, huffing as she too began to pace. "Future? What is she saying brother?"

Sapphire growled almost to the point where Kaerisk couldn't understand her words. "More than future. Must be future."

"Destiny. Whose destiny?" Kaerisk asked.

Sapphire shook her head. "Not-dragon."

"Well, no dragon made this place. So we're going up!" Zala exclaimed, padding over to the start of the steps and scampering up them. As her weight pressed onto the fourth stair, part of the stone gave way, taking her with it. Her claws scraped against the rock as she struggled to keep from tumbling into the open pit and stairs below. Kaerisk and Icia scrambled after her, pulling her up by her foreclaws as she locked her hind claws into the weakened stone. She flopped onto the stairs like the fish Father had told him of, wriggling a bit further from the edge.

Icia breathed a sigh. "That was too close..."

"Don't be so reckless, Zala!" Kaerisk exclaimed, slowly rising to his feet. Some of his and Zala's crystals had fallen from their scales, resting unlit at the bottom of the hole. He looked for them in vain.

She lowered her head. "Sorry."

As Sapphire joined them, they continued up the stairs. When they reached the top of the cliff, several columns came into view. They looked as cracked and weathered as the stairs, but held up a ceiling so high that the hatchlings could not see it from the meager light of the crystals they had taken. By the time they rounded the first of the columns, they could no longer see the walls.

"Is this the inner most chamber?" Kaerisk asked.

Sapphire crossed her arms close to her body, but then walked in front of the group. Curious, Kaerisk began to follow her. She looked a bit lost at first, but as she came to rifts in the stone floor carved for some unknown purpose, she seemed to grow a bit more confident. She followed them to a large stone pit, carved into the shape of a dragon's head, its open maw screaming to the heavens.

Cautiously, she came to Kaerisk and took two of the small purple stones from him and struck them together. They lit a little brighter and she set them into the empty eye sockets of the statuary. Light, an off-color purple white, erupted from the statue. He risked peeking within; a strange riftcrystal rested there, one that seemed to glow even brighter as the magic within the eye-stones faded and shattered to dust. The channels in the floor began to brighten with the same light, ultimately terminating in still more pits, which erupted in massive flames. Unlike the dragon effigy before them, the burning braziers depicted several piles of suffering dakael, toiling around the flame.

Icia gasped. Kaerisk dug his claws into the ground, all his instinct warning him of danger. He followed her gaze to the wall. A mural at least three elders long covered the far wall. Faded paint could not take away from the drama of the scenes depicted. It seemed to tell a story. On the left, an act of battle screamed in red hues. Dakael and dragons – no. Not dragons, but something else. They stood against dragons, which breathed fire on the land and in the sky. The creatures with the dakael resembled dragons, but had no wings. The battle gave way to great mountains, struck by lightning.

The center of the mural continued with the mountains. Rising from them was a not-dragon that dwarfed the mountains that had covered it. Its ruby eyes stared directly at Kaerisk, as though it had moved to lock eyes with him. Shuddering, he looked away. The mighty not-dragon led a huge army of dakael with spears. A barrier protected against the dragon flame and spears riddled those unlucky dragons on the ground. The final scene showed the dakael safely in the coils of the not-dragon, reaching up above to pluck the very Eye from the sky.

"Sapphire... what is this place?" Kaerisk asked, staring at her.

She shuddered, backing away from the mural, her gaze locked on the ruby eyes of the not-dragon. "Not - not safe."

Icia stepped up to the glowing dragon statue in the middle of the room, dancing a foreclaw over the detail. "The dakael had to have built this place. But how? It's huge. More than I could have imagined even dragons making."

Zala backed up towards her brother. "I don't like it, Risky." She turned her head from the mural, eyes fixating on the path they had taken to reach this chamber. "Adra and her cronies better get here soon."

Sapphire moved towards one of the side braziers, peering at the imagery on the stone. Kaerisk joined her and she jerked back at first, but then smiled and placed a hand on him. "Not all dragons same." She pulled her arms back, the smile fading as she regarded the tortured reliefs again. "Not all dakael, either."

"Shhh! I hear something!" Zala exclaimed. She padded up to one of the columns and listened. Everyone was still. There was a sound, scraping of a hard substance against stone.

Dakael? What was that human we saw before doing here?

Kaerisk stalked away from the flame, cursing himself for looking into the light and ruining his vision. He took a place at a column with Sapphire at his side, but Icia remained where she was.

Scrape. Scrape. Scrape. The sound grew closer, coming from the path opposite the one they had taken. Kaerisk steeled himself, reviewing every lesson his father had taught him while Sapphire's admonition rang in his ears. It stopped. There was a moan, amplified and altered by the shape of the cavern.

What if it's a not-dragon? I couldn't fight something like that!

He shuddered, but Sapphire pushed into his side. Feeling her there brought some comfort to him, though her face was as tortured as his.

"Wish had spear now."

"Me too, Sapphire."

"Have claws. Fire."

"I mean, I wish you had your spear." His statement must have been no comfort to her, as she began to shiver too.

Purple light emerged from the tunnel, followed by purple-speckled figures. Kaerisk breathed a sigh of relief as he recognized them as normal winged quadrupeds. He composed himself before stepping out from behind the column. When Adra came into view, her eye began to twitch wildly, as though she had some dust in it.

"Looks like we got here first, Adra," he said, unable and unwilling to not lift his head proudly at the remark.

"I can't accept this! I refuse to accept this!" she shrieked. Delaan moved into the chamber while Rilla tried to calm her companion.

"Where are we?" Delaan asked.

[89]

"We don't have a clue," Zala said, walking over to him. Kaerisk tilted his head at the act, considering the two seemed like enemies and he certainly didn't like Delaan, but he decided it was due to the fear hanging in the air.

Delaan examined the mural quietly. The eerie stillness of the chamber, however, was drowned out by the angry raging of Senadra. She pushed Rilla away and rushed at Kaerisk as though she might attack him. Kaerisk got on his guard, but she stopped before reaching him.

"This is unacceptable! I refuse to lose to you! I refuse!" She slammed her tail against one of the columns in anger.

The ground began to shift. Dust fell from the damaged ceiling and columns. Kaerisk wasn't sure if it was a quake or Adra's impact against the weakened stone, but the shaking didn't stop. Kaerisk's head whipped about, to the column, the ceiling, his friends, his enemies, as the ground began to cave.

"This place is going to collapse! Run!" Delaan shouted, turning around and bolting the way he came. Rilla and Adra joined him. Icia tried to break into a sprint, but the ground gave way. Her claws raked against the stone as gravity tried to pull her into the opening pit. Behind her, the dragon-head tumbled hundreds of feet into total darkness.

"Icia!" Zala shouted. She rushed over to where Icia dangled, heedless of danger. Kaerisk followed, but Sapphire kept her distance, moving back and forth as though torn between abandoning them and staying.

"Hang on!" Kaerisk dove. Seizing her forepaws, he tried pulling her up; however, even if Icia would have had the strength that Zala had, there was no traction for her hind claws to help him. His sister pulled on his tail so hard she drew blood, but the hatchlings could not lift her.

"It's… okay. You have to get out of here. Please-" Icia struggled, but her effort dwindled as her muscles began to fail her.

"I'm not letting go! Just hang on!" Kaerisk shouted.

I can't – I won't lose her!

Another dragon came to his side, grabbing her other forepaw. He thought it was Zala at first, but he could still feel her teeth pulling at his tail. As their combined strength hauled Icia onto the unstable ground, Kaerisk discovered Delaan beside him.

"You?"

"I couldn't leave you here. C'mon, we have to go now!" he exclaimed. The four of them scrambled to their feet. Delaan made for the path he knew, but the tunnel collapsed and he turned to follow Kaerisk's group.

Sapphire had begun to run ahead of them as soon as she saw Icia was safe. Kaerisk followed her rapidly, surprised how fast she could move on those two legs. She stumbled down the stairs, bracing herself for support against the cliff before making it safely away from the pit. Kaerisk moved to follow, but the shaking intensified and the stairs crumbled. He slid to a halt, avoiding the certain death of toppling into the darkness.

"We're trapped!" Zala screamed.

"We can glide using Riftwind! C'mon!" Kaerisk exclaimed. He took a deep breath, channeling the energy of the dragons. A warm chill shot through his muscles as his body glowed, those few remaining purple speckles in his hide shining. Locking his claws to the edge of the cliff, he vaulted forward. He had never tried this in a dangerous situation before – once or twice to test it from the waterfall dais. He felt air whistle by him as he cut through it. Rocks fell all around him, threatening to take out his wings. He outstretched his legs as he landed, trying to get traction while opening his wings to act as a break. He nearly skid into Sapphire, but he landed safely. "C'mon!" Delaan followed as easily as he had, but Icia and Zala were left behind.

"Risky! I can't!" Zala exclaimed.

"Yes you can, don't be afraid!" Kaerisk shouted.

"No, you idiot! Luxari hasn't taught me how to use the Riftwind yet!"

Kaerisk's heart sank. Without Riftwind, a dragon was too heavy to maintain a glide. Zala would seriously injure her wings and plummet to her death.

"Zala." Icia's voice was soft. Kaerisk could barely make it out over the shifting stone. "You and I made a promise, remember? We would fly together someday."

Zala's tears were apparent even at a distance. "Icia, I-"

"It's okay. Today's the day, Zala. Remember? My parents have made me use the Riftwind since I was little. Just relax, spread your wings, and let yourself fall." Icia closed her eyes and a pale glow came over her. She placed her forepaws onto Zala and the glow transferred into her friend. She panted. "Go - quickly. It won't last long."

"You'd better be right behind me!" Zala exclaimed. She turned, closed her eyes tightly, and leapt. She narrowly evaded a falling boulder half as large as she was, from luck more than conscious effort.

Icia focused again. The luster of her silver scales faded and blood leaked from her eye sockets, but the glow surrounded her. Zala landed just as Icia took to the air behind her, but it was too late. The ceiling began to cave. Despite the rumbling, crushing stone, and the shrieks of his dakael companion, all Kaerisk could hear was his sister screaming. When the rocks hit Icia, she was still smiling. The stone dragged her down into the darkness. Zala immediately tried to leap after her, but Kaerisk caught her. He pulled her back as dust obscured everything else.

<u>Committal</u>

Even as he stood beside the lava beneath the statue of the Firstbourne, Kaerisk felt cold. Luxari parted the circle of dragons that had come to stand reverently around the pool. In his hands was a stone box. Normally such a casket was unnecessary, but they had not been able to retrieve Icia's body. Kaerisk stared at the coffin, but all he could see was the same image that had haunted his nightmares for the past two weeks: Icia, smiling, blood on her teeth, blood dripping like tears from her eyes, struck by a stone and swallowed into darkness.

Through blurred eyes, Kaerisk could see Zala, standing beside Icia's parents. All three of them wept bitterly. He wanted to wail and cry with them. He wanted to scream, but a constant, insistent glare from his Father, fixated upon a distant horizon prevented him from doing so, from moving, almost from breathing.

Across the pit was Delaan. He had bolted like a terrified rabbit when the stone had hit Icia weeks ago. Gone was the arrogant smile, the confidence he had once possessed. He was shaking. He could not even look at the coffin as he pressed into his uncle's side for comfort. The elder covered over him with a wing. Zala, too, received this protection from the pair of silvers.

Why does Father deny me the same dignity?

Luxari's voice broke the surreal moment. "We stand before the ancient hearth, which has served us well in all the centuries since our arrival. This cauldron bubbled in the days of the Firstbourne. Firstbourne willing, it shall burn forever. Always has it brought us comfort and warmth, light in the darkness, and the reminder of the awesome elemental powers that birthed us. This flame – this eternal flame – is the outward manifestation of our souls. As it burns, so do we. From the fires of passion and love are we born. And to this flame, we commit our dead."

It was awkward for him to lift his paw. The stone casket was significantly heavier than a hatchling would be, but he did so, as if showing her to the Firstbourne towering above them. He then slowly lowered the casket and slid it into the lava. Shortly thereafter, it began to sink into the molten rock, an orange glow cascading around it.

"We often stand before this pool and commit a hatchling who has passed to the Illness, but Icia's loss is especially poignant, for she was overcoming the trial that had been given to her at birth. While I taught her, she was always mature, happy, and aware of how others felt. Her sacrifice was great. She gave her all for those dragons around her that meant everything to her. She lived for them. She died for them. May the elements accept her boundless spirit and gift her with a new form that lacks the flaws of her last, be it the Firstbourne's will."

Kaerisk could not stop the tears now. He turned his head away as his Father's glare fell upon him. He could not see that scowl, nor could he bear to watch the last corner of the stone sink into the lava.

Shifting. The elders began to shuffle away from the somber scene, most with faces like statues – stoic, heedless, unfeeling. Luxari joined Icia's parents and bowed his head low.

"I truly am sorry for your loss. The Glor clan had a magnificent hatchling. I shall pray to the Firstbourne your next clutch will be even more successful. I paid for the recovery from my own hoard, but do not seek to repay it. You have lost more than enough already."

They thanked the elder in strained words. Kaerisk could hardly make them out. The gold's head lowered to Zala and nosed her gently, but it did little to comfort her cries. Kaerisk's claws tensed against the stone.

If only I had realized she couldn't… I never want to see Zala cry again.

The gold came over to Father, carefully avoiding Kaerisk. "Two weeks of digging and we still haven't reached the chamber they saw. We are worried that it might have been completely destroyed."

Father lifted his head a bit higher, inhaling sharply. "It could have all been a fantasy of fear."

Kaerisk wanted to say something, but Luxari preempted him. "Do not make matters worse, Kaevaeri. Even you did not have a tough hide when she passed." Father lost his stoic posture, turning his glare from the horizon to his golden friend. Luxari did not flinch. "The Sen clan is gone now. These events will pass. But I urge you to reconsider your daughter's training. If Zala had been taught to use the Riftwind, as she would have wanted, Icia would be alive right now."

Father growled. "Don't ever speak to me about what she would have wanted. Even if you are my oldest friend, I will not tolerate such undue slight. My daughter's training will remain unchanged. Hopefully, she can find some real friends now."

"With all due respect, Kaevaeri, there are fewer true friends than those that would give their lives for others. But I see you will not be dissuaded. I hope your hide remains this thick when your choices come to bite you in the night, for I can do no more than this. I wash my wings of this matter. Excuse me; I have business to attend to."

The gold smiled at Kaerisk before he slinked up the Path of Fire. Once he was gone, Father swiftly retrieved Zala. Kaerisk followed in a daze. His sister cried the whole trip home.

[96]

The roaring water could not fill the empty feeling of the lair. As soon as Zala and Kaerisk were inside, Father curled around the entryway, blocking it bodily. Resting on his side did not make him seem languid; perhaps it was the harsh gaze he directed on his children, especially Zala, who continued to cry softly.

"Now that one matter of awful business is through, I have another to discuss with you Kaerisk. Go to your room, Zala," Father said.

"I'd rather stay here, Father," she said through her tears.

Father glanced away from her. "These matters do not concern you, as a female or even as a member of the family. Go to your room."

"How can you just ignore me?" Zala suddenly demanded.

"Did you just ask a question of me, daughter?" Father asked, turning his molten gaze onto his offspring.

But Zala did not flinch. Even with her eyes filled with tears, her muscles tensed and her tail lashed behind her. She lifted her head to her sire in spite. "Yes, Father, I did! Don't you care about me at all?"

"I do. If I did not, I would have spent my time more wisely today. I am aware that your friend has passed-"

"You don't know anything about Icia! I made her a promise – we promised – we would fly together… "

"I warned you before you attached yourself to the living dead. You knew this could happen, but you chose not to believe it. You waste your tears on her. As did my son, which was even more disgraceful."

"What?" She scratched at the ground in a rage. Kaerisk's jaw hung half open.

Why does Father speak so low of Icia? She was my friend too. If she hadn't sacrificed-

[97]

His sire's mighty talons flexed, as though he would do harm to his offspring. "You heard me. She struggled brilliantly, but she ultimately failed to live. A dragon's life is a series of trials. She could not overcome them all. It is best that she has passed on to the elements, so that her spirit might move on to find a better form. Hers was a disgrace to the perfection of dragon kind."

"Take that back! If it weren't for her-" Zala shouted.

"A dragon never speaks what he knows untrue, daughter. Icia is gone and it is time to move on."

Kaerisk stood rigid. "Father, how can you-"

"You Honorless dragon!" Zala leapt against his paw, slashing ineffectually with her untrained talons. "You didn't care when Mother died! Did you forget about her too? Did you move on? She probably hates you too!"

The paw she battled struck with incredible speed. It seized the whole of the hatchling and lifted it to eye level with the elder, where his hateful stare fell upon his own child. She yelped. Her struggling ceased so suddenly that Kaerisk thought that his sister was dead.

"You ingrate! You insolent whelp! Ignorant failure! You dare speak to me of her? You dare accuse me? You never even knew her! You will never come close to her unmatched grace and majesty!"

He shook her. Zala squeaked as she could not draw breath with her father's tight grip around her.

"Father, please!" Kaerisk exclaimed. But Father continued to squeeze. His sister hung there, her ferocity fading with her lack of breath. "You'll kill her!"

With those words, the elder slowly loosed his grip. His eyes fell upon some distant point before he released her onto the upper level. She coughed and gasped for breath, but Father refused to deviate from that empty point into which he stared.

Save for the bitter weeping of pain from his sister, there was an eerie stillness that descended upon the moment. Kaerisk wasn't sure he remembered to breathe.

"She wouldn't give up either... Go to your room, Zala." Zala rose on shaky legs. Kaerisk moved to join her on the second level, but his father's low growl stopped him. Slowly, his sister limped into the brood-chamber. His father finally looked away from his point, turning his full focus to Kaerisk.

The hatchling flinched. "W-what did you want to discuss, Father?"

"You got lucky. You don't know how lucky. Delaan's testimony stated that Senadra's tail hit the column and then the place began to shake. The Council was split on whether or not she was indirectly responsible for Icia's death, but the Sen clan has decided that they should move to the new colony in the north until the matter can be resolved or forgotten. They won't trouble you or anyone else again."

"I see."

Father snarled. "That is not all. Senadra attempted to claim she had evidence of you being a biped lover. She was drowned out by the Council, who saw it as a ploy to alleviate potential punishment. But I thought to myself, 'Kaevaeri, what would make your son so foolish as to go to a hidden and forgotten dakael hole with everyone he knows and cares about?' And so I confronted Delaan myself."

Kaerisk swallowed.

"He revealed that you had been blackmailed. An Honorless tactic, but it was all true. Bring the biped here. Now."

"But Father, I-"

Father fixated one eye on his son, widening it.

In the mood he's in, he might do to me what he did to Zala! But if I bring her...

Kaerisk's tail twitched, his head bobbing a bit from side to side. But when his father began to growl, he turned and slowly ambled to the pet chamber.

Sapphire waited at the bars. She had paced about since Icia's death with extreme worry. In the days that had passed, she spoke quietly, if at all. She had only known Icia for a short time, so her actions puzzled Kaerisk, who saw them as empathy. Now he realized she had, over a week ago, come to the same conclusion he had just now.

"Heard roars. Is safe?"

"No." Kaerisk placed one of his forepaws on the bar. Sapphire's face contorted. She reached a hand through the bars, resting it on his paw. "I... we have to see Father."

She squeezed her fingers around one of his. "Not be stopped?"

He averted his eyes. "No. But I'll fight for you."

Her face cracked at the mouth with an uncomfortable smile. "Fight for self." Her hand slowly fell away from his paw. She stepped back and took a deep breath. "I ready."

Kaerisk pried open the bars and led her into the foyer. His father's tail lashed against the ground at the sight of her. She flinched, as did Kaerisk, but when he recovered he pulled her along. When he stood before his father, he realized just how much larger Father was than the two of them. The elder's head glowered down from on high like the Eye of the Firstbourne.

"I want to hear it from your own lips. Have you been teaching the biped to speak our language?" Father asked.

"Yes, Father." His voice was barely a whisper.

"Why?"

"Because bipeds are sentient. All this time, you told me that bipeds were nothing more than animals and we should kill them as such, because they were dangerous. But Sapphire is not dangerous. She is as intelligent as any dragon I know, and Wise too. She can do things that I cannot, would never even think of doing. And I – I gave her a spear. And she did not use it against me."

Father's growls intensified. "You gave her a weapon?"

"Yes. And everything you said, about bipeds killing a dragon at every chance they got, about how I should hate them and fear them, all of it – was wrong."

The elder snarled, rising up. "Son, it doesn't matter if bipeds are sentient or not! They are still animals! They lack all culture and history. They are completely amoral beings – murderers, every last one of them! It is in their blood to kill. I gave her to you so that you would learn what a burden that bipeds are to civilized dragons. A burden we would do better to destroy. The depth of your failure astounds me."

Kaerisk stepped forward. "But we don't have to be at war with them! If we can communicate, can't we find a way to share what we have?"

"Can share. Be friends," Sapphire said in the best draconic growls she could muster.

Father was still a moment at her voice. And then his scales bristled. "Still you defend them? Haven't you figured it out yet?"

Kaerisk opened his mouth to speak, but his father was fast. Too fast. Father's claws were like quicksilver on lava rock. The human's hopeful eyes became forever locked in that false veil. And as her blood coated the floor and the walls, as it coated the young blue's scales and the old blue's talons, she did not scream. She was already gone.

"Again and again I heard that same story about Mother Mountain," the elder said.

"F-father-"

"Be silent! The rusty valley – her blood, leaking from a wound – was caused by a dakael! The bipeds killed your

[101]

mother, my mate! I always left before you finished it because her death carved a wound in my heart larger than the whole of your body! If they could understand us, they could cause untold damage. Sanrex drove them into the Deep because, if he did not, the dakael would learn from us. Take our gifts and our teachings, use them to destroy us completely. You not only risked your dream of becoming Sanrex, you risked all of dragon kind teaching a human to speak our language."

Kaerisk couldn't speak. The warm blood on his scales already began to chill as it ran in rivulets down his scales.

Father looked away. "Clean up this mess, and then join your sister in the brood-chamber. Neither of you are to leave until I call for you. I need some air." The elder turned, claws splattering the crimson like errant paint around the entryway, before he ascended the ramp and took to the sky.

Kaerisk's claws went weak as Father disappeared. He fell to his joints in the blood of his pet and friend.

"Sapphire. I'm so sorry. I didn't know it, but you were right all along."

He closed his eyes and dipped his head until his snout touched the cooling liquid.

"Dragons are monsters."

The First Decision

Kaerisk didn't know what kind of funerary rites that humans had. Such a morbid topic never came up when he was attempting to learn her language. In absence of this knowledge, he decided it was only right to give her a dragon committal. He collected her scattered parts and placed them into the cauldron of lava, causing a lot of whispering from the few dragons wandering between the caves and the molten rock. As the elements consumed the corpse, Kaerisk said a prayer to the Firstbourne, but he didn't know if the Firstbourne would care. All of a sudden, he didn't know anything.

He returned home, still covered in her blood. Zala stood at the doorway, waiting. When he came near, she cringed back. It was how Kaerisk thought he should feel, but at that moment he was numb, still shocked by the weight of Father's action and the revelation it in turn brought. They didn't speak a word. There was nothing they could say.

Kaerisk went to the waterfall. He placed the whole of his body within it, crimson fouling the pool below. Bit by bit, the blood was washed clean of his body, but not his soul. Even as the strange process of Riftwind filtered the blood away into the rock, the stain of it was not cleansed. He lifted his head into the water so that Zala did not see his tears.

When at last he stepped free, he took a deep breath and composed himself. The mark of blood still lay on the stones, but he would not clean that. He wanted that to remain. He wanted Father to see it every day.

"Kaerisk?" Zala's voice broke the silence. He turned his attention to her as the water dripped from his scales. "I – I'm leaving."

He sat before the stain, staring at it as though trying to will Sapphire back to life. "What are you talking about?"

"I'm going to run away." Zala's words finally pulled his attention away from the blood. "Father never loved me. He only ever had room in his heart for you."

"That's – that's not true."

"Don't even try to defend him, Kaerisk!"

Am I still defending him? After what he did?

Kaerisk's wings drooped, even as he lifted his head to her. "Where are you going to go?"

"I don't know. Anywhere but here."

"You don't know how to defend yourself. You don't hunt for yourself."

"I'll learn."

"Have you had your First Flame?"

"No."

"You'll die out there."

Her scales bristled. "So what? I have to do something! I can't stay here anymore, Kaerisk. Father nearly killed me! You heard what he said about Icia!"

Kaerisk rose up and walked over to her. She pulled back, but he pressed his head to her chest. "Zala, I have lost everything in my life that matters to me except for you. I can't lose you too."

Zala hesitated a moment, and then lifted his head with hers. "Then come with me." He peered at her with furrowed brow.

I don't want to see this mark every day. Here I could become Sanrex and lead our city... but would they ever accept my ideas? Father knew they were sentient and he still killed them. Even if they did-

He leaned against Zala a bit harder. He could not bear to tell her what Father had told him about their mother's death.

[104]

"I can't be Sanrex anymore. I can't be Father's child. We will find some place where dragons and bipeds can live together. We'll find a new home, Zala."

Zala cracked only the faintest of smiles as she pressed back against him. "I'd like that."

"I'll teach you everything I know about hunting and Riftwind - but Father never told me anything of the world outside of San'Lux. We need a direction – some place to go."

Zala bit her lip thoughtfully. "We can ask Delaan."

"Delaan? But he'll rat us out."

"There's no one else we can ask. And he'll know. He knows all about the outside world."

Kaerisk sighed, fixing an eye on hers. "You're sure?" She nodded affirmatively. "Alright. Wait just a moment."

Kaerisk scurried up to the brood-chamber and collected the dragon statuette Icia had given him. The golden object was impractical to take with him, but he wasn't planning on it. He scurried downstairs and left the cave, Zala close at his heels. He then found a secluded spot away from the lair and buried it in the dirt. As he rested a paw over the upturned earth, he tried not to tear up again.

I wish I could take you with me. I wish you were still here Icia. Someday, I will come back for you.

Zala nosed him gently and he took a deep breath. Lifting his head, he led them from the site. As the statue of San'Lux loomed in the distance ahead, Kaerisk glanced back once more to the home that had been his sanctuary, his prison, for the whole of his life. Zala nuzzled him briefly and scampered ahead. Following her lead, they rounded the crater rim as Kaerisk had only a few weeks ago at the races, with similar urgency. He swallowed as he heard the elders below, talking amongst themselves. The two kept away from the rim to avoid being spotted.

After passing the crater, the ground became hilly and uneven. Several circular mounds jutted up from the landscape, rabbit holes magnified to magnificent dragon proportion. Each hole led down into a lair. The suburban lairscape was always strange to Kaerisk, having spent so long apart from all the others. Zala led him into one towards the middle, sneaking into the shadows and hissing at him to follow.

Shouldn't enter without the permi- I suppose that's not a thought for a dragon on the run. Wait a second...

"Why do you know where Delaan's lair is?" Kaerisk whispered.

"We were friends for a short while, before it became a contest between Adra and me. Now shush." Zala leaned her head over the spiraling pit that led down into the deeper parts of the lair. When all was perfectly silent, she suddenly dipped her head into the hole. "Hey Delaan! Are you here?" she shouted.

Kaerisk winced. "Not exactly stealthy..."

Zala shrugged her wings. "If Delzaran were here, we'd have heard him entertaining company. Never once saw his uncle without a guest."

A moment passed. Small claws clicked against igneous floors. Delaan appeared at the curl of the entrance, peering up at them. "Zala? ... Kaerisk? What are you doing here? Hold on." The black hatchling scampered up the ramp, joining them near the top. "You two are lucky uncle is out. What are you doing here?"

"We need to ask you something very important," Zala said, resting on her hind legs.

Delaan did the same. "I'll help if I can. I never thought things would come to this. Icia was-"

Zala interrupted him. "Don't say it. Please." The black lowered his head.

"You tried. That's enough to earn a measure of my respect, for what little it's worth," Kaerisk said, coming to sit beside Zala.

Delaan regarded him. "The respect of Clan Kaer still has merit."

"We're not Clan Kaer."

To leave without Father's permission is to forfeit all titles, all right to hoard and lair – even my name. But Mother Mountain gave me this name, Father. So I'm keeping it.

Delaan tilted his head. "Is something going on?" Zala's head bobbed slowly, but she couldn't find the words.

"Zala thinks you know more about the rest of the world than we do," Kaerisk said.

The black scratched the back of his head. "Probably. I've traveled a lot."

Kaerisk nodded. "Are there any other dragon cities out there?" Zala gave him a dull look.

Delaan chuckled a bit. "Okay, I do know more than you about the outside… There are a lot of cities. I didn't come from here, you know. I'm from Ur'Del."

Kaerisk growled a bit, but attempted to hide his irritation at the flippant remark. "Is there any city that works with dakael? Views them opposite the way we do in San'Lux?"

Delaan curled his tail around himself protectively. "Well. The only city I know of that is really kind to bipeds is Luminous. They're a relatively new city-state, not like San'Lux or Ur'Del. But if you're thinking about taking your human friend there, you can forget it. It's far to the south around the Deep Mountains. They settled in the jungles there, I think."

"How far?"

"She'd never make it, and neither would you. The trip to Ur'Del alone is three days by wing, and that's not even halfway there!"

Kaerisk nosed Zala. She nodded. "We'll have to try."

Delaan laughed a bit and shook his head. "You're crazy! Just release her back into the Deep. Save yourself, and her, the trouble."

Kaerisk's head lowered. "Sapphire is dead. Father killed her just a few hours ago."

Delaan blinked. "Then why are you...?" The pair was silent as the wheels in Delaan's head seemed to click into place. He suddenly stood up, wings flared. "You can't be serious. You're running away?"

Zala leaned heavily into Kaerisk. "The further, the better."

He pushed her back and nuzzled her. "No. We are not running away. We are going to find our own way through life." She peered at him a moment, and then nodded, rising to full height.

Delaan backed away. "You'll just give up everything and walk away? To your deaths? You won't stand a chance out there! The world's a dangerous place without other dragons and a lair, you know!"

Kaerisk rose and stood beside his sister. "Delaan, I may not know much of other dragon cities, but I have been hunting alone for years. I've had my First Flame. I've a strong body and more combat training than I'll probably ever need. I will reach Luminous."

"What about Zala? She nearly got killed less than two weeks ago!" Delaan exclaimed.

Zala glared, though it wasn't directly at the black. "I nearly got killed today, too." Delaan's wings drooped at her words or her somber tone, Kaerisk couldn't be certain. "I'll learn. Please don't tell anyone about this."

He stepped near her. "Zala, I can't keep quiet about this. I already feel like I have one dragon's blood on my paws. Please don't make it any more."

She pulled away. "We make choices. We live with those choices. And we see them through to the end. Icia taught me that."

Delaan sighed, dropping to his belly in an undignified posture of defeat. "Fine. But if they ask me, I won't lie. You'd better get going."

It's more than I expected out of him. It's too bad things didn't turn out different between us.

Kaerisk nodded and pressed against Zala with his tail. "He's right. We should go now. I know the southlands well. We'll be fine for a while. Move silently and follow me."

Zala agreed and Kaerisk turned to lead them out of the cave. As he glanced back to Zala, he caught sight of Delaan, who rested his head on the floor as though his spine had gone out of place.

Hunted

Kaerisk had gone hunting at night from time to time, but it was rarely a successful one. The cascade of moonlight made the ashen ground appear seamless and did not provide enough visibility to spot deer at a distance. The best he could do was to dig up a rabbit burrow, but they were usually gone. A midnight snack was rare to find.

But never before had he slept outdoors. Strange birds called in the darkness and the sky sparkled as brightly as the hoard he had forsaken to find his new destiny. Occasionally bushes would rustle. His golden eyes scanned the darkness in vain. No predator came; dragons and dakael were the only predators left, Father had said.

I hope he was right about that.

Zala stirred. The moonlight made her scales shimmer. She had fallen asleep not long after lying next to him. She cuddled against him. After Father gave him Sapphire, the siblings began to sleep separately. It had been some time since they had been so close, and yet it felt as though that time had not passed at all, save for the hollows carved by those that had died.

Does she sleep so well because she is ignorant of the dangers or is it because she trusts me? Either way, if I don't get any sleep, we won't get fed tomorrow.

He rested his head on his paws and closed his eyes, only once more disturbed by a passing animal just out of sight.

The sun rose early and crashed upon the treetops. Light and shadow sprayed across the ashen forest. A rumbling brought his vision into focus. He lifted his head to look for the cause, only to realize he had been hearing his sister's stomach, growling for food.

He grinned a bit and shook her awake. "C'mon. It's time to find some food."

She groaned. "It's too early."

"We'll never get anywhere if we sleep through half the day. We have a long way to go yet."

She blinked awake, hopping to her feet. Her head swung back and forth before she peered up at the sky. She shaded her face with a wing, squinting at the bright blue beyond it. "Oh. Right."

Kaerisk leaned into her. "You don't sound too sure today."

She let her wing and head fall to their normal heights. "It just. I'm sort of realizing how long it's going to take is all."

"You can still go back you know."

She flicked the back of his hind legs with her tail. "No. Luminous is a good a destination as any. I'm staying with you 'til the end."

He smiled. "Is that a promise?"

She nodded sternly. "It is. Swear?" She pressed a wing forward, motioning with the wingclaw. Kaerisk turned so that he could properly extend his own wing and link claws with her. "Good. You know I keep my promises. Icia taught me that."

Kaerisk retracted his wing from hers, forcing a smile. "Me too. Let's go."

He turned to leave, but the familiar sense of Riftwind stopped him in his tracks. He pounced Zala as quickly as he could, forcing her into the bushes that had kept him up all night. She tried asking what he was doing, but he hissed for silence. A moment passed.

The treetops shook. A red dragon soared overhead, his eye trained on the terrain below. He flew so close that the ash fell from the trees overhead, creating a grey cloud. A second dragon, this one green, alighted in a nearby clearing. She

[111]

looked about, sniffed at the ground, and then raised her head to the sky.

"Kaerisk! Zala! Are you here?" she called. Kaerisk lay perfectly rigid.

Zala shifted. The dragon turned her head towards them. Kaerisk glared at his sister and Zala froze, not even breathing. The green continued to stare in their direction for the longest time before a rabbit suddenly bolted from a nearby bush to another. The green snorted and returned to the sky, flying onwards.

As soon as she was free, Zala began coughing. Some of the ash had landed on her snout. "What was that?"

Kaerisk left the brush and shook himself off with a grunt. "Looks like Delaan sold us out already."

Zala frowned as she joined him, her scales splotched with grey. "We don't know that... what are we going to do?"

Kaerisk examined the ground. With light, it wouldn't take long for a Wise dragon to start following their tracks. It would lead to Delaan's lair and from there into the Ashen Forest. That bought them a little time. Father had taught him how to backtrack, hide his trail, and take a different path – but Zala lacked that knowledge and there was no time to teach her. The only way to throw them off the trail would be to do the unthinkable.

"We're going home."

"What? But you promised-"

"And I'm going to keep it! But they will find us if we go south. We're going to have to take a different path." He lifted his head as high as he could, closing his eyes and sensing for any more vibrations of Riftwind in the air.

None for now. If Delaan told them we were going south, then we'll have to go north. Those hard rocks may not make for good hunting or travel, but even Zala won't leave a trail in them easily...

He opened his eyes. Zala stared at him, an unsure frown painting her face. Kaerisk tried to smile and it seemed to brighten Zala's demeanor. At the very least, her drooping wings lifted and she stood in upright posture.

"Lead the way," she said.

Kaerisk darted from tree to tree, his sister on his heels. Both of them breathed hard as they moved, kicking up ash as they traveled. There was no attempt to hide their trail; their speed trumped all other concerns, save when the presence of Riftwind was felt. Twice, Kaerisk directed his sister to hide behind trees and under bushes as elders flew overhead.

As they neared the border of San'Lux, the bushes were too thin and small to hide them. Again Kaerisk felt the presence of Riftwind; a gold dragon flew nearby. Kaerisk and Zala took shelter under a large stone, barely able to squeeze inside a rift between it and the ground. The dragon landed nearby, stepping closer. The adult was nearly as large as Father; when he stepped, Kaerisk could feel the vibrations. His paw came to rest on the stone. Kaerisk heard it shift over his sister. She stared at him, wide eyed. The dragon above sniffed once, twice, and then stepped back, taking to the air. As soon as they were sure he was gone, they piled out of the hole. Kaerisk watched as he followed the trail they had left in their haste.

There isn't much time.

Kaerisk darted for his lair, his sister trailing behind him. She could barely keep up, her lungs heaving for air. Rather than venture near the entrance, they took a wide path near the foot of the Deep Mountains above it. The hills hid them fairly well, but he sprinkled his sister's back with a new layer of ash as she fell to her belly in the dirt, gasping for breath. As soon as she was camouflaged, he turned himself over, writhing about in the ashen dirt until his back too looked like a natural feature.

A dragon came near to the lair. Kaerisk flattened his body against the ground, laying still and praying his camouflage would protect him. The dragon did not even look his way – his focus was on the occupant. After a short time, the dragon left. Father emerged from the lair to follow him. Kaerisk glared after the blue.

Were you not even helping in the search? Why even bother trying to reclaim us then?

He rose up and regarded Zala. Her eyes were watering and she was still, save the rise and fall of her sides, which slowly began to normalize. It was fortunate he put as much distance from the lair as he did; had they gone any closer, Father would have surely heard her panting.

"C'mon. We can take it a bit easier now. Let's see if we can find anything to eat to the north," he said.

Zala groaned as she rose. "I hope so. All this running around is making me hungry."

The two scampered down the hills and turned north. Their ashen concealment thinned with every step as particles of dust trailed behind them, but it was the same color and consistency. So long as it held and they followed the curve of the mountain, they would be difficult to spot by air.

But it was not by air that they were spotted.

"Wait!"

Zala froze, but Kaerisk wheeled about, expecting to face an adult dragon. Instead, it was Delaan; he raced up to them, coming from their lair. When he arrived, he took a moment to catch his breath. Kaerisk muttered obscenities out of earshot.

Now what? He's seen us. He'll just sell us out again. We can try to go east, but...

"Delaan! What are you doing here?" Zala asked.

"Please, you have to reconsider! Kaevaeri was angry, but he was honestly worried about you two. He drilled me for information as soon as your trail led to my lair."

Kaerisk snorted. "So you did sell us out."

Delaan's head darted towards him. "I had no choice! And it is for your own good, too! Hatchlings die just growing up, and that's with the protection of elders and a lair – I don't want anyone else to die!"

Zala stepped forward pensively. "Delaan – I didn't…"

Kaerisk moved in front of her, glaring at the black. "I am not going to be my father's puppet anymore. I'm not going to live his dreams."

"Then don't!" Delaan stood to full height. "Just talk things out with your dad. He'll listen."

Zala shook her head. "We've said all there is to say. I'm not Father's little statue either. Go back and tell him that." Delaan blinked at her, mouth agape.

"C'mon sister. We need to get going." Kaerisk started moving north and Zala followed.

But so did Delaan. "I can't just let you go. Please, let's just go back."

"Back off, Delaan! We're going and nothing is going to change that!" Kaerisk hissed. Delaan hesitated and Kaerisk picked up his speed.

Yet again, Delaan followed. "Hey! Everyone! They're here!" Delaan began to shout.

Kaerisk wanted to turn around and claw his throat out, but that would only cause more problems.

Only one other option then…

"Zala, run!"

She bolted forward and he followed her. Delaan chased at their heels. Kaerisk soon outpaced his sister, but Delaan kept up with her. As the black panted for breath, his screams stopped. He kept running, faster and faster. The ground began to shake. At first, Kaerisk thought some elders had joined the chase, but when he looked back he found none. Instead, Delaan and Zala struggled to keep moving forward as the ground shifted below them.

A quake? Not now!

Kaerisk returned his vision to the fore just in time to see the earth open. Kaerisk prepared to jump, but the tear in the earth kept widening. He skidded to a halt before it. Zala and Delaan stumbled up against him, knocking him closer to the hole. He tried to push them back.

The torn earth yawned wider, swallowing them whole.

The Forgotten

When the shaking stopped and the dust settled, Kaerisk lay on his back, staring up at a half-sealed sky. The rock had slid over the hole they had fallen through; only a glimmer of light from the falling Eye shone through the hole. It seemed too small to fit through, even if Zala could summon the Riftwind to scale the near-vertical slope.

Zala!

Kaerisk writhed about, pushing away the smaller rocks that covered his wings and rolled onto his feet. Rubble had fallen through the hole, half-burying Delaan and Zala, who still lay dazed in the rocks. Kaerisk leapt towards them, digging his sister free; she coughed up a lung full of dust as Delaan dragged himself from the stone debris.

"Are you okay, sister?"

Zala coughed again, rubbing her head tenderly with a wingclaw. "I-I think so."

Delaan shook himself off, coating the siblings' paws in dirt, and then examined the environment. "Oh Firstbourne... We are so dead."

Kaerisk glared. "Relax. This wouldn't have happened if you had just kept your mouth shut and left us alone."

"I just didn't want you to kill yourselves! Now we're all going die just like Icia!" Delaan began to pace about nervously, rearing up on his hind legs to test the wall. When it shifted, he immediately dropped down and cringed.

"We'll think of something," Kaerisk said. His voice wasn't as loud as before. Icia had died in a similar manner; Delaan was justified in his fear.

"What's that?" Zala asked.

[117]

She was staring at a small hollow in the wall leading further under the Deep Mountains. From it came a dim, but noticeable light. Kaerisk approached it carefully, pulling one of the loose rocks aside. Below was a half-shattered riftcrystal. Kaerisk grasped it. The natural magic within the crystal responded to the energy within him, illuminating a narrow passage half buried in stone.

Riftcrystal isn't natural as far as I know. It's grown. That means this had to have been a lair that belonged to a dragon, so...

"There might be another way out." Kaerisk ducked down to examine the hole, lighting it with the broken crystal. It would be a tight fit for his wings, but the chamber beyond seemed larger.

"You're crazy. Even if there is a way through that, that path leads into the Deep Mountains! If the rock doesn't crush us, the bipeds might!" Delaan exclaimed.

Kaerisk pulled his head from the hole to regard Delaan. "I left my lair to live. If you want to stay here and wait for the next earthquake to kill you, go right ahead. Zala?"

Zala crept carefully over the fallen stone. "I'm with you brother. But you shouldn't be so mean."

He only nearly got us killed. I think I'm a little justified here.

"F-fine! I'm coming too!" Delaan exclaimed.

Kaerisk rolled his eyes, took the light into his maw, drew his wings as tightly to him as he could, and slithered into the passageway. The abrasive surface dragged against his scales, pulling a few of them free. Wincing, he pushed forward. The air was dull and earthen; at its tightest points, Kaerisk could barely expand his body to fill his lungs with air. Crawling with tiny steps and pushing with his tail, he popped free of the tight confines.

The area beyond was unlike any lair Kaerisk had ever seen. The walls had clearly been shaped by Riftwind for they were smooth and unnatural, but whoever had carved this lair was a true artist of the craft. The lines of the wall were perfectly symmetrical and the roof of the passageway formed an exact arch as far as the light allowed vision. Stone reliefs covered the walls, geometric pictures of dragons in flight and in combat against dakael or imaginary foes. The only mars upon the architectural and artistic perfection of the tunnel were the large cracks that ran throughout the floor and all around the area of the collapse. Shining the light upward revealed that the arch began to ascend at that point, suggesting the path might have led up and may have been a reason for the structural deficiency.

Zala and Delaan crawled into the chamber after him. The black scurried like a rat, his claws scraping against the stone and finding purchase in the cracks. His eyes watered, though Kaerisk wasn't sure if it was from the dust or the black's fear, which had begun to manifest itself in shaking. It only slowly faded as Delaan inspected the same strong architecture that Kaerisk had moments ago.

Zala drew close to him. "What is this place, brother? Luxari never said anything about a place like this..."

Kaerisk switched the crystal to a paw. "I don't know. It must be ancient if Father or Luxari never mentioned it... the craftsmanship is incredible."

Delaan pressed a paw upon the strange, angular reliefs. "I wonder how many old ruins are hidden in the earth like this. Buried, forgotten - just like us..." Delaan sniffled as he trailed off, his paw falling to the ground and his tail curling tight to his body, his shivering beginning anew.

"Quit sniveling! If you don't like things, then change them!" Kaerisk exclaimed.

"I liked them just the way they were! I want to go back to uncle's lair and learn from Luxari and play with everyone – except you!" Delaan shouted back.

"Enough!" Zala darted between them, slapping her tail against the ground. "We can talk after we get out of here. Right?" Kaerisk sneered and took the crystal into his maw again.

Why does she keep taking his side?

Kaerisk followed the tunnel, watching sidelong as the reliefs passed. They seemed depict a dragon without wings that gained them, and then led his people into the sky. Father had told similar stories about the Firstbourne: how he had been born without wings, but gained them through many trials such as challenging the sky and swallowing the great blaze. Kaerisk had once asked where the other dragons came from, but Father had said they were always there. That was how the Firstbourne willed it, Father said.

The tunnel opened into a small chamber. The walls bent inward at a slight angle, while the ceiling rounded off into a dome. In the center of the room was a perfectly square platform; at each of the four points of the dais, four green riftcrystals rose. As the yellow light from the broken crystal shone upon the platform, the true purpose of this place was revealed: lying on the dais was a massive skeleton of a dragon. Its black eye sockets stared at them, its mouth open in an eternal scream. Looking at it made Kaerisk shudder and Zala cringe. Delaan cowered against the slanted wall, as though trying to wedge himself into a crack where the skeleton could not see him. Metal links rose from the stone and entwined with the skeleton, including rings around what had once been the joints of the paws. Behind the dais, another path continued deeper into the complex.

[120]

Kaerisk transferred the crystal to a paw. "It's a tomb… Father told me that lesser dragons sometimes bury their dead in the ground rather than commit to the flame as we do. Maybe that's why we didn't know about it."

"If this is just a tomb, then why does that skeleton have chains on it?" Delaan whispered.

Chains? What are chains?

"It's creepy, brother… we should move on," Zala said.

"I don't know about the chains, but I'm sure we should just leave him to his rest. Odd, though…" Kaerisk began to limp around the side of the dais as quietly as he could, almost as though he might wake the skeleton.

"Wh-what's odd?" Delaan asked, crawling along the side of the wall.

"The crystals on the dais should have lit up when we came near."

As they passed around to the back of the skeleton, the riftcrystal that Kaerisk held suddenly flickered out, as though something had drained it of its power. Delaan screamed in the darkness. Two green flames erupted from atop the dais. They rose from the eye sockets, burning in midair. Around them, a glowing, translucent form began to rise, as skeletal as the bones from which it pulled. Kaerisk couldn't move. He could hardly breathe as the skeletal apparition turned its head towards him.

"Four thousand years, I have waited." The voice seemed to emanate from all around them, echoing in his head. The words were draconic, but a strange dialect that arranged the words in an odd manner. Kaerisk shrunk back against the wall, just as Delaan continued to do. He bumped into Zala, who was already behind him.

"Oh Firstbourne, we're all going to die!" Delaan exclaimed, covering his eyes with his paws.

The phantom lifted its boney wings. "Death holds no meaning here. No meaning, 'til death assured."

Father had once scared Kaerisk with stories of Miasma Dragons – dragons who in death refused to pass on to the elements. Bound to wander for some unknown slight, they would snatch up unwary hatchlings from their nests. Kaerisk prayed to the Firstbourne that Father was wrong about this too.

Kaerisk tried to put on a brave face, even as his heart pounded in his chest. "Wh-what do you want?"

"Ask you I the same. For I had wished my wait to be over, and yet you ask of me this? I was at rest, but not at peace." The Miasma turned; his long, transparent spine angled down towards them like an arrow. His skeletal maw could convey no emotion, but his voice rose as though in anger. "My pledge and burden, not yet lifted. My knowledge and experience, wasted and not consulted. Speak hatchling! Why have you intruded upon my chamber?"

"We are lost, a-ancient one," he squeaked.

"Derelict! And not are you sheltered in my Academy, why? All is undone." The Miasma paused for some time, looking around the chamber as if he could see through the walls. Perhaps he could. "Yes, I see. But duty still remains. I seek peace, not rest. And I sense you may be the one to give it to me."

"Please don't eat us!" Zala cried out, covering her eyes with her wings much as Delaan did with his paws.

"Hide not your eyes from me, child. You are no Wurm." The Miasma turned his glowing green gaze onto Kaerisk. He could feel frigid Riftwind coursing through him, but he could not turn his eyes from the Miasma.

Is it trying to possess me? Firstbourne save me!

"I see. Worship they still, the false goddess. Go now, quickly, to the chamber behind me. There is a bridge. Cross it, and I will send you on your way."

"You'll send us home?" Zala asked, daring to peek with one eye.

"Go quickly, while I have both strength and patience!"

The violent voice shook loose the tension holding Kaerisk's body in place. Without waiting for Zala or Delaan, he began to run for the other exit. Only after he reached it and beheld a stone walkway suspended above a massive pit did he pause to look back. Zala and Delaan were right behind him – and behind them, the Miasma. The ghostly skeleton floated through the air, its gaping maw half open, threatening to swallow them whole. Turning, Kaerisk bolted in pure terror. His claws scraped against the perfectly flat stone, trying to gain additional traction. He only stopped when the bridge came to an abrupt end, terminating inside an egg-shaped room. Hanging above him was a massive egg-shaped crystal, connected to the ceiling with odd clasps of gold. As Delaan and Zala piled into him, pushing him against the far wall, the Miasma came to a stop outside the chamber.

Suddenly, the crystal began to turn. It shined a bright red light, washing down on them and forming a barrier over the entryway. The Miasma's form became distorted as the crystal above rotated faster and faster.

"Hatchlings born of Heart, Rage, and Innovation. Find her, you will. She is the last. And when you do, remember that you are dragon."

Zala latched onto Kaerisk and squeaked as the light intensified. Delaan screamed into his tail, curled up into a ball on the floor. The light became so bright that Kaerisk couldn't see them, and then he couldn't feel Zala or anything at all. But he could still hear: the whirring of the crystal above, the fearful screams of his companions, and somehow above that cacophony, the Miasma's voice.

"I've put a tail on you, little one. I've put a tail on you."

Distance

The whirring began to slow. The light began to fade. The screams had stopped, but Zala was crying. The sobs stirred anger in Kaerisk's heart.

I never wanted to hear her cry again. Not after...

"It's okay, Zala. It's over."

"Where – where is the ghost?" Delaan asked.

The chamber in which they stood almost seemed the same as the one they had entered moments ago. Only, Kaerisk was sure he had been up against a wall, but now an open space rested beside him; moreover, the crystal overhead was blue instead of red. Poking his head outside of the new opening revealed a much altered landscape. Instead of a narrow bridge over a dark, endless pit, the chamber beyond was a perfectly shaped dome. Dim light still shone from a massive hanging Riftcrystal, suspended from the middle of the room. The surface kept this perfection in most spots, smooth, flat, and unadulterated; however, large scores had been made in the floor from what looked to be massive claws. A large stone rise, once a half-circle of stone that protected the strange room of light, lay sundered. Small bits of Riftcrystal remained on it.

"He's not here. We're far away now," Kaerisk said.

Delaan poked his head outside. "Then where are we?"

Kaerisk shook his head. "I have no idea where the Wurmway took us."

Zala sniffled. "What's a Wurmway?" Kaerisk regarded her with furrowed brow.

I don't know. Wurm – that was the Miasma's word. Why do I know it?

"We have to get out of here! The ghost could come back at any minute!" Delaan exclaimed.

[125]

"Shut your maw!" Kaerisk exclaimed. Delaan cowered back as Zala rose. "We need to be rational about this. Let's figure out where we are and look for a way out." Kaerisk stepped out of the egg-shaped chamber and into the dome.

Delaan took a deep breath. "Sure, let's be rational. We just got transported somewhere we don't know, underground with possibly no way out, by a ghost that refuses to pass onto the elements." Delaan hung his head. "Nope. That really doesn't help." Zala brushed by him, giving a slight smile through water-stained eyes. He followed her out of the egg.

Kaerisk gathered another crystal from the sundered rock and led them through the room. The chamber could have fit three elders side by side with space for more. Crossing the scoured floor to a far archway, the dim light of the crystal revealed a large hallway with many branching paths. Taking some comfort in the options, Kaerisk pressed on, taking the first path to the left. Curving around at least a hundred feet, it terminated in a large domed chamber, larger than the first.

Tiered shelves rose from the walls, each a bit higher than the last. Small desks of stone still rested upon them, along with slightly raised platforms behind them, serving for seats. In the center of the room was a ring just a bit larger than an average elder, slightly elevated with a small trench between it and the arena-style seating. Kaerisk crept into the chamber as quiet as a rabbit, ascending the hatchling-sized steps to the ring in the middle. It reminded him a bit of the platform that rested before the eyes of the statue in San'Lux. Like the first chamber, the area had been damaged; several of the desks and seats had been destroyed. More claw marks marred the surfaces here, but many of them were too narrow and straight to have been made even by a hatchling's claw.

Was combat held here, too?

"What is this place, brother?" Zala asked.

Delaan scrambled onto one of the rings and peered under a desk. With a bit of a heave, he pulled free a large stone tablet, which he rested atop it. Perhaps it was the large domed ceiling, but his voice was steady. "I think this was a school."

"A school?" Zala asked.

"Kaerisk, can I get some light?" he asked. The blue complied. When the light shone on the table, the faded letters came into view. "I can't make it out clearly. But these tablets are just like the ones we still use today in Luxari's class, just bigger. See? The surface is weakened by Riftwind." Delaan scrapped a claw across the bottom of the tablet, moving through it almost like it was clay. "This is either ancient or the penmanship is atrocious - or both."

Kaerisk hopped over to another desk and placed the crystal on it so he could speak. "Maybe one of the other tablets has something we can read." Checking below, he found another tablet, though it was cracked in two. Carefully, he picked each piece up, put them back together, and then lifted the Riftcrystal over it. "They sound like notes of some kind. 'Professor demands attention, again.'"

"You can read it?" Delaan asked.

"Yeah. Father insisted I learn common and elder draconic. It's really not that different, but the words have more possible meanings and a strange order." Kaerisk traced his fingers gently over the symbols. "It reads, 'Can't wait for this day to be over. Professor interrupted. There was shaking! Entrance collapsed. Great, stuck here after school. More shaking, it better be open. Screams-' ...it just ends there."

Delaan planted his face into his wing. "The entrance is collapsed? It's official; we're all going to die."

Kaerisk sneered. "Will you grow a spine?"

"Brother, please." Zala pressed up against him, trembling. "Why were there screams?"

Kaerisk shook his head. "I don't know. But I don't like it." Kaerisk traced his fingers over the letters again. Somehow, he felt a strange and profound sadness, but he wasn't certain why. It was as though something important had once been here and now was gone. "Let's keep looking for a way out."

Taking the Riftcrystal, Kaerisk led the two hatchlings back the way they came. The branching paths seemed endless, but as he stared at them, he felt the urge to pick one over the others. Following it was difficult; several statues had once line the hall, but all of them had been damaged or destroyed. Their debris coated the path. Stains remained on the rocks, as did the signs of struggle. Zala pressed closed to him. He could hear her heart beating over the silence as the hatchlings held their breath. It seemed like every shadow might hide whatever creatures had attacked this place.

The path terminated again in a large chamber with a wide entrance. What had likely been a statue dominated the center of it. Light came not from the dim crystal hanging above, but from the far opening. Fresh air invaded Kaerisk's nostrils. Delaan rushed for the exit, as did Zala. Kaerisk followed, but paused as he passed the statue. A name had once rested on its base, but all that remained were the letters LAR. The strange sense of weight returned, but as he felt Zala and Delaan pulling away, he stumbled over the rubble after them.

The area beyond was flat, almost as flat as the once-perfect floors of the cavern behind them. Tall grass obscured everything they could see, taller than any grass Kaerisk had ever seen in the Ashen Forest. Pressing stalks of it aside, he bent his head down to smell at the earth. The robust smell carried no hint of ash.

Wherever we are, we're nowhere near San'Lux.

The shadow of the Deep Mountains lengthened as the Eye continued to set behind them. The umbra raced across the swaying tips of the tall grass, threatening the descent of night, though the sky above remained a healthy shine of blue. Zala shifted behind him and a vicious growl rumbled from her stomach. He regarded his sister, who gave a sheepish smile.

"You two stay here. I'm going to see if I can find something we can eat out here," Kaerisk said.

Zala stepped up to him, pressing her nose to his. "I want to help. You promised to teach me."

He churred gently. "You can. And I will. But we need to figure out what might be out here first."

Delaan lifted up on his hind legs, clawing at the Deep Mountain as he stared up its unassailable height. "Zala, you are remarkably calm considering we seem to be on the other side of the Deep Mountains with no chance of rescue." He shivered, his claws scraping against the stone.

She pulled away from Kaerisk, wrapping her tail tightly around her legs. "Delaan, I'm further away from San'Lux than I ever imagined. And right now, that thought makes me the happiest I've been in years."

Kaerisk smiled a bit and leaned into her, even as his own stomach growled. "We'll be fine, Delaan. I agree with Zala; so long as she's with me, I know everything will end up alright."

"You're all crazy." Delaan slid down the rock, his head falling hard against the dirt. He stared into the unending field of grass blankly, as though his spirit had left him. Only the slow rise and fall of his sides revealed that he was still alive, the tears welling in his eyes the sign that he was still cognizant. The sight made Kaerisk sneer.

Zala nuzzled her brother quickly. "Go, see what's out there. I'll stay with Delaan."

"Don't waste too much energy on him. We'll need it for hunting, especially with three mouths to feed." He turned

[129]

before the weight of his sister's frown fell on him. He darted into the grass without waiting for a reply.

There were many new scents in this area. Everything smelled exceptionally crisp, not dulled by familiarity and ash. Occasionally he would stop to poke his head above the grass, finding nothing but a sea of green waving in the fading light and the looming dark mountains. As he traveled away from the Deep, he could feel the heat of the Eye and an intense moisture rising from the plants; the humidity was almost intolerable and it wasn't even the peak of the day. Bugs buzzed in large number, all around him. The drone was maddening as, staring into the grass, he could never be certain if something was stalking him, ready to pounce.

The wind shifted. It brought three distinct smells – the first was freshly cut grass, sharp and familiar. It meant that something had to have been eating it recently in fairly large quantities. The second was another familiar smell – dung. The third was something he had never smelled before: strange, crisp, and moist. The westerly wind felt cooler against his scales and temporarily dulled the humidity clinging hotly around him.

He ran into the wind, fast as he could. There was no attempt to hide his approach; though uncertain if the creature he stalked was edible, his rumbling stomach drove him onwards. The grass flattened behind him. Sound broke upon him – a startled, high pitched whine unlike anything he had heard before. Skidding to a halt, he jutted his head up through the green curtain.

Its paws were deer-like – flat and hooved as they swung wildly in the air. The face was too long and there were no horns on its head; its ears were more floppy and a strange fur ran down its neck, like the hair that once grew on Sapphire's head. Its coat was short, brown. Quadruped: it landed on those

[130]

flailing hooves and bolted, hair-tail whipping behind it. The creature, far more muscular than a deer, didn't sprint as quickly, but its size was worrisome; it was larger even than he was. Taking it down alone would be difficult and possibly deadly – if those hooves swung against his head, he'd be out cold or worse. The most promising thing was that as the creature galloped away, several others of its kind did the same.

A herd animal. If we can figure out a way to bring it down safely, then we might just survive out here.

Kaerisk came forward, sniffing where they had been to memorize their scent. When he entered into their space, a salty gust of air stung his eyes. After blinking a few times, he stumbled out of the grass. The sight beyond caused him to gasp. A small bar of fine sand rolled down a short hill. Beyond it lay the largest lake Kaerisk had ever seen. When the white humps on the water crested before they hit the beach, he realized this was no mere lake, but the ocean.

Father once told me of it – water so great that even elders could not fly over it.

His rump fell to the ground. He sat and stared at the water for a time.

We really are on the other side of the Deep Mountains. I can survive. Father taught me… but what about Zala? Or even the black? Can I really take care of them too? When I couldn't save Icia? Or Sapphire?

His head fell and, for a moment, he wanted to sink to the same position he had left Delaan. The thought of sinking that low caused him to shake with self-disgust. He strained to stand. His legs were unsteady as he turned around, tail dragging through the grass as he followed the path he had made back towards the leering Deep Mountains.

Group Hunt

A gnawing pain woke him. It felt as though he had swallowed an egg and it had hatched in his stomach, and now the poor hatchling was trying to claw its way out. It had started sometime in the night as he lay curled with his sister, far closer to Delaan than he would have liked. It hadn't occurred to him until the morning sun rose, purple sky turning red as the burning Eye sprinkled swaying shadows through blades of grass, that he had never before gone a full day without a meal.

Zala groaned when he pulled away from her. As he stretched, she wiped her eyes with a wing. "Brother? It's too early."

"If we don't find something to eat, we're going to die."

"Don't be so dramatic."

"Don't be so naïve. The longer we go without a meal, the harder it's going to be to get one."

She clawed her forearms forward, lifting her rear and arching her back with a pop. "Alright, I'm up." She stood and hopped a bit. "Today's a good day for a lesson!"

Delaan grumbled, and then suddenly came awake. His tail lashed behind him and he jerked, his feet planting into the ground as his wings flared and his head swung back and forth. The move startled even Kaerisk, but thankfully the black didn't notice as the moment passed. Delaan looked at the grass with tired eyes. "Right…"

Kaerisk growled. "I swear to the Firstbourne, Delaan, you'll get us all killed out here."

"I shouldn't be out here at all!" Delaan turned sideways, a hind leg scratching at his flanks. Several scales had fallen out; a few more were dislodged by the motion. Kaerisk frowned as the now-grey scales fell to the ground. They joined several others piled up around their sleeping site. Kaerisk moved towards him and the black cowered back.

He's even more stressed than I am.

"Brother…"

"Well, you are. You might as well help out too." Kaerisk gathered up several clawfuls of scales and put them into his scale pouch.

Zala trotted over to Kaerisk at his words and pressed into him with a smile. "Yes! Come hunt with us!"

Delaan pulled his wings tight to his body. "I should stay here. Hatchlings should wait for help if they get lost, that's what the elders always say."

"We're not lost. We're on a journey!" Zala exclaimed. She hopped over to him. "I know you weren't supposed to be on it. But I know with us all here, everything will work out fine. We'll have fun, okay?"

Delaan just blinked at her.

"Let me put it another way, Delaan. You can stay here and starve or you can pull your weight and get fed. Which is it going to be?" Kaerisk asked.

Delaan's head bowed low, so far that his nose almost drooped into the pile of scales he had left behind. His hind legs pushed up into a stand and he wobbled towards Kaerisk. Zala followed alongside him, churring encouragingly.

Kaerisk turned to the sea of green around them, trampling down the tall stalks of grass. "Stay close. It's easy to get lost in here."

"Should we hold tails?" Zala asked.

Kaerisk's head jerked back at the suggestion. "What?"

Zala slowed her step at the motion. "I, um. It's something Luxari suggested when I was younger." Delaan nearly bumped into her.

[133]

"Is that why you bit my tail and followed me around when we were growing up?"

"I grew out of it."

Kaerisk smirked a bit.

"You didn't say what you were going to teach me."

He poked his head above the stalks, inhaling deeply. The ocean air was strangely refreshing to him, as if it was something he had been missing all his life. The scent of his prey was still far off. "Actually, it's something you already know."

"I do?"

"You remember the story of Mother Mountain, right?"

Delaan peeked ahead. "Mother Mountain?"

Zala spoke before Kaerisk's low growl could grow louder. "A story that was very important to us as children. It was all we had of-"

Kaerisk frowned as he pushed through the grass.

She hopped after him. "I remember. What about it?"

"The six-legged monsters. We fought them off together. Do you remember how?"

Zala shuddered. "I can't believe we ever ate bugs."

"Do you remember?"

She hummed loudly. "The spear-beaked monsters would never stay long. To defeat them, we had to circle and attack from front and back. I'd scare them, and then you pounced."

"We're going to try that again, but with these muscle-deer I found. I'll teach you about up and downwind, too, but first we have to find them. They ran south when I saw them yesterday."

"What are muscle-deer?" Delaan asked.

Kaerisk rolled his eyes. "I don't know what they are. If you have a better suggestion, be sure to let me know."

"Are you sure they're edible?"

"I'm fairly certain they're made out of meat."

Delaan sighed, but was silent for the rest of the trip. Every few minutes of walking, Kaerisk would pause to stick his head above the grass and inhale. He explained what he was doing to Zala, who absorbed every word of it. He told her of how he had hunted using scent markers and trees in the Ashen Forest and why they could not use that tactic here. Their trip was halted only once, when Zala got her first glimpse of the ocean. She hopped around as though she were still a child and demanded to touch the water. She chased the water as it withdrew and was washed back onto shore by a cresting wave as she attempted instinctually to swim. Kaerisk shook his head, wondering where she found the energy.

As the Eye climbed into the sky above, the moisture of the grass became intolerable. Kaerisk had never experienced anything like the clinging humid air that pushed down at him on all sides. It made it hard to smell anything other than grass, but when they discovered some chewed stalks, Kaerisk was reassured they were on the right track. Hearing was dampened too, as buzzing insects were lured out by the moisture or the heat. They swarmed around the hatchlings, landing on their scales and wallowing about on them before being chased off by a flapping wing or scratching paw.

At last, brown and tan crests rose from the grass in the distance. The muscle-deer bent their long necks down and tore lose several stalks before lifting their heads up to watch as they chewed. They craned their necks back and forth, short ears flopping against the side of their head, chasing away the same insects that scourged the trio of hatchlings.

"I see them brother!" Zala exclaimed. Kaerisk immediately shushed her, but the animals did not seem to notice.

"Those are your muscle-deer?" Delaan asked. Kaerisk nodded. "Those are horses."

"Are horses edible?" Zala asked.

Delaan grimaced. "They're made of meat, yes. But I hear there are strange dakael that accompany them sometimes. They were only ever seen once. They were all slaughtered, horses and all."

Kaerisk furrowed his brow, poking his head up to stare at them. The horses didn't seem to mind. "How were they strange?"

"My dad called them symbiotes. They were connected to the horses."

Kaerisk placed a paw to his stomach, pushing against it as it growled in revolt. "I didn't see any yesterday and I don't see any now." The black sighed. "Delaan, I need you to help me with the kill."

Delaan staggered at the words. "W-what?"

"Why not me brother? I could do it!" Zala exclaimed.

"You already have an important job, Zala. The horses are larger than I am and their feet are tough. I can't just bring it down like a deer and if I get hurt, I don't think any of us will be able to catch a meal."

Zala, placated by her brother's words, bounded around to the other side of him and nosed Delaan. "I'll sneak ahead." Kaerisk glared at her; the sudden action had unnerved the horses, but they had not bolted. Their black eyes focused on the hatchlings as their maws still chewed the grass within them. Zala took a measurement of the wind by licking a wingtip and lifting it, and then slowly began to circle through the grass. Every crushed blade, every crackle of displaced earth caused Kaerisk to grind his teeth.

Once the plants blocked sight of her, Kaerisk grunted at Delaan to follow him. Delaan did so, but the black's tail dragged across the ground audibly. Kaerisk lashed with his tail, whacking the tip of Delaan's snout.

The black immediately recoiled, pawing at his nose. "Ow! Hey, that hurt!"

"Get your tail up and pay attention! I'm not going to starve out here because of you!" Kaerisk hissed.

"Without me, you're going to starve!" the black hissed back.

Kaerisk blinked, and then glared. "If you think that I truly need your help-"

"Kaerisk, stop! Please! This isn't a contest. This isn't a joke. You said you need help to bring them down and you're right. Maybe you're well and trained to be a feral, but I'm not. I've never hunted alone before. I'm worried about myself, and about Zala, and even about you!" Delaan huffed, pulling back and wrapping his tail around him. "I don't know why you're so angry with me. I know I probably won't be much help. But I'll try. So please - try to be patient with me."

The horses chewed their grass, oblivious to the hatchlings' conversation. Kaerisk wasn't sure why he was so mad at Delaan either. He had been so happy when Zala had suggested they leave that hateful place of lies, because then he wouldn't have to leave alone. It was not Delaan's fault that Icia died. He had tried to save her in the end. It wasn't his fault that Sapphire died; that was Father's choice. Maybe it was his fault that they fell in the tomb with the ghost and got sucked through the Wurmway, but what if they hadn't?

Father would not have stopped until he found us. And it would have been just as hard to catch a meal.

Kaerisk rose and tiptoed over to Delaan, who cowered back. Kaerisk lowered his head before him. "I'm sorry. I've been holding all this anger... but really, I'm worried about Zala

[137]

and you too. It's like she said. We're all on this journey together, right?"

Delaan's tail slowly relaxed and he tilted his head at the blue. "Your sister may be naïve... but she's got more heart than both of us you know."

The thought hadn't occurred to Kaerisk. "I know."

Inhaling, Delaan crouched down and peered through the swaying green sea. "Alright, I'm ready."

Kaerisk turned towards the herd. He could not see Zala on the other side, but the swaying of grass suggested her position. She came close to the horses, but they didn't react as before or as expected – they began to shift. Rather than run from her, they simply walked away. When they had moved closer to the two males, Zala popped out into the ring of mowed grass with a frustrated look on her face, waving her wings and roaring in a decidedly non-threatening squeak. Kaerisk couldn't help but smile, as did Delaan.

"Now what?" the black asked.

"We wait. They're still coming. Shhh."

Though they were not running, the herd slowly stumbled towards the location of the hidden hatchlings. Delaan tensed, but Kaerisk glared at him to wait. All was still. Kaerisk tried to keep from breathing.

A horse's wail. One of them had spotted the two hatchlings. Several reared up and began to run. Kaerisk and Delaan darted forward, leaping into the flanks of one of them. Deep their claws tore and, though the beast writhed magnificently, it fell still. The three finally ate their fill.

As they lay in the freshly chewed circle of grass and stared up at a darkening sky, Kaerisk smiled at Delaan. The black almost looked relieved.

The Riders

"See? You're already being really helpful!"

"You're just lucky I'm here."

"We'd have gone south anyway."

Delaan had risen in spirits considerably since they started hunting together. It was almost enough that Kaerisk wished he had not apologized to him. But no matter how he considered it, the information was still helpful, as was Delaan when he wasn't blubbering. He had explained that the closest city should be Lan'Dal, Heart of the Firstbourne, and that it would lay beyond the plain and a watery place called a 'swamp.' It was slow going. They had been traveling a week and the endless sea of grass never appeared to change. The only interruptions of the sameness were the occasional small streams from Deep Mountain run-off. By midday, they flowed enough to drink from, but not enough to impede progress.

They hadn't gone directly south, either. Since the herd of horses was their primary source of food, they were forced to follow them. They tried to guide them south as wind conditions allowed. They were working on the problem: at nights, Kaerisk would teach Zala of the Riftwind, while making packs out of their combined shed scales. It was the strangest-looking scale pouch Kaerisk had ever seen, black and blue and ever-growing, but Zala was exceptionally proud of their work, as well as what the pack symbolized.

Kaerisk wasn't sure he ascribed to the symbolism, but the pack was soon large enough to hold meat from the slain. It would not keep for long, but a dragon stomach could handle a little rancid meat if needed. He was expecting it, if the swamp Delaan had promised was truly filled with water.

"We'll need another pack before we can leave the herd and try to push south."

"Here brother." Zala plucked some lose scales from her forearms and nosed them towards him. They sat huddled together, as they did every night to chase away the cold. Kaerisk picked up one of them and stared at it. Gone were the manicured and preened scales Zala once had; in their place had grown thicker, tougher scales, much like his own.

I hope that no matter how much you change on the outside, you'll always be Zala.

"Kaerisk?" Delaan asked. He regarded the black, who was trying to offer his own scales. Kaerisk took them. "The last one is for me then?"

"Yeah. We each need a pack, and I should probably enlarge mine. But once that's over, then-"

The ground rumbled as the wails of horses erupted through the darkness. Kaerisk leapt to his feet, poking his neck above the grass line. He blinked twice and shook his head to make sure he wasn't hallucinating.

The horses are being attacked by other horses!

It was a strange sight, but some of the horses appeared to be striking out against their kin, driving a choice few away from the others and out of sight of the blue hatchling. The rest disappeared to the east, running away from the apparently malicious mustangs.

Zala leaned into her brother, tail thrashing nervously. "What's going on?"

"It's too dark, but something is chasing the herd. We need to go after them," Kaerisk said.

"Why? If something is out there that can hunt the horses like we can, we should hide," Delaan said, crouching into the grass.

"Delaan, do you know of any other predators besides dragons and dakael?" Kaerisk asked. The black shook his head. "Then we need to know which of those it is."

Zala furrowed her brow. "What if we get caught?"

"We have to take that risk. C'mon."

Kaerisk scurried off after the diverted horses. Behind him, Zala and Delaan fell into a reluctant trot. The horses whipped back and forth in the moonlight ahead of them, as though in some primal battle. The sound of hoof against crumbling dirt hid their approach. In the parting grass, an orange light hovered. Kaerisk squinted, and then turned his eyes away from it.

A flame. Mustn't ruin my night vision.

Kaerisk moved closer as the dance came to a non-violent end. One group of horses paced and trotted nervously around in a circle, but the other calmed and kept their distance. Drawing nearer, the hatchling nearly bumped his head into planks of wood. They stood like sentinels, barring further passage, but also preventing the horses from escaping. The area within the wooden circle had been cleared of grass and reeked of horse spoor.

Zala and Delaan joined him at the wooden circle. His sister reached out and touched it experimentally. As she did, the pack of captured horses began their horrible wails, turning away and pacing nervously on the far side of the pen. Another sound came then, one not animal. Dakael voices began to shout and, in the dim firelight beyond, Kaerisk could see them – they had been riding the aggressive pack of horses! They charged towards them, hoisting spears.

"Run!" Delaan shouted, taking off into the grass.

Kaerisk and Zala sprinted after him, but the bipeds, held aloft by their quadruped symbiotes, easily surpassed even Kaerisk's speed as he pulled ahead of the fleeing black. They were quickly surrounded, the ocean of grass parted by a river of horses. They yelled and shook their spears. Zala cowered down and covered her head with her paws. Delaan backed up against her, but stayed in defensive stance. Kaerisk inhaled.

Now it is the moment of truth. Can we exist together?

He stepped forward and lifted his head, shouting as loud as he could in the language of the Deep. "No harm! No harm! We no harm!" His words were rough and likely lacked all syntax.

They had an immediate effect on the riders. They leaned back on their steeds, their spears still held, but their yelling stopped. The horses kept their circle at a safe distance, but the dakael themselves sat shocked.

One of the bipeds stopped his horse and moved it a little closer. When the steed refused to go any further, the biped leapt down from the horse on lanky legs. The rider had a stilted sort of walk with a great reach. His dark skin made him hard to focus on in the dimness of the night. He came near the dragons. Zala still pressed tightly against her brother, but he tucked his forepaws under him, trying to signal his passivity.

"Be careful, Kaerisk! He's still armed!" Delaan exclaimed. The sudden shout startled both the dakael and Kaerisk. The blue hissed at him, then looked back to the dakael with a lowered head, as if in apology.

The biped had jumped back and pointed his spear again. After a moment, he slowly lowered it. "If you no harm, why you here?" he asked. There were other words he had used, but that was all Kaerisk could really understand. It sounded like Lindorm; the words seemed to be the same, but the flow was different.

"We lost. Look for dragons, other dragons," Kaerisk said.

The biped regarded his companions, and then the hatchling again. "How we trust you?"

"Put hand on my nose, and I not bite," Kaerisk said. The biped was apprehensive, but soon took a deep breath, came forward, and placed his hand almost fearlessly on the blue's snout. Kaerisk lowered his head submissively, which felt awkward for him to do, but the biped seemed to get the unspoken message. The biped's cheeks pulled back and a wide grin danced across his features. He removed his hand and gave a cheer.

"You come. Meet leader! We eat!" the man exclaimed.

The other riders began to speak rapidly at the dakael's proclamation, sometimes furiously, but mostly with tenors of fear that did not need translation. The man would come near the others, lifting the hand that had touched Kaerisk before them like some sort of ward, causing them to shy back. It was somewhat humiliating to think that his scent was driving the other dakael away, though he was not sure if it had to do with the scent at all.

The riders began to leave, though a few stayed behind, casting suspicious eyes on the hatchlings. Zala finally relaxed and greeted the man, who could not understand her draconic and took a step back. He beckoned for them to follow and they did, the suspicious riders behind them with the man's abandoned horse in tow.

"Kaerisk, are you sure about this? They could be leading us into a trap, just like they did with the horses," Delaan said, keeping his voice lower this time.

Kaerisk glanced to him as they walked. "I left San'Lux so that I could help bipeds, elevate them. I left because Sapphire showed me there was a different way for dragons and dakael to live together. It has to start here – with trust. I don't want her death to have been meaningless."

"Or Icia's." Zala added quietly, subdued. They were quiet for a time after that.

The man called himself Geen. He slung his spear over his shoulder as he walked, expressing his relief that they did not have to fight. At least, that's what the hatchlings understood. He spoke freely and clearly, but it only showed the ignorance they had of the language. Delaan followed his words better than Kaerisk; the black spoke a language called 'Geldinese,' which was similar to Lindorm.

Geen explained that he had been a hunter for a number of years. He was proud of his bravery, being not only the first to ever interact with dragons – well, being eaten notwithstanding – but also the first to touch a dragon and live to tell it. Initially, Kaerisk found this viewpoint odd, but soon came to understand that bravery was one of their virtues, as Pride was one of his.

Nearby the corral, as Geen called it, lay the source of the orange light. A bonfire had been set up in the middle of several animal hide tents, held up by slender pieces of wood. Near it were placed slabs of meat, which were cooking next to the searing flames. It made the hatchlings salivate, but they tried to hide it lest they offend or frighten their hosts.

Before they could enter the village itself, several of the other riders began to argue with Geen. They spoke too quickly for Kaerisk to understand, but the raised voices or the dragon scent began to agitate the horses locked in the corral. It soon drew the attention of other dakael in the village, primarily female judging from the high-pitched wails that began to flood the town. Several more men and even some children spilled from the tent village, carrying spears and surrounding the hatchlings.

"This looks like a trap," Delaan said. His tail whipped about as he maneuvered backwards towards the wood of the corral, trying to keep the dakael in front of him.

Kaerisk tried to remain still, lowering his head as he had to Sapphire ages ago. "Die there or die here, at least we tried." Zala leaned into Kaerisk, trying to hide her shaking from the crowd.

"I'd like to pick the option where we don't die. Is there one of those?" Delaan peered over his shoulder, hindlegs twitching as though he were going to bolt over the fence.

The shouting began to die down as a new figure parted the circle. His face looked as though it had collapsed a long time ago; the dakael's skin fell in wrinkles across his brow and under the eyes. He spoke in angry tones to the crowd and motioned downwards with his hands; at his command, the spears were lowered or at least pointed away from them. He wore thick leathers with fur that was different from a horse. They seemed important or valuable to Kaerisk, perhaps because the other riders had been dressed in thinner, less elaborate clothes. The elder dakael suddenly came forward and knelt before the dragons, staining his robes in the mud.

"Forgive, please. Not kill us dragon flame." The elder lowered his head almost into the mud before the dragons. Kaerisk stood mouth agape and even Delaan stopped looking for an exit. Several of the other riders did the same, though Geen and a few of the men remained standing.

Zala leaned in close to her brother. "Does he not realize they could skewer us?"

Kaerisk glanced to his sister before addressing the elder. "We no harm. We lost. Look for other dragons."

The elder did not seem to relax at these words, but Geen came forward into the ring and pulled the elder to an upright position. They spoke quickly and Geen waved his hand at the

[145]

elder, speaking about his promise. The elder pulled his robes tighter to his frail body, and then nodded.

The elder finally spoke to them again, though Kaerisk could only discern part of the message. "Up a tent outside village. We will there." At these words, the crowd began to disperse, often bumping into one another as many kept their eyes on the dragons instead of where they were going. Zala found this humorous, but her laughter did not translate well and the dakael hurried away from them as though she might pounce at any moment.

The elder and Geen led the hatchlings to a small clearing just outside the village. It appeared to be part of the feeding ground for their horses, as much of the grass was already chewed to a reasonable height. Several men came with sticks and skins. While they began to work, Kaerisk looked into the village from whence they came; several dakael crowded around the large bonfire. Many of their structures were temporary and shabby from a dragon perspective, constructed in conical fashion using long poles of wood and thick leather hides. To Kaerisk, they were ingenious. No dragon would have considered uses for otherwise ignored material.

Once several poles were in place, the dakael attached the skins to one more pole, which they began to drag over the framework. Curiously, while most of the village consisted of homes of a single cone, this one had been constructed with two, connected together by an extended triangular roof. Once the spacious accommodation had been finished, the elder beckoned the hatchlings to enter, followed by several of the men and Geen.

Once inside, a small pit was created and filled with pieces of wood, which were quickly set ablaze. It warmed up the room and was a welcome change from sleeping in the cold. Food was brought in from the village bonfire on clay platters and placed before both man and dragon. Delaan thanked them to the best of his ability and the hatchlings waited a moment to see if their hosts would eat first. Several nervous moments passed before Geen lifted his platter with a smile and began to eat, giving the hatchlings leave to do the same. It did not take long for the hatchlings to finish their dakael-sized meal, but several of the other riders offered their food to the dragons as soon as the hatchlings finished. Zala didn't realize she was supposed to refuse, swiftly tearing into the second helping. When she noticed Kaerisk giving her the evil eye, she slowed her eating with a silly grin.

After the meal, the elder said he would relate 'times long gone,' which the hatchlings reasoned to be the history of his people. They were initially worried that they would be unable to understand the story, but one of the younger dakael brought in animal hides that had been painted by some means, which helped to tell the story pictographically.

This is what the hatchlings understood.

Long ago, these dakael – Ishluke – were cast into the Deep by the great dragons of old. A great war was fought, biped against biped, for the resources and the territory beneath the ever-looming mountains. After a generation of bloodshed that painted the caverns red, the Ishluke became enslaved. And so, they began digging and searching for another exit. Eventually, they created a way out. One of their bravest and fastest caught the first horse and the horse begged for its life. The dakael spared the horse so long as it would help him catch other creatures, and so the horse took him on its back and showed him the whole of the plains. At last, all of the Ishluke emerged into the sun, far away from the dragon lords. Here, they began a nomadic life, waiting in fear for the day the dragons would come again.

The chief added that some dragons had come before and slaughtered a sister village; however, as they were not cast into the Deep, they did not believe that the prophesy had yet come to pass. He asked if the hatchlings were there to warn or begin this apocalyptic time, but the dragons firmly refused.

Despite this, the Ishluke did not relax, but they did express thanks to the dragons. The elder and his men politely excused themselves, though Geen lingered at the entrance to the tent.

"No worry. I trust if you trust," he said. And with that, he left.

Delaan briefly peered after Geen before returning to the still-burning fire. "I don't know that this is ideal, but it beats sleeping outside. And death."

Zala licked her lips. "I am just glad I didn't have to hunt for the food! Though, this meat doesn't taste like horse."

Kaerisk joined her and nuzzled her tenderly. "I think it's great. We got to join in a dakael culture today. I am glad we found them."

"I don't know, Kaerisk. Something still seems a little off. They are almost being too nice," Delaan said.

Kaerisk grumbled. "Can't you just be happy for a little while, Delaan?"

"Well, like I said. It beats death." The black curled up on the other side of Zala. Kaerisk frowned at him, but then settled beside his sister as well. Cuddled together, the hatchlings drifted off to sleep. Despite the oddity of it, Kaerisk somehow felt safe again.

Truth and Murder

For two days and nights, the hatchlings remained with the Ishluke. Morning rose on the third day as it always did: at first light, the village would spring to a sluggish life. The womenfolk tended to heavy stones, which they used to grind strange seeds and plants with smaller stones. The menfolk traveled to the corral and joined with their symbiotes. Their brows had grown more and more creased as the days there had passed, and when Kaerisk stood to watch them leave, several avoided eye contact. When they rode off, they crossed distances that took the hatchlings days.

Next the children would come. Some would assist their mothers at the grinding stones or would turn to needlework similar to what Kaerisk had seen Sapphire do, what seemed like ages ago. A few went to the corral with the handful of menfolk that had not ridden away and they worked to forge bonds with the wild horses. At the time, Kaerisk didn't think much of the process; they would keep the animal caged from their natural hunting ground and provide food for it, creating a bond of trust between it and the animal. It seemed a decent arrangement really – they worked together and each got what they wanted.

All of these observations, however, were made outside of the village. Kaerisk mostly looked inwards from the spacious tent they had been provided. Both he and Zala had made trips into the village itself a few times over the past few days, but they always resulted in one or two reactions: screaming, apology, or both.

Zala poked her head from the tent with drooping eyes and scampered off into the tall grass. Though the Ishluke fed them very well every night, during the day a few of the children would offer the ground seeds that the Ishluke women worked.

She had developed a taste for them and they in turn had domesticated her stomach quite well.

"We should go." Delaan slinked from the tent, a steady eye watching the corral. One of the stallions ran wild in a circle around the fence.

"Why the rush? The Ishluke have been exceptionally generous. This is a chance for me to see if we are truly able to live and work together," Kaerisk said.

Delaan sat and curled his tail around his forelegs. "How long do you think this little village can support three hungry hatchlings?"

Kaerisk's tail flicked against the ground. "That is where they go, do they not? To hunt the animals we did not see, the not-horses, the luyak. They even are smart enough to store what they cannot eat in the, um. Pots, I think was the word."

For a time, only the sound of stone scraping stone and the chatter of dakael words passed between them.

"They did look worried," Kaerisk admitted.

Delaan nodded. "I heard the elder and Geen talking about possibly moving north, to be closer to the prey. I'm not sure, but I think we might have scared the luyak further north than usual on our way down here."

Kaerisk sighed, sliding down onto his belly, kicking up a bit of dust. "Does that mean I'm wrong? Can we not coexist?"

Delaan tilted his head towards him, and then shook it. "We're still hatchlings, Kaerisk. We're not coexisting right now. We're being allowed to stay here."

Kaerisk curled his neck to rest his head on his forepaws. "We should be helping them. Maybe we can go hunting with them."

"We'd only slow them down. I know this is important to you and I certainly don't want to leave what little safety we have here, but we can't stay."

Zala emerged from the grass and was accosted by children bearing more of the ground plants for her. She smiled at them and tried to say hello in Lindorm, but it sounded off. They shied back a moment before offering a few choice bits from the millet, but at least they did not scream.

Kaerisk smiled. "It's a start. If the Ishluke and their horses can live together, maybe someday we dragons can live with them too."

The tip of Delaan's tail rose and fell. "Just so long as you don't become the horse."

Kaerisk struggled to lift himself, shaking off the dust that clung to his scales. "I'll talk to the elder. We will set out tomorrow if they can provide us some food for the trip." He then ambled into the village, trying not to make a scene. The villagers all tensed at his passing, but he tried to ignore the reaction as he had for the last two days.

The elder had a smoke stick in his lips again. It was part of his morning ritual, one initially done outside. Zala had found it quite funny to see a dakael puffing smoke like a dragon, but Kaerisk was fascinated by it. As best as he could understand, the practice was soothing, rather than emulative. Upon seeing him, the elder took the stick into one hand, pulled it away from his lips, and bowed low.

"Thank you, great dragon. How can help?" the elder asked, again using more words than the hatchling actually understood.

Kaerisk frowned, coming forward and lowering his head even lower than the elder's. The first few times he had done this, the elder had nearly fallen onto his face trying to get lower. Zala had found it funny, but Kaerisk did not. "Please, elder. Am friend."

The elder dakael cautiously rose back up to a sitting height and put the pipe back in his maw.

[151]

"Need help, yes. We, um. Need go south. Can help?" Every word Kaerisk spoke made him cringe internally. He had helped Sapphire speak his language, but he had not spent enough time learning hers. He remembered her with every word.

The elder gripped the pipe again. "South dangerous. We help. Cannot go swamp, but Geen take you there."

Kaerisk smiled. "Thank you."

The elder bowed his head once more and Kaerisk crept out of the tent. He took in the settlement for a brief moment before the villagers noticed he had come out, and then rejoined Delaan at the dragon tent outside of the village.

"I told her not to go, but she never listens to anyone she doesn't want to," Delaan said.

"What?" Kaerisk asked. The black motioned with his head towards the corral. Zala sat at the edge of the fence, watching the wild horse run. Her head traced the creature's movements, eyes fixed on it like she was preparing to pounce. "Zala, get away from there!"

Zala hopped to her feet and bounded over as the horse passed her. It must have truly startled the horse, because it screamed its high pitched wail, turned abruptly, and bolted towards the opposite fence. One of the dakael handlers jumped out of the way before the horse trampled him. Zala looked back just as the creature attempted to leap from the pen – and failed. Its legs caught and the whole of its body toppled over like a rolling log. When it landed, its legs took the strain of impact, bending awkwardly. It loosed a horrible, pitiable wail and then whined in agony as it tried to stand again, but could not. Zala cowered back, head arched low and wings up, an utterly guilty look on her face.

The dakael began to shout, though the words came too quickly for Kaerisk to understand. Tail tucked between her legs, Zala retreated behind her brother as the elder rushed from his tent towards the disturbance. They spoke quickly, examining the horse's leg.

"Why didn't you listen?" Delaan hissed, joining them.

"I-I'm sorry! I didn't mean it!" Zala exclaimed.

Several of the men held the animal, while the elder spoke a few words. He then accepted a tiny spear with a long blade and sliced the creature's neck. The horse struggled, and struggled, and then slowly relaxed. A few minutes later, the horse fell completely still.

The elder spoke to a few of the menfolk who had held the horse. One mounted a steed and left the corral, heading south. The rest rushed into the village, collecting sticks and skins for some purpose. The elder walked to the hatchlings, his robe stained with blood.

Zala poked her head out from under Kaerisk's wing. "Brother, what is the word for sorry?" Her eyes filled with tears.

Delaan grumbled. "It's like she forgot we've been eating them for the last week…"

"It's not the same!" Zala exclaimed.

Kaerisk flicked them both with his tail. "Quiet, both of you!" He lifted his eyes to the elder, who stared back. The strange cracks around the dakael's eyes creased deeper. Kaerisk swallowed.

The elder fell to his knees, eyes welling with tears as he once more took the submissive position. His words were strained, even as he spoke the same words he had so many times. "We forgive. It is – nothing." The last word seemed to stick in the elder's throat, almost failing to escape his maw.

Kaerisk's whole body shook. He spread his wings wide, the sudden action startling the elder who at last lifted his eyes to him. Kaerisk saw the anger and the frustration, the hopelessness. "No."

"No?" the elder asked, for once only using one word.

"I am sorry. I take punish."

Zala knew little of Lindorm, but she recognized his use of 'I.' She tried to push in front of him. "Brother, no!" Kaerisk hissed at her and held her back before lowering his neck to the elder, who still clenched the tiny spear in his hand.

The elder was still for what seemed a long time. When he finally found his voice, it was gravelly. "You hurt horse. Horse passed, and spirit free. We lost brother." He lifted the blade. "Only one punishment."

Kaerisk closed his eyes and winced, but the deathblow never came. Instead, warm liquid and a rough hand dragged across his forehead. When he opened his eyes once more, he saw the elder had taken blood from the blade and anointed his forehead.

"Not understand," Kaerisk said, when the elder withdrew his hand.

The dakael cleaned the blade on his bloodied cloth and put it away. "You subject to laws, and I respect. Now I understand. Punishment is. You horse as you travel." Kaerisk still did not understand as the elder stepped around him and reentered his tent. The blood leaked down from his muzzle.

Delaan's tail shook nervously. "He said, you'll carry the horse as you travel. I hope he means it's food for us to set out with tomorrow. You're lucky he didn't kill you."

The day passed more somber than the last. The hunting party returned with another heavy sled of meat and bones, while the man who had gone south returned with a great amount of wood. An even larger bonfire than usual lit up the night as the Ishluke sung dark songs with sorrowful faces that

Kaerisk could only attempt to understand. The blood had dried, but he could still feel it there.

Unlike before, the hatchlings were allowed in the village. The fear had changed into something else, but Kaerisk no longer knew what. The Ishluke carried the dead horse on a sled, adorned with fur. They beat the skin-pots called drums and spoke of brothers. They lifted their hands to the sky and pressed them to the earth. Each came, everyone in the village, and placed their hand upon the dead horse. Kaerisk walked forward and did the same. The people seemed to approve, for some smiled and none frowned.

The men returned and pushed the sled into the flame. They carved a circle in the dirt around it as the sled and the horse began to burn. They stepped back and watched as the sled, the fur, and the carcass all went up in flames. They spoke words like 'release' and 'free' in somber sounds with sad smiles.

"They're not cooking it, are they?" Delaan asked, just above a whisper.

No, they are not. They are Committing the horse to the elements.

Zala leaned into Kaerisk. "It is like what you did with Sapphire, isn't it brother?"

He nodded and nuzzled her gently. "The Ishluke and their horses are truly as one."

The black sighed as the sweet smell of roasting meat wafted through the village. "Such a waste of good food…"

As the horse was slowly consumed, the elder stepped forward and addressed the crowd. "Today, we lost brother, but today, we gained brother. It known Kaerisk one of us. And he leaves us tomorrow, horse goes him, we all. Pray that future creates one of brotherhood."

The crowd cheered at this, though Kaerisk did not fully understand why. He felt their eyes upon him like the council of San'Lux and, like before, he could still say nothing. But, for the first time, he no longer felt judged.

One of us. We can respect one another, I know it. Sapphire – I wish you could be here to see it. Icia should have been here too. As this horse, this 'brother' lives on, so too must you somehow. I hope you both are watching over me.

Kaerisk smiled, watching the horse as its body was released to the elements and remembering his fallen friends.

First Flame

Delaan was scratching his neck again when the tree line first came into view. The black had been saddled with leather straps and bags much like they placed upon their horses, which had been a constant nuisance to him. He said that the leather was chafing his scales and that he wanted to just eat it and the meat inside the bags. Kaerisk had offered to take the baggage from him despite Delaan's earlier admonishments, but the scale-pouch Kaerisk had constructed for himself refused to be fused onto Delaan's scales, possibly because he continued to shed. His new scales were tougher and Kaerisk thought they suited the black quite well.

Geen had traveled with them, though he did not stay out in the open with them. His steed allowed him to simply leave as the hatchlings continued south so that he could return home and be with his people, but faithfully he returned again every morning, sometimes before they had even risen. Over the past three days, he regaled them with half-understood stories about his hunts of the luyak and how he had become famous for his bravery in dealing with the dragons. Kaerisk fought with his pride and vocal cords to expand his knowledge of the language, but Geen was more than happy to teach him the Ishluke's Lindorm.

The grass near the trees became noticeably shorter once they entered into it. It was as though it had chosen to stop growing at the point where large trees with fan-shaped roots and canopies cloaked the grass in shadows. The ground grew moist and, through the parted grass, small ponds of stagnant water could be seen pooling in shallow recesses of the ground. They looked as though small clumps of land had risen and moved away, leaving behind holes for water. The ground was infirm and Zala slid a bit when she tried bounding over it.

"Strong trees. Good trees. Deeper, not all good," Geen said. Unlike the elder, he spoke simple words to convey his point, which Kaerisk appreciated. "Stay here a day. I get food. Then, travel alone." The hatchlings agreed to wait and Geen left towards the village. He returned late in the evening and filled their packs from his saddlebags with more luyak meat.

Rather than return home, he stayed with them that evening. He directed them to gather wood and set it to flame with dry leaves and sparking stones. It was the first warmth the hatchlings had had since leaving the village; they huddled around it, inconstant firelight whipping about their features.

Geen rolled out a mat of fur and leather close to the flame and rested on it. "Swamp dangerous. Cannot travel with horses. We not travel there."

"What dangers?" Kaerisk asked.

Geen struggled with this for a time, before taking up a handful of grass and tearing it from the roots. He then bundled it up and showed it to them. "Danger."

Delaan actually laughed. "The grass hasn't killed us yet and there doesn't seem to be much of it in the swamp." When he realized Geen did not understand his draconic, he added, "No danger."

Geen grinned at this and nodded. "Dragons. No danger."

Zala stared up at the canopy above them. On the outskirts, the stars could still be seen through the branches, swaying in the chilly ocean breeze. "Dragons in swamp?"

Geen shrugged at her. "Don't know. Dragons south."

"You see dragons?" Kaerisk asked.

The dakael shook his head. Zala lowered her head to her paws.

Delaan nosed her gently. "It's alright. The Deep Mountains haven't changed, no matter how far we've gone. If we keep following them south, we'll find Lan'Dal eventually. And then we can get home."

"How far is it from Lan'Dal to Luminous?" Kaerisk's tail rose and fell slowly.

Delaan lifted his head. "You still mean to keep going?"

"Yes."

Geen regarded them quietly, and then lay back on his mat. He closed his eyes, but Kaerisk could still see him twitch with the dragon's words, perhaps trying to learn a few words of his own.

Zala pressed against Delaan a little more firmly. "We haven't seen anywhere else yet, besides San'Lux. It's not all open fields and dakael, right? We'll find a new home out there."

The black deflated, his body drooping to the ground, snout close to the crackling flame. "I can't go with you any further than Lan'Dal. You may want your own path, but I was happy enough in my own. My family must be throwing a fit right now."

Zala licked Delaan's snout. "We know you didn't mean for this to happen." Kaerisk grimaced at the action, but nodded supportively. "Brother and I will be fine on our own. You said there were deer in Lan'Dal's forests, right?"

Delaan pawed at his snout where Zala had licked him after some time had passed, as though removing it was reflex rather than desire. "But I don't know what lives in the area beyond the Lan'Dal forests. At least consider arranging for a flight to Luminous. I'll be trying to get one to Ur'Del."

"Could we trust that they would take us to Luminous and not San'Lux?" Kaerisk asked.

[159]

"If you don't trust them, then tell them you're from Luminous. You could say that you were there during the festival, got lost with me, and then tell the truth from there. Sheesh, they'd probably believe that more than they would two hatchlings from San'Lux working with bipeds anyway," Delaan said.

Zala twiddled her claws. "You mean lie?"

It's dishonorable, but...

"It might work. Hopefully, they won't ask too many questions." Kaerisk nuzzled Zala and then laid flat beside her. "Let's get some sleep. That terrain does not look easy to cross." There, he tried to sleep, but Zala kept turning beside him.

The Firstbourne's Eye felt far brighter without a tent over head or a wall of tall grass to protect from it. The shadows of the trees stretched like claws towards the Deep Mountains. Morning had brought moisture to the air, driven up by the sea; it had embedded itself in the ground and the trees. The mud of the night before had grown only more copious. Geen's horse grazed near him as he rose with a mighty yawn.

"Time to go. Good to meet you, Kaerisk, Zala, Delaan. Come back soon," the dakael said.

Kaerisk stretched out his wings and smiled. "Someday, we visit." A wide smile parted the Ishluke's lips. He joined with his symbiote and began trotting off towards the village, now far beyond sight. Kaerisk nosed Zala. His sister groaned at him before wobbling to her feet and gathering her scalepouch.

Delaan was already testing the mud, sinking several inches into it before pulling back and shaking his paw free. "This should be a lot of fun..."

"You're the one who said we had to go, Delaan." Kaerisk stepped around the black and into the mud, sinking even deeper than the black had. He pulled back, his elbows stained with the mud. Delaan grinned at him, so Kaerisk flicked some mud at him. "Guess we'll try to find the firm ground."

Zala walked forward with her forepaws while her hind legs remained stationary, back arching and stretching out. "We'll be fine. There's lots of places we can use. Right?" She scampered to them, and then hopped over the mud onto a patch of land with grass sticking from it. It held her weight.

Kaerisk glanced towards the ocean. White fog rolled from it, heading inland towards the swamp. "Don't go too far ahead."

"Well then, keep up!" Zala exclaimed, sticking her tongue out at her brother. Delaan and Kaerisk began to follow her path, weaving through the grassy areas. After they passed the initial circular pools, mounds of plant matter rose in small humps throughout the moist landscape. "We'll just use the hills. See?"

"Maybe it won't be so bad," Delaan said.

Zala scampered up the first of the hills, peering further through the branches of the sickly swamp trees. Almost as soon as she did, the earth began to tremble. The mossy hill lifted up, bucking Zala. The blue lost her footing and tumbled down the hill into a nearby pool of water. The hill kept rising like a boil ready to pop, and then detached itself from the mud and moist pit in which it had been resting. It left a round indentation like the others they had just crossed.

"Zala! Get out of there!" Kaerisk shouted.

The plant-beast turned on stubby feet of woven vine. The hill had been twice as large as Zala; now as it stood, it completely dwarfed her as she floundered the pool. Its body seemed composed completely of vines and moss, save for its face. Glowing eyes of amber peered at Kaerisk as though sensing prey. Its maw, shaped like the gullet of a frog, opened. Rows of sharp, petrified wood served as teeth. The vines pulled together, taut like muscle, and the creature began to amble towards Zala. She tried to scramble out of the pool, but the beast began to move faster as if sensing the hatchling's escape.

I have to do something! I won't lose her!

"Stay away from her!" Kaerisk charged over uneven ground, stumbling in the mud. He impacted the side of the creature with all his might. The beast did not budge.

"Kaerisk, be careful!" Delaan followed him, far more cautiously. By the time Delaan reached the side of the beast, Kaerisk had already scrambled atop it, carving into the vines with his claws. The thick plants did not slash easily, but his claws found purchase and cut through several of them. The beast reared up violently, gullet over the top of the trees. Kaerisk's hind paw caught in the vines and twisted hard as he tumbled from it.

He cried out in pain. It was a horrific sensation of burning pain coursing from the joint of his hind leg. He was sure he had broken it. He dangled for a moment, and then was jerked once, twice, three times on his injured paw before the beast finally whipped him from its tangled mass. As he impacted the mud and water with a dirty splash, teeth grit so hard that he could taste his own blood in his mouth, he almost forgot the battle and held completely still.

The beast fell, splashing into the small pond in which Zala had fallen. She had already scrambled out and shaken herself off, bouncing around on the grass. "Brother!"

Delaan tried to slash from the solid ground. It retaliated faster than expected, one of its vine-paws extending out of their curl and whipping him in the side. The mass was enough to send the hapless hatchling skidding back through the mud several feet.

"Delaan!" Zala exclaimed. She began to move towards him, but the vine creature turned on Kaerisk. Her brother struggled to crawl away on three legs through the dense mud without rousing any more of the nearby hills, which he reasoned might be more of the creatures. Its maw opened. "Brother, no!"

A shaft of wood flew through the air and embedded in the eye-socket of the vine beast. As Kaerisk clawed his way around the thick mass of the plant beast, he could see Geen, standing unarmed. His spear had shattered its amber eye. This seemed to infuriate the beast; it turned and began shambling towards the dakael.

Now's my only chance!

Kaerisk sneered, took a deep breath, and focused on the fire within him. When he exhaled, a gout of flame rushed over the marshy landscape, turning water to steam and impacting the back of the beast squarely – but to no effect. The vines of the creature had been soaking in water; though it now steamed with lost moisture, it did not catch fire. It kicked its feet back towards him, digging up a large chunk of mud and burying him in it. His wing bent at an awkward angle and vied for attention over the burning sensation in his paw.

No! I won't be able to breathe fire again until I've eaten!

The beast charged Geen, sending shockwaves through the ground. The lanky dakael leapt out of the way just prior to the behemoth ramming him; the creature instead hit a tree with enough force to snap the trunk.

Firelight again lit up the misty swamp. Kaerisk looked to Delaan, but the black was still moaning near the tree he had impacted, slowly rising. It was Zala. Fire wreathed her form as her first dragon flame struck the creature. This time, the moisture-stripped vines caught fire and a foul-smelling odor, like burning refuse, spewed from its sides.

The flame caused the beast to rampage, charging Delaan and slinging mud around. He scrambled out of its path, narrowly avoiding being trampled. The beast hit the tree which Delaan had; it was snapped in half. Before long the flame had engulfed it and its vine-paws could not support its massive bulk. It toppled to the ground and writhed as it smoldered, slowly dying to the flames as noxious gas rose up into the sky.

Geen came over to Kaerisk and helped to dig him out of the mud. Kaerisk thanked him, stretching out his wing and finding no real damage. He left his injured paw half-submerged in the mud, the cool earth providing some relief.

"All okay?" Geen asked.

Delaan limped towards them. "Not much hurt." The black scales hid it well, but Kaerisk imagined his whole side had to be bruised from the creature's attack.

Zala stood off to the side, watching the creature burn. She wasn't looking at it so much as she was staring towards it, her body trembling slightly. As the flames began to die, Geen hopped over the mud towards the corpse.

Kaerisk hobbled over to her. "You did well, Zala."

"It was my first flame, Kaerisk. My first flame."

Kaerisk leaned into her, hiding his injury. "You did it."

"Icia should have been here to see it."

Kaerisk frowned, twining his tail with hers. "I know."

Geen pulled away some smoldering vines and reached the other amber eye of the beast. He plucked it free with a small spear-like implement he had heard the Ishluke call a knife. He tossed the heated amber from one hand to the other as he walked towards them. Once it had cooled, he took a thin strip of hide and wrapped it up. He then attached this to a second piece of leather, making a sort of leather necklace.

"Behemoth strong. Hard to hurt, hard to kill. Take power with you," Geen said.

He placed the pendant around Kaerisk's neck. The hatchling tried to peer down at it. It still glowed, as though the creature had not truly died. When he reached one paw up to grasp it, he felt it – Riftwind. Somehow, the creature had stored the energy in its body or perhaps its eyes. He had heard his father warn him of the misuse of Riftwind; if a dragon were to use too much Riftwind, it could affect the land itself and cause creatures of living stone to rise.

Is this 'behemoth' a golem? And if so, who had created it? And...

Geen smiled at him and he smiled back.

What do the dakael know of Riftwind? When he says strength, does he know what this truly is?

"Look hurt." Geen motioned towards Kaerisk's injured hind paw, which he had been favoring as he held the crystal. Kaerisk dropped his paw to the ground, trying to look as it always did and not grimace in pain.

"Not hurt," Kaerisk said.

"Brother..."

His tail squeezed hers. "I'm fine, Zala."

"Danger, here. Be safe. Yes? Rest, again? One day? Give food to you."

"Yes! Yes!" Delaan exclaimed suddenly. The ferocity of it startled the group. The black's head drooped. "Sorry. But Geen is right. We should recover before we try again. We are lucky he was able to help us at all!"

Kaerisk sighed and then nodded. "Let's head back to the edge of the swamp. We can rest there awhile longer."

Geen led the injured group back to the campsite from the previous night, and then returned to his people with the news. There, Kaerisk spent the day off his foot, trying not to think of the pain while Delaan paced and sought another path.

Zala stared off into the swamp where the creature had fallen for the rest of the day.

<u>Behemoth Swamp</u>

The morning brought no relief for Kaerisk. His paw had swollen, but he tried his best to ignore it and hide it from his sister and Delaan. He stared at the swamp as Zala had the night before, taking a deep breath. Crossing it would be hard enough if he were well, but like this he had little chance of escaping the lumbering giants. The behemoth-eye pendant swung from his neck.

Delaan and Zala moved ahead into the swamp, trying to stay on patches of ground where the plants clung, keeping a wary eye on the many mounds poking through the morning fog. Each looked to the burned husk of the behemoth as they passed, but Kaerisk lingered. In the center of the burnt vines and cinders was a circular stone, carved with strange symbols he had never before seen. He reached towards it.

Don't touch it.

"What, why?" Kaerisk asked.

Zala paused before making a leap. "What, brother?" Delaan also paused, tail landing partway in the mud. He sneered back at it.

Kaerisk furrowed his brow as he stared at the stone. "I heard... nothing." Zala pulled her tail close to her and peered at him as though he had something on his face. "I'm sorry, let's keep going."

"C'mon Kaerisk, keep it together. If you're not well, we can try to signal Geen or something," Delaan said.

Kaerisk placed his paw down, pain immediately shooting through his body. He bared his teeth, but kept his mouth shut. "I'm fine." Delaan turned back to the swamp ahead but Zala retreated, nosing him. He smiled to her and pushed her head away with his, towards the southern swamp. Reluctantly, she turned and hopped to the next bit of firm ground. Kaerisk followed. He landed heavily, trying to keep his injured paw from hitting the ground too hard.

The hatchlings had expected to clear the first few mounds of behemoths and have only the swamp behind them to worry about, but the further south they went, the more hellish living hills they found. The wide spacing between them lessened and lessened until they became rows of living walls, impeding progress.

Kaerisk crept forward, trailing behind Zala and Delaan. Every step was agony, for the fear that they might awaken the beasts, and for the swollen paw that could hardly support his weight. Every time the sharp pain jolted up his spine, he was reminded that if they woke even one of the plant monsters he would have no chance of escape.

The ground shook and shifted. The hatchlings pulled close together; he could feel Zala shaking as she pressed against him. They looked from hill to hill, but none of them were moving. Nervously, Kaerisk took the lead, pushing past Delaan and through the row of hills. As the sun rose higher, the shaking ground grew worse and they could hear the sound of wood snapping.

"Something's coming for us!" Zala exclaimed.

Delaan turned to her sharply. "Shh!" Zala's ear frills lowered as Delaan reprimanded her.

Finally, they cleared the wall of slumbering behemoths. As the fog cleared away, they discovered yet another wall of the creatures, too densely packed to try sneaking through them. And there, in the middle of the path created by two lines of hills, was an active behemoth. It hobbled backwards several feet and then charged forward, slamming the whole of its mass against a tree. The trunk had begun to snap and splinter; the impact of the behemoth finally toppled it. The creature slid off the now shattered tree and began to devour the splinters, grinding them up on rows of petrified teeth that had threatened the hatchlings yesterday. Its amber eyes glowed dimly as it fed.

"What are we going to do?" Zala whispered, pressing firmly against her brother, which did little to help the pain in his foot.

Delaan's tail shook erratically. "Maybe we should turn back."

"No. We go forward," Kaerisk said.

Delaan glanced at him, and then motioned with a wing towards the lumbering lumberjack. "And how do you propose we deal with that?"

Kaerisk swallowed. "We don't. We're going to walk right past him."

"You really have lost your mind or something!" Delaan jerked his head down when he realized his voice had raised. The behemoth did not seem to notice, nor did the living rows flinch.

"They're not smart – they're just animals. And an animal with a kill isn't going to chase after another and leave its prey behind," Kaerisk said.

"That – thing – is not an animal."

Zala lifted her wings a bit. "I believe in brother. If he says we go forward, we do it."

Delaan opened his mouth as though he were going to say something, so Kaerisk stepped away from him and towards the behemoth. He could feel Zala behind him, her nose against his tail as though she might bite it as they did when they were children. His heart raced in his chest as he veered to the left, near the new wall of hills, but there was still only a hatchlings-length between the feeding monster and the dragons. Its maw dripped with sap, dark as congealed blood. Just a bit further and they would pass it!

It lifted up its head as the hatchlings reached the halfway mark. Kaerisk froze, his sister bumping her head into his tail before freezing as well. Its paws dug into the loose ground, finger-tendrils rooting. Its sap-stained maw turned back and forth. Kaerisk's chest began to burn in need for air, but he dare not draw a breath.

Its dim amber eyes found them. Its maw turned close to Kaerisk and his claws dug into the ground. Every muscle tensed.

I'll have to run! But I can't! I – I...

The behemoth lowered its head down to where the pendant hung around Kaerisk's neck. It then quivered all its vines and spit a bit of sap on his face before returning to its tree and taking a large bite from it, as though claiming it. The creature had mistaken Kaerisk for another behemoth!

"Move, now!" Kaerisk hissed as he began to creep faster, still hindered by his paw and by fear of waking the line of behemoths. As soon as enough distance was placed between them, the behemoth returned its attention to its kill and the hatchlings breathed in relief. Kaerisk wiped the sap from his face, or attempted to. It left a stain of black ooze on his head.

Delaan exhaled slowly, pulling towards the center of the path. "That was way too close."

Zala nuzzled him, and then took the lead. "We're fine, see?" She shook as she walked, but her voice was steady.

They pressed through one last row of the behemoths before they finally broke free. Once more the behemoth hills became sparse enough to pass between them. When they finally cleared them, Kaerisk gaped at the landscape ahead. The area was cratered with behemoth-sized holes, many of which had lost their shape as water and time had worn them away. The trees were sparse, almost non-existent in the wasteland. Reeds, brown and sickly, drooped as they clung to their last remaining days of life. The vegetation that had held the ground together in the behemoth rows was now completely gone, leaving nothing but endless dead bogs, mud, and gnawed trees.

How are we supposed to cross this?

The hatchlings sat down on the last tuff of remaining solid ground and ate lunch in silence.

When they resumed, the first step Kaerisk took into the wasteland sunk him half a foot into mud. The moist ground sucked at him, as though trying to pull him down into the mire. He wrenched his paw free and tried stretching further, but the ground was just as yielding there and his belly slapped the mud audibly. There was no grinning now as there had been when they tried to ford the swamp yesterday. Now, as Kaerisk flailed about in the mud, half-swimming, half-dragging himself through the sod, there was only worried looks and nervous hatchlings following him.

Once his body had sunk into the mire almost up to his wings, he took a deep breath, pulled his forepaw free, took a step forward, and then drove it back into the muck. He repeated this process again and again, each foot taking intense effort, and one feeling intense pain as it struggled free. He bit his lip, keeping his head high as his neck stained with the lifeless filth, silently praying his scalepouch would hold and not let any mud into the meat. Occasionally, there was a flailing to his left or right; Zala and Delaan would stumble or try to spring forward from the hungry earth instinctually, flinging mud around like whelplings outside of the lair for the first time. Even when they splashed him, he said nothing. An impenetrable silence hung over them. No bird flew overhead and no insect made a single noise. It was as though the world had ended behind the wall of behemoths. Only the hope that dragons lay beyond this mired abyss drove him forward.

[171]

The line of behemoths was still in sight as the sun went down, lost only when the mist began to rise from the distant sea. Zala groaned, her eyelids drooping, her snout dragging along the mud, moving forward out of sheer will power, or perhaps habit. She stumbled when her paw could not lift out of the earth. Her head fell to the mud and did not rise again. In fact, it began to sink.

"Zala!" Kaerisk shouted.

She lifted her head weakly. "I just. Need to rest a minute."

"We can't sleep here! Isn't there any place solid we could go?" Delaan asked. He was in no better shape that Zala, his wings covered with a coat of mud. The bags that Geen had provided were equally saturated in the black earth.

Kaerisk craned his head from left to right, but the only remaining pieces of vegetation were a few crooked trees that had somehow remained standing. The mist closed in around them, obscuring sight and hope. His head spun from exhaustion and pain.

The tree.

Kaerisk stumbled towards it. The thick trunk had stood even against the behemoths' passing. As he drew closer, the teeth marks of the angry plant creatures became visible, deep and filled with protective sap. When at last he reached it, head nearly bumping into the scarred bark, he placed his hand upon it. The branches couldn't hold them.

"What are you doing?" Delaan asked. He and Zala followed at a much slower pace.

"Making our nest." Kaerisk slid his forepaw back into the mud and reached down. The plant's roots went deep, but the land had given up all its bounty to the passing tide and left none for the tree. He grit his teeth as he pulled back against them, his hind paw burning in agonizing pain as he used it for leverage.

His claws began to slice the emaciated roots, one by one. When he could feel no more, he stepped forward and leaned against the tree. It began to tilt, but he did not have the strength to push it down. He rested against it for just a moment.

Suddenly, Zala and Delaan were next to him; as they began to push, he realized he must have fainted. Joining them, the tree finally fell, slapping hard into the mud and sinking. Though most of the trunk rested within mud, a small island had been created in the sea of earth and decay. The hatchlings rounded the sides, climbed atop it, and passed out. It was the most peaceful sleep Kaerisk ever remembered having.

When he woke, it was to the sensation of little cold pokes against his scales. Groggily, he checked his sister, but she lay curled up and fast asleep. Dawn's light struggled to penetrate the rolling fog, but above them, dark clouds hovered ominously. A droplet of water slapped against Kaerisk's snout.

Just great. Once we lose the Eye's light...

He nosed Zala awake, who groaned and stretched, trying in vain to ignore him. Her claws poked against Delaan, who also stirred with a whine. His sinuous black neck rose, peering out at the same weather Kaerisk had assessed.

"It's so cold..."

"We'll be alright, Delaan." Kaerisk struggled to right himself on the round, uneven log. He opened his scale pouch, relieved that no mud had gotten onto his share of the meat. "Check your food." With a low moan, Delaan popped open the bags he had been saddled with. Though the outside had been coated with the dark earth, none had made it inside.

Zala lifted and peered at her pouch. The uneven scales, black and blue in uneven pattern, had held to her body, but not tightly enough. Slowly, she pulled free globs of mud and dirt from her pouch, flinging them away; the rough seal of their

[173]

scales had broken. Finally, she reached the meat, which she tore loose and was about to fling away.

Kaerisk arrested her paw. "No."

Her face was wracked with exhaustion and confusion.

"We have to eat it."

"But – brother. It's dirty."

"We can't waste any food."

"But-"

"None, Zala. We don't know how far this swamp goes." He took the meat from her, brushed it off as best he could, and put it in his mouth. It had a dead, flavorless taste, as though it too had been sucked of life like the swamp around them. He tried to ignore the crunching sound the dirt made against his teeth as he devoured it.

Zala watched aghast. "You're serious?"

Kaerisk swallowed. "Eat. And share with Delaan."

She took out a piece of the mud-encrusted meat and handed it to the black. He groaned at it, scraping off as much of the mud as he could before chewing on it with tears in his eyes.

"I-I've... had worse." Delaan's words were almost unintelligible with his mouth full of mud and meat. Zala choked down what she could as the light slowly faded behind the ceiling of clouds.

When the three set off, the rain had not yet begun to fall in earnest. The first few hours were as slow as the day before, one paw in front of the other. Every muscle in Kaerisk's body screamed for relief, none more so than his still-swollen paw. Still, he trudged through the thick earth, leaving behind him a shallow trail through the mud.

And then the rain began to pour. At first, it was a welcome addition, washing out the mud and sap from the day before; however, the earth became more slick and treacherous the longer it stormed. It was easier to move it aside, but also was it easier to lose footing and stumble. More than once did Zala fall victim to this fate, plopping down into the mud, her sapphire scales coated in the sterile brown ooze.

Time seemed to stand still. Even as they pressed forward, there was no light overhead to measure their day. Only the lack of the line of behemoths and their one refuge in the wasteland brought any sense of progress. Once they had passed from sight, it was hard to say if any headway was being made at all. Kaerisk's stomach rumbled in the desolation and runny mud.

"We're going to die out here," Delaan suddenly moaned. His eyes fixated on the sky above, even as water fell into them.

Kaerisk grunted as he slogged through more of the endless mud. "Don't say that. We'll make it through this."

"I should never have tried to help you."

Zala slowed her advance. "Delaan…"

Kaerisk growled, slipping through the mud as he pushed towards Delaan. When he reached him, he lifted his paw as though he might strike the black.

Delaan turned his head to the blue, the water in his eyes not from the rain. "I don't want to die, Kaerisk. I don't want to fall into the mud and be swallowed up by the elements. I don't want to disappear into the earth like Icia. I don't want to die."

Kaerisk stumbled, not certain what to say. He too remembered the falling rocks and the screaming. He too had once considered what it would be like to be buried alive. He pressed his head under Delaan's chin and lifted it. Delaan rested there as Zala joined them, three hatchlings mired in the mud.

<u>Survival</u>

It took two days before the landscape began to change. It was almost unnoticeable at first, small grasses poking up through the sea of mud and brackish water. The more they began to appear, the easier it was to maneuver in the mire. They even began to find clumps of dirt that could hold their weight for more than a few moments. It almost brought a smile to Zala's face, until the corollary to the grasses became apparent: water. Large pools of almost unpalatable water had formed from the damage of the behemoth tide. Most of them were likely collapsed potholes from where the land-ravenous beasts once laid.

Kaerisk stepped into the water and shook off one of the many layers of mud that had formed over the past few days. It was a welcome relief for his injury; the cold marshy water was of some comfort to his paw, swollen almost half again as large as it should be. His friends joined him and the once-black pool was painted brown with their shed earthen skin.

While most pools were avoided by zigzagging through the corridors of water, some had grown so large that the only way to cross was by fording them. As they swam through the algae-encrusted water, Geen's packs buoyed up and down on the surface. Delaan might have been fortunate that he had been saddled with them; unlike Zala or Kaerisk, he had difficulty swimming. Though he blamed it on exhaustion – a fair thing to blame, for they had suffered much – it was clear from his rapid, frantic movements that he had not had much practice swimming before, while Zala and Kaerisk had grown up with the pools of their father's lair.

When they reached the other side, trees came into view in the distance. They sped up to reach them as the Eye began to set, muscles still burning from the days of hard trudging. Kaerisk remembered the Ashen Forest, the solid ground it possessed, and the delicious deer that called it home.

I could eat a whole deer right now…

When they reached the tree line, they nearly toppled into yet another pool of brackish water. This was still not a forest like the one he had known, but instead it was a swamp just as difficult to maneuver as the last biome they had passed. Delaan collapsed against one of the trees and just lay there. Zala paced about the edge of the water like a trapped animal before finally settling on the shore.

Kaerisk tried not to sigh. "Let's eat."

Delaan opened the packs, pouring out the water that had seeped inside. While it had held up well to the mud, the water was another thing, as was the algae, which painted their meat a sickly green.

Zala grimaced. "We can't eat that."

"We have to, sister."

Delaan crumpled. "I don't know if I can keep that down…"

"Enough, Delaan." Kaerisk took a piece and hobbled over to his sister.

She made a face. "I don't think I can either, brother."

"Do you remember Mother Mountain?"

His words tore her view away from the meat. "Of course I do."

"You remember the sapphire slopes?"

"Yes."

"When we still lived there, meat would rain from the heavens."

"I remember. It was the most delicious thing I ever had."

"But it wasn't always. Not at the end."

[177]

Zala pulled her paws under her, frowning.

Kaerisk lay down beside her, brushing off as much of the unintentional seasoning as he could. "By the end, the pieces of meat were rancid. That is why we turned to hunting the bugs, ascended the slopes, and found the lake of rust. We survived then. We can survive now, right?"

She took the chunk of meat from him, turning it over a few times. "We did, but…" She sneered suddenly, and then shut her eyes tightly and shoved the meat down her gullet. Kaerisk nuzzled her and stood.

I know, Zala… but Father's not coming this time.

Kaerisk returned to Delaan, who was trying not to turn as green as the algae he scraped from his meat. Kaerisk checked one sack, and then the other – only a small bite of meat remained. He took it out, whispered a prayer to the Firstbourne, and ate the last of their food.

That night, while the other hatchlings slept on the first piece of firm ground in three days, Kaerisk rested alone, his injured paw in the water. He wasn't sure if it was the algae, or the exhaustion, or the pain, or the hunger, but he began to see things. Overlapping the trees and stretching even higher were spectral spires of stone, airy and insubstantial. From perches carved in the rock, ghostly dragons took to the night sky, flying in and out of the foggy cloudbanks. Below, a phantasmal road stretched over his companions; pale white apparitions of dragons walked over them, oblivious to their existence. The hatchlings too, slumbered without acknowledgement of the scene. At the base of a nearby spire, a purple elder without a tail watched Kaerisk with one eye at all times. Though just as ethereal as the rest, he was the only one graced with color. When Kaerisk locked eyes with him, he smiled.

"Fear not Death. Only Regret holds power over dragons. Sleep, Orban. There yet, you are not."

Kaerisk laid his head down on the ground and covered his eyes with his paws, trying to will the vision away.

By morning, the hatchlings of hunger had returned to his stomach, but their incessant growling and gnawing at his insides had to compete with the pain from his foot, which had shrunken only a little from resting it in the water the night before. Doing so had left it stiff and numb; moreover, his toes didn't appear to be the right shade of blue anymore. He tried not to think about it or the apparition in the night.

At last, after fording one final brackish pond and pushing out through the undergrowth protecting the bank, Kaerisk and his friends broke through to something slightly more familiar. The forest lacked much in the way of pooled water and infirm ground, but made up for it in trees, trees far taller than even the biggest tree Kaerisk had ever seen in the Ashen Forest. The branches were too far up for a safe climb, even if he did have full use of his paw. A thin, manageable layer of grass and weeds waved through the massive trunks. Kaerisk examined one of them closely; it had been torn by flat teeth.

He collapsed in relief. "Thank the Firstbourne..."

"What is it?" Zala asked, coming to his side quickly.

"There's food in these woods."

Delaan gained a burst of energy at this, hopping over to him. "Well? Let's go get some!"

Kaerisk lifted his wing and directed them to look at his swollen paw. "I can't. It was hard enough to make it through the swamp, but I won't be able to chase anything down like this. I'll have to rely on you two."

Zala peered at it, aghast. "Why didn't you tell us? We could have stopped!"

Delaan frowned off to the side. "Because if we hadn't kept going, we'd never have made it through the swamp. Don't tell me you didn't notice his pain."

Zala's tail drooped. "I did, but…"

Kaerisk nuzzled her. "It's fine, sister. Go and get us some food, and then we can spend some time taking it slow. I'll get better in no time."

"I'll do my best, Kaerisk," Delaan said, but his head was still cast to the side. Kaerisk stared at him.

"We'll be back soon. Just rest for now, okay?" Zala nosed him quickly and then hopped off to push Delaan along. The two then disappeared into the forest.

As soon as they were gone, Kaerisk began to cry. All of the pain he had held back, all the self-doubt, began to surge out of him once he was alone. Had they gone but a few feet more, Kaerisk wasn't sure he could have prevented himself from collapsing like Delaan. His paw throbbed like a beating, broken heart, and he felt as though he never wanted to move again. Why had he agreed to leave home with Zala?

He dug his forepaws into the dirt at this question, fighting back the tears once more and inhaling. He hadn't suffered all the way through the swamp, and through the plains, and the Miasma's lair to give up now. Zala was the most important thing to him in the world, especially having lost everyone else who had ever mattered to him. Perhaps that hallucination he had seen was right: regret was a luxury he could not afford.

Kaerisk dried his eyes and stuck his paw back into the water. Looking upwards, the ashen trees of his forest home had no compare to the monsters that towered before him. As the thick clouds of fog above him parted, light fell like a curtain through the trees. They stretched upwards into the sky, higher than he had seen some dragons fly before. Even if he climbed all day, he did not believe he could reach the top, where the narrow leaves swayed in the ocean breeze. The trees themselves seemed as rigid as rock. The only thing that dwarfed the massive plants was the Deep Mountains themselves. He squinted as the Eye's light fell upon him, but he continued to stare up at the trees and wonder if he would live to fly.

Some hours later, Delaan and Zala returned with an exceptionally unlikely meal. On her back, Zala carried not the carcass of an animal, but a pile of vines and roots crowned by a pink flower. A sheepish look crept over her when she spied her brother. The vines were dumped unceremoniously before him.

"I'm sorry brother. This was all we could find."

Kaerisk pulled his paw from the water and stood up, wincing a bit as he set his paw down. "I don't think we can eat that."

Delaan sighed. "That's what I told her, but she seemed to think it was a good idea to bring it back here. I'm not even certain it's dead."

Kaerisk blinked. "It?" Worry that this might be a baby behemoth gnawed at him, but as he inspected the pile closer, he began to realize it wasn't a pile at all. The vines wove together like muscles. The flower and sunken, empty apertures below them looked almost like the skull of a human. "Wait, this is a grassman!"

Delaan nodded. "Thought you knew that. Wasn't your dad constantly teaching you about the dakael?"

Kaerisk's tail lashed about. "Yes, but he didn't tell me much about them since they weren't supposed to be a threat... did you attack him?"

Zala came around sniffing at his injured paw before nosing him. "It's alright, brother. We didn't fight. Actually, I think we scared him to death. We came near him and he just fell over and didn't move."

[181]

Kaerisk hummed. His father had mentioned little about the grassmen, only that it was difficult to tell if they were alive or dead. The only way to be sure was to check their flower; normally, killing a grassman was as simple as removing the flower, but Father always insisted Kaerisk was thorough. When the flower was removed, a seed would pop forth. If it was not destroyed, they could grow back 'like any other weed,' he had said. Gently, Kaerisk peeled back the flower petals and tried to have a look inside.

The moment he did, the vines sprung to life. It rolled onto its feet, arms waving about for a moment, and then freezing in position, one outstretched, one up, one leg partly raised. Kaerisk wasn't sure if it was a defensive posture or a dance.

"We sorry," Kaerisk tried. "Can you speak?" The creature remained still, perhaps pretending to be one of the large trees behind it. Father had never really explained how the grassmen could see or hear or if they even could. Kaerisk waited, lying on his side partly to seem less threatening and partly to relieve some stress on his paw.

Delaan shook his head. "This is a waste of time. It's a plant."

Slowly, the grassman lowered its limbs. Its strange, turnip-shaped head peered with its empty eye sockets at Kaerisk, and then rooted its feet, literally, into the ground. The vines looked like wiggling toes in the dirt. The creature went still again, and then suddenly widened as though its torso was blossoming. Delaan and Zala crept back, but Kaerisk remained where he was. The vines of its torso reformed even tighter before, and then slowly condensed. A sweet air washed over Kaerisk, followed by unusual, but recognizable sounds.

"You different. Not them. Why here?"

"We no harm. We lost. Hungry. Look for dragons," Kaerisk said.

It relaxed its torso and then reached into small slits in its body. Its writhing hand procured a small red-yellow object. Its skin was shiny. The grassman reached out towards the dragon with the object.

"Food?" Kaerisk asked. The grassman nodded. Kaerisk grasped it with a forepaw and took it. He sniffed at it; it smelled strange.

Sapphire, I want to trust the dakael. Help me.

He took a bite. It was a strange flavor: somewhat bitter, somewhat sweet, and definitely not meat. He had a hard time breaking up the pieces with his sharp teeth, but when he swallowed them down, all that seemed to happen was the void in his stomach filled a little.

"Brother?" Zala asked.

The grassman breathed out another pair of words. "Fruit. Good?"

Kaerisk nodded, though he did not mean it. The grassman reached into its torso once more and procured two other similar pieces of fruit for the other two dragons, though they were not as large as the others and one was greener than the first. It handed them to Zala and Delaan. The black, who got the green one, wrinkled his nose at it. Zala quickly took a bite, head writhing back and forth with a silly grin on her face.

"It's tart!" she proclaimed. She must have liked the tart flavor, as she immediately devoured the rest.

Kaerisk returned his attention to the grassman. The dakael was leaning backwards, almost diagonally against the light of the Eye. "Thank you. Can help find dragons?"

The grassman writhed like a snake and then stood upright and puffed out to speak. "I help you, you help me?"

"Help how?" Kaerisk asked.

[183]

"Come and see. Danger here."

The grassman took a few steps back before turning and walking deeper into the forest. Its gait was wide, rooting and uprooting with each step.

Delaan took a bite of his fruit, and then cast the rest aside. He seemed to have a hard time swallowing. When his throat was clear, he helped Kaerisk to his feet. "I don't like this, Kaerisk. We should take our chances in the forest. These trees are right for Lan'Dal; it has to be nearby."

"How do you propose we find it? This woodland is much thicker than the Ashen Forest and, between the fog and the canopy, we won't see dragons flying overhead."

"Kaerisk, they don't eat meat. I don't think they can help us."

"I like the fruit stuff, though!" Zala exclaimed. Delaan covered his face with a wing, shaking his head.

"It's not much, but it's a start. We need to regain our strength and they know the area. He helped us after you basically kidnapped him – we should return the favor if we can."

Zala agreed. The two hatchlings followed the grassman deeper into the forest, finding its lumbering method of walking rather curious. Delaan trailed behind with his tail swinging low.

A New Battle

Talking with the grassman as they walked was difficult, as expanding and contracting his entire ribcage often required a firm grip on the ground. They were able to determine that his name was Correth, that his people were called the Vitis, and that they had lived in the forest for a long time. Delaan insisted he had never heard of Lan'Dal allowing the Vitis to survive, but Correth said that they were rarely bothered by dragons. They were, however, often harassed by the chirop, which none of the hatchlings had heard of before. Kaerisk suspected it was a name for another of the races that the dragons had never bothered to ask, once Zala determined Correth wasn't just chirping.

Halfway through their journey, Correth suddenly rooted himself. His arms writhed about as his toes wriggled in the dirt. Before they could ask what was wrong, he approached Kaerisk and leaned to his side, almost completely diagonal. His hand reached out to the injured paw and unwrapped into several vines, which then gripped around it. Kaerisk winced and Correth went as still as he had when he had first been spoken to.

At last, his ribcage expanded. "You hurt."

Kaerisk grit his teeth. "It is nothing."

"I help." Correth wrapped his vines even tighter around the paw, which caused Kaerisk to cry out.

"Brother!" Zala moved forward, but Delaan stepped in front of her, watching avidly.

The vines twisted and formed around the wounded limb, wrapping it up exceptionally tight. The pressure was uncomfortable, but after a while it began to dull. The turnip-head popped up, flower tightly sealed. "Now cut."

"Cut?" Kaerisk asked. Correth nodded, motioning with his free limb to an area of his arm. "Wait – cut your arm off?" Again the Vitis nodded. "I can't do that! Don't you need your arm?" Kaerisk had reverted to speaking draconic in his surprise.

Despite this, Correth answered him. "You hurt. Not grow back. I grow back. Cut."

Kaerisk stared into where his eyes should be, and then down to the arm that held his foot. Slowly, his maw crept down to the place Correth had indicated. He closed his eyes. "I'm sorry." He opened his jaw and brought it down on the vines, severing them. Green, ooze-like blood spurted momentarily from the wound; it tasted far bitterer than the fruit he had been given.

Correth himself quivered, but otherwise seemed unperturbed by the whole matter. He tied up the now-severed vines around Kaerisk's foot and slowly massaged his blood into the paw. It had a strangely comforting burn to it. When this was done, he brought his severed arm up to where his mouth should be and bit it, for lack of a better term. It seemed to have no effect, as the ooze had already stopped flowing, but it stopped his quivering.

"Now walk," Correth said when his arm had vacated his maw.

Kaerisk's gait was a bit uneven at first. He was not used to the vines beneath his paw, preventing him from flexing it as he moved, but after a time walking became easier. The pain was still present, but the pressure helped. "How did you learn to do that? You don't have any reason to know how to heal a dragon," Kaerisk said, still speaking draconic.

Again, Correth answered. "Vitis carry memory. Some broken, some pieces. Remember before birth, before birth, before birth. Not unlike had helped before." With this, Correth began his lumbering walk, continuing without further comment. Kaerisk followed behind in wonder.

The three hatchlings and their guide arrived at the home of the Vitis. Kaerisk had expected the groves his father had told him off, a cleared circle in ample sun where they would sit together and worship the Eye like a god. But this was not the grassman grove Father had spoken of in his hateful lessons.

It looked to be a giant corral to Kaerisk's eyes. Fallen trees had been turned into walls. The Vitis had taken axes to the trees – implements Father had spoken of that they used to make spears – and turned those trees into fortifications. Thorn bushes coated the outside of the walls and the gate was moved by no less than four Vitis, their vines struggling like strained muscles in silence. The grassmen quivered at the hatchling's arrival, but they lacked the panic that Kaerisk had seen with the Ishluke – the Vitis did not build these fortifications to keep out dragons. As soon as they were inside, the grassman sealed the doors behind them.

Correth took them to a circle of the Vitis. Their arm-vines were connected and their toes had rooted deep in the soil. They swayed together, stopping only at Correth's approach. The circle parted, allowing an elder Vitis, age apparent only from how low its vines sagged and how wilted its flower seemed, to pass. Correth and the elder wrapped their arms together, writhing about in silence, speaking some secret language of touch.

"We shouldn't have come here," Delaan whispered. "They look like they're preparing to fight." He motioned up to the walls, where the grassmen patrolled the platforms cut into the tree. Every last one of them was armed with a spear.

The elder's chest rose and fell, but the seal was not as tight. His words were faint and airy. "Welcome. We give food. We ask help. Chirop come. Hurt follow. Help?"

[187]

"You have more fruit?" Zala asked. The elder nodded and pointed to a pile of the stuff behind the circle. Zala eagerly hopped over to it.

"Zala, wait!" Delaan exclaimed, following her.

She took the fruit and bit down, her whole body quivering at the bittersweet taste. "It's tangy!"

Kaerisk couldn't help but grin. "Zala, you are so weird some times." She made a face at him and then claimed a small pile of the stuff for herself, much to Delaan's displeasure. Kaerisk returned his attention to the elder. "I don't want to hurt any dakael if I can. Could we scare them off?"

The elder nodded. "We hope yes. Chirop fear dragons."

Kaerisk leaned forward, speaking almost as softly as the elder. "We will help, but promise me one thing." He glanced to Zala. "If anything happens, make sure she and Delaan get to the other dragons safely. I can't run like this."

"I know." The elder nodded solemnly. "We protect if we can."

Kaerisk smiled. "Then we agree." Delaan heard that part and fell to his belly with a groan, chewing on the fruit pile. Kaerisk joined them and they ate their fill of the strange, bittersweet fruit.

The circle of elder Vitis broke once more, vines quivering. The hatchlings watched them as they quickly took up arms and manned the walls. Kaerisk listened, but he heard nothing. Curious, he followed them with Delaan and Zala ascending after him.

The trees beyond the wall blocked most sight beyond two hundred feet, but the undergrowth that had characterized the massive coastal trees had been cleared away. Through them, the first signs of the enemy were seen: fox-men.

The term was a misnomer. The legendary creature with orange fur and pointed snout looked nothing like the fox-men in body, only in the face. They were small, lithe creatures, with odd skin down the sides of their body, from arms to legs. They waddle-ran when they moved and had a hard time lowering their arms, as though they were meant to be quadrupeds and refused to admit it. In their arms, they carried two small, sharp implements.

Delaan furrowed his brow. "They have daggers..."

Zala lifted her wings confidently. "It's just a few of them."

Humans began to follow, armed with spears and daggers longer than any weapon Kaerisk knew. They were straight blades, attached to the hilt, some nearly as large as the man that carried them. They moved through the forest at alarming speed and their numbers only continued to multiply as they surged towards the fort.

Delaan paced about the wall beside them, his nervous tail nearly knocking one of the Vitis from the battlements. "There are too many of them. Kaerisk, we need to go before they circle this place!" They came closer.

Spreading his wings wide, Kaerisk placed his forepaws upon the battlements, took a deep breath, and loosed his most powerful roar. Though a mere hatchling's cry, it was as thunder to the bipeds, grassman and enemies alike. Seeing the hatchling on the makeshift ramparts, with his proud wings spread wide and teeth sharper than the daggers of the chirop, the bipeds scattered. Zala joined him, perhaps emboldened by her brother's actions, though she loosed no cry of her own.

"They seem to be running away. Are we going to be okay?" Zala asked.

"I hope so sister. But try to look menacing."

Zala put her paws on the battlements and growled fiercely. The grassmen seemed terrified, but her brother felt it was not believable at all.

Below them, new shouts rang out from behind the line of trees. The bipeds who were terrified slowly regained composure, so long as they had two or three peers at their side. A new type of human came to the fore, one that Kaerisk had never seen before, but had heard his father speak of many times: the dragon slayer. His body was adorned with scales, heavy, thick - draconian. His head was covered in a helm of scales and dragon fangs, long enough to obscure his face. In his hand was a long strip of leather, which he struck against some of his own fleeing troops. Those who felt the sting of their master's whip quickly fell in line. Delaan took one look at him, and then charged to the opposite wall.

"Delaan! Wait!" Kaerisk shouted after him, but he did not stop his retreat. He leapt over the battlements and peeled off at full speed to the south. Kaerisk sneered, claws raking against the wood.

Only a coward saves his own skin at the expense of others. I guess you were no different than Senadra after all.

"Brother..." Zala quivered as the grassmen did beside her. Gone was that confidence she had but a moment before.

He didn't face her as he spoke. "You should go with him."

"But I can't leave you here!"

"We can't hope to win this, and I can't run."

She pressed against him firmly, almost pushing him from the battlements. "I'm staying with you."

"Promise me."

"That I will stay?"

He shook his head. "No matter what happens, you do not get caught. Run if you have to, run as far as you can and find the other dragons."

"Risky, you're scaring me..."

"Promise me, damn it!"

Her head lowered at his sharp tone, tail threatening to knock a nearby grassman from the battlements.

"I promise, Kaerisk."

The male turned his head back to the dragon slayer.

"What about you?"

"I won't be caught."

The dragons watched from the walls as the general spoke loudly to his troops, using words like 'glory' and 'death.' The warriors below chanted at the direction of their general, perhaps to scare the grassmen. It certainly worked. The yard below was filled with armed, grown grassmen, whose vines quivered with fear. Kaerisk wished there was something he could say to calm them as the dragon slayer had the enemy.

Correth came amongst his people. He stood on the highest battlements and wrapped his leg vines around them. He leaned back, his one good arm waving behind him as though he were caught in a great storm. Slowly, his injured arm stretched forward, and then the other, which held a spear. He righted himself, and then lifted the spear above his flower. Kaerisk did not need a translation for his wordless speech and it did seem to rally the Vitis, who again took to the battlements with spears at the ready.

Screams erupted from outside the walls. The other side had begun a charge, humans hacking at the plants with their crude blades. They began to circle the encampment, as though searching for some weakness. The thorn bushes did well as a deterrent; though the enemy attempted to cut the thorns away, the long reach of the grassmen's spears kept them from making much progress. Nonetheless, the humans flung themselves against the thorn-bush walls, carving into the plants as the thorns and spears cut into them. Zala watched with horror as the blood began to spill.

"What should we do?" Zala asked, fixated on the conflict.

"Go down and watch the entrance. If they break through there, yell for my help."

"What about you?"

"I'll help here, just hurry!"

Zala fled down the makeshift steps to the entrance, where several grassmen prodded their attackers over the thorn brush and wood. Kaerisk paced on the battlements, chiding himself for looking like Delaan.

Unless they get close, I can't use my claws. And my fire and Riftwind, what little I know of it, won't be useful more than once, if that!

The branches overhead began to rustle. Kaerisk spotted several chirop, who had climbed the trees during the assault. The grassmen had removed several branches that would have otherwise extended over their walls; it seemed as though the fall would kill anyone trying to make the jump. When the chirop leapt, however, they spread their arms and used their fuzzy flaps of skin to glide like a dragon.

"They're coming from above!" Kaerisk shouted. The grassmen on the wall moved their bodies to and fro, as though searching for them, but until the chirop connected with them or the ground, they did not react. The dragon slayer laughed below.

That is his plan. The grassmen can't see anything not touching the ground!

The chirop were vicious and tore at the flowers of the grassmen with their daggers and teeth. The hatchling rushed to their aid, knocking the lightweight creatures from their victims with ease. Some tried to swing their daggers at him. They cut into the scales of his forelimbs, but most lost their arms in the process and toppled onto the human advance below. Several

[192]

more of the creatures prepared to jump into the fortress; they would surround and make short work of him if the jump were successful. He had only one option.

Bristling his scales and turning his body towards the tree, he drew in a deep breath and let the flame well up inside him. Grasping the edge of the makeshift wall, he blew a jet of flame as far as he could, fire bridging the gap between the wall and the tree. The tree proved to be more resilient to fire than expected and did not combust, but the chirop shrieked in fear and abandoned their attack. As the fox-men dove off the trees and scattered, the hatchling gasped heavily, feeling drained; he had not eaten anything but the fruit and he would not be able to do that again.

Some of the enemy had scattered in fear of the fire, but not the dragon slayer. The general stood firm, put down his whip, and tore one of the scales from his armor, even as the fire burned behind him where it had fallen onto the grass. Holding the scale in his hands and speaking something under the din of battle, a blue aura enveloped him. Kaerisk watched in horror as he moved it outwards and flame came to his hands.

"That's impossible... that's Riftwind!"

The dragon slayer shouted. The flame flew from his hand and towards the thorn-bush wall. Kaerisk tried to leap out of the way, but his hind paw refused to cooperate. When the flame impacted, a great blast of air and fire followed, collapsing the battlements. The blue dragon tumbled outside of the walls into the now-burning thorn brush, head whipping against the ground. Everything became fuzzy. The dragon slayer stood over him with an insidious grin from behind those stolen fangs. Some humans surrounded him while others charged up the walls. The last thing he remembered hearing was his sister, yelling for help.

[193]

The Deep

Powerless.

He tried in vain to stretch his paws. They had bound him in mitts of metal that crushed his talons tightly against his own scales. A ring fit over his snout and neck both. His wings were painfully bound to his sides. They carried him. He didn't know how long they had hauled him, but by the time his body and mind had recovered, they stood within a massive cave in the Deep Mountains. Carved out by nature, by time, and by hand, each successive builder widened it until it was shaped like a maw that could eat several dragons alive. Through that maw, the hateful bipeds toted Kaerisk like a platter of meat.

Down was he taken, though the sprawling caverns. They stretched out in all directions, column after column arching up to support the weight of the rock above. Some paths wound down, some up, some level – all directions seemed possible within the Deep. And the dakael! This was no small collection of statues in his father's lair. The masses of humans and chirop writhed in excitement. He did not know if it was over his incarceration or the victory in war. He realized that he was not the only one detained when the crowds continued to jeer even after he had passed. Straining his head against the chains that bound him, he saw captured grassmen, forced to follow in his wake. His heart filled with dread.

Zala... did they capture you as well?

The procession turned, but he was carried elsewhere. Through the columns, he spied a massive waterfall, rumbling along with the crowd behind him. Makeshift structures of wood and cloth housed the human population along the banks of the underground reservoir. Their children played without a care to the horrors of war. Here in the dim light granted by flame and luminous moss, they were safe. Kaerisk longed to feel that way again, hating himself for it.

The paths narrowed and became dark. The humans carried him into a winding tunnel leading down. One of them took a piece of wood and struck some stones together several times until fire erupted on the log. He remembered when he had seen Sapphire demonstrate such skill and ingenuity with wonder. Now it terrified him, even as he tried to hold onto those good memories of his lost friend. Those memories fought with the fear instilled by his father, of being delivered to some butchery where his scales would be removed while he still drew breath.

The stone shook. They passed through an open area. In the darkness, the hatchling could barely discern strange figures shuffling. Their chalky bodies moved ever-ponderous through the dimness. Crystal-covered fingertips clawed at the stone of the wall, pulling forth bits of rock that were delivered to the crystalline mouth of the geode creature. It devoured the gravel with a sickening series of crunches. Others watched the human procession through their territory with calcite eyes, glowing in the torchlight.

Father never told me of such creatures...

Deeper still they took him, until the air grew stale, and then foul. Some nasty things had defecated all over this area. Above him, some of the chirop hung upside down, sleeping. Their fox-faces scrunched up peacefully as though they were dreaming dark, pleasant dreams. Father had always said that the fox-men sucked blood from dragons who went out at night.

In this darkness, is it not always night?

He tried to pull his legs closer to him, but the chains prevented it.

At last, they came to the final chamber. Here, a corral had been built like the one he had seen in the Ishluke village.

[195]

Foul, pale, pink-skinned creatures wallowed in the darkness, snorting with crushed noses at the dirt. One of the men led them away and fed them refuse in a trough. They squealed wildly as they ate the disgusting contents. Beyond them, the captors dumped Kaerisk into a corral all his own. There, the men secured a chain to the binding around his neck and removed the ring on his snout. One of them said something about seeing him again soon and the men laughed. Then they left, taking their light with them. In the darkness, all Kaerisk could hear was the repulsive squealers, devouring the garbage the bipeds left for them.

Time became impossible to follow. Hours, days, weeks, all seemed possible within that unrelenting darkness. The only break was the occasional visitor to feed the creatures in the next pen. They fed him the same refuse, which he would not and could not eat. Pride aside, it was inedible. Even the foul creatures that rolled around in their own waste began to seem appetizing to him.

The dragon slayer came, accompanied by two other humans. Kaerisk wanted to ask where his sister was, but he could find no words. Between the darkness and the teeth of the helmet, his features were still unclear, but he could see the slayer sneer. He did not speak. He directed his companions to take one of the beasts from its pin and bring it before the hatchling. The pale pink creature squealed in fear at the nearness of the dragon, but only for a moment. The general knelt and took a dagger to the beast's throat, slitting it and ceasing the noise. The smell of blood was intoxicating to the dragon. He salivated out of subconscious thought, jaw quivering with hunger.

The dragon slayer stood. The grin was gone, replaced by a look of unbridled cruelty. He placed the carcass just out of reach of the dragon, at the limit of the chain that bound his neck. Try as he might, the chain could not stretch far enough for the dragon to eat. Kaerisk tried anyway, weak and still bound limbs sliding across the ground. Eventually he collapsed, eyes blurred with tears.

"You want?" the general asked.

"Yes."

"You speak. Bad, but you speak."

The general put his foot on the carcass.

"You are pet now."

"No."

"You mount. I ride."

"No."

"You want this?"

"Yes."

"No."

"No?"

"No is what you tell me. Goodbye."

The two men picked up the carcass at the dragon slayer's urging. They took it with them as they returned the way they came. The general's torch flickered and his face became monstrously joyous.

"I eat tonight."

And with this, the general left. All Kaerisk could do was lick up the dirt and blood. His stomach rumbled its revulsion.

Sometime later, the two men returned. They carried a piece of meat from some animal; the hatchling doubted it was one of the beasts next to him, for they had made no noises beyond their usual snorting. Each took turns climbing awkwardly onto Kaerisk's back, their legs pressing hard against his bound wings, reminding him of the dull ache that had been forgotten. At first, the hatchling tried to buck them, but it was of no use with his paws still bound and his body so weak. When he stopped trying, they gave him the piece of meat. He ate it quickly, immediately feeling sick for having done so. The two men left, trapping him in the darkness again.

This repeated three times that Kaerisk could remember; it was hard to tell in his delirium. He no longer tried to fight it. He just let them on his back like a Rider's horse. Slowly, the food they brought was restoring his strength, but not his will. Bitterly, Delaan's warnings echoed in his head about becoming the horse.

I was wrong. I was so wrong. They were not symbiotes... there was no equity...

At last, they removed the bindings on his wings. Kaerisk tried to stretch them out, but doing so hurt terribly. The humans tested their ability to ride with the wings out and found they could fit them atop the unused appendages. This proved to be even more painful than when they crushed his wings with their clumsy legs, for if they felt unbalanced they would always kick their legs out and inevitably hit the joints. He screeched in pain, but still, he did not fight them.

Somewhere in the darkness, he saw his father.

Father was looking at him with that stern look, that perfected scowl that always appeared when Kaerisk had not performed a task adequately. He sat as he had at the council meeting what seemed years prior, tense and ready to spring. The hatchling stared at his father with begging eyes, but the elder did not move.

They killed your mother, Kaerisk. Now they will kill you too.

Kaerisk looked away from that imaginary spot. He felt an overwhelming urge to run, to leave, to escape. It was no well-planned thought or even a conscious one. It was an instinct that drove him to run, like the deer in the forest.

I have to get out, I have to get away!

While the men were gone, he slipped his paws from their bindings. In disuse and starvation, they had atrophied enough for him to remove the uncaring metal. He tried standing. It took an immense effort, but he could do it. As soon as he was sure he could, he sat back down to his belly, just as he had been left. He needed to see the chain that still bound his neck, for he did doubted he had the strength to break it. And so he waited in the darkness for one last ray of light.

The men returned. He did not lock eyes with them, for he knew they would see the hunger for freedom in his eyes. One stood back and held the torch while the other took to his back. He moved his neck ever so slightly, as though he were trying to get it more comfortable. There, with one eye, he saw it: the bipeds had connected the chain to the same wood that made up the corral. Wood could be destroyed.

He waited, mentally preparing himself. The man pulled at his neck, as though trying to issue commands. Kaerisk did not resist, but nor did he obey, his whole mind focused on that critical moment. And then it came: the man slid down from his back. He barely had time to scream as Kaerisk leapt up from his now-useless bonds and tore into the man with all his strength. As he fell, the other dropped the torch. The dull thud from it hitting the ground was barely audible over the squealing of the fat, dirty creatures in the other pen. The remaining human scrambled to grab his light source, but Kaerisk came close. The biped abandoned it, fleeing up the stairs from whence he had come. Whatever reason the dragon had left begged him to flee, but he could not help but sate his hunger on the corpse he had made.

Shouts came down from the tunnel stairs. Light followed. Kaerisk abandoned his meal, turning as swiftly as his injured body allowed. Over the yelling, he could hear several unnerving steps, echoing down the tunnel. One, two, one, two.

Escape!

That one overwhelming thought consumed him. He clawed rapidly at the wood where the chain held. Splinters flew everywhere and even dug into his weakened scale. He tried to ignore the pain and whispered a prayer to the Firstbourne begging that his claws were still strong enough.

At last, the chain fell from the wood with a satisfying clank of freedom.

Kaerisk took the torch in his teeth and climbed over the fence. He had to hide somewhere. He had to escape. He ran, dodging stalagmite after stalagmite that seemed to appear out of the darkness as he plunged through it. The chain rattled behind him.

His paw didn't land when it was supposed to hit ground. He tumbled forward, hitting against a far wall, torch fumbling from his grasp. He continued to spin as he plummeted, unable to see an end to the pit. He almost resigned himself to die.

Then he remembered Icia's final, blood-coated smile. He spread his wings and summoned the Riftwind on instinct. Immediately, his body rebelled. Pain spread in his wings and throughout his starving form; he coughed up blood onto his own teeth. As the torch hit the ground, his descent slowed. It was not enough to stop him. He crashed onto the torch, plunging the area into darkness.

Deeper and Deeper

"Look at what you have become."

The voice struck down upon him like a peal of thunder. Through tired, empty eyes, Kaerisk looked up and saw his father, standing on a dais above him. His perfect scowl accompanied his booming voice the way lightning accompanies thunder and it struck the hatchling with equal force.

"Father, I did all I could."

"No, son. You let yourself become one of them. An animal."

"They – the dakael – they aren't that bad."

"Is that so? Is that why you are nothing but scale and bone? Why your wings were bound like some flightless bird? Why, perhaps it is a new hatchling fashion to wear a chain around your neck?"

It wasn't until his father mentioned the chain that he felt its weight around his neck, choking him. He could no longer lift his head and the chain clanked against the ground, link by link, like a snake made of metal.

"Did I not warn you? I told you of their bloodlust, of their hatred for their betters. Did I not discuss, at length, the implements with which the bipeds try to kill us? Have I not explained the dangers of dragon slayers – the worst of the biped kind – and that you would be no match for one? Did I fail to mention what they did to your mother?"

Kaerisk tried to answer, but the chain seemed to choke him. He could not find wind or words.

"Furthermore, what justification do you have to abandon your family? Amorous, uncultured bipeds will mate with whatever they can find, heedless of the offspring they might create, but we dragons? Who understand the value of our children, for so few of them survive? Every moment I could spare and even some I could not, I spent with you. Nurturing you. Raising you."

"You tried to control me-"

"I tried to give you the best chance at life I could. This world is unforgiving, Kaerisk. You made a single mistake and now here you are, in the Deep, sure to be recaptured and broken or die from starvation. The world does not care. You're just another hatchling, a fledgling bird that has fallen from the nest. A bird would not care either – it would find another to make an egg with, giving no thought to the bones beneath its tree.

"But not a Dragon. A dragon would commit those bones to the elements. They would remember in private every day the ones they had loved, cared for, and lost, despite the cold exterior of reason to which they cling. A Dragon must be hard, inside and out. They must stoke the Rage of the Firstbourne in their hearts and be hard to the pain, to the pleasure, to the world. Then and only then is Time truly our ally, Kaerisk. For all of us have regrets. To be resilient against them is the only way to be allied with Time, else they will destroy you."

Kaerisk closed his eyes. His body felt so light. "Was I wrong in everything I did? Was the trust I put in bipeds all a mistake?"

A familiar voice answered him, but it was not his father. It was a small, almost cute growl, but it was more fluid than he had ever heard it before. "No. Suffering does not invalidate your dreams. It tests them. Was that not a part of dragon life as well, Kaevaeri?"

His father was silent. Through blurred eyes, Kaerisk looked up. Standing beside him was Sapphire, alive and well, smiling brightly. Beside her was the wild horse that Kaerisk had seen mercifully killed and committed.

"But, I – I saw…"

"Shh. You did not walk into the Deep, Kaerisk. You had the help of Geen, to make it across the plains. He saved you from the behemoth. The Ishluke feared you at first, but you gave them reason to trust you. As their brother and with their food, you crossed the swamp you could never have crossed alone. The Vitis healed your paw, as best as they could – is that not Correth's own arm, wrapped around your injury?"

As Sapphire petted the horse, he stared at the bound paw. Even in his emaciated state, it had held to him strongly.

"These biped know only fear and hate. Do you not remember how terrified I was of you when we first met? This fear and hatred is a cycle – bipeds are harmed by dragons and they in turn harm dragons, which in turn harm them. If no one breaks this cycle, it will not end until one or the other is completely destroyed."

Kaerisk struggled to lift his head towards his father, though the weight of the chain seemed heavier than ever. "Could a Dragon instead live by Honor and Pride? To make choices that do not result in regrets, but instead to be sure of them?"

His father gave a throaty chuckle, but still his scowl remained. He shook his head from side to side, like a tree swaying in the wind. His wings spread out suddenly as though he would fly.

"All Dragons should try to live this way, but can they truly? Do you not regret it now? The foolishness of youth that led you down into the Deep? Away from my lair? Your journey was a mistake, my son. It has cost you everything: your right to name, rank, and hoard; your dignity as a Dragon; your very right to be more than an animal; and of course, your sister's life. If you do not regret that last one, then you truly have become a beast."

"My sister? She's... she's dead?"

[203]

"Think, Kaerisk. Did not that armor your captor wore seem familiar? Biped tools are inferior to dragon claw and Riftwind; they might have turned you into a piece of armor as well, had they felt they could. But your sister, who had only recently known the torment of the world, her scales were hard enough to be of value, but soft enough to work. Just right for armor, don't you think?"

Kaerisk's eyes opened in dread.

"Sister!" he gasped, his voice hoarse and his body weak.

Father was gone. So were Sapphire and the horse. No – they had never been there. He had been dreaming a foolish hatchling's dream, one where Father would deliver him from the Deep alongside Sapphire.

Was it just a nightmare? Or are those fears true?

Squeaking noises roused the hatchling from his stupor. As he groaned in pain, the curious squeaks became those of horror. The rats that had been examining his body fled in all directions. Everything was darkness. Carefully, he lifted his bruised and battered form so that he could pull free the piece of wood jabbing into his stomach from where he had landed. He tried to cough up a flame, but all that came was hot breath from an exhausted and broken dragon. He lay there for a time until his eyes became more accustomed to the blackness; a bit of luminous fungus grew in the area, but it did little more than outline the surrounding tunnel.

There were no shouts of bipeds here. If they had found his fall, they had not been foolish enough to dive after him. Perhaps there was no way out. The thought filled him with a dull dread, memories of Icia's death haunting his thoughts.

And yet, that painful fall was nothing compared to the pain of nearly losing everything that made him a dragon.

His grip on the stick loosened as he tried again to summon the flame from his lips, but once more nothing came.

[204]

He could feel the pieces of the man he had eaten digesting within him. The thought somehow sickened him, but that revulsion was as dull as his fear of death. Having been so long without food, any meat was welcome in his emaciated belly.

Kaerisk wept. He was quiet, for the one fear not dull was discovery. Still he wept, tears falling onto scales scuffed and claws dulled by his horrible journey.

Sister, how could I let this happen to you? Why did I think we could get away? I knew nothing of the real world! All I had were some fool ideals that overwrote years of solid teaching from Father. How disappointed he must be.

A third and final time he tried and failed to light the torch. It was no use. Until he digested the meat, he'd have no chance of calling forth fire or Riftwind. Animal instinct drove him to rise. The chain scraped against the stone as he moved, rattling as though he were some forgotten ghost shackled by his mistake. In the darkness, he moaned and wailed his physical anguish and emotional suffering wordlessly.

A rat scurried by him. He turned as fast as he could and threw himself upon the small beast, crushing it. It was hardly a clean kill. Kaerisk gobbled the furry thing quickly. Before he had left home, he would never have thought to demean himself as to eat a common rodent. It wouldn't have been a snack to him. Now it was all he had. He wept again, the collar of iron around his neck making it too difficult to lift his head again.

Is this all I amount to? Curse Sapphire! Curse her and all of her kind! If she had not...

"Do you really feel that way, Kaerisk?"

Even in the darkness, the silver scales of Icia shimmered. Kaerisk reached for her, but his exhausted paws could not find the strength to touch her.

"If so, I must have meant nothing to you – you chose her over me."

[205]

Kaerisk's brow furrowed, his lip quivering. "I never chose her over you. I loved you."

Icia slinked forward, placing a paw onto his. "I loved you too."

His head drooped, eyes fixating on the connection. "I let everyone down, Icia. I failed you, I failed Sapphire, and now I failed my sister. Everyone that matters to me is dead."

She nuzzled him. "Do you really think so low of your sister? The Zala I knew was stronger than any other dragon, including you. She always smiled for my benefit, even when she was sad. Don't tell me you didn't see it on your journey."

Kaerisk's claws clacked against the ground, vision blurring.

"She didn't ask you to follow her. You chose this path."

"She wouldn't have survived on her own."

"Then you chose it for the right reasons."

"I don't understand anything anymore. Did I really leave my dream behind just to protect my sister?"

Icia smiled. "Think, Kaerisk. The world isn't as simple as you have been taught and still want to believe, even after everything you have seen. Change is not made in a single moment, but through a lifetime of action and effort. So I ask you. Did you leave your dream behind to protect your sister? Or was there something more?"

I wanted to prove my father – no. That's not it. I wanted to live by the virtues he taught me. There is no Pride and Honor in tormenting the dakael. We have killed each other for too long. It has to stop.

Kaerisk jerked awake and rose. Icia was gone, if she had ever been there. He pulled the chain up and rested it on his back. The movement caused the collar to pull and from it dropped the behemoth's eye. It was shining. Something in the

Deep caused it to glow. He turned one way, and then the other, discovering one direction caused a brighter shine than the other.

Only a source of Riftwind can make a crystal like this glow. Zala...?

His paw wrapped around the amber gently as he remembered who gave it to him, and then followed the light further into the Deep. Quietly, he risked hope that his sister was still alive.

The Wurmqueen

The further down the tunnel he traveled, the stronger the glow became. Nervously, his tail flicked slightly like his sister's would. A second light appeared at the far end of the tunnel. He heard a soft, continuous roar from his destination, filling him with dread. He paused a moment, letting his eyes adjust. His mind was a flurry of thought.

What if it's not my sister? An evil cabal of biped magic users, perfecting their art in the safety of the darkness? Or some horrible golem, brought to life by a forgotten nexus of energy, waiting to crush any fool enough to come close?

Kaerisk tried to stop thinking. Each possibility seemed more horrible than the last.

He snuck close, quiet as a graveyard, and peered into the cavern. The pocket within the stone was circular and massive. The arched ceiling had been painted with brilliant blues and whites, though these had faded with time. At the center was a shaft of reflective metals, from which descended a warm beam of light that illuminated the chamber. Beyond the tunnel through which Kaerisk had traveled, there were two potential exits, grafted into the walls. They had been painted and crafted to resemble natural cavern entrances, though one was far smaller than the other. Lavish cloths and pillows decorated the room, as did several stone platforms, larger than an elder dragon. A waterfall lay at the far end of the chamber. It had been the roaring sound that he had heard, which brought the hatchling some comfort.

And there, laying on one of the pillows in peaceful repose was a dragon.

Kaerisk pressed into the chamber, believing he had found refuge, but stopped when he drew closer. This dragon was different. Its scales were thicker than he had ever seen. Its hind and forelegs throbbed with muscles. Its wide and thick tail sported dangerous spikes of bone towards the tip. The crest was off – the horns weren't more than slender spindles; they pointed up, and then curved down towards the muzzle. And its muzzle was rounded and short, not long and triangular. And its wings – no, it had no wings at all!

It's a not-dragon like the one on the mural! I have to get out of here before it wakes!

The hatchling tried to backpedal, but his sensitive hind paw fell too hard against the stone, causing him to buckle. He twisted his body to keep his balance, but the chain fell to the floor and the resulting clang reverberated throughout the massive chamber.

The not-dragon's eyes opened. A black cat-like pupil swam in its sea of gold towards the hatchling, who now cowered back. When it lifted its muscular neck, it did so with a bright, inviting smile, just barely showing its dagger-like teeth.

"Well, well. A visitor, I see," the creature said. The voice proved her to be a female, but also dated her – the language was draconic, but very old, with intonations and dialects that Kaerisk had studied as dead language.

"H-hello," the hatchling said.

"Hello? Is that all you can manage? A proper greeting should include your name, especially should you happen into another's lair by mistake or whimsy of fate," she chided.

"I'm sorry, I – my name is Kaerisk."

"Dawnbringer. A powerful name, to say that you bring the dawn. I am Nao'Dariva. Do you know those words?"

"I believe it means… All-Knowing Tyrant."

"No, my dear hatchling, not tyrant. Queen. The name by which I was born died the day I received that title."

"Title?"

"Of course. I am the queen of my people, though sadly I am the last of my kind. Thousands of years ago, I was known as Nao'Dariva, the Wurmqueen."

Kaerisk faintly remembered that word from the strange cavern he had fallen into months ago. It all seemed a blur. This not-dragon creature before him, this wurm, was strangely alluring and incredibly powerful. It was she who had lit his crystal, and that was while she slept.

"You have a strange sense of fashion, little Dawnbringer."

"What?"

"Your collar. It woke me."

Kaerisk lifted a paw to it for a moment. "I am sorry. I do not wear it by choice."

"Then you shall not wear it at all."

Nao lifted herself on one paw, with the other reaching towards the hatchling. Stroking the side of his face, Riftwind passed through him and into the collar, which snapped open and fell unceremoniously to the ground. The transfer made him shiver.

She can snap metal so easily?

"There, that is better. The jewel suits you. Ah! But I am shameless, for I wear nothing at all. Wait a moment, my dear."

The Wurmqueen sauntered to the pile of cloth that Kaerisk had seen when he examined the chamber earlier. With careful paws, she lifted the silken cloth, placed her head into it, and then stepped forward. Soon, a robe-like garment had covered her body, leaving her neck free. Her forepaws and tail had flaps through which they hung, allowing her forearms freedom of motion and her hindquarters to be covered without the cloth dragging into her hind legs. She turned towards him with surprising grace and sat comfortably on her dress.

"Now then. I suppose that jewel is all you have? Dragons do not have the same sensibilities – no, wait. What is with the vine?" She peered at the wrapping that Correth had given of himself.

"I was injured before I got here."

"Those are Vitis vines. I am surprised you know of their healing properties."

"They have healing properties?"

The rounded face of the wurmqueen pulled back into a wry smile. Again she reached out and stroked the side of his face, a larger jolt of Riftwind passing through his body and into the vines, which began to wither. "Long ago, we wurms lived with the dakael and discovered much of them. A pity that your race has lost so much of what we had given them." When the vines fell to the floor, broken and sapped, Kaerisk's paw had receded to normal size and the pain was almost completely gone.

Kaerisk tried to hide worry with wonder when his gaze returned to the wurm. "I'm afraid I know nothing of your people."

"I'm not at all surprised. I'm sure all knowledge of us was stripped from your history. You have forgotten, as a people, all that you owe to us and to mine. Without the wurm, the dragon would not exist."

"I don't understand."

"Then let me tell you a story. Long ago, wurms ruled the land. They were great and powerful, physically unmatched and magically unrivaled. We – wait a moment, you look famished. Are you hungry?"

Kaerisk lowered his head, unsure how to answer. His stomach, however, rebelled at the mention of food and growled audibly.

"You do not impose on me, little one. A moment."

The wurm lifted her head and roared. The cavern shook with her impressive lungs. Kaerisk cowered a bit, which caused Nao to smile toothily at him. Within moments, bipeds flooded the chamber through the smaller exit; they were the same type of stone-creature he had seen through the darkness on his descent. Gemstones pierced and fractured their stone skin, seemingly at random. Their eyes glowed, even in the light of the chamber. The hatchling feared he had been caught again and would be dragged back to that horrible stall. But they did not attack him. Each and every one bowed down low before the queen.

"Fetch my guest and I some meat at once!"

The dakael scrambled away. Within moments, a large tray was delivered with heaps of meat torn from the bone. It was so quick that Kaerisk wondered if they had been waiting just outside with it.

"Now leave us!"

Once more the bipeds followed her command and disappeared as suddenly as they had arrived, save two guarding the entrance from which Kaerisk had come.

Kaerisk regarded her, astonished. "W-what are they? Golems?"

Nao loosed a laugh. "They are dakael, not some misused Waydeep. They are called the Waylund and few dragons even suspect they exist. Do not feel too ignorant."

Waydeep? Does she mean the Riftwind?

"Where was I? Oh yes. Eat, little one, you look terrible."

The hatchling followed her command with the same reverence and confusion that her biped servants did. Fear kept him from eating too quickly this time.

"We ruled the world. Bipeds all over bowed before us as they did just now. They fashioned us clothes and jewelry, to

[212]

fill our coffers and hoards. They entertained and made us laugh. They hunted for us, lest they become the meal. And we in turn built magnificent palaces of stone, moved the earth itself to our needs, and held dominion over all living things.

"But we were 'imperfect' in the eyes of would-be dragons. For you see, dragons did not exist then. They came from us. The first of them was the worst. He taught his followers that the strong could not coexist with the weak. That the strong had to fight and change to remain strong. Ignorance! Hatemongering ignorance bred from a tiny mind that felt thrill from violence. And so he and his followers changed. That wurm became the first dragon after he had swallowed the fire, tamed the wind, mastered the water, and defeated the earth. But it was not enough, was it? No. Now that they were stronger than the wurm, they could not coexist with the wurm. They would make the wurms serve, as the bipeds had. And so war came to this realm.

"It raged and raged, but the First Dragon won. His followers were few, but vicious and deadly. Even our great strength and mastery of the Waydeep was rendered impotent before them. And when at last it was over, all of the wurms but I and a few others lay dead. We hid here, in the Deep, until one by one, each of them died from starvation or age. We have suffered so much at the hands of dragons."

She stared at him as though he was the meat he ate. Kaerisk placed his paw on the tray and slid it towards her, which caused her to smile.

"Worry not, little one. I do not hate you for the sins of your fathers. Indeed, I have a great deal of hope for you... and an offer."

<u>Egress</u>

The Wurmqueen devoured the platter of meat completely. It was obviously too little to sate her hunger, but it made quite a spectacle. Indeed, she might not have been hungry at all. Her massive maw tore the meat apart and then lifted it up to let it slide down her throat, face contorting as if savoring each exquisite taste. All Kaerisk could think about was how quickly the food was gone. She licked her lips with a long, muscular tongue, and then smiled at the hatchling, almost benignly.

"Come with me, little one. I wish to show you something."

She stood. Despite the silken covering, she was able to move efficiently towards the only exit large enough for her to use. Kaerisk trotted behind her, still amazed that his hind paw no longer hurt.

The tunnel was less well-cared for than the chamber from which they had traveled, but another light waited at the end so bright that it made it impossible to see anything but the path.

"You see, little dragon, it has been very lonely for me. I have suffered greatly in the darkest reaches of the world, hiding from my cousins. But this offence, this genocide, cannot go forever unpunished. Sooner or later, they must be made to suffer for the choices they have made, for – as they say – survival of the fittest always goes on."

The tip of her tail flicked from side to side as the golden pools of her eyes fixed their blackness upon him. The spikes on her tail tip mesmerized the fearful hatchling.

"You are a hatchling, a child, long removed from your parents. Tell me, child, would I be wrong to assume that you left them behind? Perhaps to find your own way?"

Kaerisk could not answer her. His lowered head told her it was true.

"I offer you a new way. A way back. Serve me as my vassal and aid me in preparing the bipeds for the trials to come. Already several of them perform well, but to see that a dragon has joined them would do so much to boost their morale. And of course – if you serve me well – I can undo the damage."

"Damage?"

"Yes, little one. I can quench the horrible fire inside you, ground you in reality and earth, and return you to a dragon's true form: the wurm. I can make you one of us; our species will be reborn."

"I would - give up my wings? My fire?"

"They are impractical. Irreverent. Symbols of a people who live through oppression and bloodshed, through constant change of whimsy and chance. You would not need them, for the bipeds would serve you as loyally as they do me. Look here: I shall show you true fire."

They passed into the light. His eyes adjusted to the chamber beyond, a massive complex of stone in hexagonal patterns with paths leading around it. In the center of the room was a pit of fire unlike any he had ever before seen. A sphere of pure, liquid flame bubbled like hot water. From it, jets of fire arched against the ceiling, where it was drawn towards red riftcrystals embedded in the center of each basalt plate.

"What is this?" Kaerisk asked, staring into it.

"Do not look into it too long, little one. You might go blind."

Kaerisk instead turned his gaze back to the wurm, who was staring over it with a grim face.

[215]

"Long ago, this fire fell from the sky and burned much of the land. We wurm buried it within the earth. It is called the Starchild, a small fragment of the Forgotten Ones. Overtime, I have learned some measure of control over it." She lifted a paw and the flame rose up; however, it wavered as though a powerful breeze moved it. "I can bequeath this flame to you, as well. More than a match for any fool dragon-fire. You shall be served by dakael, live as a god to them. Is that not fitting?"

To not go hungry again, to live with hoard and servants... my fire and my wings have never saved me, have they? Is it really such a thing to give up for luxury and safety?

Something within him turned at these thoughts. He was taught to have Pride in his wings and fire, in his dragon form, and in dragon life. He was to act in a manner worthy of Honor, not live off the backs of hapless bipeds. He was to be Patient in the face of hardship, even starvation and death. And his Wisdom told him to consider all things.

"Do not trust her."

He looked about for the voice, but Nao did not appear to have heard it. She watched him with a curious furrowing of her temple. The voice was faint and feminine, but somehow deep and intense.

"What do you suppose she intends the biped to do?"

Kaerisk blinked at the question.

What trials would she put them through, unless –

"Nao'Dariva, what trials do you intend to have the bipeds face?"

The wurmqueen was terribly displeased. Her tail beat against the ground, causing dust to fall from the ceiling. Where it impacted the Starchild, little wisps of smoke and bright flame followed.

"The dragons believe that each creature must strengthen itself to survive. Our people were unprepared when we fought.

We were overpowered and defeated. We are not fools, my dear hatchling. We learn. We learned what they have taught us."

"And that is?"

"That in order to defeat them, we must also evolve. Not become them, for that would be folly, but to surpass them. A unified force that has mastered new techniques never before seen."

Kaerisk remembered the dragon slayer. His scale armor was thicker than any dragon hide. His magic could not have been haphazardly learned.

I was not followed because they knew where I would fall!

Nao'Dariva's smile became twisted as she watched him realize the truth.

"You – you are the one who is causing the bipeds to go to war?"

"Yes, little Dawnbringer. I gave bipeds the knowledge of magic. I helped them craft weapons of war. And unified by my banner, we have tunneled out from the Deep, right under the nose of the doddering dragons. Their crimes are unforgivable, Kaerisk. I have lived this long by stoking the furnace of my hatred and forging tactics and stratagems more deadly than anything my bipeds or the dragons themselves wield. You have figured this much out. Then, perhaps, you might understand the true offer I am making you."

"You've giving me a chance to live - by becoming one of you."

"Close. You would have to earn your place as a wurm. I will not suffer the arrogance of the dragons and, though you are still young, their taint is near-everything you are. I'll not share that honor with anyone who does not deserve it."

"And if I refuse-"

"You know that is not an option. Least, not one you could live with. My champions would break you. They almost did, even though I ordered them to go easy on you."

Kaerisk shuddered. He could not go through that again. The thought that they were holding back terrified him. And yet, he could not willingly kill his own people, despite whatever crimes they may or may not have committed. He stared at her, torn. If he agreed, he would be a traitor to all he had even known. But if he said no...

"Do not give up, Dawnbringer. Whether you realize it or not, you have brought help. Be prepared to run."

The light flared up from the Starchild. The shadows of Nao and Kaerisk danced against the walls. The wurmqueen's silhouette was huge and monstrous; it seemed to writhe as though something was trapped within it.

Nao'Dariva narrowed her eyes suddenly. Kaerisk feared she was about to make the choice for him, but she wasn't staring at him. She peered behind him to the wall.

"You have two tails," she said.

He didn't see it at first, but as he watched his tail, he saw that a shadowy double of it seemed to follow just a step behind his own. "What?"

The shadow stopped moving, as though it knew it had been found out. A low laughter filled the chamber and the wurmqueen grew tense. The gem around Kaerisk's neck shone with light and, from within the hatchling, the skeletal Miasma Dragon arose. He appeared even more fearsome than when Kaerisk had seen him in his tomb, almost solid and with a vicious, laughing snarl on his nearly-translucent scales.

The Miasma's wings flared, casting a shadow even larger than the wurm's. "Finally have I found you, Nao'Dariva, the fallen queen. Graciously has my host brought me – and you – to the exact spot I required."

"It can't be. You died!" Nao'Dariva shrieked.

"You should have died thousands of years ago, but still you live. You have passed a deadly fire to children who know not how to use it. But I have faith in *my* people, Wurm. And now I'm going to kill you."

The crystals directing the flame from the Starchild suddenly shattered. The skeletal structure of the Miasma reared up in battle stance, spreading its bony wings as powerful jets of flame surrounded him and the Wurmqueen.

"You have not forgotten my mastery of the Starflame, I trust? You should not have laired so close to its greatest source on this world!"

The flames wreathed the Wurmqueen. As her silken garments burned away, her screams echoed throughout the tunnels.

"He cannot maintain this ruse for long, Kaerisk. You must run down the tunnel from whence you came. It will lead to an exit. From there, head east. Do not stop until you find your people, little one! They must know the Wurmqueen has done!"

Kaerisk sat there, flabbergasted and afraid.

"Run, Dawnbringer!"

The hatchling turned and fled as Nao'Dariva battled with the flame or the Miasma – Kaerisk couldn't tell. Behind him, human, chirop, and Waylund alike flooded the burning walkways, coming to the aid of their queen. Their voices echoed far down the tunnel the hatchling desperately traversed. As Kaerisk reached the sky-painted chamber, his heart seized in his chest. The smaller tunnel from which the bipeds had come with food lit up, threatening to deliver death instead of a meal.

He dashed through the room and leapt over one of the lavish pillows, peeling towards the entrance from whence he had originally come. He bounded up, only to skid to a halt before the Waylund guarding the exit.

[219]

No, Nao foresaw this possibility too!

He cowered back from the stonemen, their glowing crystal eyes on him. They moved forward, and then parted, leaving a wide gap between them. Kaerisk stared at the now-exposed tunnel, shivering.

"Go. Waylund says you must escape." The voice did not emanate from any mouth, but one of the stonemen's head crystals had begun to glow.

Kaerisk tensed and sprung, charging through them. He didn't know what was going on, what was up or down, but he had to run. Behind him he could hear shuffling, moving, running, screaming. His claws dug into the scored stone as he put his healed paw to use, sprinting as far away from the Wurmqueen as he could.

He wasn't sure how long he had run, but his pained joints burned as though they were melting from the inside and his heart rebelled within his chest. And yet, even as his lungs could barely get enough of the stale air to keep him conscious, he saw a light at the far end of his path. On and on he pressed for it, as if the one thing he wanted to possess in the world was that light. Only when he passed beyond the threshold of the mountainous Deep into that blinding light, he allowed himself a moment of rest.

He stood in a narrow valley with a few sparse trees. Two mountainous arms wrapped around those trees protectively. The rock above the exit looked curiously like a dragon snarling; it may have been a statue at some point, but was weathered by time. He could hear the sound of water flowing. Above the northern arm, a waterfall spilled down the mountain. A short walk around the hill revealed a river. Kaerisk immediately indulged himself in a long drink, which was the sweetest water he had ever tasted.

Shouting came from the exit he had left behind. Several bipeds armed with spears and nets broke from the mountain and shielded their eyes from the light.

They already caught up with me!

He turned and followed the river east as fast as he could, pinning his sore wings to his body. Behind him, he heard the bipeds give chase. Lindorm words nipped at his heels in cacophonous tones. Where the river meandered, he leapt, plopping into it for a moment before hopping out onto the other side. A net brushed along his scales, but did not catch. The hatchling tried desperately to run faster.

Behind him, he heard splashing. He dared not turn his head, but he knew they were crossing the water. He hoped it slowed them. Darting in and out of trees, he ran and ran, once more his body begging him to stop through the molten pain in his joints. Sheer, animalistic will to live forced him to keep going.

I will not be made a slave to the Wurmqueen or a pet to the bipeds!

The ground suddenly ended. Below him was a fifty foot drop to stone and a small pool that could not be more than a few feet deep. The falls became a river choked with dense trees and overgrowth that stretched to the horizon. Sparse grass flanked both sides of the tree line.

He looked back now. They were still coming and would be on him in seconds. He took a deep breath, spread his wings, and held to the gem around his neck with one paw. Summoning the Riftwind, he leapt over the edge of the cliff. Even with the amulet's assistance and his meals, the use of the Riftwind burned throughout his body as though still hungrily consuming him from within.

Hold it together, Kaerisk!

The descent was much smoother than his fall in the cavern, but the landing was no better. In focusing so much on keeping aloft, he failed to turn before hitting the tree line – literally. He crashed through a series of tree branches and scraped his belly against the top of a trunk. The trunk caught him, bringing his forward momentum to a sudden halt and sending him toppling down several more branches to the thorny brush below.

Horizons

The orange sky shone through the broken trees and branches above him. He wasn't sure how long he had been unconscious, but the watchful Eye drooped in the eastern sky, soon to pass below the distant horizon. The horizon itself was obscured by the trees and bushes that grew fervently throughout the river valley. Several tendrils of broken branches and uprooted bushes gripped at him as he tried to rise.

It was not easy to do so. The whole of his body had been battered in the poorly directed descent, adding to the already bruised wing from his earlier fall in the Deep and the utter exhaustion from his starvation and torture. The thought of food caused his stomach to grumble and he sucked in his slender gut, trying to stop it in vain. Peering up to the cliff he had leapt from revealed none of his pursuers, but he wasn't sure he had lost them yet.

Taking a deep breath, he began walking east. It was slow going; between the injuries and the heavily overgrown terrain, he couldn't make much progress. In the back of his mind, he worried that he was leaving Zala behind. He did not know if she was alive, dead, or worse, but having witnessed the Wurmqueen for himself, he knew there was no hope of rescuing her on his own.

After pausing to take a drink, he walked away from the river to where the plants began to thin out. Despite how well the plants around the water thrived, the area beyond it was quite desolate. Little grass clung to the sandy ground and deposited rocks made the path uneven and dangerous. It did give him a clear view of his surroundings: directly east, a large hill jutted out of the earth. Behind it, smoke rose. His tired eyes followed the trail into the sky as wind blew fiercely through the valley.

He froze at a welcome sight: a dragon flew overhead.

He called out, but the wind must have muffled his scream. It flew over the hill without turning back for him. He sighed, but it was one of relief as much as pain. He had to be near something. It filled him with hope.

The dragon had not heard his call, but someone else had. Biped voices shouted wildly, spreading knowledge of his call. Kaerisk saw a few through the trees, but their heads were not turned towards him. Kaerisk immediately dove into the bushes, taking cover. The instincts drilled into him by his Father demanded that he charge the unwary bipeds and silence them before they could alert their comrades, but both fear and logic prevented him from going through with it. These dakael were trained by the Wurmqueen to hunt and kill dragons – he'd stand no chance against them, even if he were in top shape.

Pinning his wings close to his body, he began stalking through the twisted tangle of narrow leaves. The gushing water hid his breathing and the sound of his passing at a distance, but he doubted it would hide him should they come close. Two were on the other side of the river; while swift, the water was not terribly deep and they could cross if they caught sight of him through the trees. He moved almost painfully slow, trying to make every rustle of plants look like a natural wind.

His immediate concern, however, was the human on his side of the river. At this point, the man was only fifty feet away and kept watching the ridge as though expecting the hatchling to come at him in ambush. Unlike the dragonslayer Kaerisk had seen in the Vitis war, the dress of this one was primarily tanned hides similar to Sapphire's clothing, but with plates of scales tracing down the arms. His feet were bound up in some sort of leather wrapping as well, making travel over the rocky terrain easier than it had been for Sapphire what seemed a lifetime ago.

He turned. Kaerisk lowered to the ground and froze. Though the man peered up and down the foliage, he made no sign of recognition that the dragon was there. He walked towards Kaerisk's position, following the tree line. His leather wrappings crushed the gravel in that unnerving one-two fashion of the bipeds. His gaze continued down the line as he ambled forward. He came so close that the dragon could smell the sweat of the human even through the heated plants and dull humidity rising from the river.

The man suddenly froze as well, his eyes going wide.

He must be able to scent me too!

Kaerisk steeled himself and leapt from the bushes, tackling the human. His body wracked in pain at the sudden lurch and impact; he pinned the man more from sheer bulk than any willful intent. The dakael's mouth opened, but no sound came from it. Kaerisk's paw lifted up, ready to tear out his throat.

As the man's terrified eyes locked with the hatchling's eyes, head twisting back and forth, Kaerisk slowly lowered his paw to the ground. He suddenly felt very heavy. It was as though at that moment, everything he had seen and experienced in the Deep caught up with him. His head drooped, but the man still winced as if expecting a final blow.

No. I saw a monster in there. I became a monster in there. I left Sanrex and that dream behind! I just have to make it to the hill and I can glide down again!

Kaerisk stood and began towards the hill. Behind him the dakael coughed violently, drawing breath once more. As Kaerisk's hobble turned into an off-balanced sprint, the man began to scream. All of Father's teaching chided him for not finishing the man, but he pushed the thoughts aside with a spark of hope that dragons waited just beyond the hill.

[225]

Shouts rang out from above him. Several dakael began to line the ridge away from the river. A few threw nets and spears at him; one of the nets nearly caught on his wing, but fell off as he barreled towards that mound of dirt. The dakael followed him with nearly the same desperation he had to reach the hill. They began plucking scales from their outfits and lifting them over their heads.

Just as Kaerisk reached the hill, the first ball of flame crashed against the mountainside, causing Kaerisk to skid to a halt before the fires. Behind him, several more of the dakael began to crackle audibly as they drew power from the scales they held. With reckless abandon, they began to coat the mountain in flame even as Kaerisk continued ascending it, veering to the left or right whenever he sensed the fires coming. Heart racing, bones aching, he could not avoid them all. More than once were his scales singed by flame, blue blackening and bringing new pain with every motion of his muscles. As he neared the top, he spread his wings, preparing to make his desperate leap.

The ground itself erupted below him in the shape of a spike. It tore into his outstretched wing, his blood coating the earth. Momentum carried him forward, tearing the hapless hatchling's wing. It cut all the way to the end of his skin, but could not break the last ring of scale as he skidded to a halt against the hill. He screamed louder than he had ever screamed in his life. As his vision blurred, his heart racing only to spill more blood onto the rocks, he realized the Wurmqueen might have successfully taken flight from him after all.

The dakael came running up the hill, but they continued to wield the Riftwind without pause. In moments, flames had nearly completely encircled Kaerisk, choking the air with smoke. There was little vegetation to burn, but what did exist was dry and spread the fire with ease. Kaerisk peered into the flames as the dakael neared his position.

The flames stared back at him.

Humanoid figures began to rise from the wildfire burning around him – no, the flame itself took the shape of humanoids. Dimly, he realized that the humans had tipped the scales of the Riftwind too far. He lowered his head, expecting to be pummeled by the newly-created golems of living flame. The heat came closer to him. It was intolerably hot and lingered for what felt an eon to the hatchling, but then turned away. Chancing a peek, he saw that the living flame had been drawn inexorably towards the energy that created it: the still-crackling hands of the bipeds.

The golems had adopted four arms and sinuous movement. They reached out with them, paused only momentarily as balls of flame and waves of earth crashed into them. The misguided mages were actually attempting to undo their mistake by the same means that had caused it in the first place. Had Kaerisk not been in such agonizing pain, he would have stood dumbfounded.

Much like the fire they created, it can only be put out by running out of fuel – wait, the fire!

The flames that had surrounded him now composed the golems, clearing his path to the top of the hill. Gritting his teeth, he stood up onto his hindlegs, pulling his wing off the spike that pinioned him. He fell back to all fours and topped the hill just as the golems reached the mages and began combusting them. At the bottom of the hill, he saw the dakael he had spared. The human had not followed the rest and stood in horror as his companions turned to ash.

Kaerisk staggered down the other side of the hill. Beyond the smoldering ridge lay an ocean of sand and a walled city of domes. From the largest central dome rose the column of

[227]

smoke he had first spied in the distance, competing in size with the one behind him. He could barely discern the forms of dragons within the city, peering up towards his location.

Salvation...

He descended carefully, leaving a trail of crimson behind him. The closer he got to the city, the harder it became to move. He felt cold, even in the heat of day. He nearly stumbled down that hill more than once, but he somehow held himself erect as he hobbled, favoring his injured wing. The sand was warm to his claws. They sank into it, making his trek even harder. By the time he reached the gates, all his strength had left him and he collapsed into a fitful sleep.

<u>Innovation</u>

It was warm. His vision was blurry at first, as though he had slept a long time. The area was unfamiliar. A foreign, oily odor hung in the air, even though there was no sight of anything that might have caused it. Incense burned nearby, perhaps to hide the smell. It was sweet and rejuvenating in some ways, but the scent of oil was still overpowering.

Across from him sat another hatchling. He couldn't make out anything except the shape, as only small fires at the end of wax sticks lit the room. They burned quietly as the hatchling sat on patient haunches. Kaerisk crawled forward, dragging his broken body across the ground and inhaled deeply in the other hatchling's direction. Familiar. Not his sister.

"Delaan..."

"I'm here, Kaerisk."

The blue whipped his paw out and snatched one of Delaan's horns with more strength than he realized he had left. He forced the head to the ground, snarling. "You left us to die!"

"I ran so I could save you! You know you could not have escaped with your foot injured!"

"Then why didn't you take Zala with you? She trusted you! I trusted you!"

"Because if it was only you there, they wouldn't have come!"

Kaerisk's eyes adjusted to the dim light. He half-hung off a slab of stone, cushioned by pillows. A light cloth covering had been pulled over him, but he had lost most of it in his lunge. Delaan did not struggle under his grip; he seemed as drained as Kaerisk and his eyes were bloodshot in the firelight.

Kaerisk loosened his grip. "What are you talking about?"

Delaan remained where he was. "Lan'Dal is like San'Lux, but in reverse. They care more about females than males. If Zala was there, it was likely they would have come."

The statement brought some reason back to Kaerisk, which also brought sensations of cold and pain. His wing was the worst; he discovered that the skin of his wing had been tied shut by several strands of cloth thread. They had been anchored through new holes that were far too small for a dragon to have made. This concerned him, but he was far too tired to waste energy on things outside of his immediate control. He slinked back and rested his head on the slab.

Above him hung a device. It consisted of several globes that rotated in a circle. It made a soft whirring sound, almost as though an insect hid within each of the tiny globes. Delaan noticed him staring at it.

"We put you in the nursery. It was the only room we had available, really, and it was the best for treating your injuries," he said.

Kaerisk did not understand at first what the nursery was, but his Pride was not injured when he did. He wondered if he would have been as close to his father had he been given a room of his own when he was a whelpling.

Delaan slowly lifted his head. "We weren't sure if you were going to make it."

"My sister? Did you at least get help for her?"

Delaan looked ashamed. His head hung low to his forepaws and his eyes stared into the tiny fire. "The dragons came, but not because I asked. Correth and some Vitis helped Zala escape." His wings drooped over his back.

My sister is safe, but...

"Where is she?"

"She's not here. She decided to stay in Lan'Dal."

"Why is she still there? Was she injur-"

[230]

A rumble and a creak interrupted him. At the far end of the chamber stood a large blockade of several wooden planks, joined together by two metal strips. Kaerisk reasoned it existed for privacy, as it seemed easy enough for a dragon to push it open or shut it closed. Through the now-open entrance stepped another dragon, an elder female. Her scales were ruddy and brownish, but they had a metallic sheen even in the dim light. She walked with poise despite her size; Kaerisk remembered that Zala had had similar lessons on poise from Luxari, though his sister only showed him a few times and often ignored them when in the lair.

"Delaan?" Her soft and deep voice washed over the chamber.

"I'm here, mother. He is awake," Delaan said.

"This is good news. I should like to hear how he has come here and how he could cause such a mess with improper use of the Riftwind."

She pulled her head back, as though she had not meant to voice the last part. Her copper scales burned warmly in the candlelight.

"I am Del'nura. It seems you have met my son. I trust he has already introduced himself?"

Her eye fell menacingly upon her offspring. Kaerisk tried to lift his head; it was an effort to do so, but he succeeded.

"Yes, he has, elder. We met in San'Lux months ago. My name is Kaerisk."

Delaan gave him a pained look.

"Kaerisk! So, you are the errant, petulant child who dragged my son off to die!"

"Mother, I told you-"

She glared at him and he fell silent. That glare was then turned onto Kaerisk. The copper scales somehow looked brown in the firelight, but Kaerisk had seen true horror in the Deep. Del'nura did not frighten him.

He raised his head proudly, almost in defiance. "He tried to get us to stay in San'Lux and became trapped after we crossed the Wurmway. I did not drag him into this, nor was it his fault either."

"Yes, I've heard his fanciful story about – wait, what did you say?" She studied him silently for a time, whatever malice she bore disappearing from her face in place of scrutiny. It was as though she tried to bore a hole through him with her gaze.

Kaerisk rested his head once more. "Where am I, elder?"

"You are in the city-state of Ur'Del, Innovation of the Firstbourn."

Ur'Del... That's where Delaan is from. This must be his home, and – hold on, Del'nura? But if Ur'Del is led by the families Ur and Del, doesn't that make Delaan...

He blinked at the black hatchling with surprise. He had not imagined that the dramatic whiner could be descended from one of the city leaders.

"I do not yet believe you. But I want you to tell me how you escaped from the depths of the Deep and reached this area so quickly," Del'nura said.

Kaerisk blinked. It had felt like months to him. "Quickly?"

"Lan'Dal, where you were taken, is several flight-days from here. There is no way you could have crossed that distance alone, underground no less, in under two weeks."

Two weeks? Has it only been that short of time?

"I'll tell you everything, elder. My sister and maybe all dragons are in danger."

*   *   *

He reclined his head after he had told the copper dragon everything that had occurred, from leaving his father's lair to his most recent injuries at the hands of the biped. At first the elder seemed incredulous and unconcerned, growing especially cold when Delaan was mentioned. The more detail he added, however, the more she grew anxious and attentive. By the time his tale was finished, the elder had reclined on her haunches, staring into her paws with uncertain eyes.

"You saw one of those not-dragons in the Deep? A Wurm? What exactly is a Wurm, mother?" Delaan asked.

"Something a hatchling wouldn't know about. This is dire news indeed. It explains so much and opens up so many questions," Nura said. She stared at Kaerisk's tail for a time, perhaps trying to determine if the second one was still there. If it was, Kaerisk could not see it.

"Everything I have said is true. I am terribly worried about my sister and I need return to her," Kaerisk said.

He tried to stand, but the elder smiled for the first time since she had arrived and loosed a shushing noise.

"Worry not, little one. I must visit my husband immediately and we will deal with your sister at once. Focus on resting; you have had an adventure far beyond what any could have imagined."

"Mother?" Delaan asked.

She ignored him and turned slowly, walking out of the room on unsteady paws. Kaerisk watched her go through the wax sticks and flames, the heat bending the light in surreal ways and distorting her image. For a moment, the blue thought he saw the Wurmqueen and he shuddered.

[233]

"I'm sorry. Mother has been like this since I came home."

"It wasn't your fault."

"I know. But they want me to have a certain level of decorum, I suppose. Can't have me running off and getting killed."

"Maybe they were just worried about you."

"I guess. That, and the situation being what it is, they decided to keep me within arm's length for a while."

"What situation?"

"The war that you took part in has everyone concerned. Not because you were in it, I mean, but because the bipeds are acting in such a way. It's uncharacteristic. Maybe this Wurmqueen you saw explains it, but I don't know. We're just lucky that it hasn't spread to our bipeds here."

Kaerisk blinked. "You have bipeds?"

"Yes."

The blue hatchling tried to stand, his weak legs shaking under his own weight. Delaan tried to arrest him, but Kaerisk pushed him back with a trembling claw.

"I can't just lay here. How is Zala? Was she injured?"

"She is fine. I sent word to Lan'Dal in secret when you first arrived. I didn't want mother or father to know who you were until you were well - didn't know how they would react."

"How'd you manage that?"

"My parents often have me run errands or send messages for them. It wasn't too hard."

Kaerisk tried to stretch his wings out, but he felt the small ties tug when he did. He folded them to his back. "Would it be alright if I looked around? I'd rather the sky be over my head right now."

"You should be resting, especially after what you went through." Delaan's words did nothing to deter the other hatchling. He sighed. "Alright, we can have a look around town. I'll show you the Manufactory. But take it easy. I'm sure my parents would have an aneurism if they realized I let you wander around in your condition."

"I'm not as weak as I look," Kaerisk said, lifting his head proudly. He didn't keep it up there for long, as his neck hurt. Following Delaan, who pushed the so-called door open, Kaerisk left the nursery.

Delaan's lair consisted of a large earthen dome, separated into several parts. It appeared to be made of sand that had been mixed with other materials and baked by sun and dragonfire. The device that Kaerisk saw in the nursery was one of many in the lair, each with varying shapes and sizes. Their uses ranged from entertainment, such as a box that contained a spinning statue and music, to devices that eased everyday living. One machine actually pumped water from below ground without using Riftwind. Kaerisk was amazed that such a thing could exist.

Outside was blazingly bright compared to the inside of the dome-lair. Desert heat fell over the blue's already warmed scales. The smell of oil was much greater out here, as the substance was used to lubricate various machines that had been set up around the city. Earthen walls rose around the city in a circle, lending a sense of safety to the hatchling.

In addition to several other dome-lairs lining wide streets of baked sand, there were also small domes that attached to one another. Kaerisk wondered if hatchlings in Ur'Del got their own lair when they reached a certain age, but no – coming out of one was a biped. It seemed as though bipeds and dragons lived side-by-side.

Kaerisk thought back to those cursed lessons once again. The bipeds here were exclusively geldin: the only race besides humans possessing a name that dragons apparently cared to remember. Geldin were small, brownish-gold creatures with green outlines around their pointed, triangular ears. They had very long, slim fingers, which were actually quite muscular compared to the rest of them. Father had said that these bipeds were the least likely to cause him trouble. Now he knew why.

The geldin walked into a large, central dome. From the dome came a great pillar of smoke – the column he had seen at a distance.

Delaan followed his gaze to it. "That is the Manufactory. Long ago, the founders of Ur'Del built it as a meeting hall to discuss new innovations to aid dragon life. It still serves that purpose, but also produces many new innovations every day." He led the blue to the building and took him into one of the large arches that served as entry points.

The inside was filled with dragons and bipeds alike, each working or speaking rapidly. There were stations of stone where tools could be used, whether they were smelters – the primary source of the smoke – or saws for cutting wood or gems. Most of the devices were for easier living, such as the water pump that he had seen inside Delaan's home. Some, however, were directed towards war. One dragon worked alongside a geldin; the dragon would cast the metal and shape its still-molten form with the Riftwind. After the claw-shaped device had been fashioned, it was dumped into a vat of water with an audible hiss. It was then passed to the biped, who began to carve into the metal with a gem-tipped tool. Fine, serrated edges designed for better rending potential took shape before Kaerisk's eyes. When the task was done, the dakael placed it in a large barrel which stood on what looked to be a door in the ground.

Delaan glanced at it. "There are tunnels under there. Don't know what for though. C'mon."

Delaan led him through the Manufactory, passing a circular pit where two dragons and a biped sat and discussed. Kaerisk lingered to listen.

"We have a lightweight alloy now. I believe it will allow us to make our resonance devices smaller. We still have to come up with a better way of generating the power on a smaller scale, though," one dragon said.

"Manual power is out of the question. No, I think if we use Riftwind crystals, we'll be fine," the other said.

"What if we used steam to capture a charge?" the geldin asked in draconic. "If we could do that, then-"

"We have a few centuries on you, little geldin. We'll come up with the best option," the first said, his Pride transforming into superiority. The geldin lowered his head and went silent as the two dragons continued to discuss.

Kaerisk glanced to Delaan. "This isn't the place I had intended to reach. Is Luminous better?"

"With bipeds? So I hear, yeah. I'll do everything I can to help you get there."

"I still don't understand why, Delaan."

"All my life, I was told that I would be the next leader of Ur'Del. Every lesson, every action, everything - all for that future. I never really thought much about it. Not 'til you left San'Lux. Not 'til I accidentally followed."

"Do you want to leave your life behind?"

"I don't know. I don't think I'd have the courage, even if I did. And I realize now that, if I don't find that courage, I won't be effective in the future already planned for me." Delaan lowered his head, glancing sidelong at Kaerisk. "Without you constantly pushing me, I would have died out there. We all might have. Now I hear what you went through in the Deep and I realize just how much strength you really have."

Kaerisk nosed his head up as he had what felt like ages ago in the swamp. "Every dragon finds their strength in time. I never thought I could count on you, but it seems I was wrong."

"Truthfully, I don't think you could have either." Delaan smiled, but it was a serious smile, as though he had decided something in that moment. "Want to see our meeting hall? It's not as fancy as the statue in San'Lux."

"Sure."

They left the massive dome and began walking towards the far end of the city. A few elder dragons sat outside of the steeper domes to which the black led the blue. They appeared to be discussing intensely. Delaan spotted his mother, who in turn spotted him; she gave him a rather irritated stare. Some of the elders followed her gaze to the pair, which they stared at curiously. From between their legs, a small blue hatchling came rushing forth at top speed towards the two.

"Risky!"

History

Zala impacted her brother squarely on his battered chest, wrapping her arms around him and squeezing against his delicate wing. He grimaced in pain, but still he smiled as his sister held him, preening his neck lovingly.

"Zala! I thought I had lost you," Kaerisk said, resting his weak neck over hers.

"And I you. You look terrible! Are you all right?" she asked.

"I'll live."

Nura stepped around the other dragons with a polite nod of excusal. The other dragons, both female, did not seem to mind and spoke quietly amongst themselves.

"I thought I told you to rest, Kaerisk. You are in no condition to be walking around, especially in this heat. Delaan should know this," she said, punctuating a cold glare at her son.

"It was my idea. I'm sorry; I couldn't rest," Kaerisk said.

"I did say I would deal with your sister. You may have lost faith in your father, but it is dishonorable to have lost faith in all dragons," she said.

"I am sorry."

She smiled lightly. "I can't begrudge you though. I should have explained, but the matter of your story preoccupied me. I was hoping you were better rested before meeting her," Nura said. She peered closely at the stiches in his wing, but they had not snapped. "Delaan, don't think I haven't figured out who sent for her. Take these two back home and let the boy rest – with our guest's leave, of course," she said, motioning to the other two dragons with a nod.

"You have it. We are glad at least this was resolved," the elder of the two dragons said. She whispered something to the other, who soon left with a polite nod. "I'll send my companion with that news back to Lan'Dal, but it seems we have much more to discuss."

"Of course. Off you go, little ones. Now is a time to rest," Nura said.

Delaan's head lowered a bit. The hatchlings said farewell and turned down the street. Kaerisk gave Delaan a little glare of his own.

"How come you didn't tell me she was in the city?"

"I didn't know. I've hardly left your side since you arrived."

Kaerisk drew his head back, and then lowered it. "Sorry."

Once they had returned to the nursery, Kaerisk bedded once more on the pillows while his sister sat beside him, looking over each of his wounds with a careful, if untrained, eye. They were quiet for a while. Kaerisk watched his sister, as if afraid she might disappear. Once she was satisfied that he wasn't in mortal danger, she returned to preening his neck affectionately.

"What happened, sister?"

"After you fell, I thought it was all over. We were surrounded and there was nothing that I could do. I attacked some of the chirop that had snuck inside."

"You fought too?" Delaan asked.

"Of course I did. If I didn't, they'd have killed me."

Zala lowered her head, looking sidelong at Delaan through the haze of the incense. She took a deep breath of it. Her tail still twitched back and forth; even though she was with her brother in safety, Kaerisk could hear her heart race and feel her body tense as she rested against him. Slowly, she exhaled and began to recount her tale.

"There was fire everywhere. Chirop and grassmen fought, the little fox-men hissing and screeching. It was horrible. Correth suddenly ran up to me and told me to come with him. His vines were writhing everywhere. I asked him about you, but he said it was too late and if I stayed I would die – well, smaller sentences, because he's a grassman. I paced about, trying to figure out some way of going to help you, brother. I was so afraid that I'd lose you. And then I remembered the promise you made me make. I wish I hadn't. I followed after Correth, thinking he might know a way out. I should have been faster, because I got attacked."

She showed Kaerisk her shoulder. A small scar had formed where the scales had grown back; the wound was about the width of a chirop dagger.

"Correth helped me though. He got the fox-man off my back, and then we ran together. The elder grassman was dead; there was fighting everywhere. It was chaos! The grassmen tore open a hole in the fort, which caused the logs to roll outwards, and then we rushed through the break in the wall. They stabbed the humans that had escaped being crushed, and then we just ran and ran and ran…"

Kaerisk could hear his sister's heart speeding up in her chest, even as her eyes closed and her tail lay still.

"Then the ground shook. I thought it was the army chasing us, but it was an elder dragon instead. She thought they had captured me. She berated me and told me that I should have known better or something, but then she realized I wasn't from Lan'Dal. She agreed to shelter me and the few grassmen who had helped me escape. Apparently, the grassmen's only plan was to run towards the dragons and hope they didn't get killed."

"Not much of a plan," Delaan said.

[241]

"It worked," Kaerisk said. Delaan shrugged.

Zala nodded. "Anyway, I told them about Delaan and you. I begged them to try to help, but they insisted I go to see their leader first. I was so worried about you, I couldn't think of anything else, even as I stood before her – Matron Laniela. She didn't seem to like me, as I was interrupting her sleeping or meditating or something. I begged her to go after you two, but she informed me that she had already sent her dragons to try to find you."

Delaan picked at a loose scale on his wrist. "Her dragons picked me up around that time, I think. I didn't get into town until after Zala's meeting with the Matron. They weren't able to reach you in time, though." His eyes fixated on that errant scale, carefully placed to avoid eye contact with Kaerisk.

Kaerisk churred gently. "It's alright, Delaan. You tried."

"I'd have liked to have been more successful."

"What happened next, Zala?"

Zala leaned into her brother. "The Matron was not happy with me, as I said. She spoke at me for a while, telling me I was frail and that I would not cry if I were a real dragoness. But when she finally asked for my name, she immediately knew who I was."

Kaerisk blinked. "She did?"

"Yes. Our mother came from Lan'Dal."

They sat in silence as the weight of those words sunk into him. Kaerisk knew almost nothing about Mother Mountain. All he knew was her sapphire slopes, her kindness, and her death.

"What – what did she say?"

Zala leaned against him more firmly. It hurt his wing, but he ignored it as he was enrapt by her words. "She told me that mother was a guardian and that she and Father fell in love during a biped hunt near Lan'Dal. She bade me tell her my

whole life story and how I got there. I told her about Icia, and
Sapphire, and Luxari's lessons, and Icia's... She seemed really
mad at Father for some reason. Before I could ask anything
else, Aleni – that's the elder who found us – came back with
Delaan and told us that you had been taken. The Matron looked
for you, but she couldn't find you."

Kaerisk furrowed his brow. "I thought the Matron was
with you."

Delaan nodded, though he still did not lift his eyes.
"Laniela has the gift of truesight; it's passed down in her
bloodline. She can see what others cannot. That was likely what
she was doing when Zala arrived. But even she couldn't see
into the Deep to find you."

Is Nao able to block such a thing somehow?

"After that, arrangements were made for Delaan to go
home and I stayed behind in Lan'Dal. I trained with them,
because I wanted to go help you somehow. I even joined a
young Wing – that's a group of females working together."

"I wanted to stay with Zala, but once they figured out
who I was, there was no choice. They sent me home," Delaan
added.

Zala nodded. "It's alright though. Aleni and the Matron
took very good care of me. The Matron said it was like having
her old friend back again. I wasn't able to learn enough in time
to help look for you, but Delaan's message came that you were
somehow in Ur'Del and I immediately came here with Aleni.
I'm so glad you're alright." She nuzzled her brother for
emphasis.

He too was glad, though more because she had not
suffered as he had. He returned her nuzzle. Delaan sat quietly,
still fixated on his paw. His eyes caught the black, but then a
thought seized him as he considered Zala's story.

"Zala... did you ask what mother's name was?"

Zala hung her head. "I was too ashamed to admit that I did not know her name."

<u>True Council</u>

Six days passed. Zala remained steadfastly by her brother's side. Delaan spent his time as a go-between for the hatchlings, who remained peaceably sequestered in the nursery. Aleni left soon after arrival, promising to return a week later. Delaan informed them that Aleni was not the only dragon who left. Several elders flew from Ur'Del with great speed, though Nura had not told her son why.

It was therefore a surprise when Nura came with another elder to ready the two for flight.

"What flight?" Kaerisk asked.

He was worried that Nura intended on sending them home. Though he had expressed his desire and effort to leave his father, Nura had made no assurances against returning him to San'Lux.

"You and your sister are to appear before the Gathering of Voices – the True Council," Nura said.

"The Council? In San'Lux?" Kaerisk asked.

"No, child, I do not mean a city council. You will stand before the True Council, the coalition of every dragon city-state recognized by our people." Kaerisk shuddered.

An even larger council than San'Lux? I couldn't even stand before one city, how could I stand before several?

"I am to go as well?" Zala asked.

"I believe Aleni intends to meet you there, Zala. In addition, your testimony may be called upon as well."

Kaerisk rose slowly, still favoring his left side where the wound had been made in his wing. He tried not to let them see his tail twitch or let his voice crack.

"Then let us hurry."

[245]

Nura explained on the way. Her voice was barely audible over the warm wind as they flew over the desert. It was rare that the True Council would meet; most of the time, dragon city-states handled their own affairs and fostered their own ideology. When a meeting was called, it was usually in response to a threat greater than a single city alone.

They sat down in the warm sand as the sun fell over the horizon. Nura and her mate, Delarrean, happily set upon the meal they had brought with them as the flight had left them hungry. Kaerisk and Zala were also given a portion of the meat. While they ate it, Kaerisk watched the stars come out and shine upon him. He remembered the first night alone with Zala and Delaan on the plains and wondered if a new journey was about to start.

The next day, they flew over the meeting place. The land had been cratered by some extraordinary event. The ground within the crater appeared to be permanently molten, with occasional jets of gas spewing up into the air. Four firm columns had been driven into this unsteady rock; somehow, they did not melt, even in the magma. These columns supported a stage large enough to hold many dragons. On the outside of the crater, four more marble poles wider than an elder dragon had been crafted. They towered into the air and held aloft a dome of similar rock crowned with gold, which covered the whole of the crater.

"This is the Site of Ascension," Nura said, "where the Firstbourne was, well, born."

Already, many delegates had gathered upon the stage. The outside of it was raised, while the inside had a small depression for speakers. Kaerisk recalled the same indentation at the top of the statue in San'Lux and reasoned it too must help the acoustics for speakers. He spotted Luxari on the other side of the stage and cowered behind Nura so as not to be seen. She and her mate pressed him rather firmly in front of them, perhaps finding the action unseemly. Luxari noticed him, but he did not appear to recognize the hatchling and soon returned to speaking with fellow delegates. Kaerisk breathed a sigh of relief; his father was not among them.

There were many more dragons than the hatchling had anticipated. Beyond San'Lux, Ur'Del, and Lan'Dal were a host of other city-states, each consisting of two to four representatives. Kaerisk counted at least seven other delegations; he wondered how many there were. Nura seemed to know as she directed Delarrean to the stage when a final pair arrived. The elder black stood and addressed his peers.

"As my couriers have already informed you, the matter for which this True Council has been called is extremely dire. We stand before a churning tide that surges forth from the Deep. Our sworn protectorate of this land, the duty handed down to us by the Firstbourne, is in grave jeopardy. A great power has been bestowed upon those who would be our enemies by sources unseen for thousands of years. We come to present evidence of this fact and to discuss what our response should be."

Delarrean went over the details: that bipeds had learned magic and that a Wurm was leading them to seek an ancient vengeance. The delegates waited impatiently as Delarrean explained these events. One of the dragons raised a wing as the elder reached a pause.

"The floor recognizes Luminous."

So that one is Luminous.

The elder, an emerald-scaled female, lifted her body and projected her voice as she spoke. "We wish it to be known that our bipeds have not displayed, overtly or covertly, any indication of displeasure towards or hostilities against dragon kind. Nor have we seen any evidence of the use of Riftwind amongst our wards. You spoke of evidence. I wish to hear it."

The emerald sat down and the Matron Laniela lifted her wing. With Delarrean's approval, she too rose to speak.

"Shortly after the battle between a nearby encampment of grassmen and dakael from within the Deep, my patrols discovered damage first assessed to be the release of fire from a hatchling who had been present by happenstance. Upon a second sweep, it was discovered that the damage was in fact a blast of fire-laced Riftwind in a concentrated area. It was not a result of hatchling fire."

"Does not the possibility exist that the hatchling caused it?" one of the other city-states asked.

"The hatchling in question was starving at the time as a result of a long journey. The use of Riftwind on such a scale would have killed him," Laniela said.

"Where is this hatchling? I should like to question him myself," another city-state said.

Delarrean beckoned Kaerisk to him. It took a nudge from Nura to get him to move. Standing in front of so many elders from so many different walks of life left Kaerisk feeling both nervous and embarrassed. He tried not to shake, but he was certain he did.

"Little one, when did you first learn about Wurms?"

"When I met Nao'Dariva, elder," Kaerisk answered. His voice carried further from the center than he thought it would. It made him feel a bit emboldened, even as he was surrounded on all sides by elders.

"You are certain you did not just read about Nao in an ancient text? Perhaps mistaken what you saw in the Deep? Even the eldest Wurms known did not live past a dragon's age, and there have been at least five such ages since the last known sighting of her work."

"Father never told me about Wurms. He taught me extensively on bipeds: what to expect and how to fight them. What I saw down there was no biped and no dragon," Kaerisk said.

That city-state sat and discussed amongst its members while another rose.

"We find some difficulty believing in your story. For an untested hatchling to go so far and survive, especially with two untrained hatchlings hampering him, is dubious at best and impossible at worst. Describe how you made it to the other side of the Deep."

"We fell into a derelict lair. Inside, we found a tomb, a Miasma Dragon, and a pathway. At the end of it was a massive crystal which I'd never seen before. It bathed us in light, and then we moved somewhere else. The area looked the same, but the crystal was a different color."

"You could have read about the ancient Wurmway leylines. No one has seen them in thousands of years."

"Where, precisely?" Delarrean interrupted. "Text about the Wurmway were once held in Eidolon, but that city was abandoned centuries ago. All we have now are sparse records of copied text, most of which remain sealed."

Luxari rose up and Delarrean recognized him. "It can be confirmed that the lair they found exists, as does the room they describe. Shortly after learning of this story, we followed the hatchling's trail and discovered the lost lair. We are not sure whose tomb it is yet, but the Miasma Dragon is now gone. All that remains are the bones, preserved by the sheer friction of Riftwind – a feat only achievable over a long period of time with a constant source of energy. A Miasma Dragon would fit this description."

"Then you recognize this hatchling, Luxari?" one of the city-states asked.

[249]

"Yes, I do. This same hatchling and his sister left their lair months ago. I am extremely surprised to find them alive, but as they are their story must be found credible," Luxari said.

"Even if their story is true and a Wurm still lives, how are we to extract her? The tunnel in which she resides is too small for a force of elders to breach," another city-state said.

"And what kind of threat could bipeds truly be? Even knowing the secrets of Riftwind, they are too small to make use of it," still more said.

"I believe that if we were to speak with the bipeds of the Deep-" the emerald from Luminous began.

"Preposterous! We could no more argue with a rock than speak civilly with the dakael," Luxari exclaimed.

"I agree with Luxari! Let us find a way to dump the mountains upon their heads!" another city exclaimed.

"We've no need to take action – the bipeds are likely to kill themselves and their queen with the powers they do not truly understand," said another.

"Order! We speak out of turn and solve nothing!" Delarrean exclaimed. No one was listening to him as the dragons continued to argue.

The blue hatchling felt something well up inside him. Seeing so many elders bicker like hatchlings was too much to bear, especially after what he had seen. He lifted his maw.

"Enough!" Kaerisk shouted.

His word was wreathed by a fire he could not control; fire and word both came from his mouth. The burning display immediately focused all attention onto him. Though he was nervous, his fury overrode any fear within him. Words flowed as if they were not his own.

"This council is the ruling body of our people. From inception designed so that ideas could be discussed safely and threats could be met. I may not understand all the rules. I'm just a hatchling. But that gives me a unique perspective. I know when things are bigger than I am. And this - this is bigger than I am. This may be bigger than we all are. When I was suffering at the hands of the bipeds, it was under orders of Nao'Dariva, the Queen of the Wurms. She had them chain me and beat me, break down my will, just so that I would know the anger she had within her. She did not know who I was. She merely knew that I was dragon. Her hate was a palpable thing and it pierced my heart. It cut deeper than the spike that tore my wing! The bipeds in the Deep will learn. They will grow. And they will follow her, as they have in eons past, as they might have been doing all this time. Even now, they dig secret tunnels from the Deep, seeking to surprise us in our lairs. She is coming to kill us all! United, we must stand. If we do not, we will surely have our wings torn from us!"

For a time, the Site of Ascension was quiet. Kaerisk lowered his head remorsefully, but none looked to punish him for his transgression. Indeed, many had heard and listened. When at last the dragons spoke, they did so in whispers amongst themselves. Delarrean lifted his head and addressed the council one last time.

"Let us recess for now. Before the month is ended, I would like us to present proposals from our city-states to decide what is to be done about this threat. Nao'Dariva was said to be ruthless and cunning both; if she has lived this long, there must be a reason why she has chosen now to move. Please bear this in mind as you prepare your proposal."

Kaerisk and Delarrean returned to their area of the platform. Zala came up to her brother and nuzzled him gently.

"I don't know how you could stand up there. I'd have been terrified."

"I was. But I had to say something."

"You are much like your father in that regard," Luxari said. The gold had crossed the stage almost as soon as the two vacated it.

"Elder Luxari," Kaerisk said. He could not hide his new trepidation in his voice.

"You stole his gift of public speaking. I'd say inherited, but given the circumstance... Kaerisk, your father has been devastated since you and Kaezala disappeared. He has cloistered himself within his lair and rarely travels from it, even to eat. I tried to tell him that you and your sister were here, but he turned me away, I who have been his friend and mentor since he was a hatchling. You have suffered so much and have reached this point a stronger dragon. Will you not reconsider your course of action now? I would gladly do all I could to restore you to your father."

"As you have said, elder, I have suffered much. I cannot allow that suffering to have been in vain. Zala and I will continue on to Luminous."

Zala stood tall beside him. "Brother is right. I value your lessons, Elder Luxari – but I found my home with my brother, and in Lan'Dal. I made him a promise and I will make good on it."

"I am glad you made it to your mother's home, Zala," Luxari said.

She curled her tail around her paws. "You are?"

"Did your Father ever tell you of how he and your mother fell in love?"

Both hatchlings shook their head.

"That is a true pity. There was once a series of great exoduses from the Deep. San'Lux has always taken its charge of protecting dragonkind seriously, and so hunted each and every one of these incursions. But Lan'Dal, too, takes this charge seriously. When the bipeds came from the Deep in

Lan'Dal's territory, your Father led a charge there; however, Lan'Dal would have none of it. Your mother came to meet them and demanded they leave this matter to them. Rather than be turned away, your father challenged her to a duel for the right to hunt there."

"A duel? Like what was held in front of the Firstbourne statue?" Kaerisk asked.

"Yes. All one had to do was push the other out of the ring. We thought it would be over in a matter of minutes. Several hours later, they still fought and we still watched, no longer cheering but mired in our own amazement at their stamina. We thought it would be over by the first night, but the battle continued. On and on they fought, neither side willing to budge an inch towards their defeat. The rest of us had to get food from the nearby forests, as the battle went on for three days. As night fell on the third day, the combatants collapsed at the same time, neither side victorious."

There was a short pause as some dragons shuffled by them.

"They were too stubborn to lose and so neither won. But they gained something much greater – for the two fell in love in that moment. You both have your parents' stubbornness. It has served you well, for refusing to give up is what has allowed you to survive what you did. And you may yet gain something even greater from this. But you should know: several bipeds escaped into the world during their inadvertent diversion. Be mindful of the unintended consequences... and take responsibility for them when they rear their heads. If your Father had, perhaps he would have been more understanding towards you."

"What do you mean, elder?" Kaerisk asked.

Luxari smiled and shook his head slowly. "That is a story for another time. Suffice to say you already know its ending."

Kaerisk frowned. Something about the elder's words felt menacing, though he had spoken with a hint of sorrow.

"What will you do now, elder Luxari?" Zala asked.

"He still believes you both to be dead. Perhaps it is best if he continues to believe it, at least for now. When he is done mourning and is at last in the right state of mind, I shall tell him what has truly become of you."

"Do what you think is right, elder. I must do the same," Kaerisk said.

"So I see. Good luck to both of you."

The gold walked across the stage again, this time in far less a hurry. As he left, Kaerisk returned his attention to Zala. She had stopped looking at Luxari at some point, her eyes fixated on the delegation from Lan'Dal. Kaerisk nosed her and she smiled at him. He wasn't sure why, but something about her smile reminded him of Mother Mountain.

"Do you want to go with them, Zala?"

She did not look him in the eyes. "I made you a promise, brother. We shall reach Luminous together."

Kaerisk leaned into her, churred, and then scampered over to the emerald who spoke for Luminous. Zala followed slowly behind him. Thanking Delarrean and Nura as they passed, they came to a halt before the emerald, who had watched the approach with a curious eye. Kaerisk bowed his head low to her.

"Elder, you are from the city of Luminous?"

"I am the scholar, Jelia. It is on my wings that the leadership of Luminous falls."

"My name is Kaerisk. By our own act, my sister and I have become orphans. We wish to join your city." Kaerisk pushed Zala forward a bit with his tail and she nodded to the elder.

"This is a twist. I thought that your experience in the Deep would have turned you back to San'Lux."

"My faith was tested, but I still stand before you, elder Jelia."

She smiled. "Indeed you do. A hatchling of your strength can go far. But a Wise hatchling would not join so readily. Perhaps what you should do first is ascertain the ideology and beliefs of the people you wish to join?"

Kaerisk lowered his head at her words. His embarrassment was no more tolerable with Zala snickering beside him.

Still, Jelia smiled. "I am not refusing you Kaerisk. Your rashness and tendency to jump into things without thinking them through is a trait common to a San'Luxian. But - they have their place. Using those same traits, you survived what would have killed lesser hatchlings. If you are to follow our path, little ones, you must begin to learn anew. Are you ready to make that commitment?"

Kaerisk lifted his head, his stare hard and determined. Zala watched him quietly. "Yes elder. Even if I must forget everything I have learned."

Philosophy and Dissention

Luminous nestled comfortably into a valley between two plateaus that arched together. On closer inspection, Kaerisk realized that the two plateaus had at one time been a single rock, carved away by dragon claws over time. It looked almost like a maw, as the city continued well into the mountain. The outer walls had originally been used for dragon lairs, but necessity or invention had left only small pockets. Into those pockets had been chiseled structures of hatchling proportion; inside, Kaerisk could see dakael working and living.

Within the mountain were the lairs of the dragons. Light had a hard time reaching the inside of Luminous proper due to the walls created by the arms of the plateau, but hundreds upon thousands of purple, blue, and green crystals had been hung by threads from the ceiling. The entire chamber sparkled with their light. A raised commons stood in the middle of the area; it was already occupied by two elders, arguing about the nature of truth when the hatchlings and Jelia arrived. They halted their debate to greet her.

"You two are at it again I see," she said.

"As you often say, debate is the bloodless battle of the mind," one of them replied.

"In which our wit is sharpened, yes, yes. My kyn, the time for debate is soon upon us, as is battle of a bloodier kind. Please rally the others. Tonight, I must present the ruling of the Council to our people. Be sure that a large meal is prepared; the flight has left us famished," Jelia said.

The two elders agreed and went their separate ways, vowing to prove their points at a later date. Despite the serious tone and looming threat, Jelia seemed cheerful; she cast a smile at Kaerisk as she rested on her belly.

"You've seen some of Luminous thus far, though there is still more to see. Of course, I need not give you a tour as yet. Hopefully, you have some questions for me."

"Of course we do!" Zala exclaimed suddenly. Something about the outburst seemed forced, like Rilla's laughter at the biped ruin. When the elder looked to her, she lowered her head, as if she never had a question at all.

For what felt like the first time, Kaerisk stepped in to upstage his sister. "Elder, my father wanted me to have nothing to do with bipeds. He did not even teach me that other city-states besides San'Lux existed. I know well how San'Lux views the biped. I want to know how Luminous does." His words had been practiced internally during their flight to the far south.

"He taught you of the Virtues, yes?"

"Yes."

"Those Virtues are the same here. Pride is foremost among them. As such, we do not see ourselves as equal to the bipeds. Our role is that of the teacher. Biped species have been leaving the Deep for centuries, as the food and space below become too little for them to survive. Some manage to escape the gaze of the dragons; most are driven back and to extinction. The dragons of Luminous believe that this should not be our only answer. We have taught the dakael our ways, culture, and language. We treat them with respect due a people developing, and in so doing, we earn that Pride."

"No dragon believes that bipeds are equal to them?"

"Bipeds are sentient, yes, but our culture has developed thousands of years while theirs has been squelched by our own policies. It is uncivilized for us to behave in such a manner."

Kaerisk frowned. "I'm not certain I agree." Zala tilted her head at him.

Jelia, too, cocked her head curiously. "With what point? You know well San'Lux has prevented their culture from flourishing, as have others."

"Then their culture is one of war and hardship; I have seen this first hand. Limited or primitive by our standards, they arrange themselves just as we would in their position. I would not be here today if not for the kindness of several dakael."

Jelia smiled gently. "So you would believe the dakael are our equals, then? That is radical even for us."

Zala pressed against him. "I always knew you were soft for bipeds, brother, but equal?" He frowned at her.

Is there no place in this world where I might find the home I wanted for Sapphire and me?

Jelia's tail twitched back and forth. "Do not forget that the Virtues are earned through action; they cannot be bestowed upon others. And while our policies exacerbate the problem, they are not the source of it. Dakael need more time before they – and we – are willing to see them as equals. That is the future we work towards here in Luminous."

If not now, then maybe someday.

"Elder, what would we have to do to join your people?"

"That depends on other factors we shall discuss later. Ask me something else."

The cryptic response was not what Kaerisk had expected, but he did not let his rashness get the better of him; the elder had already warned him of this.

Zala, however, had apparently not learned. "Why is it such a secret?" Jelia frowned at her.

Kaerisk poked her with his tail. "Have Patience Zala." She frowned and said nothing more. The lights above twinkled like a night sky in the awkward silence. Absently, he recalled Delaan's words before he had left San'Lux. "I have heard that

Luminous is a newer city-state than San'Lux. How was it formed?"

"There were five primary cities that formed thousands of years ago after the death of the Firstbourne. As you might have gleaned, those cities were founded by two families joining together under similar ideals and many of them maintain both their ideals and linage today. As time passed and dragons learned more about themselves and the world, new ideas began to form. A few dragons with common ideology would sometimes splinter from their cities and attempt to found new settlements. Some dragons would follow if their hearts believed in those new ideals, as you have. The rest would be passed down to hatchlings born to the new city-state. Not all survive, of course; Eidolon was mentioned, for instance. But Luminous has stood for three hundred years since the time I founded it. It won't be going anywhere soon."

"Because it was new, you didn't use your name?"

"We dragons have Pride, but mine's not that great. I preferred a word rather than a name, because words last. They speak ideals where names can only stand for them. They always reemerge when we need them most. Luminous is to shed light on old practices and adapt new ones – a shining beacon of Wisdom."

Kaerisk thought the idea sound. The purple crystals lighting the chamber gave the emerald elder a surreal look.

"How do you try to reach your goal? What is it you teach bipeds?"

"Philosophy, civics, and architecture. Would you like to see?"

Zala stepped forward. "Wait." The elder regarded her curiously. "I do have a question."

"Ask."

"What is Luminous' stand on the importance of community?"

The elder smiled and stood. As she walked back towards the entrance to the city, she explained. "Our society is built upon the interconnection of our people. Despite this, each and every one of us must be self-reliant. Here, our focus is knowledge. We learn together – but we are ultimately judged upon our own merit." Zala's tail twitched as she walked. Kaerisk frowned when he saw it.

She's not satisfied with that.

Light from the fading Eye still bathed the canyon arms in warmth. At the end of one arm was a dragon, overseeing several bipeds working metal tools into the rock. The bipeds consisted of two races, the catmen and the lizardmen. They worked without guile towards each other or the dragon who was watching them.

"This rock can be quarried and transported through a variety of methods. However, the assembly can sometimes be difficult if there is not an image in mind of what the end result will be," the dragon said.

"We planned our dwellings, did we not?" one of the lizardmen asked.

"Yes. The plans were scrawled upon tablets that you neglected to bring today. As such, the image is what we have to keep in mind. How will this stone work?"

The elder placed a paw upon one of the large stones that had been cut from the cliff.

"It will serve as a foundation," a catman said.

"It is much too thick to transport with ease. And a foundation must be a flat, long stone. This could not hold more than one of you."

"What if I only mean to hold one of me?" the catman asked.

"You'd have little room to sleep. And what of those around you? Would not they like a dwelling too?"

The cat sighed in frustration. Jelia led the hatchlings away as the elder continued to instruct on the finer points of design.

Once out of earshot, Jelia spoke again. "To return to our teachings: the first thing a society needs is a place to be, a way to live, and an ideology. These three things have always been the cornerstone of our civilization. Luminous has the caverns I showed you for a place to be. Our way of living, that of scholars, in which we are all treated as equals and united in our experiment to see the biped races elevated – our ideology."

"You are not held in higher regard than your peers, elder?" Kaerisk asked.

"I do not rule Luminous. I said that leadership fell on my wings, but it falls like a heavy stone. Leadership is a burden. And, to be honest, that burden has hampered me greatly these three hundred years. I may be held in higher regard, but it is not by choice, nor do I accept it when I see it. I am but one scholar, nothing more."

Kaerisk paused his step. Zala kept walking for a time before she also came to a halt, regarding her brother with an arched brow. When the elder noticed the hatchlings had stopped, she turned to face them.

"Elder, why would you not answer what we would have to do to become members of your city?"

"You are a sharp one."

She sat upon her haunches, looking about. Spying bipeds and passing dragons, she guided the hatchlings quietly back into the cavern and around the steps of the commons.

On the other side, Kaerisk discovered a short tunnel that opened into a large cavern. Parts of the ground had been left un-carved – shelves, which held row after row of stone tablets or delicate parchment. A few dragons read quietly here, honing their minds. Kaerisk looked at the repository with wonder; he had never seen so many texts all in one place. Indeed, Father had used only two tablets in his lessons.

In the back was still another tunnel, against which a large rock had been laid. Jelia pushed it aside and stepped into the chamber beyond it. It appeared to be a study or foyer of some kind, with still more tunnels connected behind it. There was a large rectangular pedestal, on which had been placed a tablet-tome, forgotten. Jelia took a seat on the other side of the table and looked down at the hatchlings behind it.

Zala came to the pedestal and placed a paw on it. "Brother, doesn't this look like the chamber we visited?"

Kaerisk regarded her. "Which one?" Jelia also listened with interest.

"The one after the ghost. With the lights."

"After the Wurmway."

"Yeah."

Jelia cleared her throat. "Perhaps what you saw was a remnant of the Grand Academy. Legends tell us there had once been a place where all hatchlings learned, but it was destroyed by a great catastrophe. Were there less pressing matters at hand, I would probably go looking for it myself."

How much of this world has been forgotten, I wonder?

"But to the question you asked me. You broke the traditional laws by leaving your father's lair. You thus orphaned yourself in that moment and became hatchlings with no father. Orphans are far from unheard of, little ones. Many dragons, especially those from the older city-states, still practice the rite of exposure."

Kaerisk had heard of the rite of exposure in his father's lessons. Couples who were unready or unwilling to raise hatchlings of their own would intentionally lay their eggs in the

Ashen Forest and leave them to the whimsy of fate. If the hatchlings survived, both being left alone as eggs and the arduous life of the wilderness and then found their way into the city, they would be lauded and praised, given their own family line or be adopted by one of the families there. The entire community would raise the children, instructing and guiding them as they grew. It sounded wondrous to Kaerisk when he was a small hatchling, but the reality of his own journey dispelled the romantic notion of it. If Kaerisk and his companions had barely survived as grown hatchlings, an egg that went through a rite of exposure was almost as good as dead.

"In a certain way, you underwent your rite of exposure; you merely did so at a later date. And so it falls on me to decide how best for you to join us. I believe you are both strong enough to make it on your own. You and your sister could easily be granted space within Luminous to build your own dwelling and I expect you would begin immediately and soon succeed. However, I do not believe you would be truly immersed within our culture in such a manner. A greater challenge I must set before you."

"And that is?"

"I want to adopt you."

Zala's earfins pinned back against her head. "What?"

"As with a survivor of the rite, you would not be true members of my family, mind you, but it would be necessary for me to oversee your instruction and indoctrination into our city, as well as provide living space and amenities."

Zala's tail lashed wildly behind her.

Kaerisk was more perplexed than angry. "I don't understand. Why would you offer to adopt us?"

"Oh? Perhaps you are not as sharp as I thought."

Kaerisk paused at those words, trying to determine if they were an insult. He reconsidered the topic discussed before their journey to the library. "This has something to do with your leadership."

"I grow old, Kaerisk. I will soon be past breeding age and I have never had time to seek a mate or even entertain the thought of suitors. For three hundred years, this city has been my world, my everything. Indeed, I still would not seek one now. I do not wish to pass down leadership through my linage. I believe that the concept is archaic and prevents new ideas from being born and discussed. If I were to take a mate, it is likely that all of Luminous would look to my children to lead them when I am gone. And that burden I would never place upon my children."

She paused, still smiling. But it had become sad, even as it hung on her lips.

"Despite this sacrifice, I cannot help but feel the need to have children of my own and pass down what I have learned to specific individuals with whom I have close ties. Your arrival presents that opportunity. I am sorry – I must sound terribly selfish to place this tariff upon your entry, but I can promise you that I will devote to you as much as I have to Luminous."

"This is unacceptable!" Zala exclaimed. Jelia's head jerked back at the tone. Her muzzle scrunched up as though she might sneeze.

"Zala?" Kaerisk asked.

"Brother, you cannot consider this offer! We have a mother. A great mother! She was respected within Lan'Dal and she gave us life! She gave me something to aspire too, something – something more than what I was allowed to be! Her story, those days we spent with her, they're… they are more precious to me than anything. I can't let anyone take that from me."

[264]

Kaerisk chanced approaching her. "But sister, isn't this what you wanted? We left Father's lair to find a new home and a new life."

Her wings lashed upwards, a rare fire in her eyes. "And we did!" When Kaerisk cowered back, she pinned her wings close to her as though she had not intended to turn that anger onto him. "I did, Kaerisk. Standing here, hearing this – I think I finally understand it. I don't hold the same values you do, brother. I don't care that much about the dakael. But when I was in Lan'Dal, I felt – I felt like I had truly come home. Like some part of Mother Mountain still lived there. That I could almost feel her presence again, like I had never really left her sapphire slopes. I made you a promise that we would reach Luminous together, but I-I want to return to Lan'Dal."

Kaerisk again tried to approach her, successfully. He covered her with a wing and leaned into her as Jelia listened in silence. "I don't know if I can let you go."

Zala pressed her nose under his chin. "Then don't. Come with me."

After all we have gone through to reach this point, should we turn back? Luminous is close to what I wanted, but...

Jelia finally lowered her head to the hatchlings' level. Zala drew back from her as though perceiving some threat, but Jelia smiled. "Orban, you grew up in San'Lux. You know what it was like to be marginalized, unseen, forgotten. To be female in a male's world – your only role to fulfill the cycle of life. Has it not occurred to you that you ask your brother to suffer the same fate?"

Zala's head jerked back, knocking Kaerisk's chin. "I – I do no such thing!"

"You think with your heart, Zala. You are a daughter of Lan'Dal. I should know." She smiled brightly. "It is where I was born. And I think that is where you should be. But give your brother time to weigh his options. Even a male as capable as Kaerisk may be overlooked in Lan'Dal - or worse, conflated with his father."

Kaerisk stopped rubbing his chin. "What do you mean, elder?"

"Lan'Dal saw your mother's death as a failure on the part of your father."

Kaerisk glanced to Zala. "Is that true?" Zala shrugged her wings.

"The circumstances were suspicious, I will admit. An elder dragon, especially one as strong as your mother, rarely succumbs to biped wounds – they simply haven't the technology or the will to pierce a dragon's hide deep enough to kill." Kaerisk began to shake, pondering the implications. Jelia's tail tipped back and forth erratically. "On the other paw, it may be that the bipeds she encountered were empowered by the wurmqueen. Nothing was ever conclusive and it is dishonorable for me to gossip-monger so."

A moment of silence passed between them as Kaerisk leaned into Zala. She nosed him gently, but avoided locking eyes with him. He frowned at the action.

Does she really suspect Father of... murder?

"In any event, I will arrange a flight to Lan'Dal. It could not hurt to hear their preliminary discussions on the broader matters at hand anyway. I will set you up in an empty lair tonight – I apologize that it will be rough. It was a collaboration between dragon and dakael at creating a lair. But considering what you have faced, I doubt it will be unpleasant."

"Brother..."

"I will think about it tonight, Zala."

Zala slowly pulled away from him, lingering as the last bit of her scales still connected to him. When contact was broken, she left the room without another word.

Arrivals and Departures

The morning felt particularly cold for some reason. The light of the Eye shined down into the welcoming arms of Luminous, but it did not carry the heat he had grown accustomed to over the years in San'Lux, or even in the deserts and plains he had so recently traversed. A purple elder with a thin and small scale pattern stood patiently as he waited for his cargo. Around his neck had been fitted a leather harness, with slots into which a hatchling could hook their legs and be secured for a trip. There was room for two on the elder's back.

Zala stared at her brother and the emerald standing behind him. Kaerisk sat on his haunches, tail curled around his foreleg as Father had. Zala lowered her head.

"I thought back," Kaerisk said. His sister lifted her neck and locked eyes with him. "And all this time, I thought I knew you. At first I was convinced that you were Father's favorite, that you always got your way. That you enjoyed emasculating me all the time."

"Risky-"

Kaerisk grinned. "There you go again. But you know, I was wrong. Not just about your relationship with Father. About everything. All this time I thought I was protecting you, but really, I needed you. Probably more than you needed me."

"Then you will come with me?"

Kaerisk walked forward until he was face to face with her, arching his neck and pressing his forehead to hers. She followed suit. He closed his eyes and inhaled, thinking back over everything he had the sleepless night before – of the time they had spent on the slopes of Mother Mountain, of the arguments they had when he was still ignorant, of the compassion she showed to Icia, Sapphire, and even to him. He kept breathing in, wanting to take in that scent one last time to remember her as she had been. He knew that it would never be the same again.

"You asked me the same in San'Lux. But this time – this time I have to stand on my own."

She quivered against him as her eyes filled with water.

"Sister. When you reach the end of your path, promise me that we will live together one last time so that I might finally find out who you are."

Zala huffed a laugh, splattering tears onto his cheek. "Only if you promise me the same."

"I do."

"Then I will. Be sure to write me often."

"All the time."

Zala reluctantly pulled back and climbed onto the purple's harness. Once she had locked her paws into the restraints, she looked back one last time with those large golden eyes and she smiled. Kaerisk did his best to smile back.

I do not know if what I saw in the Deep was a hallucination or if it was real, but it certainly was right. Stay safe, Zala.

The purple took off into the sky as Jelia walked forward, resting on her haunches behind him. Kaerisk lowered his head to his paws, wiping his eyes.

"I cannot call you mother."

"I know. I will be content to be your mentor."

Kaerisk stared up at her. "Why did you not offer that to my sister?"

"Were it only her discomfort, I would have offered. But it was not, Kaerisk. She said herself that her heart was not in the dakael. Your sister's heart lies in the Heart of the Firstbourne. She needs to know her mother and she will find her in Lan'Dal. I know this must be hard for you, but you and your sister have made the right choice. Already you are becoming elders."

Kaerisk frowned. "That brings me little comfort."

"Then take comfort in the difficulty. Her heart will always be with you, too."

Kaerisk craned his neck to watch the purple disappear into the morning sun before following Jelia back into Luminous.

At first, the arrangement was awkward for the two. Jelia had never been a mother before, Kaerisk had never had a mother before, and neither of them would admit the elder was a mother. The emerald had offered to hunt for the hatchling, but he insisted on hunting for himself. She showed him the surrounding land and he found an excellent spot to ambush prey. Whenever the elder would teach him, it was always in public under the watchful stares of others. Kaerisk was unused to the attention and didn't care much for it either, and so learning anything proved difficult at first. Worst of all, Jelia's lair behind the library desk consisted of a single chamber and was hardly suited to a second occupant. Since neither thought it proper for them to share a room, Kaerisk had been sleeping in the study. This was problematic because if the stone was left open, any number of curious scholars would barge in looking for the emerald, but if it were closed, Kaerisk could not leave on his own power.

One day, he woke to find Jelia discussing with another dragon just outside his room. Blinking the sleep from his eyes, he approached Jelia's side and addressed the other elder.

"Kaerisk. Good to see you again," she said.

"Elder Del'nura! What brings you to Luminous?" Kaerisk asked.

"As I was explaining to the Scholar, it is time again for Delaan to spread his wings. We believe this city is most suitable," Nura said.

"In location," Jelia said. Nura did not argue the point.

Kaerisk caught sight of Delaan, hiding behind his mother's legs. He had a strangely guilty look on his face, as though he had done something wrong.

I wonder if his mother is embarrassing him?

"Mother, may I have a look around?" Delaan asked, his voice near a whine.

"I'll be happy to show him around if you will allow it, elder," Kaerisk said.

Both mother and son regarded him: one with respect, the other with relief.

"This hatchling is one of the most remarkable I have met in some time, Jelia. You're quite lucky that he's come to you," she said.

"Indeed I am," Jelia said, not expounding further.

"Very well, show him around. I will discuss at length in Jelia's chambers now that you are awake, Orban," Nura said.

"Excuse us," Kaerisk said, rounding the elder black and leading her son from the library.

"Thanks for getting me out of that," Delaan said.

"It's nothing. I'd like to repay the favor of showing me around Ur'Del," Kaerisk said.

"You have gotten sharper when it comes to dragons."

"When it comes to people, Delaan. A hard and costly lesson to learn."

Luminous was a bustle as the two hatchlings entered into the glowing cavern. In the early mornings, the central platform was used for teaching and debates between both young and old. As the two ascended, they listened to a heated exchange on how much freedom should be given to bipeds. In the audience were a few elders, but many hatchlings as well.

Kaerisk had not met many of them as yet; whenever Jelia taught him on this same platform, Kaerisk felt exposed to their stares. None thus far had approached him and all of his communication had usually began and ended with a respectful greeting. Being the unofficial child of Jelia had its disadvantages too.

Delaan, however, had no reservations - not about Kaerisk, and most certainly not about the other hatchlings. He gave a few of the females a cheesy smile. The blue poked him in the side with his tail to keep him on track.

"From up here, you can see most of the important places," Kaerisk said in a hushed voice, leading Delaan around the edge. "Several of the lower level lairs have been taken for research or learning. That one down there focuses on the healing arts, for instance." The blue pointed to one of the lairs; a biped held its hand gingerly as it went inside.

"What about those?" Delaan asked.

Kaerisk followed the point of the black's wing. Not far from the healer's chamber lay a series of large steps, leading up the wall. Luminous proper resembled a compressed sphere; the stairs led up to the mid-point and several ledges wrapped far around the hollowed plateau. On these ledges were many rocks leaning heavily against the wall, each covering a hole.

"The upper lairs are for residents. They don't have fancy 'doors' here, so rocks seal the lairs shut when not in use or at night."

"How am I supposed to get out if I'm in there?" Delaan asked.

"I'm still working on that. Just have to wake up at the same time as the elders, really," Kaerisk said.

"That early?" Delaan asked.

Kaerisk turned his head. For some reason, hearing Delaan whine made him smirk. He wasn't sure if it was because the black was uncomfortable or because it brought back memories of their trip.

"So tell me, Delaan, what made your parents send you here?" Kaerisk asked.

Delaan was quiet for a moment. The counterpoint argument between the elders behind them got under way, warning of the dangers of too much freedom without supervision.

"After my parents saw how I took care of you, they thought I might have been more responsible. Or at least, that you were a good influence on me. So Luminous became my next destination."

"Aren't they still concerned about the bipeds?"

"Yeah. But Luminous is pretty far from the Deep. Don't think we'll see any humans or chirop out here. But now that the cities are coming up with plans, I think they're feeling a little more confident. My next trip was supposed to be Lan'Dal, but they thought it was way too close to the bipeds."

Kaerisk grimaced at his words, pressing himself against the stone railing of the platform. Delaan watched him with a tilted head.

"Is something wrong?"

"Zala's in Lan'Dal right now."

Delaan blinked and lowered his head. "Sorry, I didn't mean-"

"It's okay. I'm just worried about her."

"I thought she was just running around somewhere. Why did she leave?"

"She wanted to be with our mother's people. I just hope she's happy and doesn't worry about me."

"You're worrying about her, though."

Kaerisk looked away.

Delaan nosed him. "Your sister's pretty strong. She's always been, though."

Kaerisk regarded him and smiled. "I know. I've known since I met Icia."

Delaan frowned a moment, but it faded when Kaerisk did not join his unhappy memory. He hummed for a moment, his head returning to normal height to peer over the railing. "What about the bipeds? Do they live here?"

Kaerisk shook his head, and then motioned for Delaan to follow. Down they descended until the light of the sun painted the tops of the canyon walls. In the shade below rested the biped homes that the blue hatchling had seen briefly on his first visit.

"Kaerisk!" a voice came as the two approached.

From one of the houses, a small bundle of fur rushed forth and latched onto Kaerisk's foreleg. She bit him playfully, which was of no consequence to Kaerisk's toughened scales. The biped child, one of the cat race, peered up at the hatchling she wrestled with curious eyes.

"You help more?" she asked in Lindorm, her own skills at language now inferior to Kaerisk's own.

"Leave the hatchling be, little one!" her mother exclaimed from the home. Her stern tone and hands-on-hips approach saw the cat child quickly dislodge herself from Kaerisk's leg.

"Sorry! We play later!" she exclaimed.

The child darted back inside, watching as her mother stitched cured furs together. Kaerisk watched the art with sad eyes, but a happy smile.

"They sure are friendly with you!" Delaan exclaimed.

"To be honest, I feel more comfortable around them. I've not been in the company of other dragons for very long,"

Kaerisk said. Delaan nodded. "It was her sewing that I noticed first. It reminded me of Sapphire."

"She's still important to you, even now?"

Kaerisk nodded and continued. "I've been helping here in the afternoons. That little biped took one of her father's tools and chipped a hole in the wall, which I repaired with Riftwork. They in turn have been teaching me the language of the Deep."

"A give and take relationship. Something like what we have with the geldin," Delaan said.

"There is a respect that is different, though. The geldin serve, but we attempt to elevate the bipeds. At least that is what Jelia has explained to me." The woman waved to the hatchling and Kaerisk nodded politely. "Actually, I've helped a lot of families around here with Riftwork. I'm glad I can learn and be helpful to others."

"Seems odd for a dragon, you know."

"Really?"

"Most dragons focus on the improvement of the self."

"There's nothing wrong with living for Pride. I find mine in helping others."

"That's what makes you weird."

"I should pounce you."

"Oh c'mon!"

Delaan shrunk away dramatically, wings flaring in front of his face as though he were trying to hide. Kaerisk was initially perplexed by it, having little experience in playing with other hatchlings. Even when he was young and wrestled with his sister, Father often intervened for fear that one would be injured. But when the cat child came back to the doorway to join the fun, Kaerisk at last understood that the action was in jest. He crouched down with a grin, as if going to make good on his threat.

The play, however, was swiftly interrupted. An elder gold dragon sauntered up to the two hatchlings and addressed them.

"Ah, Kaerisk, there you are. It is good to see you, as always. This must be Delaan, then," he said. Kaerisk tried not to frown.

See me yes, but never speak.

"I am, elder," Delaan said, coming beside Kaerisk.

"My name is Zelbaran. I will be putting you up in my lair for the duration of your stay here. I will also be serving as tutor and mentor. As such, you will begin classes with me starting tomorrow," the gold, Zelbaran, said. "I have also heard all about your visit to San'Lux. As such, I shall be keeping a vigilant eye on you." Delaan's head drooped a bit.

"Elder, would it be alright for me to join Delaan in your lessons?" Kaerisk asked.

Zelbaran tilted his head for a moment. Delaan gaped at Kaerisk as though shocked anyone would ask for more schooling.

"You are being taught by Scholar Jelia, though. And I can assure you her lessons are of the highest quality," the gold said.

"It won't interfere, elder. I merely want to learn as much as I can and I would also like to keep Delaan company. Both of us are a bit displaced here," Kaerisk said.

"I suppose it wouldn't hurt then. I will clear it with the Scholar later. For now, Del'nura wishes to see you, Delaan. Hurry back to her and then we will get you situated," he said.

The two hatchlings thanked the elder and headed towards the library. As they walked, Delaan looked at Kaerisk sideways.

"You didn't have to volunteer for my sake," Delaan said.

"Maybe not, but I said it before. I find my Pride in helping others."

"Thanks… for being a friend."

Kaerisk absorbed those words with tempered curiosity.

When did Delaan become my friend?

Still, he smiled. "You're welcome."

Delaan grinned, his tail tip flopping back and forth as he pranced ahead.

"You're still weird, though!"

The Second Decision

For two weeks, Kaerisk grew used to his new life. Delaan allowed him to meet other dragons more easily than on his own, just by being near him; the black had always proven to be more loquacious than him. His days began to follow a pattern: mornings were spent with the black and Zelbaran in school; afternoons spent hunting with Delaan, who had become more proficient from their journey; late afternoon with the dakael, at which point Delaan would leave him; and finally evenings with Jelia, learning from her and recounting his day.

One day, Kaerisk and Delaan solved a riddle and returned with a dillwhip. Zelbaran accepted the plant from Delaan and congratulated him, but to Kaerisk he gave narrowed stares. The blue asked if he had done something wrong. The elder shook his head, but told him to see Jelia immediately. Kaerisk agreed and soon returned to the library. As he traveled, every dragon who saw him gave him dark and dubious looks.

When Kaerisk arrived, Jelia was speaking with some of the most elder scholars in a circle. Spotting her pupil, Jelia quickly dismissed the elders and led the hatchling into her study. She took the other side of the desk and stared down at it with pensive eyes.

"What is the matter, elder?" Kaerisk asked.

Jelia regarded the hatchling she had adopted, and then promptly returned her stare to the stone. "The plans were voted upon. The consensus of Luminous is that we must use a team of bipeds to assassinate the Wurmqueen. The people also agree that this plan would be voted down in True Council if that team was not led by a dragon. Unfortunately, due to the size of the tunnels, only a hatchling could suffice."

"That does seem the most logical from our point of view. They'd make fine allies under the command of some hatchling," Kaerisk said.

Jelia shifted as though she were uncomfortable. "The consensus of Luminous is that the plan be carried out by drawing out the forces of the Deep near Lan'Dal, while the team uses the tunnels from which you escaped. But there is a problem."

"What is that, elder?"

"You are the only one who knows where those tunnels are and how to navigate them."

Jelia was very still. The blue hatchling blinked.

"You want - me? To lead the biped force?"

"There is no one else we can think of who may be better. We dragons of Luminous are strong in the art of Riftwind, Kaerisk, but battle is not what we teach our hatchlings. The hatchlings are young scholars, tutored in the art of study. But this is a time of action, little one. You are the only one who might succeed."

Jelia's tail tip beat against the ground in dull tones that shook the stone.

"I cannot and would not order you to go. And there is the possibility that a different plan will be adopted. The thought of putting you through this, even disregarding my personal... It is shameful that I present this choice to you, Kaerisk. But as leader of Luminous, I must. Please consider taking on this role."

The thought of risking the Deep again sent shivers down the hatchling's spine. When he left Father's lair, all he wanted was to reach Luminous. He did not want to uncover some great and terrible plot against dragon-kind. And Nao'Dariva – she was at least as strong as an elder, if not several times stronger.

What chance would we really have? And if we fail, what she'll do to me...

Kaerisk took a deep breath and closed his eyes, trying to shake that thought. There was no doubt logic behind the scholar's suggestion. No one else might find those tunnels and, even if they did, the hatchling saw many passages that he ignored in his hasty flight. They might lead search parties in circles for days.

But still, if I failed...

"I – I need time to think about it."

"I understand, but this plan is to be presented within the fortnight. I wish I could give you more time. I wish... Take your time."

Jelia stood from behind her desk and retreated into the back room of the lair. Her motion was slow, as though a heavy weight was tied to her tail. Kaerisk moved with similar speed in the opposite direction.

He walked past the gleaming veil of Luminous proper, past the biped houses he had frequented so often, and out into the gentle plain before the jungle forests to the south. It was not to the forest he marched. Instead, he rounded the arms of the plateau and headed north to an unnatural series of hillocks. A vigorous wind began to blow.

Grass-covered hills rose like bellies full of eggs. Some had not yet eroded into the perfect domes that described so many of them; no, some of them retained the shapes of the dragons they had been in life. Where San'Lux committed their dead to fire, Luminous hid their faded lights in the earth. Such a fate could be his if he accepted the role asked of him – or worse.

The specter of his Father seemed to hang over the sacred mounds and his words over his head. 'Kaerisk, you may think that I am overbearing and cruel to keep you so close, to

[279]

teach you at length and to supervise you always. But in truth, most hatchlings, even those who hatch healthy, do not tame the sky,' he had said. Kaerisk had come to Luminous to escape those teachings and that place. And yet, even now as he stood on Luminous' soil, all he could remember was his father.

I might have to fight other bipeds too… to kill, just as he wanted. I don't want to be a monster.

"Kaerisk!"

Delaan ran up to him. He was out of breath; he must have run all over Luminous looking for him until someone pointed him to the Site of Committal.

"Did they tell you?"

"Yes."

"You're not really–"

"I don't know. I'm trying to make sense of it."

Delaan caught his breath and came to stand before the mounds. He must have been thinking the same morbid thoughts that Kaerisk had, because he gave the blue hatchling an eerie stare.

"If nothing is done, Zala could die. All of us might."

"But you don't have to be the one to do it. No one would blame you for turning this down."

"I'm glad Zala isn't here."

Delaan titled his head. "Why?"

"She'd want to come along."

"You're thinking of going through with it?"

"I think I am starting to understand why Zala left to be with our mother. She warned me, even then. Even with her last breath."

"What are you talking about?"

Kaerisk placed a paw reverently on the dragon-shaped mound before him. He smiled, though the smile felt incomplete, as though something was still missing.

"Right before my mother died, she told me not to be sad, because pain, suffering, and the loss of those closest to me would make me stronger. I didn't understand her then. I think I do now."

"Well I don't. What good will come of you dying in some forgotten tunnel in the Deep?" Delaan asked.

Kaerisk put his paw down and turned to face his friend. He sat on his haunches with a stern face.

"When I left San'Lux, I did so in anger and fear. I thought that everything that Father taught me was a lie. And while it was tainted by hate, I have used it to protect my sister and you. To survive the journey we went through. And now I have the chance to use those same skills to help all of dragonkind and every dakael still in the Deep. Father taught me how to fight with hate. But there are some things worthy of being hated in this world. The Wurmqueen and what she plans to do to our race – that is why Father taught me all those years. This is what he taught me to do."

The wind howled. Delaan looked at him much as he had several months ago when Kaerisk and Zala left San'Lux. This time, however, Kaerisk was not angry. He had not forgiven Sapphire's death or Father's needless hate. But he did feel regret for leaving as he did.

"I made my mother a promise before she died. I have not kept that promise yet. That is why I know. I can go into the Deep and come back. Because I can't die – I won't die – until I tell my father what she wanted me to tell him."

Delaan was utterly still as the wind whipped at his newly toughened scales. The wind's howl carried anguish that was not its own.

"Did - did you hear that?" Delaan asked.

The two hatchlings skirted the graves-hills near the edge of the Site of Committal. Rounding one last reverent hill, they spied a biped, fallen to the ground. Delaan stood at a distance, but Kaerisk neared the biped in haste. As he approached, he realized it was not one of the cat or lizard people of Luminous – this was a human. He slowed his pace, wary of a trap. No other biped could be seen and the plain stretched quite a distance; the hillocks might conceal someone, but they had just rounded the Site of Committal and saw nothing. The human was terribly injured. Bruises and blood painted his body like a canvas of crimson and black. His feet were uncovered, calloused, and cut from the rough journey he had made.

"What is a human doing here?" Delaan asked.

Kaerisk didn't know. He stood over the human just as transfixed as Delaan. Something about the wounds did not seem right, as though he looked at them from the wrong angle. He tried hard to find the balance between his father's teachings and his ideals.

"We should leave him."

"No, Delaan. He's injured. We'll take him back to Luminous."

"But he's human! One of the Wurmqueen's proxies!"

Kaerisk pushed his head under the man's broken body and rolled him onto his back. The man groaned in pain. "I am my father's son. But that does not make me my father. That is why I am here in Luminous today, Delaan. C'mon." Kaerisk didn't wait for Delaan to respond. He swiftly marched back to the city.

The human's arrival caused a great commotion. Bipeds and dragons alike did not know what to make of him, but Kaerisk stood with the human on his back at the entrance to Luminous proper. The uproar soon summoned Jelia, who called for aid. An elder took the human from the blue and disappeared into lair designated for healing. Jelia and Kaerisk followed.

"What happened? Where did you find him?"

"Near the committal site. He was injured when I arrived, but completely alone."

"I suppose we'll have to get the story from him when he is able."

"Mentor, I've reached a decision."

Jelia paused at this, but then quickly began to move again. "And?"

"I agree with the elders. I will accept this duty."

Jelia's head drooped as she walked, even though some Pride showed in her voice.

"Then we must have you meet with the bipeds free of Nao'Dariva's control."

Jungle Lizards

Emerald wings carried the hatchling southeast of his new home. Though this was his third flight by dragon-back, it felt more frightening for what was to come. The air grew humid and warm. The verdant plains gave way to a lush emerald canopy. Kaerisk had never seen trees like these in all his life; soon, he was to meet a people he had only encountered as isolated individuals in Luminous.

"What do I need to know?" Kaerisk asked, his voice barely carrying over the wind.

"Above all, respect their culture and do what is necessary."

Jelia's words whipped by him. He could barely hold on to them.

"I have to admit to some concern. The bipeds might not agree to risk their own lives against the Wurmqueen."

"Why not?"

Jelia's wings beat faster against the air as though contemplating an answer. "The Setkaa and the Shiris both have long left the Deep. The Setkaa in particular... You will see. We are almost there."

An unnatural break occurred in an otherwise endless canopy of green. The elder slowed her pace to set down within it. Kaerisk slid from the harness on her back and looked around the area. The humidity seemed even greater without the rushing wind of flight. Insects buzzed incessantly around him: in the air, in the bushes, in the dirt. Small animals scattered at their arrival, escaping into trees and the lush jade sky.

"From here, we must walk. If I feel the need, I may instruct you while we are with them."

Kaerisk groaned. "You aren't going to use the Riftlink, are you?"

Jelia smiled a bit and walked ahead of him, saying nothing.

The two dragons walked for half an hour before reaching their destination. At the end of the path stood four monoliths, which marked the entrance to the lizardman city. Stone had been brought from some source that was utterly unseen in the jungle. Most of the buildings consisted of small, crude houses built by stacking several stones upon one another, though some of the newer houses showed signs of significant construction improvements. In the middle of the village loomed a lizard-like face, carved from what was once an even larger rock. Its tongue hung out as though it was hungry and its eyes were ravenous rubies that looked down upon the hatchling with sparkling glee.

As Jelia and Kaerisk arrived, many lizard folk came from their dwellings. Each had been occupied in some task; the butcher was the first that Kaerisk noticed, because the biped reeked of blood. Though more lizardmen than he had ever seen before emerged into the jungle city from their dwellings, it seemed as though several of those houses went unused. One of the older lizardmen came forward to greet the two dragons. His scales, orange and black stripes, were odd patterns to the solid blue dragon.

"Scholar Jelia, you honor the people of Setkaa with your arrival. The stars have changed their season many times."

"Kaerisk, remember what I said. Above all, respect their culture."

Jelia's voice echoed through the Riftlink. Only Jelia knew how to use that magic, she had explained, the knowledge having been lost to Eidolon's fall. While it wasn't the first time he had heard someone in his head, her magic felt different, like someone scraping the inside of his skull with sand and rock. His head jerked in response, eliciting a curious look from the elder Setkaa.

"It is rare that you would bring one of your young so far. I fear there must be a dire reason for the transit."

"This is my adopted son, Kaerisk."

Kaerisk glanced up at her at the comment, surprised she would call him that after declaring her contentment with 'mentor.' She smiled at him and he smiled back, but he was not certain he truly shared the sentiment.

"He may be tasked with a great mission, but we will require your help to face this challenge," Jelia said.

"Have you come to ask us for aid, great scholar of the dragons? Or have you come to require it?"

"I ask."

"Such a matter must be humbling to a creature of Pride. Yes – I remember all that you taught me when I was but a child. There was always one thing, though, that you steadfastly held for yourself."

Jelia was silent.

"Some have heard what troubling winds bring your emerald wings. Indeed, look around you. This village once held more of my people, but no longer. We slaved to build this city. Our backs broke to move the stones, to carve the wood, to forge our metal. Such a task would have been easy for a dragon; the application of your inherent magicks would have made life much less difficult. At least, that is what you told us – that it was inherent. Not something we could learn."

Jelia remained still. She did not change her stance nor waver her eyes.

"So when they heard that they could learn the magic, they left. They joined with the Great Lizard Under The

Mountain. Seduced, they were, by this power. By its luxuries and ease."

"And yet, old friend, you remain here," Jelia at last said.

"Indeed I do, my mentor. For I moved those stones, carved that wood, and forged that metal. I earned through my effort more than what dragons were given. I found a different kind of magic, one that perhaps you intended all along. The magic of self-respect. The magic of Pride."

Jelia smiled.

"I take pride in this city, as do the people who live here. We owe you much for giving us both the chance and the direction we needed at a time when we were little more than scared animals. You can be sure that we will follow you into battle, even if it is against our fallen. In fact, I believe many of us would prefer to face our fallen as a matter of pride." The elder paused a moment, looking to the hatchling. "But you brought this one. Which means you had a request."

"This one may be leading a force of bipeds into the Deep to kill the Wurmqueen," Jelia said.

"A dangerous gambit. Do you feel up for the challenge, Kaerisk?"

"I do," the hatchling said.

"I wish you to stand before our idol. Stand there until it is time to stop."

"How will I know?"

"You will know."

The hatchling walked by the elder to stand before the menacing face, gazing up into the looming maw. The ruby eyes seemed to glint at him with bitter hunger.

"Come Jelia, while the hatchling acquaints himself with our idol. I should like to discuss the details of your plan."

"Of course." The elder turned and walked out of the village by the same path they had taken before. Kaerisk did not turn to look, but he could hear her exit, presumably following the Setkaa elder. He patiently stood there and waited.

All around him, he could hear the Setkaa shuffle back into their dwellings and resume whatever task they had been doing before the dragons' arrival. As he waited there, he considered the word 'idol.' In Luminous, he had learned that bipeds believed in 'gods' – a personification of the natural elements and the presumed creators of their various species. It seemed rather silly to Kaerisk, who respected the Firstbourne and fire alike, but worshiped neither.

Is this idol a representation of their god?

It struck him that, if it was, it looked very little like a Setkaa. Its face was too blunt, too pushed in, too round. Its vicious teeth were long and sharp, more elongated than anything the Setkaa sported. It might have been a dragon, but it wore some sort of helmet which a dragon would not, or maybe they were horns – it was hard to tell, as the stone dictated that the appendages had to be very close to the head.

Looking into those ruby eyes, Kaerisk began to feel strange. Energy tingled throughout his body, but it wasn't Riftwind. The eyes began to glow. Kaerisk wasn't sure if it was a trick of the light.

What is this eerie feeling? The tongue, was it always on the right side of the maw? Did I move or has the statue gotten closer? Why is this statue so familiar?

That maw, its lewd grin of pure ravenous hunger, seemed to open wider, wide enough for a hatchling to fit within. *"Because my people owned the lizardmen long before yours!"*

Kaerisk clawed at his head with a forepaw, hearing the familiar voice project into his mind. Even as he did, he could not look away from the horrific sight as the statue laughed devilishly. He could barely find breath.

[288]

Nao'Dariva!

"I saw you the moment you stepped into my temple with those other hatchlings months ago. You are beginning to understand, aren't you? My eyes and ears are everywhere. I already know what you plan to do. You managed to elude me once, but do not think I have not already concocted a hundred plans to see you returned to my tender, loving care."

No! I will not be captured again!

"I will find you, Dawnbringer. I will drag you back into the Deep. I will tear your wings from your back!"

Never!

Kaerisk leapt forward, breaking the spell of the ruby eyes. He crashed into the statue and clawed at it ineffectually, stopping only when he successfully tore loose one of those spiteful ruby eyes.

A peel of thunder roared overhead. The sudden sound broke his concentration, causing the hatchling to jerk back and fall to the ground. Through the rich canopy, Kaerisk could barely perceive the blackened clouds that would soon rain. All around him, the Setkaa had emerged from their huts and surrounded him. They stared at him. Jelia, too had returned, looking at him aghast for his vandalism. In his paw, the ruby eye still shimmered at him as though sparkling with hate.

"Kaerisk! What have you done?" Jelia asked.

The hatchling tossed the eye to the ground. "Did you know? Did any of you know? Nao'Dariva has been watching this village from the start!"

"Why do you suppose I had you stand in front of the statue, young dragon?" the elder Setkaa asked. Jelia jerked her head back at this. "Long ago, our people worshiped her as our great progenitor and she used us for our talents. When we learned of the Shiris protected by Luminous, we asked to be freed. The Wurmqueen allowed it. But still we bare her mark, the connection between us and her." He pointed to his eyes.

"You are her eyes," Kaerisk said.

"Yes."

"That is how you knew she offered magic! She still speaks to you!" Jelia exclaimed.

"Yes."

"Then how can any of you serve to catch her off-guard? To go with me into the Deep itself?" Kaerisk asked.

From one of the huts, a final Setkaa emerged, dressed in an orange robe. Half his chest was exposed as the top of the garment draped over only one shoulder. His muscular tail hung out the back. His pattern was a bluish purple, stripped with black. His eyes were covered by a black blindfold, tied tightly to his head. Despite the impediment, he walked over to Kaerisk without delay.

"I will go with you."

"But how...?"

The Setkaa reached out his hand towards Kaerisk's muzzle. Kaerisk went still, curious. When the lizardman touched his snout, he felt something like the Riftlink in him and his eyes felt warm in his head.

"I see what you see. She sees nothing but darkness." The Setkaa removed his hand and frowned. "A storm approaches. Rains are a sign of change, young dragon. If you complete the task you have been given, things will change."

"Will it be for the better?" Kaerisk asked.

"Rain brings life when it falls gently. When it falls in torrents, it floods and life is taken away. But this is your storm. You shall determine what rain may fall."

"I will do everything I can to make change for the better."

[290]

"Then I would call you brother." The lizard's face cracked a wide smile. "I am Kiaron. Should the time come, I will accompany you into the maw of oblivion itself."

Doubt and Faith

"I still do not understand. Why was this secret kept from us?" Jelia asked.

The Setkaa elder had been extremely accommodating. They stretched a mat of several woven leaves over the Jelia and Kaerisk when the rain had begun to fall in earnest. As lightning crackled in the distance, the lizardman had answered all the questions Jelia had asked of him.

"There was no secret. We have always told you that we worshiped the Great Lizard Under the Mountain. We have always told you that our spirits were linked by her. We have always told you that it was by her will that we left the Deep. If you did not hear us, it was by choice, Scholar Jelia."

The emerald dragon furrowed her brow, earfrills slapping against the side of her head. "Tell me this. Does the Wurmqueen know of our plan?"

"Though she can see what we see, hear what we, I suspect she already knew of your plot. Her eyes and ears are everywhere, and we were retired only because we were no longer necessary. But my brothers in the Deep know now. They know the dragons will come for them. And I pray it will give them reason enough to turn back to us."

Her head drooped. "We may have to start all over and be more careful as to what our ultimate decision is." A moment of silence passed before the elder rose to her feet, nearly dislodging the tarp above her. "I must return to Luminous and hold a second vote with this new information. Come along Kaerisk."

The blue also stood, but did not make to follow her. "Elder, might I stay here until you hold your vote?"

Jelia tilted her head. "Do you not think it unwise?"

[292]

"Nao is not here and I have nothing to reveal. And if we do keep to the plan, I should like to know these dakael better."

Jelia tapped her chin with a wingclaw before nodding. "Very well. Please watch over Kaerisk until I return; I should have a course of action before tomorrow ends."

"As you like, Scholar Jelia. I am glad we were able to speak again, though I wish the circumstances were less dire."

Jelia forced a smile. "As do I, old friend." With this, she left the protection of the tarp and exited the village on foot. Through the trees, Kaerisk saw her take to the sky, subconsciously spreading his previously injured wing.

I wonder if I could fly in a storm someday. Or at all.

The elder addressed him. "Please make yourself at home, dragon Kaerisk. Any of the empty houses will do for the night; you should be able to fit inside them."

"Thank you for your hospitality, elder."

He smiled. "I am happy to host Jelia's child. She has done much for us and Setkaa do not forget. Please excuse me; I wish to discuss matters with my people."

Kaerisk bowed his head low out of respect and the elder Setkaa took his leave. As he did, the hatchling realized that the orange-robed Setkaa, Kiaron, had returned home. Despite the blindfold, he had moved swiftly and without notice, surprising the hatchling.

Though the town had returned to work once the tarp had been strewn, with Jelia's departure it once more ceased to function. The elder directed the other Setkaa into a small circle in front of the now-defaced statue and spoke quietly to his people. Kaerisk did not know what was said; the rain fell too loudly against the leaves above him. He did notice, however, that Kiaron was not present.

Curious, Kaerisk stepped out from the protection of the tarp and followed the Setkaa to his home. Like all of the houses, there was no door or covering over his entryway. The inside was quite simplistic at first look: a slab covered with furs, a table or pedestal of some kind, and a chest of stone. The chest had been left open; it contained at least one other orange robe. Kiaron himself sat at the table, carving a small stone object with a sharpened tool.

"May I come in?" Kaerisk asked.

Kiaron paused his whittling only for a moment. "Of course."

The blue dragon stepped inside and immediately rethought his concept of simple. The floor had been carefully carved with small bumps that Kaerisk noticed even through the thick scales of his paw. Peering closer, he found similar, but different bumps on the floor for every part of the home, designating some area within it. At first, Kaerisk wondered what purpose the textured served, but when his gaze returned to the blindfolded Kiaron, it made sense.

"You never remove that blindfold?"

"Never."

"Why?"

"This is what I have been chosen to do."

Kaerisk shuffled inside to get his tail out of the rain and sat on his haunches next to a free stool. "Would you tell me about it?"

Kiaron stopped his whittling and put his tool down. "You and Jelia have been speaking to the elder for some time now."

"You could hear us all the way in here?"

Kiaron shook his head. "Not exactly. I could listen through the elder's ears and see through his eyes. But to the point: you already know a bit of our history."

Kaerisk had learned more about the Setkaa in the few short hours spent here than in all the time he spent in

Luminous. The Setkaa had been the favored pets of the wurmqueen for a very long time, acting as her spies or agents. Though the elder Setkaa had not been particularly specific as to what they had done in the past, he had at least assuaged Jelia that their being there was not one of Nao's plots.

"There came a time when we were not as favored. And when this occurred, the Setkaa were able to look with eyes unclouded by the Great Lizard. They saw the plight of the other dakael and knew they would share their fate – pitted against one another, denied food when it was scarce, and potentially even purged. The Setkaa of old feared the last one the most. While we had witnessed humans, Shiris, even chirop being killed in great numbers when they disobeyed, we had always been spared the Wurmqueen's wrath."

From the little time I spent there, the Deep was a horrible place…

"However, we knew it was inevitable that we would suffer a purge. And so we required someone to which the Wurmqueen did not have access, to keep secrets and plans. For instance, one of my predecessors kept the Setkaa's desires to leave the Deep a secret until she allowed the Shiris to go. Fortunately, we never suffered a purge while under the Wurmqueen, but now we face that same fear – except that we must do it ourselves."

Kaerisk frowned at the thought. Outside, a chanting began to rise. Peering through the doorway, the dragon discovered the meeting had turned into something else. They stood in a circle around the defaced statue, chanting the same words nearly in unison.

"What is going on outside?"

"They are praying."

Kaerisk blinked. "Praying? To the Wurmqueen?"

Kiaron nodded. "But how - why? Isn't she your enemy?"

Kiaron rose, taking careful steps towards the entrance. Kaerisk stepped aside for him, but he placed his hand on the hatchling's side and a curious energy passed between them. Kaerisk could hear the words of the circle as clearly as if he had been standing beside them.

"Great Mother, grant to us the return of our brothers and sisters. If this is not possible, let them see the error of their ways. Grant us the strength to persevere if it comes to battle between us. Temper our forgiveness so that we might accept them back one day."

Kiaron removed his hand and the voices again muted. "Our actions may be conflicted, but so too are we."

Kaerisk frowned. "It isn't right for us to ask you to do this. Dragons – we never fight our own kind. Not like this. Not to the death."

"You do not ask what is not right."

"What do you mean?"

"We are a people of dissonance. We are desperate for change and willing to sacrifice for it, even if we do not agree on the path we must take. This is a matter that must be concluded; that we are given the opportunity sooner rather than later is neither good nor bad, it simply is."

Dragons separated themselves on ideals, but never fought each other for them. If our roles were reversed - could we make the horrible choice they must?

Kiaron tilted his head. "You seem pensive."

"It's nothing."

"I still appreciate it."

"What?"

"That you would question your right to ask this of us. You are unlike others we have met, even Scholar Jelia. I am looking forward to working with you, Kaerisk – no matter how dire the circumstances."

"What if the plan changes and your people do not need to go to war?"

"I would still prefer to see the Wurmqueen defeated with my own eyes. But if this is not possible, I hope you continue to visit as I will still wear this blindfold and cannot go far."

Kaerisk finally smiled. "You have my promise on that." As Kiaron returned to his table, the hatchling followed him. "What were you working on when I came in?"

"I carve little statues to serve as talismans or to communicate ideas. Would you like to try?"

"I'd love to."

For the remainder of the day, the two worked on carving a new statuette depicting a vanquished Wurmqueen.

<u>Shiris</u>

When Jelia returned, the rain had not yet stopped. She spoke briefly with Kiaron outside of the village, and then called for Kaerisk to join her. As the lizardman passed the hatchling, he placed a hand on Kaerisk's shoulder and smiled.

Then the council's decision remains unchanged.

Kaerisk followed Jelia out of the village and secured himself into the harness she wore. "Mentor, where do we head now?" Kaerisk asked.

Jelia drooped a bit at the word mentor. "Luminous stands firm, so we must travel to the Shiris. Hold on, Orban."

With several beats of her massive wings and a strange tingle of Riftwind, Jelia lifted him into the air. Kaerisk held tightly to her neck.

The elder's voice barely carried over the wind. "Do you think it is possible what she said is true? That she had her eyes on you from the start?"

"I don't know. When I stood before her, I felt as though anything was possible."

Jelia frowned, flying a bit lower to avoid some buffeting winds. "You did well, Kaerisk. But the Shiris will be a bit more stubborn."

"What can I expect?" Kaerisk asked.

The people of Setkaa were much different than the docile and attentive bipeds living in Luminous. He was not sure if it was living separately that had emboldened them or if it was their own form of Pride as the elder had proclaimed.

"The Setkaa are a spiritual people, but the Shiris preferred to hone their bodies and hunt. You may have to prove yourself to them as well."

Kaerisk didn't like the sound of that.

The trip did not last more than an hour. The elder flew closer to the trees as another clearing came into view. With a mighty beat of her wings, she landed upon the moist dirt just as rain began to fall. Her stomach rumbled as Kaerisk slid down her back, but she tried to hide it. Even one as practiced in the art of magic as she did not do so without suffering some ill effects; doubtless, she was famished.

The two entered the village. The Shiris worldview reflected in their structures; hides of animals had been draped over trees or poles that had been permanently staked into the ground. They were more rectangular than conic, though with an arched roof to keep the rain from collapsing the structure. A few buildings had been constructed with stone, but all construction on them appeared to be long abandoned.

They remind me of the Ishluke, but these are simpler.

If any of the Shiris had learned of the Wurmqueen and her teaching of magic, none had decided to join her. Several cat-people emerged from their tents and the jungle itself at the dragons' arrival. Unlike all of the other races he had thus far seen, the Shiris largely ignored clothing. A few had a scrap of leather here or there, but it made Kaerisk wonder if it was simply a matter of their fur concealing everything or if they wished to be more like dragons themselves.

Also unusual, the Shiris did not venerate an elder as their leader. The female who came to stand before them was rather muscular, youthful, and had an almost feral gaze. Kaerisk wasn't sure if they were coming to meet the two or eat them.

"Scholar Jelia. Your presence in this place is rare. Have you come to entertain challenges again, as you did in years past?" she asked.

Jelia twitched a bit at the cat's words.

"Oh, no, I am afraid not. But soon, there will come a test of that prowess, good Shiris."

"After they adopted this militaristic culture, they started challenging me to duels. I entertained them at first, though they were always one-sided; however, I came to realize that it would only foster animosity towards us if I continued to beat them."

Kaerisk scratched his head as the elder's voice scraped through it. The action drew the attention of the feline.

"Perhaps he will, then?"

"Oh, um. No, that's not why we're here exactly," Kaerisk said.

"Why, then?"

"War is coming between the bipeds of the Deep and the dragons. They are allied behind a fierce lizard much like a dragon, but not," Jelia explained.

"The Wurmqueen," the feline said.

"You know of her?" Jelia asked.

"Scholar, we have always known of her. You dismissed our ancestor's tales three hundred years ago as myth and legend, but the Wurmqueen was alive even then. We were the first to break her hold, though our only option was to run and try to find allies on the surface. That is why we were the first. She called you enemy. That is why we sought you as ally."

Jelia blinked at this information. Kaerisk had begun to notice that, whenever Jelia was surprised by something, she would always scrunch up her snout like she was about to sneeze. At that moment, it looked as though she might have blown the village away if she had.

"Please forgive me, all Shiris. Had I stopped to consider the possibility…"

"Scholar Jelia, you believed in us. It did not matter that you did not believe in our facts. We knew what was true. And in truth, it was you who shielded us from the claws of Lan'Dal and gave us refuge. For this, we remain grateful to you. If you go to war with the Wurm, then we Shiris will join you. We have a score to settle."

Jelia bowed her head low. "You do me honor. But I must ask one last thing of you. It is our intention to send a team of champions to face the Wurmqueen and kill her. It will be led by this hatchling. Will you lend your champion to him, my adopted son?"

The cat's eyes fell upon the hatchling with scrutiny. She must have been determining if the young dragon was worthy of a fight. Her ears were pinned back and her teeth were bared. The light rain matted her fur and made her look even more feral.

"He must tell our champion himself that he is to lead her."

"Where is she now?" Jelia asked.

"Deep in the jungle. Hearing of the Wurmqueen's rise, she has been training day and night to kill her and her vanguard. Let him see if she is so willing to follow him."

Jelia lowered her head to the hatchling and nodded. Kaerisk took a deep breath and walked by the feral cats, careful of their pensive tails that swished more rapidly as he passed.

Though the jungle was quite unfamiliar to him, frequent travel through the brush had worn down the foliage, marking a clear path. The drone of falling rain against endless green vegetation was maddening; it was difficult to tell how long one walked while in the humid flora. It was equally surprising when the plants cut away into a cleared piece of land.

The area consisted of flat, upturned dirt and a few trees that had been stripped of all leaves. The trunks sported several claw marks, indicating their purpose. With the vegetation cleared, the continuous rain had turned the area into a pit of mud. It felt a bit uneven as Kaerisk stepped into the ring; his weight caused him to sink an inch or so into the earth.

In the middle of the ring, tearing at one unlucky tree, stood a white feline with black spots. Sweat matted her fur from her excessive training regime. Her own blood stained the tips of her fingers from the callous use of her claws. As soon as the dragon entered, she turned to him. Emerald eyes caught him in a savage death stare. She raised her claws to him, tail flickering back and forth wildly.

"Have you come to fight me? I will accept your challenge, hatchling!" she bellowed in Lindorm.

Fortunately, Kaerisk had grown more adept at the language. "No, I'm not here to fight. Your people are going to fight against the wurmqueen and her followers. You and others will go and assassinate the wurmqueen herself."

"Then I shall lead this mission to victory!"

"No, you don't understand. I am to lead that party."

The cat hissed. "I accept orders from no one weaker than me. You will prove yourself or you will find another!"

"I don't want to-"

The time for words had apparently ended as she charged him. Her nimble feet moved gracefully over the mud. The blue tried to get into stance, but the mud was too slippery; when the cat leapt into him, he slid and fell to his stomach. Despite the hardness of his scales, she found ridges on which to hook her claws. She tore them loose, drawing blood. He roared in pain.

Digging his claws into the mud, he whipped the whole of his body around. The full force of Kaerisk's muscular tail slapped against her side and sent her flying back. She landed on all four limbs, skidding across the mud. The hatchling rose to his feet as she charged him a second time, but now he was sure of his footing. He snarled as he swiped his claws at her. Instead of catching her, she soared over his head. Turning midair, she dug her claws into his back and held on, riding him as she tried to tear the wings from his back.

Feeling her there drove Kaerisk into a frenzy. All the hatred he had for the wurmqueen and her minions surfaced at that dreadfully familiar sensation of someone on his back. He bucked wildly, hopping to and fro. Still she held on tightly, unable to do more. He couldn't pry her loose with his teeth at that angle and so he did the unthinkable. Throwing his head down and to the side and his tail and wings up, he leapt with his back feet only. His body jackknifed. The cat was taken completely by surprise as the sky flipped upside down and Kaerisk landed atop her. Her body sank halfway into the mud under his form.

As soon as he had accomplished this, he rolled rapidly onto his feet, slinging mud everywhere. The cat lay dazed on the ground as the rain began to intensify. He snarled at her as bloodlust clouded his vision. He held his muddied claws to her throat, choking the wind from her. Her claws dug into his scales as she tried to pry his grip from her neck. Gradually, her eyes turned from anger to fear.

It was in that moment he remembered the man whose life he had spared near Ur'Del. The eyes were the same then. The urge to kill was the same then, every fiber of his being screaming to finish off the threat as Father had always taught him. Father had been right then. If he had killed that man, he might have made it to Ur'Del without tearing his wing.

I might never fly because I –

He released her throat and drew away from her. She immediately began coughing and gasping for air. Kaerisk's tail curled around his forepaws, which seized it in a shaking grip. As she rolled over, stumbling to her feet, Kaerisk trembled.

I don't wish to become a monster. Sapphire, help me...

The cat tried to get back into a fighting stance, but when Kaerisk did not follow suit, her head dipped forward and her

[303]

shoulders slumped low. She swallowed to clear her throat. "You have bested me."

Kaerisk inhaled deeply and released his tail, trying to stand proud even as the ground he stood on felt as unstable as the earthquakes he had felt as a child. "Will you follow my command?"

"I will follow you anywhere. My life is now yours."

"I don't understand."

"I do not accept this defeat. Until I am ready, I will serve you. But when that time comes, I will fight you again. And I will win."

Kaerisk blinked, all haze of self-doubt fading at this odd turn of events. "You want to serve me?"

"No."

"Then why?"

"It is my way. I am Myrra, the strongest of the Shiris. I want someday to defeat you. The only way I can ensure that the day comes is to follow you."

"I still don't understand."

"Then do not. Return to my people and tell them what I have said."

She returned to attacking the log even more viciously than before and ignored all further words from Kaerisk. With no other option, he trudged back through the intensifying rain.

<u>Agency</u>

"We are going to have a chat about proper etiquette when dealing with unusual cultures on the flight home, Kaerisk."

The hatchling scratched at his head as Jelia's Riftlink invaded it once more. The dakael had accepted his words more readily than he had expected and far more graciously than Jelia. He no longer felt like a pile of meat in their eyes, but he was not sure if that was a good thing after Myrra's unusual proclamation following the fight.

"Shall we continue, elder Jelia?" the lead huntress asked.

"Yes. I need to know everything you can tell me."

The Shiris had not covered Jelia with a tarp of leaves as the Setkaa had; instead, only the huntress herself had a leather roof over her head. Some of the population had retreated into their leather tents, but most stood in the rain, fur matting to their bodies as they stared up at Jelia like sentinels. Kaerisk stood beside the emerald, who protected him from the rain with a wing. If the elder was mad, it had not overridden her maternal instincts.

"The city of learning was wiped out by the stones she had placed. All of them grew sick and died. After this, she sent out the Setkaa to watch the other cities for a time, to see if they found the cause, but none of them ever did. After that, a great feast was held, but my people were not invited, even though we had hunted the food."

Jelia's claws twitched. "I knew it! I was not somehow resilient or had better blood at all!"

"Elder?" Kaerisk asked.

"If I am right, the city of learning was Eidolon. That city was completely wiped out by the Illness, the first and only recorded outbreak affecting both hatchlings and adults. It was only at Eidolon that the Illness was contagious. When a few managed to escape the city, they recovered, but the other dragons stigmatized them. They were never again allowed back into society and settled somewhere in the mountains. The Illness isn't an illness at all – it's something external!"

Kaerisk whipped his head between the elder and the huntress. "Wait, are you saying the Wurmqueen created the Illness?"

"Yes, hatchling Kaerisk. The Wurmqueen did," the huntress said.

Then Icia's suffering, her death... I can't tell Zala. She wouldn't understand.

"There is only one thing that perplexes me. We never figured out that this was an intentional attack – why did she not repeat the process with every dragon city?" Jelia asked.

"We rebelled."

Kaerisk turned away from his thoughts and again listened to the huntress. The sound of the rain against leather and scale could not drown out her powerful voice.

"The humans and the Shiris could no longer brook the disrespect of the Wurms. Only a few of them existed and yet they ruled us like they were gods. A great war shook the Deep, biped against biped, biped against Wurm. For the first time, the Wurm did not win – the fighting dragged on for years upon years. It was only when a turncoat human sided with the wurm that the war ended and peace was declared – as though we were all friends once more!"

All of the Shiris hissed along with their leader.

"Our people tried to leave the Deep, tried to find help. We were instead slaughtered. Those that returned did so in chains! Slaves no longer to the Wurm, but the humans who had come to rule. Before a lifetime was out, all races of the Deep had nearly starved to death and the useless humans turned back to the Wurms to beg them for help. And the Wurms granted it to them – no longer did they rule the Deep like gods: they became gods!"

Jelia frowned. "I have heard this story many times, though you did not call them Wurms."

"We called them monsters. Monsters, you could choose to understand."

Jelia's head drooped. "That is the second time I have been told that. And I apologize to you as I did to them. But please tell me, if the Wurms again gained control, why didn't Nao attack with the stones?"

"Something changed. Nao was the only Wurm left, but still called herself queen. For the first time, she began teaching dakael magic, though not the Shiris. The Shiris were granted freedom instead and we took it, even if it meant death. Then we met you. The rest you know."

Jelia frowned. "She is the only Wurm left – her people have no future. That kind of hate and desperation…"

"Tell us, Scholar. How long must we wait before we can attack?" the huntress asked.

"I ask that you wait for three weeks at least. There is the possibility that the dragons will not accept our plan."

The huntress' tail fur stood on end at this information. "That is unacceptable. Regardless of what the dragons say, the Shiris will fight the Wurmqueen."

"Please, have patience-"

"We will not!"

As the two began to argue, Kaerisk spied Myrra walking into the village. With Jelia's admonishment still itching inside his cranium, Kaerisk shuffled towards the Shiris champion, hopeful to somehow undo whatever it was he had done. The moment he did, however, she changed course to intercept with the same fierce eyes she had when she had attacked him.

Maybe this was a bad idea-

He tried to backpedal, but it was too late. Myrra reached forward and grabbed him by the horns, but she did not strike him as Kaerisk expected. "I am not yet ready to challenge you again, dragon. But soon."

He pulled his head back, but Myrra held firm. "My name is Kaerisk."

"Then I am pleased to know my rival's name."

Kaerisk shook his head free. "I am not your rival!"

"Then what are you to be? My captor? My master? You have defeated me and I have nothing left to give!" she hissed. Fortunately, the argument between Jelia and the huntress kept the attention of the others from the rising agitation of Myrra.

He took a deep breath. "Please Myrra – I don't want any of these things."

"Then my line is pledged to you until I defeat you."

"What? No!"

"What do you want from me, dragon? We Shiris have lived in the shadows of the great lizards for the entire history of our people! Even here in the light of the great flame, we are still cast in the shadow of Luminous. We are not illuminated by your people; we are plucked like weeds, grown like Vitis! We pace at the boundaries in this invisible cage, looking outwards to the lizards above and fostering the same anger for them as we had for the lizards within the mountains. All while the dragons try as the wurms did, to breed out the anger and the strength from the Shiris so we are docile. So I ask you again. What do you want from me, dragon?"

Kaerisk lifted his head. "I want to be your friend."

Myrra jerked. "What?" She leaned forward, peered into his eyes for a moment, and then pulled back suddenly with a laugh. "You are a trickster! A jokester. I am amused, but I am not fooled. You maintain what is and will remain to be."

Does she really find my words so meaningless? Do the Shiris truly begin to hate the dragons like they hate Nao?

The hatchling frowned, distracted by the tension between Jelia and the huntress. The huntress spoke to Jelia much in the same way Myrra had to him, with puffed fur despite the rain. She decried the wurms as monsters they had to fight.

"Myrra, do you hate the dragons?"

Her moment of levity passed. She considered the question with a serious expression, though her feline face made it difficult to tell her mood without the obvious emotions of anger or humor.

"… No. I hate the fate given to our people. Dragons and wurms are just parts of that fate."

"I don't know that I can, but I want to change that fate someday. I do want to be your friend, Myrra. I want to be a friend to all the Shiris, all the dakael."

She snorted. "You are young, and stupid." The rain began to lessen overhead as the argument between Jelia and the huntress concluded, the elder's statesmanship somehow calming the Shiris. "But, I suppose, so am I. My pledge remains and my line will serve you, until you or I break the chains."

"I accept this Myrra – but know that you, and your line if necessary, will be more than servitors to me."

She grabbed his horns again with teeth bared, but she did not seem angry when she spoke. "We shall see, dragon Kaerisk. In the meantime, watch your tail." She released him and flicked his nose as she walked by him into one of the tents.

[309]

As her tail slipped inside and Jelia finally caught sight of him, he tried to figure out if he had made things better or worse.

<u>Ambassador</u>

The rain finally ended on their short flight back to Luminous – not that Kaerisk could enjoy it as Jelia not only censured his actions regarding Myrra, but also informed him that they would be leaving Luminous to head north almost immediately. While Jelia ate and Delaan learned of the success of their trip, Kaerisk questioned how they could ask the other dakael if they were not under Luminous' protection. Jelia replied they would need all the help they could get, and that if both the Ishluke and Vitis were to assist, it would help cement their right to be outside of the Deep. Kaerisk wondered if the injured human he found would be asked as well and if he could even be trusted.

Delaan kept staring at Kaerisk when he thought the blue hatchling wasn't looking, as evidenced by a quick jerk of his head whenever Kaerisk's eyes caught his.

Is he that worried about me? Maybe he should be, but...

With the meal complete, the pair began the trip north. The flight from Luminous to Lan'Dal took two days; the emerald's wings beat cold air as he held on for his life. The hatchling felt in awe of himself. The land below seemed to span forever and all of it he had somehow crossed. As he lay awake below a brilliant canopy of stars on that first night, he questioned if he truly made the journey or if he had been dreaming the whole time.

On the third day, the Deep Mountains loomed high into the sky and the forest of Lan'Dal came into view. Two dragons escorted the pair into the village, where the Matron greeted them with dignified respect. The dragons remained on constant alert, as the forces of the wurm rested less than a day's march away.

The rolling grass domes teemed with activity. Kaerisk looked to them in wonder; though they were similar in shape to the domes of Ur'Del, these were sunken into the ground and covered over by the grass that grew wildly throughout the forest. A male elder stood in the entrance of one of these domes, looking at a passing group of females – one of the Wings of which his sister had told him. In his arms was a very young hatchling, perhaps still a whelpling, unable to yet voice its thoughts.

Jelia said that it was like San'Lux, but in reverse. True, the males seem to be isolated and care for the children, but...

The passing Wing discussed quickly, and then bounded from the village. As they took to the sky, another Wing returned, almost like clockwork, each dragon carrying a fresh meal. Kaerisk marveled at it. It was only now that Kaerisk understood why Zala had asked about community back in Luminous.

So this is the community Zala sought. In San'Lux, dragons stood alone, but here, they stand together.

"We have kept this city secure with our vigilance and diligence. But I take it you are not here to merely visit, Scholar Jelia," the Matron said. Her words returned Kaerisk's attention to the matters at hand.

"Luminous prepares for its plan for the Council."

"Would you share it, daughter of the heart?"

Daughter? That's right. Jelia was born here, wasn't she?

"We wish to muster a force of bipeds to drive the Wurmqueen's horde back into the Deep and strike at the wurm herself."

"Biped against biped? A dangerous concept, but with plenty of precedent. I'd not so willingly put my trust in them, but I know your ways are different. I respect them."

[312]

"And what is Lan'Dal's answer?"

"We believe that a force of hatchlings would more than suffice to bring down the bipeds of the Deep, once they had been coaxed into battle with the elders."

The thought of more hatchlings descending into the Deep sent shivers down Kaerisk's spine. His paws tightened and his eyes fixated on the Matron. "What about Kaezala?"

The Matron's face wracked with displeasure at his unsolicited voice. The blue bowed his head in apology before she answered him. "Her Wing is too young for such an attack."

"I know well your ways, Laniela. And I know that your hatchlings are surely the only ones who could accomplish what you would have them do, for they are both powerful and dedicated to the survival of their peers. But even knowing this, I am not sure I could support that plan. It is with heavy heart that even one hatchling should be risked," Jelia said. Her wing brushed against Kaerisk.

The Matron frowned at this. "The Heart of the Firstbourne is indeed a heavy one, Jelia. Such a decision would tear at me for the rest of my days – the fate all of us fear. If you are not in a rush, I should like to discuss this with you in private."

"I would gladly discuss at length, but there are some pressing matters. Fortunately, I have my ambassador." Jelia gave a slight grin to her adopted son.

"Ah, yes – Zala's brother," Laniela said.

"Laniela, would you have someone lead Kaerisk to where the grassmen are?"

"Of course." The Matron spoke quickly with another dragon, who left soon after. "Wait here, little one, and someone will be with you shortly. Jelia, please join me in my lair." The Matron led the Scholar into her dome lair without any more regard to the hatchling.

[313]

The trees of Lan'Dal towered far above their hillock homes. Kaerisk stared at them much as he had nearly a month ago after crossing the hellish swamp. One of the trees had its green head of leaves shaved clean and atop it had been grafted a great platform; it occurred to him that it was the first time he had ever seen a draconic structure built of wood. He wondered what purpose it served, but it was large enough to hold at least two elders.

"Would you look at this one? He doesn't seem to know what's going on."

Kaerisk blinked and returned his attention to the earth. He found himself surrounded by three female hatchlings, peering at him with scrutinizing eyes and smug grins. Their leader, a green with piercing purple eyes, leaned in close to him and then blew a ring of smoke into his face. He coughed a bit.

"I thought that foreign males were supposed to be tougher than ours. He doesn't look that impressive to me," she said.

"He's seen some scraps, looks like," a red one said. She jerked her chin towards the wing that had been torn at Ur'Del. He held it closer to his body, acutely aware of how asymmetrical it had become.

"Don't think he'll even be able to fly," the last one said.

"That works for me. Might as well keep a male close to home," the green one said.

Kaerisk cleared his throat. "Excuse me, but are you the ones who were supposed to take me to the Vitis?"

"I did not ask you to speak," the green one said.

Kaerisk rose to his full height, his wings spreading behind him. "I did not ask permission."

She laughed. "Who do you think you are?"

"Kaerisk!"

[314]

Zala's voice broke the circle of hatchlings. She nearly ploughed into him as she embraced him in a wing-hug.

"Kaerisk? Your brother?" the green asked. "The one who-"

"Yes." Zala nuzzled her brother and turned towards the others. "Was Tyraisa giving you trouble, brother? She always leaps before she looks."

The green turned her head away as her name was called. "I-I didn't realize. I apologize, Kaerisk."

He regarded the green and her entourage. "Who are they, Zala?"

"They are members of my Wing. The red is Gella, and the purple is Ydel." Zala smiled at them brightly, despite whatever mischief she may have thought they were getting up to.

He rubbed the back of his head. He faintly recalled that Zala had joined a Wing, but they had not discussed it much while he was recovering in Ur'Del.

"They asked us to take you to the Vitis. Did you come to practice your language with them?" she asked.

"Something like that. Actually, Jelia wasn't sure if Lan'Dal had destroyed them or not."

Zala beckoned for him to follow and the group left the village. They fell into a diamond formation, which make it somewhat difficult for him to walk beside his sister, who took the lead. The path they traversed was not well traveled, but it had seen increased activity as several of the plants along the footpath had begun to wither.

"Most of the Vitis did die that day. Those that remain here tend to their garden, but the Matron believes we should protect them for now," Zala explained.

Kaerisk tilted his head. "Why?"

Tyraisa pushed past his tail. "The dakael always go for the Vitis, so they're bait."

Kaerisk frowned. "What garden?"

"You'll see."

Zala wasted little time getting caught up on Kaerisk's trials in Luminous. She was surprised that Delaan had joined him there, but she seemed glad of it. He failed to mention the reason for his coming.

Zala, on the other hand, was open about her time in Lan'Dal, far more so than Kaerisk expected in front of others. She related that she was placed into a Wing that was a bit younger than her. Before her coming, Tyraisa had been the eldest; initially, she did not take kindly to Zala being there. The two shared a laugh as they remembered their first hunt together as a Wing and how Tyraisa had been so confident before the hunt, but could not bring herself to kill the deer after they had caught it. Even Gella and Ydel spoke fondly of the event and looked at Zala with pride. The whole interaction made Kaerisk smile.

Jelia was correct. You did make the right decision, sister.

"We wouldn't have caught the deer in the first place if we hadn't followed Zala's instructions," Tyraisa said.

"It was just what brother taught me, Raisa. If it hadn't been for him, we wouldn't have made it through the swamp or survived on the plain." Zala leaned into him, resting her head against his.

Kaerisk churred. "I wouldn't have survived without you either, Zala."

"Zala's told us a little bit about San'Lux. The Matron probably wouldn't be pleased with the idea, but I'd like to see what you can do someday," Raisa said.

Kaerisk frowned a bit. "The skills I have were given by my father. I am just glad I could find a positive use for them." Before he could consider the idea further and remember why he came, Zala nosed his head up and smiled at him. He smiled back and then looked to Raisa. "Why would the Matron not be happy about that?"

"She has chilled considerably towards San'Lux. My mom told me they used to hold hunts and contests together, but they don't do that anymore. Most of us didn't even go to the Festival of Flame," Raisa explained.

Kaerisk's frown returned. Zala's smile was not enough to counter it this time.

"We are here."

Kaerisk looked up and found that his somber face was quite a home in the Vitis garden. It consisted of upturned earth and grassmen, standing half-rooted in the soil. A few flower buds bloomed at their feet, gentle shades of green, pink, and white. They sang with the wind, a sort of low, whispering melody that left the area feeling paradoxically morose and tranquil. A few hushed their tune at the arrival of the hatchlings, but most continued on, as though they slept where they stood. Maybe they did. With no eyes, Kaerisk could never tell if they were alert or not.

One of the Vitis uprooted and hurried over to them, his roots moving carefully through the earth. He then waved one arm and one half-regrown stub at them frantically, as if warning them not to pass.

Kaerisk smiled. "Hello Correth. It has been quite some time," he said in Lindorm.

The grassman paused his movement and then withdrew one step, slanting backwards. Suddenly, he lurched forward, wrapping his arm-tendrils around the blue hatchling. Zala's entourage tensed at the action, but Kaerisk smiled. He had been around bipeds long enough to know the action was one of happiness.

"Kaerisk, are you alright?" Raisa asked.

"We'll be fine. Give us a minute, okay?" Zala asked. Her Wing agreed and retreated some distance to chat amongst themselves.

Correth withdrew from him and expanded his ribcage to speak. "Elder brother, good to see. Thought perished." Correth too spoke in Lindorm, perhaps wisely hiding his knowledge of the draconic tongue.

"Elder brother?" Kaerisk asked.

Correth motioned widely to the Vitis behind him. "Different understanding, of time and family. No disrespect." Correth's vine-body writhed a bit in embarrassment.

"You don't need to be so apologetic to me, Correth. You tried to help us and you saved my sister when it mattered most. That's all I care about."

Zala hummed sheepishly, tilting her head. "You really have improved at the biped-speak, brother. I can barely follow what you're saying."

I'm counting on that, Zala.

The Vitis's body stopped twisting about, its tiny leaves stretched up towards the sun. His good arm reached forward and twisted its vines around Kaerisk's arm somewhat awkwardly. Kaerisk remembered faintly that he and the Vitis elder had once locked arm-vines together, and he wondered if the gesture was one of friendship.

Correth's chest-lung expanded once more. "Why have you come?"

"The one who sent the bipeds upon you, the Wurmqueen Nao'Dariva, seeks to use bipeds to fight the dragons. The dragons of Luminous believe that a force of

[318]

bipeds would be best to combat her in the Deep, while we dragons fight out here."

"Want our help?"

"Yes. Two races have already agreed."

Zala listened carefully. Words like fight and combat caused her brow to furrow and her eyes glanced to her brother. Kaerisk felt her gaze on him, but tried not to show it.

Correth made another sweeping gesture to his brethren. "Remain free. The rest, killed or captured to be harvested for their excrement."

"Excrement?"

Correth reached into his body and produced one of the fruits he had given to them to eat some time ago. The blue hatchling felt a little green at the realization, but Zala seemed to miss its meaning.

I wonder if Zala still likes that stuff?

"Vitis will help. But some must remain in this sacred garden."

"What is this place?"

Correth drooped at bit, and then stood up rigid. He brought his good arm to where his throat should be and wrapped around it, slowly tilting back while his half-healed arm thrashed wildly. He then stood and motioned to his flower, flipping his hand forward. Next, he knelt down and made a small hole in the dirt. He mimed picking something up, and then placed the imaginary thing into the hole, closing the soil up again. At last, he returned his attention to Kaerisk.

"Your dead still live here?" Kaerisk asked. Correth nodded. "This place is grave and egg-shelf both." He cast his gaze upon the garden-graveyard with reverence. The strange and haunting song seemed to convey the mixed emotion of the plot. Correth looked a bit wilted, perhaps thinking of those he had lost.

[319]

Zala already had some idea of the garden's purpose, but it was not until her brother held that moment of reverence that she fully understood. "Oh! I am sorry Correth, I didn't know what this place was really for." She stepped back some. Correth reached out and placed his vines on her maw gently, as though to say he felt no offense.

"Any help that you could give would be appreciated, Correth. But there's one more thing," Kaerisk said.

Correth regarded him.

"Our plan calls for a team of bipeds led by a hatchling to kill the Wurmqueen. Are there any among you who would go?"

Zala's brow furrowed ever deeper as the two spoke. Each word seemed to concern her more and more.

Correth picked up a nearby stick and placed one end on the ground. He held it as though it were a spear. "All others gone, I remain. I shall repay you."

Kaerisk nodded in thanks. He nearly bumped into Zala's head as she blocked his path.

"Brother, what hatchling is to lead this team?"

Kaerisk tensed up. "Did you understand all of that?"

"Enough. We can recognize some dakael words because we need to know when someone is going to fight or not. There is a team and it's going to be killing something. There's only one thing I can think of – that creature you saw in the Deep. So who is leading?"

Blast it! I didn't want you to know… or worry. But I can't lie to you!

"… I am."

"That's too dangerous! You can't go back down there alone!"

Zala's sudden change in mood drew her Wing back to her. They gathered behind her like a wall of scale.

"Everything okay, Zala?" Raisa asked.

"No! No it's not! Kaerisk is going to fight the Wurmqueen!" Zala exclaimed.

The scaled wall drew back at this. "You mean that thing everyone's afraid of? The wingless dragon?" Raisa asked.

"I won't be alone. I'll have powerful bipeds with me. And the other dragons might not even-"

"But the Wurmqueen nearly killed you! I can't let you go alone. I won't risk losing you again!"

"Zala..."

"I have mother's fire in me, brother. You even said you needed my protection when we parted in Luminous! When I lost you to the Deep the first time, I was devastated. It was like losing Icia a thousand times more! I will not go through that again. I will not let you go alone!"

"Zala, are you serious?" Raisa asked. Her face was wracked with surprise and horror both.

Kaerisk looked away, trying to think of anything that might dissuade her. "You can't go, Zala. It's not even my decision. This is Luminous' plan, not Lan'Dal's."

"Then we'll see what the Matron has to say." She turned her tail to him and stormed back through the forest.

Old Friends

"You haven't said anything since you found out. Are you alright?"

Jelia's voice cut through the wind. Kaerisk could barely hear it, but he made no indication that he did. He felt a little betrayed, but more than anything, he was worried.

I can't believe Jelia agreed to it. It's one thing to risk my own life, but...

"The Matron has faith in your sister. You should as well."

"I do, but..."

"It's politics. They agreed to support our plan at the meeting if Zala joined the strike team. To be honest, it makes me feel a little better. Another dragon couldn't hurt."

The Matron had promised to give his sister special training for the mission. If this training was anything like the Matron herself, it was likely to be terribly harsh and demanding.

Even with it, though, will you be alright? Do you truly understand the horror of the Wurmqueen as I do?

Night descended upon the green and ever rolling plains. The herds of horses he had chased at the beginning of his journey settled in to rest while the nocturnal creatures – chirping insects especially – woke for their nightly days. The village he had visited was not exactly where he had left it; they had moved further north and settled once more into the tent city. The two had discussed the Ishluke long before their flight; Jelia worried they would scatter upon seeing a full grown dragon, but the hatchling was sure that if she approached by foot, it would be less frightening.

They landed a short distance outside of the village, but the Ishluke immediately rode out to meet them as though they had been watching the skies. They circled the pair of dragons and Jelia ushered Kaerisk closer to her as she lifted her wings in battle stance. Kaerisk pulled away from her when he spotted someone he recognized.

"This is very familiar to me, Geen."

One of the circle broke ranks and dismounted. His sudden action caused the group to slow, all eyes focused on Kaerisk and Geen.

"You return! Your speech is much improved. It seems you found other dragons."

"I have. And I've seen and learned a lot too."

Jelia relaxed as Geen rested his spear on his shoulder. The other riders came to a stop, though they still formed a circle around the dragons.

"What brings you to this place?" Geen asked.

"In my travels, I encountered a ferocious beast called a Wurm. We have come to ask for your help."

Geen and his men grew tense at this revelation. Jelia shifted, her weight leaning on her hind paws as though ready to pounce. After turning to his men, he gazed at the hatchling with uncertain eyes.

"It would be best if you came and saw," he said.

"We can't take them back there! It could be a trick! We have already panicked with-"

Geen lifted his hand to him. "Have you forgotten that with this hand, we avoided dragon-flame? Did you forget that Kaerisk is our brother? Let him have his voice as our culture demands!"

The Ishluke who had spoken wriggled in his seat, but his eyes fell upon Jelia. "The green one is much bigger and she is not one of us. She should remain here."

"Anywhere my hatchling goes, so too will I," Jelia said. The Ishluke, even Geen, tensed a bit at this proclamation.

"Please Jelia, let me do this," Kaerisk said.

"How can I just leave you here?"

Her eyes were focused on the riders. Each still carried their spear, though they weren't currently pointed at either dragon. Kaerisk placed a paw on hers and peered up with some effort; she craned her neck down to him.

"I put my trust in the Ishluke before. I still trust them now. If Luminous truly believes in helping bipeds, it has to start here."

Jelia gave a bemused look. "Listen to you, dictating to me on the nature of dragon-biped relations. I suppose it is harder when the hatchling-" She stopped herself, biting her lip. "I will be waiting." The emerald dragon lay down, her green scales blending in with the verdant plains.

"I won't be long," Kaerisk said. Jelia nodded and the hatchling walked beside Geen, who began leading him back towards the village.

Even though the village had relocated since the last time that he had seen it, much of it remained the same. Strong wooden sticks still held up the animal hide tents and a bonfire burned in the middle of the village, enticing him with cooking luyak meat as it had months ago. He shuddered at the corral as they passed it, but no one seemed to notice. The women still clung to their young in terror at the sight of the dragon, but their children were more curious than afraid, perhaps because they recognized Kaerisk.

One thing was vastly different. In the far back of the village, looming high over all of the tents, stood a stone pillar. This pole of rock had been carved and shaped, each rung depicting some terrible fate, be it fire from dragons, or teeth, or claws, or bipeds fighting other bipeds. But the very tip of the pillar was a pressed in dragon head, rounded and open mouthed as if in a roar. If Jelia had stood next to it, the eyes of the head would have peered into her own. Kaerisk recognized the face. He had seen it before.

"Nao'Dariva..." he uttered. His words sent some of the Ishluke fleeing in terror.

"What ill fate has come to us? Have you come to enact the doom promised by the Wurm?" the elder asked. He stood in front of his tent, wrinkled face twisted between fear and rage, but entirely wracked with displeasure.

"No, elder of the Ishluke. I have come only to talk," Kaerisk said.

The elder paused a moment, before nodding. "I will speak with my brother. Come inside and we will discuss." He went inside without waiting for the others to follow.

Once Geen, several other riders, and Kaerisk were inside, they sat much as they had on the day he first arrived. The tension had returned. The elder stared at the blue for a very long time before speaking, as though expecting Kaerisk to be the first to speak. He tried, but every time he did, the elder would hum loudly, as if displeased or impatient. At last, he spoke.

"I cannot decide what omen you are. Since the arrival of you, your sister, and the black, strange occurrences have showered upon us."

"What has happened?" Kaerisk asked.

"First, the luyak moved even further north. Something must have frightened them. Then the wild horses ran through our village, trampling one poor soul to death. But the worst has been the totem."

"Totem?"

"You saw it outside. The totem of Nao'Dariva."

"She was here?"

"Her emissaries. Humans, dressed in scale. They came amongst our people with powerful weapons and toppled our horsemen with ease. They did not slay us, but they did warn us that death approached. They told us that dragons would come to kill us all, because we did not have the protection of the great and wise Nao'Dariva."

"You think we-"

"We said we had met a dragon before and that they did not wish us harm. And to this, the champions laughed. One of them lifted his jewel-covered hand and the ground itself trembled. Fire and earth rose up, carving itself to his whim. Each time he spoke, another scene would form, telling us – death by fire, by tooth, by claw. And atop it, she watched. Nao'Dariva, the Wurmqueen."

Geen slammed his fist against the ground. "We could do nothing."

"They promised to teach us what they had learned – the magic. But only if we would swear our loyalty to the Wurmqueen as our people once had before our history had even begun. Only if we would fight the dragons. We did not know what to do. If we trusted in dragons, in you, then Nao'Dariva would surely send her champions to slay us. They defeated us with ease – we would have no chance against them. But if we sided with them, we faced the same deaths that they swore to protect us from – those prophesized by our ancestors, the great horse-tamers who abandoned the Deep."

"What did you decide to do?" Kaerisk lowered his head, much as he had when he accepted the punishment for his sister's murder. His eyes closed, he waited, half-expecting them to either capture or slay him.

What we would ask them is no different than what the Wurmqueen does. No other dragon is their brother as I am, so what kind of promise can I really make them?

"We told them that we would not return to the Deep."
The hatchling looked up, a bit of Pride in his face.

"We told them that we would need time to decide what
we must do. They were displeased, but they promised us a full
passage of moon-darkness. We still know not what we can do.
But we mustn't lose our way of life or our lives."

Kaerisk's tail curled around his forepaws. "We dragons
learned of Nao'Dariva recently. I met her myself as I tried to
find other dragons. She was terrifying. She harmed me just
because-" He paused. He would have finished 'because I was a
dragon,' but such a reasoning had seen many bipeds killed. He
frowned at the thought and continued. "She had so much hate.
And she was powerful, yes. But the dragons are stronger. We
have no desire to harm you. Indeed, we have come to ask for
your help."

"Our help?" Geen asked. The elder also looked shocked.

"Our elder dragons cannot descend into the Deep, where
the Wurmqueen roosts and the bipeds hide. We wish to lure the
bipeds out into a battle, defeat them, and then push them into
the Deep. There, several bipeds and hatchlings will chase them
even further and strike down all of the followers of
Nao'Dariva."

"The Deep frightens us, great dragon. Those who were
our enemies are now even more bitter and powerful still. All we
have are our spears and our horses. None of us will venture
inside," the elder said.

"I would," Geen said.

"Geen?"

"I have fought by the side of the great dragon and his
kin. You know my courage; you know my strength. These
dragons mean what they say. Will our foretold end never come
or is it only delayed? I cannot say. But if I can delay it further

with my spear, aiding those who I know to be good creatures, then I shall for the sake of all my people."

The elder lit his pipe and took a puff of it. His arm shook ever so slightly. His fellow Ishluke seemed invigorated by Geen's words.

"We will fight with you, dragon. But what can we do? It is not long before the champions of Nao'Dariva return," the elder said.

They can't just wait here… it's a gamble; if the True Council does not vote to accept this plan, then…

Kaerisk took a deep breath. "Gather your people and head south to the dragons of the forest – of Lan'Dal. They watch over the Vitis, who suffered as your people might. They may help you as well. When the time comes, we will drive them back into the Deep," Kaerisk said.

The elder stared at his shriveled hands. "We will need assistance to cross the swamp. At the very least, a path carved through the behemoths."

That place was terrible to cross… I hope Lan'Dal will assist them, because I do not know if we have time to do it ourselves.

"I will try to secure aid for you within a few days."

"Then we will begin preparations in the morning. I know not how many will share Geen's courage to go underground, though."

"I will only need Geen if it comes to it. I will be leading a force to kill the Queen herself."

Geen puffed his chest proudly at this piece of information. He appeared ready to slay the wurm at that moment.

<u>Preparations</u>

To Kaerisk's surprise, Lan'Dal readily agreed to assist the Ishluke in traveling through the swamp. Three elder Wings were dispatched, setting ablaze a path through the swamp by strafing it repeatedly with dragon flame. Jelia assisted as well, directing the effort and striking down the behemoths with careful interest, especially directed towards the stones at the creatures' core. The burned-out path left behind was far more solid than the one Kaerisk himself had taken and every step of the horses on the fire-blasted sand cracked with a strangely satisfying crunch. Watching the elders work was both fascinating and terrifying and he began to have a sense of just what could be accomplished if the dragons worked together.

Four days later, a famished Jelia and a tired hatchling returned to Luminous. Biped and dragon alike gathered at the arms of the plateau when they arrived, though not with a much needed meal. "Scholar Jelia," one of the dragons said, "the human has woken. He refuses to speak to any but you."

"Then I shall see him immediately. Prepare food for myself and my hatchling," she replied. She walked past the gathering, but it followed her. Kaerisk was caught up in the crowd.

"But Scholar! We believe that he might be a spy sent from the Wurmqueen," the dragon said.

"Even we bipeds think so!" one of the Shiris gathered exclaimed. His voice drew the rousing agreement from several others among the mob. Jelia turned abruptly, causing the mob to collapse against itself.

"If this is so, how are we to know for certain unless we ask? Not long ago, I was reminded just how important it is to lend a certain amount of trust to those who would otherwise not have it. Let us treat him with respect, until such time as he proves unworthy of it."

No further argument was made; the elder would not be dissuaded. She entered into Luminous proper while the mob discussed amongst themselves whether or not she was right. Kaerisk pushed through the intellectual melee.

Once inside the twilight cavern, Kaerisk spotted Jelia entering into the medical cave. He followed her immediately. The spacious chamber appeared to have been a dragon's personal lair at one point, but had been repurposed into an aid station and place of study. Two dragons practiced the healing arts within its walls and served as doctors to those with injury.

The human had been laid on a raised stone shelf covered with leaves that served as bedding. His wounds had been dressed with herbal compacts that sped the healing process. Indeed, the canvas of his skin was less black and crimson and more pink and green. Kaerisk lifted a wing to his neck, the compacts reminding him of his old injury.

The human looked up at the emerald elder with strained eyes. "Are you the one they call Scholar Jelia?"

"I am."

"My name is Vandys. I was one of the humans that served the Wurmqueen. When the Setkaa joined us, they spoke of dragons that were good to them, but did not share the secret of magic. I pried and learned that they were not kept as pets or slaves, but allowed to live free."

"Then you come seeking amnesty?" Jelia asked.

"No. I've come to seek help."

"Help?"

"Nao'Dariva. She has taught our people magic, yes, but she has done so at the expense of our freedom. We are her slaves, though no one will speak this truth. Most follow out of fear, some out of ancient loyalty. But all who follow are made slaves to the Wurmqueen."

"You would ask us to liberate your people?"

"I would gladly fight to do so myself. But I haven't the power to face her alone."

Jelia mused on this for a time. When Kaerisk came beside her, the human noticed him. Confusion painted his pink face.

"You… seem familiar," he said.

"I was the one who brought you here," Kaerisk said.

"You did that for me?"

"It was the right thing to do."

Jelia watched the interaction silently. The human reached out to the dragon. Kaerisk hesitated. Vandys waited. After a moment, the blue came to the human's side, who placed a hand on his scales. It was awkward, for both of them.

"Do you wish to kill the Wurmqueen?" Jelia asked.

"Elder?" Kaerisk asked.

"With everything that I am," Vandys said.

"Then focus on healing. If you are well enough, you will have your chance."

With this, Jelia turned and left the room. Kaerisk slowly pulled back, letting the man's hand drop, but his eyes spoke a new fire. Vandys lifted his hand onto the bed-shelf and stared at the ceiling as though trying to bore a hole in it with his gaze. Kaerisk did not know why, but something about it seemed horribly familiar and left him unsettled. He fled from the aid station to rejoin Jelia.

"What was that about?" Kaerisk asked as soon as they were safely away from earshot.

"The humans deserve a chance to liberate themselves. Besides, you'll need all the help you can get," she said. Already she was directing a dragon to her, carrying a meal of venison.

[331]

"That's not what I mean. Are you sure we can trust him?"

"Kaerisk, I haven't the time to explain my reasoning right now. I have delayed the Council by ensuring our plan can work. I leave for the Site of Ascension immediately."

"What?"

"I'll explain it all later. For now, spend the rest of the time preparing. Speak with the elders in the library. You need a plan to beat her."

"Mentor…"

Jelia nearly pounced upon the meal brought with little more than a half-choked thanks. The other elder did not seem to mind and left shortly after. Kaerisk followed him outside. Jelia could be just as stubborn as he was and it availed him nothing to speak to her when she was so set on her path. Following her direction, he traveled to the library.

Inside the normally quiet chamber were three elders, already discussing. One was green, one was red, and one was the gold, Zelbaran. Delaan also stood by Zelbaran's side, but contributed nothing. Kaerisk came over to them and their conversation immediately halted to greet him.

"We were just beginning to debate. Scholar Jelia told us you'd be coming," Zelbaran said.

"She did?" Kaerisk asked. He was impressed; Jelia had been out of his sight for no more than a few minutes and she had already planned a trip across the country for herself and a meeting for him.

"Yes, yes, come. Have a seat," the green said. Kaerisk did so next to Delaan.

"Did you meet with all the bipeds?" Delaan asked.

"I did. We have their support," Kaerisk said.

Delaan looked shifty for some reason, but said nothing more. Zelbaran cleared his throat as an indication to be silent.

"The first strategy is the most obvious: send the bipeds in close to strike her," the red said.

"Direct, but there is the problem of her scales. Legend says that only the strongest dragons could cut through their hide; indeed, most Wurms were killed by crushing. Superior weapons would be needed for such an assault, sharper than dragon claw," Zelbaran said.

"Dragonhide has been pierced before, I don't see why wurmhide would be any better. Especially where the plates meet the scales. Moreover, where would we get superior biped weapons?" the red asked.

The green peered at Delaan. "While their smiths have never crafted biped weapons before, their knowledge of metallurgy is uncanny; surely they might know of metals that could pierce wurmhide."

"Ur'Del?" asked the red.

"Of course. We shall send an envoy asking for the weapons to be made. Who will be amongst you, Kaerisk? And tell us what you know of their ability to fight," the green said.

Kaerisk blinked and shook his head before answering. He felt as though the conversation was moving too fast. "A Shiris – she was training with her claws when I met her. A blindfolded Setkaa; I don't know if he'll stay blindfolded or what martial skills he has. An Ishluke rider and a grassman... I saw both wielding spears, so they likely know how to use them. And my sister."

Delaan stiffened at his last words.

"Two spears, claws, perhaps a weaponized hammer of some sort for the lizard? It would be hard to miss even blindfolded if it were large enough and it fulfills our need for crushing implements," Zelbaran said.

"Kaerisk brings up a good point; we should not fail to ready the hatchlings either. Perhaps claws for them as well," the green said.

"Good idea. I've a list now. Kaerisk, the legends say that the Wurms were extremely powerful in magic. Is this true?"

"Yes. Even asleep, she lit crystals," Kaerisk said.

"It will be a part of her attack, for certain. Let us discuss ways you might counter it while the bipeds work," Zelbaran said.

Minutes lengthened into hours. Again and again, the elders taught him of how to disrupt the flow of Riftwind and he practiced it with them until he felt hungry enough to gnaw his own arm off and devour it. Delaan looked on silently.

At some point in the training Delaan had left the library, but Kaerisk did not notice it until Zelbaran called the meeting to a close. Kaerisk's stomach rumbled in revolt; the elder offered to hunt for him that day, to which he gladly agreed. Instructed to wait at Zelbaran's lair, Kaerisk left the library.

Delaan waited for him, just outside. "You're really going through with this."

"I must, Delaan."

"It's going to happen."

"What?"

"The Council will agree. Ur'Del will support your plan as well."

"You don't know that for sure."

"I do. Kaerisk, do you know why I was really sent here? To San'Lux even?"

The blue blinked. Delaan pawed at the ground as though ashamed.

"It's not just to learn. My parents send me to other cities to spy on them. I learn what they're planning and we have time to choose to support them or not. I don't like it, but it's what I have to do. It's just how politics works for us."

"Why are you telling me this?"

"Because I wish I could have lied. Told them something else, anything else. I don't want to see you or Zala get hurt. I've never had a friend like you before, Kaerisk. Most befriend me because of my family line, because I am to be the next leader of Ur'Del. But not you. Not Zala. I don't want to lose what we have. Lose you."

Kaerisk smiled lightly and walked beside his friend, leaning into him. Delaan's head drooped as low as Kaerisk's foreleg.

"Come with us if you're so worried."

"My parents would never allow me. And I'd just be in the way."

"My father didn't allow me to leave."

"I'm still not that strong, Kaerisk."

"You are stronger than you know."

"… I'll find another way to help you. I swear it."

"I'll hold you to it."

Delaan lifted his head and scurried off into the sparkling crystal twilight. The next morning, Delaan was gone. Kaerisk trusted him to keep his word. And so he returned to the elders to continue preparing for the battle to come.

<u>Tensions</u>

"Jelia, I have a bad feeling about this. Are you sure he can be trusted?" Kaerisk asked.

Vandys stood alone, staring out from the twilight of Luminous proper into the shadows of its arms. He watched the bipeds and dragons as they prepared for travel and war. Most of the bipeds who planned on rejoining their people had already joined the march.

"Sometimes the hardest thing to do is trust," Jelia said.

Each day had been torturous. Every moment passed agonizingly slow, whether he was hunting in the forest, claw-striking at trees, speaking with the remaining bipeds on the nature of their warfare, or learning more of countering both Riftwind and the Queen's stratagems. Jelia stood aloof all that time, ever watchful of her adopted son, but also ever silent to him. Truthfully, Kaerisk wished she had not been so quiet and hated himself for it.

"I know. I'm just afraid."

"So am I, Kaerisk."

"He recovered just in time for us to leave."

Vandys turned, as though sensing the elder and hatchling speaking about him. At a distance, he waved to them and smiled, but it looked wrong somehow, as though there were something more behind his eyes left unseen. Kaerisk tapped his adoptive mother's hind leg with his tail.

"I see it too," Jelia said. "Keep an eye on him. But never let your suspicions ruin your chances."

"My chances?"

"To turn an enemy into a friend. The fate of humanity might lay with this single man."

Kaerisk frowned.

I want to trust him. All humans, even. Is it just memory of my suffering that taints me with distrust? Or is it Father's lessons, still clawing at my mind?

"You need all the help you can get, Kaerisk. It may be convenient for him to appear now; we do not know if the Setkaa transmitted our plan. But trust first."

The hatchling sighed. He turned his gaze upon the human and never let it falter. Vandys stared back with the same intensity.

An hour passed and they took to the skies. Jelia flew ahead of them. Kaerisk had been relegated to the back of the elder red with which he had discussed the plan to kill the Wurmqueen. It wasn't that Jelia could not bear to carry him to his dangerous future – well, not that alone – but rather, for the other passenger on the red's back. None of the other dragons would take the human for fear of treachery; the red only agreed if Kaerisk was present as well. The blue held tightly to the harness around the red, claws hooked securely into the ridges of the crimson scales below the leather. One arm and part of his body extended over the human, who had less natural ways of maintaining a grip. Kaerisk was not only guard, but also an additional harness for the human. Wind whipped past them. Vandys smiled at hatchling that held him the same as he had on the ground. It made Kaerisk uneasy.

"Do your people tell stories?" Vandys asked.

"Of course," Kaerisk replied. The wind nearly drowned out his words.

"We do too. I am reminded of an old story my father told me."

"About flying?"

"No, swimming."

"Swimming?"

"Yes – a scorpion wanted to cross a pond, but couldn't swim. He asked a frog if he would take him across the water. The frog refused, knowing the scorpion would sting him."

"Makes sense."

The red below dove to avoid more turbulent winds. Vandys held tighter to the harness, but his eyes never left the hatchling above him. As the elder righted, the human continued.

"The scorpion argued that he would die too if he stung the frog. So the frog agreed. Halfway across the water, the scorpion stung the frog."

"Why'd he do that?"

"Frog asked the same thing. The scorpion told him, 'it's my nature.' They both ended up dying."

Vandys laughed and finally averted his eyes from the hatchling. He seemed to be looking at the mountains to the north, but Kaerisk could not be sure. A thought seized the dragon.

"Which are you more afraid of? The story or falling?"

Vandys grinned at him as the dragons turned north.

"The story."

Two days later, Vandys, Kaerisk, Jelia, and the red arrived in Ur'Del. The dragons and geldin of the city had anticipated their arrival and the city was warm with the aroma of cooking meat, almost hiding the odor of burning oil. The elders ate their fill ravenously; they would be leaving for the front as soon as they had a chance to digest and rest. Vandys wandered to the side, examining some of the innovators' machines.

Two dragons from Lan'Dal were the next to arrive, bearing Geen, Correth, and his sister. She scampered to him and embraced him in a winghug.

"It's good to see you, brother."

[338]

"It's good to see you, too. Did the Matron train you well?"

"I've the bruises to prove it."

He smiled, but his tail paced back and forth in time with his sister's nervous twitch. Despite their positive tone, Kaerisk feared what was to come. They turned their attention the bipeds, who were getting used to their footing again and marveling at a city that could survive in the desert.

Correth turned his sightless eyes to the sun, covered his face with one arm and then slowly crumpled like he was wilting.

"I thought Vitis liked the sunshine," Geen said; apparently, Geen had gotten used to their interpretative language in the time Kaerisk had trained.

Correth writhed and then hid his flower from the sun with his hands.

A final dragon arrived from Luminous. He had been about an hour behind the red, as he had to visit both Setkaa and Shiris villages to pick up his cargo: Myrra and Kiaron. They had remained behind while their people had already departed for the north.

"What is that whirring noise I hear?" Kiaron asked, earfins slapping against his blindfold. He followed Myrra by keeping a hand on her shoulder.

"Who cares? It's too hot! Let's get inside!" Myrra exclaimed.

"Why are you complaining? You're naked," the lizard said with a smirk.

"This fur is meant to keep me warm, you know!" she exclaimed, the hair on her tail standing on end.

"Why is she naked, anyway? And how does the lizard know that with the cloth on his eyes?" Geen asked.

"Ah, there you all are," Delaan said. The group turned to face him as he arrived from the Manufactory. He was accompanied by a stocky Geldin wearing gold-rimmed spectacles. "I don't envy you. Not one bit. But a part of me wishes I could come with you."

"There's still room for more, if you feel up to it," Kaerisk said.

"My place is here. Maybe someday, I'll choose my own grand adventure. But not today. Follow me and bring your bipeds. I kept my promise. We at Ur'Del have been preparing some gifts for you."

Delaan turned and began to walk away. Kaerisk called for the bipeds to follow and they did, though none appeared to notice Vandys at the far end of the line.

Delaan led the group into the Manufactory. There, several geldin rushed to them, each bearing items and weapons that might be of some use. Naturally, the dragons were fitted first: shimmering claws of metal, reinforcing their natural talons. It fit the two well. The amber which Kaerisk still wore around his neck was then charged by several Riftwind crystals that the geldin had brought.

"Master Delaan helped to forge those claws himself," the old geldin added to the hatchlings.

Next, Correth was given a specially designed spear. Rings adorned the length of the shaft, into which the vine-like body of the Vitis could entangle and tie. The only way he could lose that spear was to have the whole of his arm severed. To prevent that, a metal ring mesh covered his torso to negate cuts to his fragile vines. Most important was a helmet of shining metal; oddly conic, its purpose was to protect and allow plenty of space for the nerve flower at the top of Correth's head.

To Geen, similar armor and weapons were given, but the helmet and spear were different. The spear functioned in two ways: a primary point, sharpened to the finest edge for the piercing of the wurm's hide, and a reverse hook for climbing onto the beast or tearing off flesh. The helmet was made of leather, but a single dragon scale rested on the left side near the eye. The geldin explained that if Geen pressed a finger upon it, his eyesight would be temporarily improved, allowing him to pinpoint where to thrust his spear.

Myrra balked at the metal claws, insisting she would tear the beast limb from limb with her bare paws. The geldin were insistent, however, as was Kaerisk - the latter to whom she relented. She also forewent the armor they had designed for her, preferring to have nothing at all besides her claws and fur and not even Kaerisk could convince her otherwise.

To Kiaron, the geldin gifted their masterwork: the Thundering Warmaul. The massive spiked ball on a stick had a charged Riftcrystal within it; each strike of the hammer would not only cause the sound of thunder, it would send a bolt of Rift energy through the victim. As with the Shiris before him, Kiaron decided against armor, preferring to focus all his strength upon holding the massive weapon.

"What about me?" Vandys asked.

The other bipeds turned their eyes upon the human perhaps for the first time. They immediately became tense, holding their new weapons at the ready. Vandys lifted his hands up as though in submission, while Kaerisk came between them; his action calmed them somewhat, but they were still wary of the surprise guest.

The geldin leading the fitting of the weapons adjusted his tiny gold-rimmed spectacles up his protruding brown nose. His fingers were long and muscular. "We were told there would be six of you, not seven. We have nothing for you, son."

"I can't very well go down there defenseless and hope to be of any use," Vandys said.

"What do you propose we do? You are to set out tomorrow morning. There's no time to forge a biped weapon of your size, to say anything of armor," the geldin said.

"Is there metal on hand? And could I have access to the forge and perhaps some assistance?" he asked.

"You believe you can craft a masterwork weapon in one night's time?"

"Yes."

Delaan looked to Kaerisk. The blue frowned to the black, uncertain.

Is this where Vandys hid his sting? Or does he truly mean to help?

Zala clicked against the hard ground, her new claws sounding as she came to stand by her brother.

"Is there any other option?" Kaerisk asked.

"A spear-tip could be forged from cast-off metal. We could make a spear in a day, but it may not be as good," the geldin said.

"It'd do nothing against the Wurmqueen. Give me a chance," Vandys said. Jelia's admonishment hung above the blue.

Vandys does deserve a chance.

Kaerisk rubbed under his chin with a wing. "No harm in trying, I suppose. Could a backup weapon be prepared at the same time?"

"It's a simple process, so I don't see why not."

"Then will you give him access to the forges, Delaan?"

"I don't know what my parents would say, but I trust you, Kaerisk. Go ahead," Delaan said, ending with a nod to the geldin. He returned the nod and led the human away.

"Delaan, where are we to rest? I think all of us have had a long flight getting here, some more than others," Zala asked.

The remaining bipeds slowly relaxed as Vandys left, revealing just how tired the flights had left them.

"We'll cloister you in the nursery again. Let's head there now," the black said, leading them away. "Try to get a lot of sleep – you'll head out early tomorrow."

"Kaerisk, why is there a human with us?" Zala asked quietly.

"Not all humans are our enemies. You remember Sapphire."

Zala lowered her head at the memory.

"I may presume to speak for all of us, but I think we share her concerns," Kiaron said. "The human is a liability. You had best be sure we can trust him."

Kaerisk regarded Vandys one last time, suspicion clouding his heart. The human wasted no time in setting both dragon and geldin to work for him. A gleam in his eyes of unbridled creativity and all of its triumphs and horrors haunted Kaerisk as he walked away.

Terror and War

"Kaerisk! You have to get up!"

He stumbled to his feet, unable to find his footing. The nursery where they had rested the night before had proven as comfortable as it had while he was healing, but now it and the ground below him shook with a mighty tremor. As dust fell from the sandstone ceiling, he scurried to the door, which Zala held open. Beyond it, he could see his biped companions fleeing towards the far exit. As soon as he was through, Zala abandoned the door and joined him in rushing after the bipeds, surprised that her speed more than matched his own. The group piled outside.

Smoke and fire now covered the city of Ur'Del. The corpses of several geldin and chirop littered the sandy floor of the Innovation of the Firstbourne. The city's inhabitants scrambled over them without pause to put out the fires and repel the attack.

Through the haze of the smoke, Kaerisk saw that the entrance he had passed through months before was now choked with battle. Humans held a line against the physically superior dragons with weapons he had never before seen, blades and hammers of horrifying make. Behind them, still more humans rained fire and earth onto the city and the dragons that blocked the entrance. It prevented the defenders from pushing out.

"Brother!" Zala exclaimed. She crashed into him suddenly, knocking him out of the way. A trio of chirop flew in over the walls using a scaffolding of earth raised from the ground like the totem he had seen at the Ishluke village. They had nearly stabbed Kaerisk on their way down. They landed just a few feet away and turned to fight with their shining metal daggers.

"Out of my way!" Del'nura broke through the smoke and lunged, a powerful claw crashing into two of them, but missing the third. The sole remaining chirop retreated into the smoke. "Thank the Firstbourne you are still here. Get the dakael into the Manufactory before you get caught up in the fighting!"

"What about our mission?" Kaerisk asked.

"We can't get you out of the city like this. You're just as likely to get attacked by our dragons in this melee! Come quickly!"

Kaerisk called to the dakael to stay together in Lindorm. Nura led the way, pausing only a moment as a blast of fire erupted from a nearby dome, igniting the oil present. The black smoke made it hard to follow the russet-colored dragon, hard to breathe. Kiaron was nearly left behind when his coughing caused him to lose contact with Myrra, who had been acting as his eyes.

A blast of air from a dragon's wings broke the smoke temporarily. Through the haze, Kaerisk saw an elder green surrounded by chirop. They chattered and screeched as the dragon roared his challenge, but they did not run. These were not the cowardly dakael he had seen at Lan'Dal. When the chirop leapt they did so as a team, latching onto the dragon's hide and stabbing their hooked daggers into the weakest spots of his scales. As his blood spilled out onto the sand below, the smoke closed again. Through it, Kaerisk could hear the dragon scream in pain, and then go silent.

"Inside!" Nura shouted. The Manufactory loomed above them, each of its entrances guarded by at least one dragon. The gatekeeper tensed as the dakael came to the fore, but Nura quickly reminded him of the plan.

"We can fight too!" Myrra exclaimed, flashing her metal claws.

"Inside!" Nura shouted again without turning back. "I must find my mate! Protect the hatchlings!"

"Elder!" Zala exclaimed, but Nura charged once more into the cloud of smoke.

"C'mon, inside. We'll figure something out," Kaerisk said, trying not to frown. The group passed by the elder sentinel and stood just inside the dome. The fires of the forges burned untended. The sounds of metal and machines were replaced with screams of battle.

"How could they have known to attack now?" Geen asked. At the question, the dakael peered at Kiaron. When Myrra pulled away from him, he tensed.

"I had nothing do to with it! Blindfold! Remember?" Kiaron tapped the side of his head where the blindfold wrapped around it.

"No. It's the one who is missing that betrayed us," Myrra said.

Missing? ... wait, where is -

"Vandys..." Correth's word came out as a wispy sigh.

Kaerisk growled. "Now hold on! It's too soon to say that anyone betrayed anyone. Where is he?"

"Brother?" Zala asked.

"They think the human did this somehow."

"... Did he?"

Zala... I don't need any more incentive to be suspicious of him.

"There you are!"

The group turned towards the voice. Delaan scurried up to them, followed closely by Vandys. On the human's back was some sort of leather casing, secured over his shoulder. His smile was met by Myrra's hissing.

Delaan drew back slightly. "Is she, er – she won't attack me, will she?"

"She's not angry with you, Delaan," Kaerisk said. The black hatchling relaxed only a bit; whatever relief he had at seeing his friends faded as he looked beyond the elder to the horror outside. "What are we supposed to do?"

"I don't know. We were working in here when it happened. Bipeds were suddenly everywhere, and then they set fire to the storehouse. They knew exactly where to strike us. It doesn't make any sense." Delaan's tail shook out of sync with the rest of him. "Father gathered most of the hatchlings and told us all to stay in here. He ran outside, trying to find the rest. Then the smoke became too much and the elders guarded the entrance – I tried to get someone to go for you, but no one would listen. Everyone's fighting, but we were unprepared for... this."

Myrra clanged her claws together as her tail flicked agitatedly. "I cannot understand the black one! Does he tell us where we must go to fight?"

"He recounts his being here. He has nothing useful to-" Kiaron suddenly stopped speaking and stumbled away from Myrra. He struck his leg against a low wall of a discussion pit, and then sat down on it.

"Kiaron? What's wrong?" Kaerisk asked.

"They are fighting," he said.

Zala rolled her eyes. "Did he just figure that out?"

"No – not this battle. Battle everywhere. My people – I have never felt anything like this."

Zala focused. "Brother, did he say everywhere?"

Kiaron shivered. "Yes. The Setkaa are in Lan'Dal and San'Lux and even Luminous – they are fighting everywhere." Zala's eyes went wide with this revelation.

"We'd better act fast then," Vandys said.

Myrra advanced on the human, flashing her claws. "This is your fault! It is always your fault! Humans are incompetent betrayers!"

"Is this really a time we should be fighting amongst ourselves?" Vandys asked, backing up.

"We do not need human help!" Geen exclaimed, following Myrra in for the kill.

"My people are as much involved in this-"

Correth lifted one arm and let its vines unravel and fall. "Weavers. Plans." He too joined the group. Zala and Delaan kept back, only half-aware of what the dakael were saying.

Sapphire...

Kaerisk leapt between the mob and Vandys, snarling. The dakael champions pulled back at the sudden action. Vandys smiled, but Kaerisk tried to ignore it. "Enough! Maybe this is all indicative of some ancient grudge yet to be settled or maybe it's the stress of this moment. I don't know. But I know this. Several months ago, I met a young human. My father brought her to me and forced me to be near her. In that time, I learned so much about who she was. Sapphire was no animal, but a thinking, reasoning being. She had hopes and dreams. She had a family, friends. When I told my father of this, he struck her down in a flurry of gore and hatred."

Zala's brow furrowed as she began to understand his words. "Brother..."

"The hatred that my father has for bipeds pales in comparison to that of the Wurmqueen. She threatens to destroy everything that dragons are, that dakael are. For the first time, we are united, equal, in a common purpose. This moment – this is why I abandoned my father's lair. Because I wanted to see a world where bipeds do not live in fear of dragons and dragons regard bipeds as I did that human: with dignity and respect. Now is the time when my hopes and dreams are tested. If I was wrong, if we do not stand united, all of us will die. Our families will die. Our cultures will die. Stand with me. Stand together. Put aside whatever anger you have for each other and vent it upon the Wurmqueen. Let us make a new future."

The smell of burning oil still choked the Manufactory, but the mood had changed. Myrra stared at her claws quietly. Correth had rooted firmly into the sand. Kiaron had risen silently behind them. Geen nodded to Kaerisk in understanding as their dragon companions sat stoically.

The smile on Vandys' face was gone. He stared at Kaerisk almost as though he had grown another head. He suddenly looked away from him, to the forge. "I apologize."

"For what?" Kaerisk asked.

"For everything. But above all, for questioning if your people told stories."

He undid the wrapping on the object strapped to his back and took hold of its cross-shaped grip. It was like a dagger, but Kaerisk could never have imagined once so large and straight. The bluish metal of the blade seemed to throb and hum as the cloth fell away. Its edge was honed to a paper-thin line; its tip was sharp enough to pierce a dragon's hide. Its golden hilt was inscribed with beautiful symbols of ancient script. A blood red ruby formed the pommel of the carefully wrapped grip.

"This blade, forged by dragonfire, will bring an end to the Wurmqueen. I promise you this," he said.

Kaerisk nodded to him. In that genuine moment, the hatchling could at last remember Sapphire when he looked at this human.

"This is all well and good, but how are we supposed to get to the Wurmqueen? We were supposed to attack while she was distracted," Zala said. She glanced over her shoulder at the dark clouds suffocating the city.

A moment of silence passed as the group racked their brains with that problem. Delaan shivered, but stepped forward to speak. "I know a way."

Tunnels

The dust still hung in the air as Delaan took his first
tentative step into the hole. He had cleared away a pile of dirt
with his tail, well-hidden behind some stone storage bins, and
revealed a small door in the ground. The tunnels below were
almost as black as the oil-rich smoke billowing up from the city
burning down around them.

"You're sure this will lead out?" Kaerisk asked.

"I used to play in these tunnels as a kid. They go all
over the place, even outside the walls," Delaan said. Zala
handed him a Riftcrystal, which he held in his free paw as he
shuffled down the stairs. Geen and Myrra looked particularly
hesitant about descending into the tunnels, but when Kaerisk
followed the black, so did they.

As eyes adjusted to the light, the extent of the system
became clear. Though the entrance they had taken was only
hatchling-sized, the stairs which they traversed were sized for
an elder; Kaerisk had to hop down a bit with each step, making
the going slow at first. At the bottom of the steps was a large,
straight passageway carved with Riftwind's perfect lines. In the
dim light, Kaerisk saw that the entrance they had come from
may have been much wider at some point, but had been filled in
by time, intention, or both.

"This place is huge! What is it used for?" Zala
exclaimed. Her voice carried much further than expected,
echoing down through the darkness ahead. Her frills lowered a
bit when Kaerisk shushed her.

"I don't know," Delaan said, leading them into that
darkness. "I kept my hideaway secret for a long time. When I
did finally ask someone, I turned to the smartest elder I knew
that wasn't in my family – he only explained that they have

always been here and that they aren't likely to be stable anymore."

"Didn't you ask anymore?" Zala asked.

"He wouldn't say more – next day, I was in serious trouble with my folks. Honestly, I'm surprised it took him that long to rat me out." The black gave a slight smile as he limped, keeping the crystal ahead of him.

Vandys held up the rear, one hand on the hilt of his blade, though it was once more shouldered. When he caught Kaerisk looking, he smiled to the blue. Kaerisk nodded and returned attention to the front.

There's no point being suspicious now. We have to get out of here and stop this.

Not long after, the tunnel came to an abrupt end. The way ahead had been collapsed with rock. Rather than be deterred, Delaan pulled a stone away from the corner and revealed another tiny passage. This one appeared to be less well-crafted than the one they had just traversed; the lines were incongruent, but natural. After slipping into the chamber beyond, the whole area lit up with Riftcrystals, which appeared to have been growing naturally in the cave. The multicolored glow left a sense of the fantastic in Kaerisk, who understood why Delaan had kept the place a secret.

"This way," Delaan said. The cave had three other tunnels leading out from it, but Delaan moved with purpose towards only one of them. The bipeds followed close behind the dragons, Kiaron having a hard time lugging around the large maul and keeping one hand on Myrra's shoulder.

At first, everything was quiet. Only the sound of the bipeds' armor and the dragons' metal claws tapping against the stone ground gave any sense of the passage of time. The tunnel opened into another cavern, webbed with pathways and pits. Below, the darkness loomed like a hungry maw, laced half-shut with rock bridges. Delaan shivered and kept to the center of the path.

"I used to love this place. But – after what happened to..." Delaan trailed off, almost catching eyes with Zala.

She approached him. "Delaan, it's-"

An eruption of sound and light flooded the walkways. Below them, dust rushed outward in a burst and hung over the pit before slowly descending into it. A throng of dakael rushed through the cloud of dirt, charging from a freshly opened crack in the wall. Kaerisk leapt forward, taking Delaan's crystal from him and covering it with a wing, hissing for silence.

After the main group of dakael had passed wielding their torches and their weapons, a pair of humans followed, wearing scaled armor that marked them as leaders of the Wurmqueen's forces. One of them appeared winded. The other appeared annoyed.

"Hurry up, Lucien. We didn't have time to finish the tunnels; we have to get this done before the attack is over," the annoyed one said.

"We're rushing into this," Lucien said, after taking a deep breath.

"We didn't have a choice. You let the hatchling escape."

Kaerisk risked peering over the side. The darkness and shifting light of the torch made it difficult to see, but he recognized the human – he had allowed him to keep his life during his dash to escape the Wurmqueen.

"Everyone was murdered by the flame monsters. The Wurmqueen never told us about them. And now we're going to break into the Manufactory and kill-"

Delaan's eyes went wide.

"Are you going soft, Lucien? The dragons kept us locked in darkness like this for untold generations! We will be free and they will all die. Old and young both."

"I won't do it."

"What?"

"I will face whatever punishment the queen wishes. But you are going on without me."

"You always were weak. I can't waste time with you anymore. Stay here and rot." The annoyed man pushed Lucien to the ground and then sprinted after the group of dakael. After Lucien returned the way he had come, Delaan turned to the group.

"They knew about the plan to hide the hatchlings in the Manufactory! They'll be slaughtered!" Delaan exclaimed.

"Should we help them?" Kiaron asked.

"If we go back, we lose our chance to attack the Wurmqueen!" Myrra exclaimed.

Delaan took a deep breath. "Follow me, now."

The black hatchling suddenly took the crystal into his maw. He turned and raced down the pathway. Kiaron struggled to keep up due to his contact with Myrra. Correth's uneven footing slowed the Vitis as well, but everyone kept sight of Delaan even as he turned through several twisting passages at top speed. He skidded to a halt before a pile of rubble, clawing frantically at one corner of it. Zala and Kaerisk assisted him as the dakael caught up to them, revealing a path spiraling upwards.

Zala began, "Is this-"

"Yes," Delaan preempted her after spitting out the crystal, "the exit is right above you. I can't go any further. I have to get back to the city and warn my father."

"But Delaan – the tunnels could be crawling with dakael!" Zala exclaimed.

"I have to try."

"Be safe, Delaan. We will put an end to this," Kaerisk said.

But... Did I-

"Delaan!" Zala exclaimed, but he put the crystal into his maw and charged back the way he had come.

Geen nodded after him. "The black is a brave one, too."

Zala tensed. "Brother…"

"Let's go."

Kaerisk slipped into the tunnel and ascended the spiral. Zala's tail twitched sullenly as she followed. At the top, he forced aside a small boulder. The bright light of the Eye shined overhead, causing him to squint as he stuck his head out of the hole. The city still loomed nearby, but the exit had been nestled in a small alluvial valley, long dried in the desert sands. Once outside, he could peek over the ridge and see that the battle still continued; a few dragons had pushed out from the entrance, but several of them had been brought down and were not moving.

Kaerisk waved a wing. Keeping low, they followed the valley away from the conflict. The dragons' wings would occasionally knock some of the sand free of the ridge, causing the whole group to pause in wait for fear someone had seen them. They huddled close to the ground, wings pinned as close to them as possible, crawling slowly away from the city.

Once enough distance had been put between them and the battle, they immediately rushed across the open sandy plain to the active river valley and began following the line of trees towards the Deep Mountains. Though they kept a brisk pace, they slowed a bit so as to not tire themselves before they arrived.

"Zala - do you think I caused all of this?" Kaerisk asked.

"What are you talking about, Kaerisk?" She trotted beside him and nosed under his chin.

"If I hadn't found out about Nao's plans, if I hadn't let that human escape, maybe she wouldn't have acted so soon."

Kiaron stumbled forward and placed a hand on Kaerisk. "Do not say such a thing, Kaerisk." Kaerisk looked up into his blindfolded face as he came to a stop. "The Wurmqueen had always planned to act. Sooner or later, this would have happened. But now your people have a chance to fight back. Ours have a chance to free ourselves of the Wurm, once and for all."

Correth stood before him, placing one arm on the dragon. The other arm motioned to the group, and then unraveled. His whole body drooped. The vines then wove back into the shape of an arm and Correth stood strongly.

"I think what he says is that we are all with you, Kaerisk. We will hold together," Vandys said. He beamed that unnerving smile, but Kaerisk found some comfort in it. He stared at the bushes where he had hidden months ago.

Maybe I did make the right choice then. Delaan will be alright. So will Lan'Dal, and San'Lux, and Jelia, and Father... Everyone is counting on us.

He took a deep breath. "Then we must hurry."

<u>Usurpers</u>

Darkness delayed the group for several minutes. Reaching this point had been surprisingly easy; the Wurmqueen's horde had tunneled much closer to Ur'Del than expected, leaving the overland strangely silent and serene compared to the devastation behind them. Even ascending the cliff had proven to be less challenging than anticipated.

This was fortunate, because any chance of success would require the element of surprise; their only guide would be the same glowing lichen that the hatchling had followed to his escape. Though the actual emission of light was low and the darkness would slow them down, once their eyes had adjusted it proved enough to see.

Far more challenging were the several paths branching off in different directions. He wished Delaan were here or perhaps had not lead them so swiftly through the tunnels below Ur'Del, because he felt quite lost in the Deep tunnels he had egressed so quickly. He remembered a straight exit with no branches, but coming from the opposite direction revealed sharp corners that he had not seen. With each tunnel, he had to crouch low to the ground and closely examine at what he had passed once in haste several months ago.

Blood. He hadn't remembered it because he was so numb, but he smelt it now. Above him, the ceiling broke into a shaft leading up to parts unknown. The blood he smelled – dragon's blood – was his own, coughed out in a stupor after his rough fall. The gem around his neck began to glow.

"We're close. Get ready," he whispered.

The bipeds tightened their grips on their weapons, while Zala and Kaerisk both lifted the tips of their claws as they walked, trying to be as silent as possible. Every breath seemed to bounce off the wall like a scream giving away their location. Fear of broken silence was more maddening than the darkness or the fear of the battle to come.

Light. Muffled sound from within the chamber thankfully hid any breathing the party made. They listened closely. A human voice speaking Lindorm bounced down their tunnel.

"My queen, the battle goes well. Would you have us join them?"

"No, I am expecting guests shortly. I have no desire to fight them myself."

The Wurmqueen. So she knew this as well.

"Your clairvoyant oracle has foreseen this, exalted one?"

"I'll tell you a secret now, my trusted minions. No one, not even I, can truly see the future. But those who have seen so much of the past know what is possible and likely. We have struck them in their homes; they already had planned attack and so reprisal is expected. The Wurmlines have not been disturbed – they will not strike with magic. And so I expect to see hatchlings. I want you to tear the wings from their back when they arrive."

"Yes, magnificent queen!"

"Now, do not disturb me until then. I shall be watching the battle above unfold."

In the tunnel, Myrra grew anxious, tail flickering back and forth rapidly. Her flexing claws threatened to crash against each other with a clang at any moment.

Correth waved his arms first towards them, and then the open cave, as if to ask the plan.

"She expects hatchlings. We should go in first," Vandys whispered.

"That suits me well!" Myrra said, barely able to contain her enthusiasm.

The rest silently agreed. The bipeds shuffled past the two dragons, coming to the very edge of the light. Myrra led the way, fur on edge. With a signal from Kaerisk, the group rushed into the light. Zala and her brother followed shortly after, no longer hiding their metal-tipped claws, which clinked against the cave floor. Screams of bipeds washed over them as they dove into the light.

Kaerisk's eyes readjusted to the false sun. Shafts of light fell upon the battered corpses of the Wurmqueen's elite guard, dead before they could even tout their precious magic or Wurm-touched weapons. Nao'Dariva beat her tail against the ground in agitation, shaking the chamber. The brown lizard was no longer in a silk robe, but plates of golden armor, reinforcing her already impenetrable hide. Her rounded muzzle turned upon the group with a sneer.

"Dawnbringer. I am ever impressed that you have set aside your fear to visit me again. Such courage to stand before your doom. But worry not. I won't kill you. I will twist everything that you are and break you until you are less than an animal!"

She roared, shaking the chamber with her lungs alone. Her body crouched low, ready to pounce upon her attackers at any moment. That they had not engaged her was proof of her ferocious appearance.

"We won't let you rule the Deep any longer, Nao'Dariva!" Kaerisk shouted, trying to look fierce. In the presence of the Wurm, his voice was smaller than the most distant of thunder.

"You've employed bipeds for your dirty work. Tell me, Dawnbringer, do you think this was a wise decision? You may see them as noble savages, but they will always be savages. I have kept them in check for thousands of years, dear hatchling. I am master and jailor both. In time, they will turn on the dragons too."

Correth's chest puffed up like he was ready to pop. "Kaerisk and Zala aided my people against impossible odds. I will stand by his side until I wither!"

Kiaron tore loose his blindfold and flung it to the ground. His eyes were as red as the ruby Kaerisk had torn from the statue. "Now I see the monster that has lorded over my people with my own eyes! Kaerisk has given me the chance to free my people. I will stand by him to see that freedom used well!"

"The time of the Wurm is over!" Vandys shouted, holding his sparkling blade high.

Nao'Dariva turned to him with a wide, snake-like smile. "Oh, that weapon? Did you forge a new Blade of Vandys? A Wurmbane?" The human held the sword before him, his furious gaze all the answer the queen required. "Very well. As I am sporting, go ahead. Strike my chest as hard as you can and let us see how your ancestor's fabled blades fare."

"So be it!" the human shouted, screaming at the top of his lungs as he charged.

"Vandys, it's a trick!" Kaerisk shouted.

The human did not listen. He rounded a large pillow and, jumping as high as he could, slashed the sword against the wurm's hide. It tore through the golden plates as though they were nothing, but it was repelled by the beast's hide without difficulty. She smiled down at him as he stared up in horror.

"My dear, favorite pet. I kept your line close to me because I knew very well what kind of vicious monsters you are. Did you think I wouldn't alter what information your family passed down to forge those cursed blades? You followed the recipe, but you failed to realize it was my recipe."

[360]

Her paw lurched, impacting Vandys squarely in the side. Kaerisk swore he could hear his bones cracking as he flew through the air, landing in a pile of pillows as his sword clattered beside him, dragged on by momentum. Correth ran on stilted vines to the fallen, lifting up his spear to protect him.

But the queen did not advance. Her spiked tail slapped against the ground as she stared at Kaerisk. "Now, Dawnbringer. Your weapons are useless. Let me show you that your touted Riftwind is as well."

She reared up, lifting her paws almost to the ceiling. Kaerisk did the same, preparing to counter her energy with his own; the moment he tried, he felt as though he were rolling down a mountain. The ground shattered beneath their feet and encased them in tombs of earth, only the heads of the victims sticking out, not by Kaerisk's interference, but the queen's will.

"Risky! I can't get loose!" Zala exclaimed. He could see his sister's neck writhing against the restraints, her body hidden by the stone.

The queen laughed. "You haven't figured it out? You've seen three and think there is but one. Waydeep is not Riftwind – any attempt to counter my energy with your own will fail."

No! Everything I trained for was for nothing?

"Don't feel too bad, though. Your people's ignorance was my goal all along. Let me give you something worth feeling bad about though: I will crush the life out of each of your biped companions, one by one, and then I will devour your sister's soul. And when that is done, I shall give you back to the dakael of the Deep until you are nothing more than a shell with stumps on your back where wings had once been!"

All of his companions began to scream as the rocks tightened around them, save Correth, who could not create the air for it. The queen seemed unsatisfied with this, and so turned her paw on him first; the squeezing intensified, popping off his helmet, which clattered to the floor. The rocks crushed his vine-body until his juices ran from the cracks. His vine-head fell to the side, the flower atop it withering. A small seed trickled down the rapidly browning petals, and then clattered down the stone prison to the floor.

"Stop this!" Kaerisk shouted, his eyes tearing, his paws unable to move in their stone prison. His only reply from the queen was her bellows of laughter as she pointed her hand at Geen.

The walls began to move. Small, biped-shaped chunks began to pick themselves from the earth, ruining the sky-like mural painted around it. The Waylund approached and surrounded the Wurmqueen, gems on their heads and bodies glowing dimly.

Nao paused her violence to address them. "I did not call for you."

"Apologies, great queen, but the master begs us speak." Their voices seemed projected, and vibrated in unison throughout the chamber. Kaerisk was uncertain if he was hearing their voices or sensing them.

"Master? I am your master!" Nao exclaimed.

"Only Waylund master Waylund."

They joined hands before the queen could react and a blinding light erupted from their gemstones. Though the queen soon broke the circle, shattering one of the Waylund against the far wall, whatever they had done already taken effect. The queen panted heavily; the earthen restraints around Kaerisk weakened.

The magic shattered around him when another source of Waydeep disturbed it. Kaerisk thought it was from the Waylund at first, but when he focused his teary eyes, he realized Vandys had been the source. Putting that knowledge aside, he emerged from the earth as his sister did, helping her to dig out the rest of their biped companions.

"And you, Waylund? Then die!" The creatures leapt upon her, tearing her armor from her body, even as she shook them violently. A few even used the Waydeep against her, spikes of earth slamming against her hide to no effect. It still seemed hopeless, until one of them drew energy directly from the queen herself. The vivid russet scales dimmed in that spot and when it was struck, the queen roared in pain.

She shook the remaining Waylund from her and retreated to the large tunnel. "You only force my escape for now. When this day is over, I will rule from a new world: the surface!" When the Waylund attempted to follow, she struck violently against the walls of the tunnel with her body, causing it to become unstable. Tons of rock fell, but the Waylund lifted their arms; the glow from their gems erupted into a bright light and enveloped them. Above them, the earth ceased to fall, creating a small corridor through which Kaerisk could see the Wurmqueen flee towards the Starchild chamber.

As his companions moved cautiously towards the Waylund, Kaerisk lingered near the crushed form of Correth. Spotting the seed, he took it carefully in his paws and held it to his chest.

I won't let you die in vain.

He slipped the seed into his scale-pouch and sprinted after his companions. He paused to look at the same ruby-headed Waylund that had allowed him freedom months before. The stone-man nodded to him.

"You know now what you must do," he said without speaking. "We have sealed her Waydeep temporarily, though she has limited command of the other Forgotten. Go quickly and end this, before she can use the Wurmway to escape."

"There's a Wurmway down here?" Kaerisk asked.

[363]

Zala tilted her head. "You mean the crystal-thing that sucked us far away?"

Kaerisk affirmed it and led most of his group through the tunnel held open by the Waylund; Myrra had already run ahead, though she was still within sight. She had paused before the flaming sphere that was the Starchild. As Kaerisk's eyes adjusted, he could see the Wurmqueen retreat down one of the side paths, leading to what seemed to be another tunnel.

Nao paused to turn. "I see you are as persistent are you are foolish. Allow me to reward you with fire!" She lifted her forepaws and flames began to wreath her; however, instead of the inferno that the Miasma had commanded, the crystals along the wall began to shatter. As the riftcrystals rained down on them, the Starchild began to lose its perfect spherical shape and the flares jutting from the living flame became erratic and violent.

"Do not tarry! I will not be able to stop myself from engulfing this chamber!"

"Starchild?" Kaerisk asked, lifting his head.

"Go!"

Kaerisk rose up and began to bolt after the retreating Nao. His companions followed behind him, with Kiaron in the rear, moving slower due to his huge maul. A jet of flame rushed before Kaerisk, causing him to pause. A second took its place when the first faded, but low enough for him to leap over it. Above him, below him, beside him, the flames of the Starchild rose up like angry claws raking the walls.

"C'mon!" Kaerisk shouted, his companions struggling to keep up with him and Zala. Kiaron made a jump, but his tail was singed and his screams echoed in the chamber. "Kiaron!"

"Keep – going!" he shouted through gritted teeth.

They ploughed forward through the intensifying heat. The Starchild looked like an egg, rising from its nest. They reached the other side of the chamber, only to discover the wurmqueen had created a thin barrier of stone between them. Going back was no longer an option as the stone path they had taken began to melt.

"Kiaron, can you strike the wall with your weapon?" Kaerisk asked.

The Setkaa nodded, hoisting it above his head, even as his body strained against the pain that surely arced through his body from the burns. The group stood back as the Thundering Warmaul crashed into the wall, blasting a sizable piece from it.

Beyond the new opening, Kaerisk saw another light: a shining crystal above an egg-shaped device. Vibrating ripples of energy formed around it and the entire chamber within which the Wurmqueen sat. She smiled at them widely, her terrible features even more distorted by the glaring energy.

"Cross the barrier at your own peril, children. But do try." She lifted her head, pointedly ignoring them. Myrra hissed wildly and made to charge.

Kaerisk caught her by the tail. "No! That energy would tear you apart!"

She growled violently. "We cannot do nothing! The Wurm must pay!"

Kaerisk released her tail and approached the barrier, placing a forepaw before it.

"Brother!" Zala exclaimed.

He smiled, but did not look back. "It'll be alright."
I hope.

Drawing energy from the reaction itself, the rippling waves began to slow. The Wurmqueen lifted her own forepaws, trying to speed the process, but the Waylund's effect on her Waydeep remained apparent as she began to curse wildly. Kaerisk shook as the Waydeep from the Wurmway flowed into him; he could feel it trying to crack him like a stressed rock.

When he could hold no more, he reared up, pointed both hands above Nao'Dariva, and sent a bolt of pure energy into the crystal, which cracked.

"You fool! What have you done?" Nao exclaimed.

The energy field wobbled and suddenly exploded outwards. Kaerisk closed his eyes, expecting to be torn apart or incinerated. Instead, when he dared peek, he found that the field had passed over him and spread out like the lava flows he witnessed as a child in San'Lux. Behind them, the Starchild's flame rose into the chamber, threatening to engulf them all.

Then the ground shifted, as though it had fallen from a great height. The areas where the field touched melted, not like lava, but like water, oozing down. Parts of the ceiling around these points collapsed, but the Starchild was suddenly absent. They had come to a new area of the Deep – and taken a chunk of the old area with them! The stolen pieces effectively blocked all large exits from the newly ruined chamber, leaving Nao nowhere to run. The field retreated into the crystal, now green, which shattered completely. The shards fell like rain upon the Wurmqueen.

"The time of judgment has come," Kaerisk said.

"Who are you to pass judgment on me, hatchling?" Nao hissed viciously, stepping out of the chamber as it collapsed behind her. "This world belonged to the Wurm. The dragons stole it from us. Forced us to hide in the Deep like rats. I was there to witness the horrific birth of the Firstbourne. I was there in the war between our people. I was there when our people fell and died at your high and mighty claws and magic. I was there as we lost all sense of pride and dignity."

She lashed her teeth forward to bite at Kaerisk, who retreated to the others. Nao began to circle them in the small, ruined space.

"I have survived this long to see justice done for my people! I put to death thousands upon thousands of your kin and still your debt of genocide goes unpaid! I led the charge to destroy the Grand Academy! I buried Ton'Plu in rock and fire! I gifted the Illness to Eidolon, sped it in every dragon I could! You think two more hatchlings and a pitiable band of dakael can end a life that has lived over five thousand years?!"

Zala began to shake. At first, Kaerisk thought it was fear, but when Zala spoke, her voice was steady. "You are responsible for the Illness?"

Nao sneered, green liquid dripping between her teeth. "I am responsible for all ill that has befallen the dragons!"

Zala's head snapped up to face her. "You took someone very special from me. Someone who struggled and fought no less hard than you, and deserved life far more. For Icia's sake, I will bring you down!"

"As will I!" Vandys shouted, lifting his dragon-forged blade.

"As will we all! For Icia! And for the freedom of the dakael!" Kaerisk exclaimed.

Nao's tail shook violently and her maw opened. Everyone scattered as she spit thick green mucus onto the floor. Where it landed, the ground began to sizzle and melt.

"Attack!" Myrra shouted. The Shiris rushed up to the wurm's side, slicing at her flank with the metal claws. The thick hide was utterly unharmed by the sharpened claws, but that fact did nothing to halt the Shiris' feral fury, striking again and again as though the Wurm was the tree outside her village.

Kiaron and Geen were next to reach the queen. The massive maul of the Setkaa crashed into the wurm's muzzle as she made to bite them. The resulting shock sent her reeling for a time, giving Geen an opportunity to get in close and use the scale on his helmet. He scanned the Wurmqueen's hide back

[367]

and forth, but his jabs were as ineffective as Myrra's claws when he finally struck.

"Zala! Did Lan'Dal ever teach you how to draw Riftwind from objects?" Kaerisk shouted.

She paused her approach. "Yes, why?"

"Draw it right out of her hide!"

Her brother focused on that task himself. Aiming all his attention to the wurm's left paw, he drew Riftwind into himself, holding it with all of his will. The queen growled and spat at him, but Kaerisk was still far enough away to avoid it, and even continue the draining. When he could hold no more, he turned the energy into a ball of fire and threw it into the face of the queen. While it caused no damage, it did temporarily blind her.

"Now, Kiaron! Try striking her left paw!"

"I hear you brother!"

The Setkaa rushed into the gap between her paws fearlessly. With a powerful downward swing, the Thundering Warmaul smashed the hand of the queen with a sickening crack, followed by a peal of thunder. The Wurm roared, this time in true pain. The use of Riftwind had weakened her hide, just as the Waylund's use of Waydeep had. Kiaron withdrew to evade reprisals.

"I'll not let you use me as an object! My hatred is unquenchable!" she shrieked.

She hobbled towards the hatchling and whipped him with her tail faster than he anticipated; it was all he could do to avoid the spikes on her tip. The wind was knocked out of him as he flew across the room and slammed his wing into the wall, breaking it with an audible crack. Even as his breath escaped him, he screamed in agony. Parts of the bone protruded from its scaly sheathe.

"Brother!" Zala shouted. The queen turned to her, eyes burning with anger. Eyes that had missed the action she had already done. "Her right flank!"

"I'll carve our past from you!" Myrra screamed.

The Shiris drove her claws into the side of the beast, slicing through it as easily as she had intended from the start. The dark red blood of the wurm spilled out into Myrra's white fur. Geen joined her, screaming Correth's name as he plunged his spear deep into Nao'Dariva's side.

Kaerisk stood on wobbly legs as Myrra and Geen were whipped away by the muscular tail. Geen's arm suffered similar injury as his own wing; his spear-arm was torn and limp. Myrra fared better, skidding backwards on all fours and avoiding a wall. They had to end this quickly, before anyone else fell.

He pushed away all sensation of pain, all worries of if he would ever fly, and focused on the queen's chest. He shuddered when he drew the magic from it; so much energy rested there, dark and wild and powerful, as though all her hatred had become Riftwind within her bosom. The queen turned towards his sister.

"Zala! Get over here!" he shouted, leeching power as quickly as he could.

His sister charged through the queen's grasp, leaping over the good claw and sliding under the injured one. The queen roared in frustration, trying to catch her prey with her tail, but Zala had seen what it had done to her brother and the dakael. She lunged into the queen's side, scaling her scales with force of will alone. Even as the queen turned, bucked, and lashed her tail, Zala leapt from her back, using the stolen Riftwind to glide. Nao'Dariva turned to the hatchlings, maw dripping with acid.

"Now Vandys! Through her chest and move away!" Kaerisk shouted.

The human complied, having slipped unnoticed by the lizard. Close enough now, he plunged the Wurmbane into the chest of Nao'Dariva. He did not have time to pull it out before her wild claws knocked him aside. It was the break that Kaerisk wanted. Transforming his stolen energy into lightning, Riftwind arced into the sword and struck against the beating heart of Nao'Dariva. Her black pupils shrank as her heart began to beat erratically in her chest. She clutched at it with her injured paw, but it was too late. She fell upon the ground, writhing and heaving. She set those narrow pupils upon her killer and sneered at him one last time.

"My hatred is undying. Death will not stop what I have done."

At last, the Wurmqueen fell still.

Vandys recovered as the bipeds cheered their freedom and success. He stalked over to the corpse and kicked it. He then set about tearing off choice scales. Even though Nao'Dariva was a wurm, the action made Kaerisk shiver. It felt sacrilegious somehow.

The words of the queen still echoed in his head. "They will turn on the dragons too."

<u>Resolutions</u>

"The Wurmqueen lies dead!" Vandys shouted. His words were echoed in wails by the bipeds further up the tunnels.

"You are certain this will get us out alive?" Kiaron asked.

Vandys was apparently quite familiar with the Deep. Once they had broken free of the ruined chamber and found their bearings, he led the way with a simple wooden torch. He did not elaborate on what the queen said to him, if he understood it himself. The Wurmbane still dripped with royal blood. He held it before him as proof. Some humans came near, but only to stare at the blood before wailing and disappearing into the darkness.

"With their master dead, the bipeds under her rule will scatter in fear, cowering in the furthest reaches of the Deep. To many, she was a god. We will find no resistance on the way out," the human said.

The stink announced that they passed through the chirop's caverns. The chirop remaining in the Deep hid in crevasses or disappeared into tunnels unseen. Their beady eyes stared and flashed in the flickering light, tiny bodies pressed tightly into the corners.

Last I passed this way, I was in chains. Now I leave victorious.

He shuddered at the memory, the action rattling his bent wing against him. For some reason, it didn't hurt as much as it had during battle. Perhaps it was the surreal situation or perhaps he could not risk showing pain in this place.

They passed into the large cavern where the human settlement lay. It was completely abandoned by the time the group arrived. The rush of the waterfall was almost eerie. It echoed through the empty chamber, a grim specter of the children's laughter that he heard when he passed these caves months prior.

Where have all those people gone?

The world outside the Deep was much changed. The forest near the caves had been torn down, used to create weapons of war. Those weapons now stood abandoned or burning. In the new clearing rested hundreds of bodies, dragon and biped alike. The carnage was almost unbearable. The ground had been stained with blood; bodies not yet corpses moaned for rescue or release.

"Aleni!" Zala shouted.

A detachment of dragons stood a hundred feet away, tending to the wounded. Zala immediately rushed to her teacher. The group made to follow, but Vandys did not move. Kaerisk held back to regard him.

"Aren't you coming?"

"No, Kaerisk. My place is with my people."

"You used Waydeep during the battle to break our bonds, didn't you?"

"I did."

Kaerisk regarded him. Standing there, in front of the cave, Kaerisk at last recognized him, taking a few steps back. "You – you are the dragon-slayer that captured me!"

He sunk the Wurmbane in the earth and took a withered scale from his pants pocket. He turned it over in his fingers, comparing it to the larger scale he had torn from the wurm.

"… Yes. Nao wasn't lying when she called me her favored pet. What I did at the order of the Wurmqueen was not my will, but I am still responsible for my actions. Had I known then what I know now…"

"Then all this time, you were sent by Nao'Dariva! But why?"

Vandys frowned. "Haven't figured it out? She knew they would send a squad of bipeds or dragons after her. She expected it would be you leading them. She found you through the Setkaa in Luminous, and she sent me. I was to cause dissension and betray you right as you came into her chamber, slaughter your allies, and capture you once more. She had horrible plans for you, Kaerisk. Ones I dare not utter here."

Kaerisk slowly relaxed. "Then, why? Why did you turn on her?"

He put the scales away and placed his hand on the hilt of the blade. "For nearly all our history, the wurm has collared us and held our leash. My father told me a story, that his father before him told, all the way back to the first Vandys – that we have always sought to be free, but that dragons would step in to rule us when the wurms were gone. That they thought of themselves higher than dakael, and always would." His fingers danced along the pommel of the blade. "But when my machinations were put down by your words, when you called us all equal in that moment - I felt something I had not felt since the time when I was a child and my grandfather told me stories of how we fought the wurms in the past: self-respect."

"Vandys-"

"After all I had done to you, even if you didn't recognize me, to still say that about dakael – it gave me a hope I had forgotten. That is why I aided you. I would stand by you to the end. But right now, my people need me more. They have yet to shed the golden chains that bind them to the Wurm and to the past. They need to learn that there may yet be an accord with dragons. That our future will not always be one living under tyranny and rock."

[373]

"Dragons will surely scour even the Deep, seeking to cull the magic-wielding humans."

"I'll be alright. My family has survived since the earliest days of the wurm – we will survive this as well."

"Will I ever see you again?" Kaerisk asked.

"I don't know."

"Vandys, I – I forgive you."

Vandys smiled brightly. He knelt before Kaerisk, as he must have many times to the Wurm. But there was no hesitation, no guile, no sense of lingering distrust. "You give me more than I deserve. If ever I leave the Deep, it is to you I will go, Kaerisk. Be well."

Vandys rose, slung his bloody blade onto his shoulder, and marched back into the Deep. The hatchling watched him go, uncertainty painted on his brow.

He joined his sister and the others with the dragons. In the fields, Vitis collected seeds and vines from their slain brethren. Shiris, Setkaa, Ishluke – all were made equal in that moment, for all they could do was comfort the fallen as they passed. The dragons had medicine, but even they still suffered losses.

"The death toll was greater than expected. Most of the fighting took place in the forest, where the bipeds could ambush even us dragons with unholy weapons," Aleni said.

"Is the Matron – and Raisa and-" Zala began.

"They are fine. They collapsed many of our lairs, but we in turn collapsed most of their tunnels and herded them all into a single point. The strike against the Heart of the Firstbourne was not as bad as we feared." Aleni looked grimly at the dead. "Especially compared to this. We were baited into acting. The dakael knew we would come for them, and they were waiting."

"What shall the rest of us do?" Myrra asked.

Aleni glared at the Shiris harshly; even though their people had fought alongside the dragons, it seemed that split blood had only made the dragon more distant to the dakael. "The Ishluke have a camp south of here. Go there, and either join your own people or wait." Her words were Lindorm, but rung harshly.

Myrra lifted her tail as if unimpressed with Aleni's draconic tone and promptly began walking away. "I'm going home, but I'll be waiting there, Kaerisk."

The other bipeds followed her after saying their goodbyes to the hatchlings. Geen held his shattered arm tenderly. Kiaron had taken to waddling to avoid straining his seared tail. It felt hollow to Kaerisk. The bipeds had performed a great accomplishment for the dragons, had suffered and sacrificed for it, but it had gone almost completely unrecognized. He made a note to visit them again soon.

"The Wurmqueen is dead," Zala said.

"The best news I've heard all day. If you two are not too tired, I could use some help."

"What do you need?" Kaerisk asked.

"The dragons on the ground – some of them are already beyond help. Some are able to be saved. But there are only so many of us able to search after the battle. Would you pan out along this area and see if there are any left to aid?"

"Yes, elder," the two said. It was a grim task, but also one that might save lives. There was no way they could refuse.

"Kaerisk, was it? Your wing is in terrible shape. Hold still – this is going to hurt." Aleni took his wing in her paws. It wasn't until she touched it that he was reminded of how much it hurt, but its break was almost negligible pain compared to what came next. She slipped the bone back into his scales and righted it. He tried not to scream. Taking a wooden splint and one of her own scales, she bound the splint to the wing, keeping it set and motionless. "Now, get moving. We are running out of time."

He nodded slowly and then scampered off with his sister, who nuzzled the side of his head tenderly. He felt the pain acutely every time he stepped; looking at the splint caused it to worsen. He tried to focus on those before him, imagining their pain as worse than his own.

For many, it was.

The fighting had been fiercest at the entrance. The evidence lay in the dead surrounding it, for all they encountered had long passed to the elements in bloody fashion. They found one who wheezed incessantly, but was still alive; they called for help immediately. Seeing his wounds treated and his breathing eased was invigorating, especially to Zala. It gave them the courage to keep looking.

Several smaller tunnels had been cut into the rock along the side of the mountain. It seemed their purpose was to ambush; many corpses, bipeds and dragon alike piled nearby them. Following the wall, they came upon more living and dying.

It was here that a great blue dragon lay in a pool of his own blood.

"Father?"

Kaevaeri, the expert biped fighter and father of the two hatchlings laid spit upon several spears. He had taken wounds like a berserker. The ground told his story: his mighty claws had rent the earth where they dug in, using them as leverage to cut down scores of his enemies, who lay littered around him. There was room enough to fly, but he must have stayed on the ground. The hole from which the ambush came was blackened by dragon flame. He stumbled – indentations in the ground several feet from his resting place confirmed it – but still he fought on. If any bipeds still lived, they ran from him, even as he surely collapsed where he now rested.

But why? Why was he here? Father would never have worked with bipeds and Luxari said he never left his lair after we had-

"That voice. Is it time? Am I to join the elements now?"

"Hurry! We need help here quickly!" Zala shouted, twisting back and forth, as though caught between running for the healers and staying with her injured sire.

"No Father. You're not dead, and neither are we," Kaerisk said. He came around to his father's head, the once mighty neck and shoulders on which he had ridden as a child now atrophied with malnourishment and injury. As a healer rushed towards them, Zala came to his side.

"I had thought I had lost you… just like your mother. And Zala? You are here too?"

"Yes Father," she said meekly, her eyes swelling with water.

"Risen from the dead. Like ashes to a phoenix. Yes, son… that is a good name for you. Ausixen."

"Please, don't talk. Help is coming," Kaerisk said. His voice cracked as though he were a whelpling again.

"Too late. Just as I was with your mother. My hatred. My hatred was my undoing. I didn't see her wounds. All I saw were the bipeds. All this time, I hated bipeds. But what I really hated was myself." The elder's eyes welled with tears as his dimming gaze fell upon his son. "I lied to you, Kaerisk. Bipeds wounded your mother, but I was the one who killed her. I left her with the eggs and did not go for help. I have always been a fool…"

The healer came upon the hatchlings and the fallen elder. She examined the wounds with clinical precision.

Shaking her head, she confirmed Kaevaeri's self-assessment before moving on to search for more survivors.

"No! Father, you can't die!" Zala exclaimed, pressing her small head into his neck. She dug her claws into the ground and pushed her rapidly moistening face against him, as though she were trying to help him to stand.

"Calm yourself now, Zala. Where have you been?" The elder wheezed between words. The spears like quills rose and fell with every mighty heave.

"L-Lan'Dal..."

"Good. She would have wanted it that way. You must carry on our family line. I know I... I have no right to ask it. I never gave you the attention you deserved. But so much of her I saw in you... what a fool I have been."

"No Father... you're not a fool," Kaerisk said, "You are the wisest dragon I know. I'm sorry. I'm so sorry for leaving you. Please, don't... don't die."

For the first time, Kaerisk truly wept in the company of his father. In this moment, there was no parental glare, no restriction on emotion. It was as if all of his loss, from Mother Mountain, Icia, Sapphire, Correth, and now his Father all loosed itself upon his body. He trembled under their weight.

"No, Kaerisk... You simply found another way... to live..."

"Please Father! This isn't what I wanted!" Zala cried.

"Father... Mother said something to me before she passed. She said she didn't blame you. She died happy."

Kaevaeri's body fell still and a look of calm came over him.

"Then so too do I... I'm proud of you... of you both."
The elder's eyes closed, never again to open.

From the Ashes

Birds flew overhead, singing their birdsong in shrill voices. Warmth filled the verdant hillside where Kaerisk stood. He held a device imported from Ur'Del – courtesy of Delaan – which allowed him to transport water and then pour it gently upon the ground. This 'watering can' had proven quite useful. A small pink bud had begun to form from the stem, lavishly devouring the sunlight and water both.

The whole of the area was filled with small hills. A few other dragons came to visit, but their interest was not in gardening. They touched the hillsides with reverence and wept bitterly. They never learned the lesson that Kaerisk had learned as a whelpling.

The cemetery represents another trial that makes a dragon stronger. They exist not truly for the dead, but for the living.

"Elder Jelia said I could find you here."

Downhill from him stood the blue female who had been his constant companion since birth. Zala smiled at him.

"Don't you find it morbid to stand on the hills? I mean – they were once dragons."

"They aren't anymore, sister. They are the elements, returned to those from which we were born. If the essence of what they were still lingers here, it is only in our hearts and our memories, giving us strength to carry on."

"You've changed."

"Do you think so? Myrra keeps insisting I'm going soft, but she still hasn't asked for that rematch in all the months since the war."

"I wouldn't say soft. Just... different."

"Are you here on business?"

"No. I came to visit you."

"Well, that's a surprise."

"Is it now? You haven't visited me in all this time."

"I have sent regular correspondence."

She sighed. "It's not the same."

Kaerisk sat on his hind legs, signaling with his head for his sister to join him. Some mourners gave her a dirty look as she ascended the burial mound, but none said a word to her.

"What are you doing here, anyway? Father was committed in San'Lux."

Their father returned home to great honors, lauding his sacrifice in the name of dragon kind. Kaerisk had watched from the ridge as he was committed under the respectful gaze of the statue. As he was still disowned, he had no right to be present at the committal itself.

"I'm not here for Father. I'm here for Correth."

"Correth?"

Kaerisk nodded, motioning to the ground. "Careful not to step on him."

Zala blinked, peering at the bud. "That's Correth? You didn't return his seed to his people?"

"In all that happened, I honestly forgot until I was back here in Luminous. I planted him right away, fearing that he might really die otherwise. I spoke to the Vitis about it; they didn't seem to mind. But he's quite beyond moving now. It'll be several years before he is ready to uproot."

"Why here? I mean…"

"It's what Father said before he passed."

"Ausixen?"

"Phoenix, yes. What better way to symbolize that than growing new life from the passing of the old?"

"I suppose that's true." Zala's tail twitched back and forth as she stared at the bud.

"How goes the reconstruction at Lan'Dal? I know you spoke about it in your letters, but…"

"Good, good. The fire to the domes caused many lairs to collapse, so new ones had to be built. Much of the old city will go unused before long. Lan'Dal decided to expand, so abandoned lairs will be used for training and memorials."

"I saw that some of the forest had been cut away, but I didn't know why. I'm glad to hear that things are going well there."

Zala tilted her head a moment, and then frowned and pulled her wings in front of her. "Kaerisk! You were in Lan'Dal and you didn't visit me?"

"No, I was at the Vitis settlement on business. I wanted to go, but couldn't."

"Oh." Her wings relaxed. "What business?"

"Apparently, I made some sort of impression on all the biped races."

"And?"

"And. Jelia thought it would be best if I acted as ambassador on a more full-time basis. Usually, I'm called in to settle disputes. At the time, I was there dealing with chirop refugees."

"I saw them. Many Lan'Dal units scoured the Deep for the remaining magic-users and ultimately rounded up most of the chirop population. Seems the Wurmqueen didn't teach many of them magic."

"Yeah. Displaced and hungry, they turned to their natural enemies and food source: the Vitis."

"They eat the grasspeople?"

"No, just their fruit."

"Oh."

Kaerisk grinned. It seemed that his sister still didn't know why the Vitis had to grow fruit regularly. "You still like fruit too, don't you?"

"Yeah, but they never complain when I ask for it. Don't know why they'd complain about the chirop."

"It's mostly that they tear it from the vine, which can kill the grasspeople."

"Ah. That makes sense."

"I mediated the conflict by structuring times and letting the Vitis control the flow of fruit. The chirop kept referring to me as the Mighty Godslayer. It was embarrassing, actually."

"And inaccurate. She was neither a god, nor were you the only one there. I was there too!"

Both hatchlings smiled.

"Oh! How is your wing?"

Kaerisk flexed it. The bend from the break was hardly noticeable. He flapped it a bit, kicking up some grass that had withered away. "Wouldn't say good as new, but the healers are certain I will fly. Soon, in fact."

"That's good news. Last I heard, you were uncertain."

"Sometimes, Patience can wear thin. They were uncertain until a few weeks ago, and thus so was I."

"I suppose so. Did you get the items I sent you?"

"Yes, but I shouldn't have taken them."

"Nonsense. They are yours as much as mine."

"I was disowned."

"Then they're a gift from your sister, since it's all mine."

Kaerisk chuckled. He wasn't going to win this argument. "Fine. The pieces from Father's hoard have brought me some comfort. There is at least one treasure I am happy to keep."

Kaerisk smiled as he thought about it. The statue Icia had gifted him at the festival had remained safely behind.

"What of the lair?" he asked.

"I've decided to leave it as it is for now. In case things change. It's nice to think it will always be there."

"Yeah."

"Luxari promised he'd preserve it until we decided to use or sell it. He sealed up the entrance with a large rock once all the hoard had been removed and transferred to Lan'Dal."

"I'm sure he would have been happy knowing that he provided for us both."

Zala simply nodded. "How's Delaan?"

"I haven't seen him."

"He isn't staying here anymore?"

"Not since the war."

"He doesn't blame you, you know."

Delaan had successfully delivered his message, but Delarrean was slain when they evacuated the hatchlings to the council chamber. Kaerisk attended his committal on his way to San'Lux, but Zala had arrived from Lan'Dal too late to witness it. He was buried with great honor in the sands outside Ur'Del.

"I still feel like it was my fault. If we had turned back-"

She interrupted. "We might have let the Wurmqueen escape and kill thousands more."

He sighed. "That's what he said, too. Either way, as the last of the Del bloodline, he's being kept strictly at Ur'Del for now."

A bit of silence passed. A cool breeze washed over their blue scales, as though mistaking them for the sky. The bud flowed with it, dancing its dance of life.

"What I said - thinking about it. I meant it."

"What?"

"Phoenix. Rising from ash. About Mother Mountain and everything I learned on her sapphire slopes with you."

He pressed his hand upon the hillside, as though it were Mother Mountain, soft and tender.

"Losing her, and Icia, and Sapphire, and now Father… all were harrowing trials that left their scars upon us. But Mother Mountain was right. Loss has made me strong. It's made me question my right to have survived, and to encourage me to spend every day earning that right. The loss is the trial. It's what we overcome. Rise from. Like a phoenix from the ashes."

He closed his eyes. In his mind, he could still remember his father's strong blue scales and powerful claws. He could see him again as he did as a hatchling, when his father was not just his father, but an ideal – the perfect dragon.

"I'd never have come as far as I have without him. The lessons that I tried to escape were the things that saved our lives, saved everyone. Even disowned, he gave me a name. Ausixen."

"Kaerisk…"

"I want to live up to that name. I want to rise above all the loss and hardship. I want to help others, to teach them what I've learned in my trials so that they might face theirs. I want to be a phoenix. A blue phoenix. It has a nice sound to it. I think Father knew that."

"… I think so too, brother."

"No matter what, Zala, I will rise from the ashes. Every trial by fire another chance to harden my scales and strengthen my Virtues. I hope you feel the same."

"It is harder for me. But I do. I miss them a lot."

"So do I."

Zala leaned into her brother's side. He placed a wing over her, hugging her to him. She sighed happily, while he remembered days long passed.

"Will you be staying with us long?"

"For a while. Jelia opened her lair to me, on the condition that you don't mind."

"Not at all."

Zala smiled at him. "Good. I still need to get my things inside; that giant stone was blocking the way."

"You get used to it."

"You, maybe. I'll see you soon, right?"

"Right. Just need to finish up here."

Zala smiled and said farewell, bounding quickly down the hill. Kaerisk picked up the can and continued irrigating, carefully spreading its contents around the bud. The shining sun cast his shadow over the ground. He examined it a moment, squinted, and then looked around.

"Two tails. Miasma?"

"I remain, Kaerisk. At least for a while longer."

The Miasma Dragon did not manifest this time, but his voice emanated from a spot next to Kaerisk. Despite being invisible, his shadow stretched next to the hatchling.

"Who are you? I mean, really?"

"Remember a title, I do: Flameborn. But my name... So committed was I to my cause – to ensure the Wurm was dead – that I lost sight of everything else. Ended is my task and I should move on. Return to the elements."

"But you haven't."

"I feel as though something has been set into motion. And yet, many generations may pass before is felt the damage of Nao'Dariva."

"Will you last that long?"

[385]

"I know not. First to you I wish to say one thing, before I return home."

The shadow twisted its neck, as if looking at the hatchling.

"Of this can I be sure: no coincidence brought you to me. A guiding paw is upon you, Dawnbringer. Proceed with whatever you choose carefully – for the future now belongs to you."

"I will act with Wisdom, but the future is not mine alone."

"In your task, never be so focused that you become blind."

"Father taught me that, as well. It was the last lesson he gave to me."

"Then ready you are. I wish you well."

The shadow blew away as though the dragon who cast it was made of dust.

The soft breeze turned into a welcoming gust. The need to rise above – rise like a phoenix – enveloped him. He spread his wings wide and the wind filled them. He closed his eyes, letting the air slice against his powerful leathery wings, but he was still too heavy. Into himself he summoned the Riftwind, burning his energy and filling him with hunger. His body was made lighter; he had to hold to the ground so as to not blow away. Turning to run with the wind, he leapt from the hillside. One thrust of his wings, two, three. Up and up he climbed, until that small flower was beyond sight. As he glided towards Luminous, he did not see it bloom.